THE KING OF THE CASTLE

by Victoria Holt

THE KING
OF THE CASTLE

VICTORIA HOLT

Doubleday & Company, Inc. Garden City, New York

1967

All of the characters in this book are fictitious, and any resemblance to actual persons, living or dead, is purely coincidental.

FOR
MONIQUE MADELEINE PAULE RÉGNIER

THE KING OF THE CASTLE

❧ 1 ❧

Even as the branch-line train came into the station I was saying to myself: "It's not too late. You could go straight back even now."

During the journey—I had crossed the Channel the night before and had been traveling all day—I had been mustering my courage, assuring myself that I was no foolish girl but a sensible woman who had decided to take a certain action and was going to carry it through. What happened to me when I reached the castle depended on others; but I promised myself I should act with dignity, and behave as though I were not desperately anxious, hiding from them the fact that when I thought of what my future could be if they rejected me, I faced panic. I should let no one know how much this commission meant to me.

My appearance I felt—for the first time in my life—was in my favor. I was twenty-eight and, in my dun-colored traveling cloak and felt hat of the same color, calculated to be useful rather than decorative, and after having traveled all night, I certainly looked my age. I was unmarried and had frequently intercepted pitying glances on that account and had heard myself referred to as "an old maid" and "on the shelf." This had irritated me with its implication that the main reason for a woman's existing was dedication to the service of some man—a masculine assumption which, since my twenty-third birthday, I had determined to prove false; and I believed I was doing so. There could be other interests in life; and I consoled myself that I had found one.

The train slowed down. The only other person who alighted was a peasant woman carrying a basket of eggs under one arm and a live fowl under the other.

I took out my bags—there were several of them, for they contained all I possessed—my small wardrobe and the tools I should need for my work.

The only porter was at the barrier.

"Good day, Madame," he was saying. "If you don't hurry the baby will be born before you get there. I heard your Marie had started her pains three hours back. The midwife's gone to her."

"Pray it'll be a boy this time. All those girls. What the good Lord is thinking of . . ."

The porter was more interested in me than in the sex of the expected baby. I was aware that while he was talking he was watching me.

My bags were now beside me and as he stepped forward about to blow his whistle and send the train on its journey, an old man came hurrying onto the little platform.

"Hé, Joseph!" the porter greeted him and nodded towards me.

Joseph looked at me and shook his head. "Gentleman," he said.

"Are you from Château Gaillard?" I asked in French, which I had spoken fluently from childhood. My mother had been French and when we had been alone we had conversed in that language, although in my father's presence English was always spoken.

Joseph came towards me, his mouth slightly open, his eyes incredulous.

"Yes, Mademoiselle, but . . ."

"You have come to pick me up."

"Mademoiselle, I have come for a Monsieur Lawson." He spoke the English name with difficulty.

I smiled and tried to force a nonchalance into my manner, reminding myself that this was the smallest of the hurdles over which I should have to jump. I pointed to the labels on my baggage: D. Lawson.

Then, realizing that Joseph probably couldn't read, I explained: "I am *Mademoiselle* Lawson."

"From England?" he asked.

I assured him this was so.

"I was told an English gentleman."

"There has been some mistake. It is an English lady instead."

He scratched his head.

"Shouldn't we be going?" I asked. I looked down at my baggage. The porter came slowly over and as he and Joseph exchanged glances, I said with authority: "Please put my baggage into the er . . . conveyance and we will leave for the *château*."

I had practiced self-control for years and there was no trace of the apprehension I was feeling. My manner was as effective here as it was at home. Joseph and the porter carried my bags to the waiting trap; I followed, and in a few moments we were on our way.

"The *château* is far from here?" I asked.

"Two *kilomètres* or so, Mademoiselle. You will see it soon."

I looked about me at the rich wine-growing land. It was the end of October and the harvest was over; I supposed they would now be preparing for the next year's crop. We skirted the little town with its square dominated by the church and *hôtel de ville*, with its branching narrow streets, its shops and houses; and then I had my first glimpse of the *château*.

I shall never forget that moment. My common sense—of which in the last year I had consoled myself I had plenty as a compensation for having little else—disappeared; and I forgot the difficulties in which I had recklessly placed myself. In spite of all the alarming possibilities which logical reasoning suggested were inevitable, I laughed quite audibly and said equally audibly: "I don't care what happens. I'm glad I came."

Fortunately I had spoken in English and Joseph could not understand. I said quickly: "So that is Château Gaillard!"

"That's the *château*, Mademoiselle."

"Not the only Gaillard in France. I know the other in Normandy, of course. The one where Richard Coeur de Lion was kept a prisoner." Joseph grunted, and I hurried on: "Ruins are fascinating, but old castles which have been preserved through the centuries are far more so."

"The old *château* has had some narrow escapes. Why, in the days of the Terror it was almost destroyed."

"How fortunate that it wasn't!" I heard the emotion in my voice and hoped Joseph hadn't. I was enchanted by the *château*; I longed to live in it, to explore it, to become familiar with it. I felt it was where I was meant to be, and that if I were sent away I should be desperately unhappy—and not only because I did not know what I should do if I went back to England.

Briefly I allowed that alarming possibility to come between me and my contemplation of the *château*. There was a distant cousin somewhere in the north of England—actually a cousin of my father's of whom he had spoken now and then. "If anything happened to me you could always go to Cousin Jane. She's a difficult woman; you'd have a wretched time; but at least she would do her duty." What a prospect for a woman who, having been denied those personal attractions which are the key to marriage, had developed a defensive shell, largely made up of pride. Cousin Jane . . . never! I had told myself. I would rather become one of those poor governesses depending on the whims of indifferent employers or mischievous children who could be even more diabolically cruel. I would rather place myself in the service of some querulous old woman as a lady's companion. No, I should be desolate, not because the dark pit of loneliness and humiliation gaped before me, but because I should be denied the infinite joy of doing the work I loved the best in the world in a setting which merely by its existence could make my life interesting.

It was not quite as I had imagined it; it surpassed expectations. There are occasions in life when reality is more exciting, more enchanting than the picture the imagination has supplied—but they are rare; and when they come they should be savored to the full.

Perhaps I had better enjoy these moments because they may be the last I would enjoy for a long time.

So I gave myself up to the contemplation of that magnificent piece of fifteenth-century architecture standing there in the midst of the vine country. My practiced eyes could place it within a decade or two. There had been extensive building in the sixteenth and seventeenth centuries, but the additions had not detracted from the symmetry; rather they gave it its character. I could see the cylindrical towers which flanked the main building. The chief staircase would, I knew, be in the polygonal tower. I was fairly knowledgeable about old houses and although often in the past I had resented my father's attitude towards me, I was grateful for all he had taught me. The aspect was purely medieval; and the solid buttresses and towers gave an air of having been built for defense. I calculated the thickness of those walls with their narrow slits of windows. A fortress surely. As my eyes went from the keep overlooking the drawbridge to the moat—dry, of course—I caught a glimpse of rich green grass growing there. Excitement gripped me, as

I gazed up at the corbeled parapet supported by numerous machicolations about the outer façade.

Old Joseph was saying something. I guessed he had decided that the arrival having turned out to be a woman instead of a man was no concern of his.

"Yes," he was saying, "things don't change at the *château*. Monsieur le Comte sees to that."

Monsieur le Comte. He was the man I should have to face. I pictured him, the aloof aristocrat, the sort who would have driven through the streets of Paris in his tumbril to the guillotine with haughty indifference. So he would banish me.

"Ridiculous," he would say. "My summons was clearly meant for your father. You will leave immediately."

It would be useless to say: "I am as competent as my father was. I worked with my father. In fact I know more about old paintings than he did. That was the side of the business he always left to me."

The side of the business! How explain to a haughty French count that a woman could be as efficient, as clever at the specialized work of restoring old paintings as a man.

"Monsieur le Comte, I am an artist myself . . ."

I could picture his scornful looks. "Mademoiselle, I am not interested in your qualifications. I sent for Monsieur Lawson. I did not send for you. Therefore oblige me by leaving my house (. . . my residence? . . . my castle?) without delay."

Joseph was looking at me shrewdly. I could see that he was thinking that it was very odd that Monsieur le Comte had sent for a woman.

I longed to ask questions about the Comte, but naturally I could not. It would have been useful if I could have learned a little about the household, but it was out of the question to inquire. No. I must put myself into the right mood; I must feel that there was nothing unusual in taking my father's place, so that I could convey this to others.

In my pocket was the request. That was the wrong word. Monsieur le Comte would rarely request; he would command as a king to a subject.

The King in his Castle! I thought. Monsieur le Comte de la Talle summons D. Lawson to the Château Gaillard to carry out the work on his pictures as arranged. Well, I was Dallas Lawson, and if that summons was meant for Daniel Lawson, then my answer was that Daniel

Lawson had been dead for ten months and that I, his daughter, who in the past had helped him in his work, was now carrying on in his place.

It was about three years earlier that my father had been in correspondence with the Comte, who had heard of his work, for Father had been well known as an authority on old buildings and paintings. Perhaps in the circumstances it was natural that I should grow up with a reverence for these things which had turned into a passion. Father encouraged me in this and we spent many weeks in Florence, Rome, and Paris doing nothing but looking at art treasures; and every moment I could spare in London was spent in the galleries.

With a mother who was not very strong and a father who was almost always absorbed in his work, I was thrown a great deal on my own resources. We saw few people and I had never formed the habit of making friends easily. Not being a pretty girl I felt at a disadvantage and there seemed to be a constant need to hide this which made me develop a far from attractive, over-dignified manner. Yet I longed to share experiences with others; I longed for friends. I was passionately interested in the affairs of others, which always seemed more exciting than anything that could happen to me. I would listen enraptured to conversations which were not intended for my ears; I would sit quietly in the kitchen while our two servants, one elderly, one young, discussed their ailments and love affairs respectively, and stand quietly listening to people in shops when I was shopping with my mother; or if anyone came to the house I was often discovered in what my father called eavesdropping. It was a habit of which he did not approve.

But when I went to my art school, for a while I began to live my life firsthand, as it were, rather than through my ears. Yet that did not satisfy Father either, for there I fell in love with a young student. In romantic moments I still wistfully remembered those spring days when we wandered through St. James's and Green Parks and listened to the orators at Marble Arch, and strolled along the Serpentine into Kensington Gardens. I could never be there without remembering; that was why I never went if I could help it. Father had objected because Charles had no money. Moreover, Mother, who by that time had become an invalid, needed me.

There was no great renunciation scene. That romance had just grown out of springtime and youth; and with the coming of autumn it was over.

14

Perhaps Father had thought it would be better if I had not the opportunity to become involved with anyone else, for he suggested I leave the art school and work more closely with him. He said he would teach me far more than I could ever learn at school. He was right, of course; but although I learned so much from him, my opportunity to meet people of my own age and live my individual life was lost. My time was divided between working with Father and looking after Mother. When she died I was stunned by my grief for a long time and when I recovered a little I felt that I was no longer young; and as long ago I had convinced myself that I was not attractive to men, I turned my desire for love and marriage into a passion for paintings.

"The work suits you," my father once said. "You want to restore everything."

I understood what he meant. I had wanted to make Charles into a great painter when he wanted to be a carefree student. Perhaps that was why I lost him. I wanted to restore Mother to her old vigor and interest in life. I tried to chivvy her out of her lassitude. I never tried to change Father. That would have been quite impossible. I realized that I had inherited my forcefulness from him, and at the time he was stronger than I.

I remember the day the first letter came from Château Gaillard. The Comte de la Talle had a gallery of pictures which were in need of attention; and he would like to consult my father about certain restoration of the *château*. Could Monsieur Lawson come to Château Gaillard, estimate what work was necessary, and if a satisfactory arrangement could be reached, stay until it was completed?

Father had been delighted. "I will send for you if possible," he had told me. "I shall need your help with the pictures. You will enjoy the place. It's fifteenth-century, and I believe a great deal of the original is there. It'll be quite fascinating."

I was excited. First because I longed to spend a few months in a French *château*; secondly because Father was beginning to accept my superior knowledge where pictures were concerned.

However, a letter had arrived from the Comte postponing the appointment. Circumstances made the visit impossible at present, he wrote, giving no detailed explanation. He would probably be in touch later.

About two years after receiving that letter Father had died quite suddenly of a stroke. It had been a terrible shock to realize I was on my own. I felt bereft, lonely and bewildered—moreover I had very little money. I had become accustomed to helping Father in his work and I wondered what would happen, for although people had accepted the fact that I was his assistant and no doubt very useful in that capacity, how would they feel about my standing on my own?

I talked this over with Annie, our elderly servant, who had remained with us for years and was going off to share a home with a married sister. She thought there were only two things I could do. I could be a governess, as many ladies had to be, or a companion.

"I'd hate either," I told her.

"Beggars can't be choosers, Miss Dallas. There's many a young lady, educated like yourself, who's found herself left—and been forced to."

"There's the work I've done with Father."

She nodded, but I knew she was thinking that no one would want to employ a young woman to do the things my father had done. That I could do them, was not the point. I was a woman, and therefore no one would believe my work could possibly be any good.

Annie was still with me when the summons came. The Comte de la Talle was now ready for Monsieur D. Lawson to begin the work.

"After all, I *am* D. Lawson," I pointed out to Annie. "I can restore pictures as well as my father could, and I can see no reason why I should not."

"I can," replied Annie grimly.

"It's a challenge. It's either this or spending my days teaching. Father's lawyers have assured me of the urgent need to earn a living. Fancy teaching children to draw when they have no talent and don't want to learn! Or perhaps spending my time with a fretful old lady who finds fault with everything I do!"

"You have to take what comes, Miss Dallas."

"*This* has come to me—so it's exactly what I am doing."

"It's not right. People won't like it. It was all very well going with your father and working with him. You can't go on your own."

"I did finish the work after he died . . . at Mornington Towers, you remember."

"Well, that was what he started. But to go to France . . . a foreign country . . . a young lady . . . *alone!*"

"You mustn't think of me as a young lady, Annie. I'm a restorer of pictures. That's quite different."

"Well, I hope you'll not forget that you're a young lady all the same. And you can't go, Miss Dallas. It wouldn't be right. I know it. It would be bad for you."

"Bad? In what way?"

"Not . . . quite nice. What man would want to marry a young lady who'd been off abroad all by herself."

"I'm not looking for a husband, Annie. I'm looking for work. And I'll tell you this: my mother was exactly the same age when she and her sister came to England to stay with their aunt. The two girls actually went to the theater alone. Fancy that! Mother told me she did something even more daring. She went to a political meeting once—in a cellar in Chancery Lane . . . and, as a matter of fact, that was where she met Father. So, if she hadn't been bold and adventurous she wouldn't have had a husband—at least not that one."

"You were always one for making what you wanted sound right. I know you of old. But I say this: It's not right. And I stick to that."

But it had to be right. And so, after a great deal of consideration and trepidation, I had decided to accept the challenge and come to Château Gaillard.

We crossed the drawbridge and as I looked at those ancient walls with their moss and ivy, supported by the great buttresses, as I gazed at the cylindrical towers, at the rounded roofs rising to conical points, I was praying that I might not be sent away. We passed under the archway and entered a courtyard with grass growing between the cobbles, and I was struck by the silence. In the center of the courtyard was a well about which was a parapet and stone pillars supporting a dome. There were a few steps leading to a loggia in front of one side of the building, and I saw the words DE LA TALLE entwined in the fleurs-de-lis, cut into the wall above a door.

Joseph took out my bags, set them by this door and shouted: "Jeanne."

A maid appeared, and I noticed the startled look in her eyes when she saw me. Joseph told her that I was Mademoiselle Lawson, I was to be taken to the library and my arrival was to be made known. The bags would be taken to my room later.

I was so excited at the prospect of entering the castle that I felt quite reckless. I followed Jeanne through the heavy studded door into a great hall on the stone walls of which hung magnificent tapestries and weapons. I quickly noticed one or two pieces of furniture in the *régence* style—one of these a magnificent table of carved gilt wood, with the delicate latticework which became so popular in France during the early eighteenth century. The tapestries, which were exquisite and of the same period as the furniture, were in the Beauvais style with Boucher-like figures. It was wonderful; and my desire to pause and examine almost overcame my fear, but already we had turned off the hall and were mounting a flight of stone steps.

Jeanne held aside a heavy curtain and I was stepping on a thick carpet in great contrast to the stone steps. I stood in a short dark corridor at the end of which was a door. When this was thrown open the library was disclosed.

"If Mademoiselle will wait . . ."

I inclined my head. The door was shut and I was alone.

The room was lofty, the ceiling beautifully painted. There would be great treasure in this place, I knew; and I could not bear to be sent away. The walls were lined with leather-bound books, and there were several stuffed heads of animals which seemed to guard them ferociously.

The Comte is a mighty hunter, I thought, and imagined him relentlessly pursuing his prey.

A clock with a carved cupid poised above its face stood on the mantelpiece, and on either side of it were two delicately colored Sèvres vases. The chairs were upholstered in tapestry and their framework was decorated with flowers and scrolls.

But impressed as I was by these treasures, I was too apprehensive to give them my full attention. I was thinking of my coming interview with the formidable Comte and rehearsing what I would say to him. There must be no loss of dignity on my part. I must remain calm, yet I must not appear too eager. I must disguise the fact that I longed to be allowed to work here, that I might succeed and so move on to win further commissions. I believed that my future hung on the next few minutes. And how right I was.

I heard Joseph's voice. "In the library, Monsieur . . ."

Footsteps. Any moment now I should face him. I went to the fireplace. Logs were laid in it but there was no fire; I looked at the painting above the Louis XVth clock, not seeing it; my heart was beating fast and I was gripping my hands in an effort to stop them trembling when the door opened. I pretended not to be aware of it so that I might gain a few seconds respite in which to compose myself.

There was a brief silence then a cool voice said: "This is most extraordinary."

He was about an inch taller than I, but I am tall. The dark eyes were at the moment puzzled, but they looked as though they could be warm; the long aquiline nose suggested arrogance; but the full lips were not unkind. He was dressed in riding clothes that were very elegant—a trifle too elegant. His cravat was ornate and there was a gold ring on the little finger of each hand. He was fastidious in the extreme and not as formidable as I had imagined him. This should have pleased me, but I felt faintly disappointed. Yet this man was more likely to be sympathetic towards me than the Comte of my imagination.

"Good day," I said.

He took a few steps forward. He was younger than I had thought he would be, for he could not have been more than a year or so older than I . . . perhaps my own age.

"No doubt," he said, "you will be good enough to explain."

"Certainly. I have come to work on the paintings which are in need of attention."

"We understood that *Monsieur* Lawson was to arrive today."

"That would have been quite impossible."

"You mean he will come later?"

"He died some months ago. I am his daughter, and am continuing with his commitments."

He looked rather alarmed. "Mademoiselle Lawson, these paintings are very valuable . . ."

"It would scarcely be necessary to restore them if they were not."

"We could only allow an expert to handle them," he said.

"*I* am an expert. My father was recommended to you. I worked with him. In fact the restoration of buildings was his *forte* . . . pictures were mine."

This is the end, I thought. He is annoyed to have been placed in a distasteful situation. He will never let me stay. I made a desperate effort. "You had heard of my father. Then that means you had heard of me. We worked together."

"You did not explain . . ."

"I believed the matter was urgent. I thought it wiser to obey the summons without delay. If my father had accepted the commission I should have come with him. We always worked together."

"Pray be seated," he said.

I sat down in a chair with a carved wooden back which forced me to sit up straight while he threw himself onto a settee, his legs stretched out before him.

"Did you think, Mademoiselle Lawson," he said slowly, "that had you explained that your father was dead we should have declined your services?"

"I believed that your object was to have the pictures restored and was under the impression that it was the work which was important, not the sex of the restorer." Again that arrogance, which was really the outward sign of my anxiety! I was certain that he was going to tell me to go. But I *had* to fight for a chance, because I knew that if only I could get it I could show them what I could do.

His brow was wrinkled as though he were trying to come to a decision; he was watching me covertly. He gave a little laugh which was quite mirthless and said: "It seems strange that you did not write and tell us . . ."

I rose to my feet. Dignity demanded it.

He stood up. I had rarely felt as wretchedly miserable as I did when I haughtily walked to the door.

"One moment, Mademoiselle."

He had spoken first. It seemed a small victory.

I looked over my shoulder without turning.

"Only one train leaves our small station each day. That is at nine o'clock in the morning. It would be necessary for you to drive some ten *kilomètres* to catch a main line train for Paris.

"Oh!" I allowed dismay to show on my face.

"You see," he went on, "you have placed yourself in a very awkward situation."

"I did not think that my credentials would be slighted without scrutiny. I have never worked before in France and was quite unprepared for such a reception."

It was a good thrust. He rose to it. "Mademoiselle, I assure you, you will be treated as courteously in France as you would be anywhere else."

I raised my shoulders. "I suppose there is an inn . . . a hotel where I could stay the night?"

"We could not allow that. We can offer you hospitality."

"It is good of you," I said coldly, "but in the circumstances . . ."

"You spoke of credentials."

"I have recommendations from people who were very pleased with my work . . . in England. I have worked in some of our great houses and have been entrusted with masterpieces. But you are not interested."

"That is not true, Mademoiselle. I *am* interested. Anything connected with the *château* is of the utmost concern to me." His face had changed as he spoke. It was illumined by a great passion—the love for this old house. I warmed towards him. I should have felt as he did if such a place were my home. He went on hurriedly: "You must admit that I am justified in my surprise. I expected a man of experience and am confronted by a young lady . . ."

"I am no longer young, I assure you."

He made no effort to refute this, still seeming preoccupied with his own thoughts—his emotions where the *château* was concerned, his indecision as to whether to allow me, whose skill he doubted, near his wonderful paintings.

"Perhaps you would show me your credentials."

I walked back to the table and from an inner pocket of my cloak took a bundle of letters and handed them to him. He signed for me to be seated. Then he too sat and began to read the letters. I folded my hands in my lap and clasped them firmly. A moment before I thought I had lost; now I was not so sure.

I watched him while pretending to study the room. He was trying to make up his mind what he should do. This surprised me. I had imagined the Comte to be a man who was rarely in doubt, who made quick decisions, having no difficulty as to the wisdom of them, since he would believe himself always to be right.

"They are very impressive," he said as he handed them back to me. He looked full at me for some seconds, then went on rather hesitantly: "I expect you would like to see the pictures."

"There seems little point if I am not to work on them."

"Perhaps you will, Mademoiselle Lawson."

"You mean . . ."

"I mean that I think you should stay here at least for a night. You have had a long journey. You are tired, I am sure. And as you are such an expert"—he glanced at the letters in my hand—"and have been so highly congratulated by such eminent people, I am sure you would at least wish to see the pictures. We have some excellent examples of painting in the *château*. They have been collected from time to time over centuries. I do assure you that it is a collection worthy of your attention."

"I am sure it is. But I think I should be getting to my hotel."

"I don't recommend it."

"Oh?"

"It is very small and the food is not of the best. You would be more comfortable in the *château*, I am sure."

"I should not care to make a nuisance of myself."

"But of course you would not. I am going to insist that you stay here, and that you now allow me to call the maid to take you to your room. It has been prepared, you know, although of course we did not know it was to be for a lady. Still, that need not concern you. The maid will bring some food to your room. Then I suggest you rest awhile and later you must see the paintings."

"Then you mean that you want me to do the work I came to do?"

"You could give us your advice first, could you not?"

I felt so relieved I changed my feelings towards him. The dislike of a moment ago turned to liking.

"I would do my best, Monsieur le Comte."

"You are under a delusion, Mademoiselle. I am not the Comte de la Talle."

I was unable to control my amazement. "Then who . . ."

"Philippe de la Talle, the Comte's cousin. So you see it is not I whom you have to please. It is the Comte de la Talle. He is the one who will decide whether or not he will entrust you with the restoration of his paintings. I assure you that if the decision rested with me I should ask you to begin without delay."

"When can I see the Comte?"

"He is not at the *château* and will doubtless be absent for some days. I suggest that you remain with us until his return. In the meantime you can examine the paintings and then be ready to estimate what is needed by the time of his return."

"Some days!" I said in dismay.

"I fear so."

As he moved to the bell rope and pulled it, I was thinking: This is a respite. At least I shall have a few days in the *château*.

I guessed my room was close to the keep. The window aperture was large enough to contain two stone benches on either side, although it narrowed to a slit. I could only look out by standing on tiptoe; below me was the moat and beyond that the trees and vineyards. I was amused that even as I reviewed the uncertainty of my position I could not stop myself assessing the house and its treasures. Father had been the same. The most important thing in his life had been ancient monuments; and paintings a good second. With me it was paintings first, but I had inherited something of his passion for buildings.

The lofty room was full of shadows even though it was early in the day, for picturesque as the window embrasure was, it excluded the light. The thickness of the walls astonished me, although I had been prepared that they should be; the huge tapestry which covered almost the entire surface of one was in muted shades of peacock blue, in fact peacocks figured in it—peacocks in a garden of fountains, colonnades, reclining women and gallants, clearly sixteenth-century. The bed was canopied and behind it was a curtain and when I drew this aside I recognized what was beyond as a *ruelle*—an alcove found in French *châteaux*. This one was large enough to be like a small room and contained a cupboard, a hip bath and a dressing table on which stood a mirror. I caught a glimpse of myself and laughed suddenly.

Yes, I did look capable. Almost formidable. I was travel-stained, my hat was pushed too far back on my head so that it was even less becoming than usual; my hair—long, thick, and straight, my only good point, was completely hidden.

The maid had brought the hot water and asked if I would care for cold chicken and a carafe of the *vin du pays*. I replied that it would suit me admirably; and I was glad when she went, for her obvious curiosity and excitement at my presence was a reminder of what a reckless thing I had done.

I took off my cloak and the unbecoming hat. Then I took out the pins and let my hair fall about my shoulders. How different I looked now—not only younger, but vulnerable. Now I could be that frightened girl behind the confident woman I pretended to be. Appearances were important, I must remember. I was proud of my hair. It was dark brown but the touches of chestnut in it were so marked that they shone almost red in sunlight.

I washed from head to foot in the hip bath and felt refreshed. Then I put on clean linen and a gray merino skirt with a light cashmere blouse of a matching color. The blouse buttoned high at the neck and I assured myself that in it I could be mistaken for a woman of thirty—when I put up my hair, of course. I disliked the gray, for I took a great pleasure in colors. I knew instinctively that a certain shade of blue, green, red or lavender would have given character to the gray skirt; but much as I loved combining colors to produce beauty I had never wanted to experiment with my clothes. The light coats I wore for my work were in dull brown, as plain and severe as those my father had worn—in fact I wore his, which were a little too broad but fitted otherwise.

There was a knock on the door as I was buttoning my blouse. I caught a glimpse of myself in the mirror on the dressing table. My cheeks had flushed a little; and with my hair which fell to my waist and spread itself about my shoulders like a cloak, I certainly looked different from the undaunted woman who had been shown into the room.

I called: "Who is there?"

"Mademoiselle, your tray." The maid had come into the room. I held back my hair with one hand and drew aside the curtain very slightly with the other.

"Please leave it there."

She put it down and went out. I realized then how hungry I was, so I came out to inspect the tray. A leg of chicken, a twist of crusty bread still warm from the oven, butter, cheese, and a carafe of wine. I sat down there and then and ate. It was delicious. The wine of the country, made from grapes grown within sight of the castle! The food and wine made me sleepy. Perhaps the latter was very potent; in any case I was tired. I had traveled through the previous day and night; I had slept little the night before that, and I had scarcely eaten either.

I felt a dreamy contentment creeping over me. I was here in the *château* for a while at any rate. I was going to see the treasures of the place. I remembered other occasions when I had stayed with Father in great houses. I recalled the excitement of coming upon some rare work of art, that glow of understanding and appreciation which was like sharing in the joy of the creator. Surely similar experiences were waiting for me in this *château* . . . if only I could stay to enjoy them.

I closed my eyes and felt the rocking of the train; I thought of the life of the castle and the life outside it. The peasants tending the grape vines, exulting in the *vendange*. I wondered whether the peasant woman's child was born and whether it was a boy; I wondered what the Comte's cousin was thinking of me, or whether he had dismissed me from his mind. I slept and dreamed I was in a picture gallery, that I was cleaning a picture and that the colors which were emerging were more brilliant than any I had ever seen before—emeralds against gray . . . scarlet and gold.

"Mademoiselle . . ."

I started out of my chair and for a moment couldn't remember where I was. A woman was standing before me—small, thin, her brows brought together in a frown which suggested anxiety rather than annoyance. Her dusty-looking hair was arranged in curls and bangs, puffed up and frizzed in a vain attempt to hide how scanty it was. Anxious gray eyes studied me from under the frown. She wore a white blouse adorned with little pink satin bows and a dark blue skirt. Her hands nervously plucked at the pink bow at her throat.

"I fell asleep," I said.

"You must be very tired. Monsieur de la Talle has suggested that I should take you to the gallery, but perhaps you would rather rest a little longer."

"Oh no, no. What is the time?" I consulted the gold watch—it had belonged to my mother—which was pinned to my blouse. As I did so I saw the hair falling over my shoulders and I felt myself flush slightly. Hastily I pushed it back. "I must have been so tired that I slept. I've been traveling through the night."

"Of course. I will come back . . ."

"That is good of you. Will you please tell me who you are? You know I am Miss Lawson come from England to, er . . ."

"Yes, I know. We were expecting a gentleman. I am Mademoiselle Dubois, the governess."

"Oh . . . I had no idea . . ." I stopped. Why should I have any idea as to who was who in this household? The thought of my hair flowing down my back was disconcerting. It was making me stammer in a way I never should could I have presented my usual severe demeanor.

"Perhaps you would prefer me to come back in say . . . half an hour?"

"Give me ten minutes in which to make myself presentable and then I shall be very happy to accept your kind offer, Mademoiselle Dubois."

She ceased to frown and smiled rather uncertainly. As soon as she had left me I went back to the *ruelle* and looked at myself. What a sight! I thought. My face flushed, my eyes bright and my hair in such confusion! I seized my hair and drew it tightly back from my forehead; I plaited it and wound the plaits into a bulky mound which I pinned up on the top of my head. I looked even taller that way. The flush was dying from my cheeks and my eyes were now dull gray. They were the shade of water and reflected the colors I wore as the sky will change the color of the sea. For that reason I should have worn greens and blues; but having assured myself that my assets did not lie in personal attractions and that if I were going to win the confidence of my employers I must present myself as a sensible woman, I cultivated dull colors as I did my somewhat prickly exterior. I believed they were the necessary weapons for a woman alone in the world with her own battles to fight. Now my mouth was set in the firm no-nonsense lines which I tried to adopt; and by the time Mademoiselle Dubois returned I was ready to play my familiar role.

She looked startled when she saw me, so I knew what a bad impression I had made in the first place. Her eyes went to my head and I felt a grim satisfaction, for now there was not a hair out of place—it was neat and severe as I liked it to be.

"I am so sorry I disturbed you." The woman was too apologetic. That little matter was over, and it was my fault for falling asleep and not hearing her knock. I told her this and added: "So Monsieur de la Talle has asked you to show me the gallery. I am most eager to see the pictures."

"I know little about pictures, but . . ."

"You say you are the governess. So there are children in the *château*."

"There is only Geneviève. Monsieur le Comte has only one child."

My curiosity was strong, but one could not ask questions. She hesitated as though she wanted to talk; and how I wanted to know! But I was in command of myself and growing more and more optimistic as the moments passed. It was wonderful what the brief rest and the food, the wash and the change of clothes had done for me.

She sighed. "Geneviève is very difficult."

"Children often are. How old is she?"

"Fourteen."

"Then I am sure you can easily control her."

She gave me an incredulous look; then her mouth twisted slightly. "It is evident, Mademoiselle Lawson, that you do not know Geneviève."

"Spoilt, I imagine, being the only one?"

"Spoilt!" Her voice had an odd note. Fear? Apprehension? I couldn't quite place it. "Oh that . . . as well."

She was ineffectual. That much was obvious. The last person I should have chosen a governess. If they would choose a woman like this for such a post, surely my chances of getting the restoration commission were good. Although I was a woman I must look far more capable than this poor creature. And wouldn't the Comte consider the education of his only child as important as the restoration of his pictures? That remained to be seen, of course. I was impatient for my encounter with this man.

"I can tell you, Mademoiselle Lawson, that to control that girl is impossible."

"Perhaps you are not stern enough," I said lightly, then changed the subject. "This is a vast place. Are we near the gallery?"

"I will show you. You will get lost here at first. I did. In fact even now I often find myself in difficulties."

You would always find yourself in difficulties, I thought.

"I suppose you have been here for some time," I asked, merely to make conversation as we passed out of the room and went along a corridor to a flight of stairs.

"Quite a long time . . . eight months."

I laughed. "You call that long?"

"The others didn't stay as long. No one else stayed longer than six."

My mind switched from the carving on the banister to the daughter of the house. So this was why Mademoiselle Dubois remained. Geneviève was so spoilt that it was difficult to keep a governess. One would have thought that the stern King in his Castle could have controlled his daughter. But perhaps he did not care enough. And the Comtesse? Strangely enough, before Mademoiselle Dubois had mentioned the daughter I had not thought of a Comtesse. Naturally there must be one, since there was a child. She was probably with the Comte now and that was why I had been received by the cousin.

"In fact," she went on, "I am constantly telling myself that I shall go. The trouble is . . ."

She did not finish, nor did she need to, because I understood very well. Where could she go? I pictured her in some dreary lodging . . . or perhaps she had a family. . . . But in any case she would have to earn a living. There were many like her—desperately exchanging pride and dignity for food and shelter. Oh yes, I understood absolutely. None better for it was a fate I could envisage for myself. The gentle-woman without means. What could be more difficult to bear than genteel poverty! Brought up to consider oneself a lady, educated as well as—perhaps better than—the people one must serve. Continually aware of being kept in one's place. Living with neither the vulgar gusto of the servants below stairs nor with the comfort of the family. To exist in a sort of limbo. Oh, it was intolerable and yet how often inevitable. Poor Mademoiselle Dubois! She did not know what pity she aroused in me . . . and what fears.

"There are always disadvantages in every post," I comforted.

"Oh yes, indeed yes. And here there is so much . . ."

"The *château* seems to be a storehouse of treasures."

"I believe the pictures are worth a fortune."

"So I have heard." My voice was warm. I put out a hand to touch the linenfold paneling of the room through which we were passing. A beautiful place, I thought; but these ancient edifices were in constant need of attention. We had passed into a large room, the kind which in England we called a solarium, because it was so planned to catch the sun, and I paused to examine the coat of arms on the wall. It was fairly recent and I wondered whether there might be murals under the lime-wash. I thought it very possible. I remembered the excitement when my father had once discovered some valuable wall-painting which had been hidden for a couple of centuries. What a triumph if I could make such a discovery! The personal triumph would of course be secondary, and I had thought of that only because of my reception. It would be a triumph for art, as all such discoveries are.

"And the Comte is doubtless very proud of them."

"I . . . I don't know."

"He must be. In any case he is concerned enough to want them examined and if necessary restored. Art treasures are a heritage. It is a privilege to own them and one has to remember that art . . . great art . . . doesn't belong to one person."

I stopped. I was on my favorite hobbyhorse, as Father would have said. He had warned me: "Those who are interested probably share your knowledge; those who are not are bored."

He was right and Mademoiselle Dubois fitted into the second category.

She laughed, a small tinkly laugh without any mirth or pleasure in it. "I should hardly expect the Comte to express his feelings to *me*."

No, I thought. Nor should I.

"Oh dear," she murmured. "I hope I haven't lost my way. Oh no . . . This is it."

"We are now almost in the center of the *château*," I said. "This is the original structure. I should say we are immediately beneath the round tower."

She looked at me incredulously.

"My father's profession was the restoration of old houses," I explained. "I learned a great deal from him. In fact we worked together."

She seemed momentarily to resent that in me which was the exact reverse of her own character. She said almost severely: "I know that a man was expected."

"My father was expected. He was coming about three years ago and then for some reason the appointment was canceled."

"About three years ago," she said blankly. "That would be when . . ."

I waited and as she did not continue, I said: "That would be before you were here, wouldn't it? My father was coming, and somewhat peremptorily he was told it was not convenient. He died almost a year ago and as I have continued with work that was outstanding, naturally I came in his place."

She looked as though such a procedure was far from natural, and

I secretly agreed with her. But I had no intention of betraying myself to her as she betrayed herself to me.

"You speak very good French for an Englishwoman."

"I am bilingual. My mother was French, my father English."

"That is fortunate . . . in the circumstances."

"In any circumstances it is fortunate to be in command of languages."

My mother had said I was too tutorial. It was a trait I should curb. I fancy it had increased since Father had died. *He* once said I was like a ship firing all guns to show I was equipped to defend myself just in case another should be preparing to open fire on me.

"You are right, of course," said Mademoiselle Dubois meekly. "This is the gallery where the pictures are."

I forgot her then. I was in a long room lightened by several windows, and on the walls . . . the pictures! Even in their neglect they were splendid and a quick look was enough to show me that they were very valuable. They were chiefly of the French school. I recognized a Poussin and Lorrain side by side and was struck as never before by the cold discipline of one and the intense drama of the other. I reveled in the pure golden light of the Lorrain landscape and wanted to point out to the woman beside me that light and feathery brushwork which might have been learned from Titian, and how the dark pigments had been used over rich color to give that wondrous effect of light and shade. And there was a Watteau . . . so delicate, arabesque, and pastel . . . and yet somehow conveying by a mood the storm about to break. I walked trancelike from an early Boucher painted before his decline set in and a perfect example of the rococo style, to a gay erotic Fragonard.

Then I was angry because they were all in need of urgent attention. How was it they had been allowed to get into this state! Some I could see had darkened badly; there was a dull foggy film on others which we called "bloom." A few were scratched and streaked with water. The brown acid left by flies was visible; and in some places the paint had flaked off. There were isolated burns as though someone had held a candle too closely.

I moved silently from picture to picture, forgetful of everything else. I calculated that there was almost a year's work in what I had seen so far and there was probably a great deal more than that—as there always was when one began to examine these things more closely.

"You find them interesting," said Mademoiselle Dubois vapidly.

"I find them of immense interest and certainly in need of attention."

"Then I suppose you will get down to work right away."

I turned to look at her. "It is by no means certain that I shall do the work. I am a woman, you see, and therefore not considered capable."

"It is unusual work for a woman."

"Indeed it is not. If one has a talent for this kind of work, one's sex is of no importance whatever."

She laughed that foolish laugh. "But there is men's work and women's work."

"There are governesses and tutors, aren't there?" I hoped I made it clear that I had no intention of continuing this aimless conversation by changing the subject. "It depends of course on the Comte. If he is the man of prejudice . . ."

A voice not far off cried: "I want to see her. I tell you, Nounou, I *will* see her. Esquilles has been ordered to take her to the gallery."

I looked at Mademoiselle Dubois. Esquilles! Splinters! I saw the allusion; she must have heard herself called that often enough.

A low soothing voice and then: "Let go, Nounou. You silly old woman. Do *you* think you can stop *me?*"

The door of the gallery was flung open, and the girl whom I at once recognized as Geneviève de la Talle stood there. Her dark hair was worn loose—and was almost deliberately untidy; her beautiful dark eyes danced with enjoyment; she was dressed in a gown of mid-blue which was becoming to her dark looks. I would have known immediately, even if I had not been warned, that she was unmanageable.

She stared at me and I returned the gaze. Then she said in English: "Good afternoon, Miss."

"Good afternoon, Mademoiselle," I answered in the same tongue. She seemed amused and advanced into the room. I was aware of a gray-haired woman behind her. This was obviously the nurse, Nounou. I guessed she had been with the girl from babyhood and helped with the spoiling.

"So you've come from England," said the girl. "They were expecting a man."

"They were expecting my father. We work together and as he, being dead, is unable to come, I am continuing with his commitments."

"I don't understand," she said.

"Shall we speak in French?" I asked in that language.

"No," she replied imperiously. "I can speak English well." She said, "I am Mademoiselle de la Talle."

"I did assume that." I turned to the old woman, smiled and said good day.

"I find these pictures most interesting," I said to her and Mademoiselle Dubois, "but it is obvious that they have been neglected."

Neither of them answered but the girl, evidently annoyed at being ignored, said rudely: "That will be no concern of yours since you won't be allowed to stay."

"Hush, my dear," whispered Nounou.

"I will not hush unless I want to. Wait until my father comes home."

"Now Geneviève . . ." The nurse's anxious eyes were on me, apologizing for the bad manners of her charge.

"You'll see," said the girl to me. "You may think you are going to stay, but my father . . ."

"If," I said, "your father's manners resemble yours, nothing on earth would induce me to stay."

"Please speak English when you address me, Miss."

"But you appear to have forgotten that language as you have your manners."

She began to laugh suddenly and twisted herself free of the nurse's grasp and came up to me.

"I suppose you are thinking I'm very unkind," she said.

"I am not thinking of you."

"What are you thinking of then?"

"At the moment of these pictures."

"You mean they are more interesting than I am?"

"Infinitely," I answered.

She did not know what to reply. She shrugged her shoulders and turning away from me said pettishly in a lowered voice: "Well, I've seen her. She's not pretty, and she's old."

With that she tossed her head and flounced out of the room.

"You must forgive her, Mademoiselle," murmured the old nurse.

"She's in one of her moods. I tried to keep her away. I'm afraid she's upset you."

"Not in the least," I answered. "She is no concern of mine . . . fortunately."

"Nounou," called the girl, imperious as ever. "Come here at once."

The nurse went out, and raising my eyebrows I looked at Mademoiselle Dubois.

"She's in one of her moods. There's no controlling them. I'm sorry . . ."

"I'm sorry for you and the nurse."

She brightened. "Pupils can be difficult, but I have never found one quite so . . ." She looked furtively at the door and I wondered whether Geneviève added eavesdropping to her other charming characteristics. Poor woman, I thought, I didn't want to add to her difficulties by telling her I thought she was foolish to suffer such treatment. I said: "If you care to leave me here I'll make an examination of the pictures."

"Can you find your way back to your room, do you think?"

"I'm sure I can. I took careful note as we came along. Remember I'm used to old houses."

"Well then, I'll leave you. You can always ring if you want anything."

"Thank you for your help."

She went out noiselessly, and I turned to the pictures, but I was too disturbed to work seriously. This was a strange household. The girl was impossible. What next? The Comte and the Comtesse? What should I find them like? And the girl was ill-mannered, selfish, and cruel. And to have discovered this in five minutes of her company was disconcerting. What sort of environment, what sort of upbringing had produced such a creature?

I looked at those walls with their priceless neglected pictures and in those few moments I thought: Perhaps the wisest thing would be to leave first thing in the morning. I might apologize to Monsieur de la Talle, agree that I had been wrong to come, and leave.

I had wanted to escape from a fate—which I knew since my encounter with Mademoiselle Dubois (Splinters, poor thing)—could be quite terrible. I had so desperately wanted to continue with work

33

I loved; and because of that I had come here under false pretenses and laid myself open to insult.

I was so firmly convinced that I must go that I almost believed some instinct was warning me to do so. In that case I would not tempt myself by studying these pictures further. I would go to the room they had given me, and try to rest in preparation for the long journey back tomorrow.

I walked towards the door and as I turned the handle it refused to move. Oddly enough, in those seconds I felt a real panic. I could have imagined that I was a prisoner, that I could not escape if I wanted to; and then it seemed as though the very walls were closing in on me.

My hand was limp on the handle, and the door opened. Philippe de la Talle was standing outside. Now I understood that the reason I couldn't open it was that he had been on the point of coming in.

Perhaps, I thought, they don't trust me here. Perhaps someone always has to be with me in case I attempt to steal something. That was absurd I knew and it was unlike me to think illogically. But I had had scarcely any sleep for two nights and was deeply concerned about my future. It was understandable that I was not quite myself.

"You were on the point of leaving, Mademoiselle?"

"I was going to my room. There seems no point in remaining. I have decided to leave tomorrow. I must thank you for your hospitality and I am sorry to have troubled you. I should not have come."

He raised his eyebrows. "You have changed your mind? Is it because you think the repairs beyond your capacity?"

I flushed angrily. "By no means," I said. "These pictures have been badly neglected . . . criminally neglected . . . from an artist's point of view, that is, but I have restored far worse. I merely feel that my presence is resented in this place and that it would be better for you to find someone . . . of your own sex, since that seems to be important to you."

"My dear Mademoiselle Lawson," he said almost gently, "everything rests with my cousin to whom the pictures belong . . . to whom everything in the *château* belongs. He will be back within a few days."

"Nevertheless, I think I should leave in the morning. I can repay you for your hospitality by giving you an estimate for restoring one of the pictures in the gallery which you will find useful when engaging someone else."

"I fear," he said, "that my niece has been rude to you. My cousin will be annoyed with me if he does not see you. You should not take any notice of the girl. She's quite ungovernable when her father is away. He is the only one who can put fear into her."

I thought to myself then: I believe you are afraid of him too. And I was filled with almost as great a desire to see the Comte as I was to work on his pictures.

"Mademoiselle, will you stay for a few days and at least hear what my cousin has to say?"

I hesitated, then I said: "Very well, I will stay."

He seemed relieved.

"I shall go to my room now. I realize I am too tired to work satisfactorily today. Tomorrow I will make a thorough study of the pictures in this gallery and when your cousin returns I shall have a clear estimate to give him."

"Excellent," he said, and stood aside for me to pass.

As soon as it was light next morning, refreshed after a good night's sleep, I arose exhilarated. I intended to have a look at the *château* grounds and perhaps explore the neighborhood. I wanted to see the little town, for the old church had struck me as being about the same period as the *château*; and no doubt the *hôtel de ville* was as ancient.

I had had dinner in my room yesterday evening and it had been excellent. Soon afterwards I had gone to bed and slept immediately. Now the morning brought optimism with it.

I washed and dressed and rang for breakfast. The hot coffee, homemade crusty bread and butter, which arrived almost immediately were delicious.

As I ate I thought of the events of yesterday, and they no longer seemed as strange as they had the previous night. I had yet to discover what sort of household this was; all I knew at present was that it was an unusual one. There was Cousin Philippe, in charge during the absence of the master and mistress; a spoilt girl who behaved badly when her father was absent, no doubt because when he was there she was in such awe of him; there was the weak and ineffectual governess and poor gray old Nounou, the nurse who had no more control over her than the governess had. Apart from that there was Joseph the groom and numerous servants, male and female, necessary to care for such a vast establishment. There was nothing unusual in such a household; and yet I had sensed mystery. Was it the manner in which everyone who had mentioned him had spoken of the Comte? He was the only one whom the girl feared. Everyone was in awe of him. Everything depended on him. Certainly whether or not I stayed did.

I made my way to the gallery, where I enjoyed a peaceful morning examining the pictures and making detailed notes of the damage to each one. It was a fascinating task, and I was astonished how quickly the morning passed. I forgot about the household in my absorption, and was astonished when a maid knocked at the door and announced that it was twelve o'clock and that she would bring *déjeuner* to my room if I wished.

I found that I was hungry and said that would be very agreeable. I packed up my papers and went back to my room, where the maid served me with a delicious soup, followed by meat and salad, in its turn followed by cheese and fruit. I wondered if I should eat alone in my room all the time I was here—that was, if I met with the approval of Monsieur le Comte. I was beginning to think of him as Monsieur le Comte and to say his name to myself with a kind of mockery. "Others may be afraid of you, Monsieur le Comte, but you will find I am not."

The afternoon was not a good time for working, I had always found; besides, I needed a little exercise. I could not, of course, explore the castle itself without permission, but I could look at the grounds and the countryside.

I had no difficulty in finding my way down to the courtyard to which Joseph had brought me, but instead of going out to the drawbridge I crossed the loggia connecting the main building with a part of the *château* which had been built at a later date, and, passing through another courtyard, I found my way to the south side of the castle. Here were the gardens, and I thought grimly, if Monsieur le Comte neglects his pictures he does not his gardens, for obviously great care was bestowed on them.

Before me lay three terraces. On the first of these were lawns and fountains, and I imagined that during the spring the flowers were exquisite; even now, in autumn, they were colorful. I walked along a stone path to the second terrace; here, laid out with parterres, were ornamental gardens; each separated from the next by box hedges and yews neatly clipped into various shapes, predominant among them the *fleur-de-lis*. Typical, I thought, of Monsieur le Comte! On the lowest of the terraces was the kitchen garden, but even this was ornamental, neatly divided into squares and rectangles, some separated from each other by trellis about which vines climbed; and the whole was bordered by fruit trees.

The place was deserted. I guessed that the workers were taking a siesta, for even at this time of the year the sun was hot. At three o'clock they would be back at work and continue until dark. There must be many of them to keep the place in such good order.

I was standing under the fruit trees when I heard a voice calling: "Miss! Miss!" and, turning, saw Geneviève running towards me.

"I saw you from my window," she said. She laid her hand on my arm and pointed to the *château*. "You see that window right at the top there . . . that's mine. It's part of the nurseries." She grimaced. She had spoken in English. "I learned that off by heart," she explained, "just to show you I could. Now let's talk in French."

She looked different now, calm, serene, a little mischievous perhaps, but more as one would expect a well-brought-up fourteen-year-old girl to look, and I realized that I was seeing Geneviève without one of her moods.

"If you wish," I replied in that language.

"Well, I should like to speak to you in English but, as you pointed out, mine is not very good, is it?"

"Your accent and intonation made it almost unintelligible. I suspect you have a fair vocabulary."

"Are you a governess?"

"I am certainly not."

"Then you ought to be. You'd make a good one." She laughed aloud. "Then you wouldn't have to go round under false pretenses, would you?"

I said coolly: "I am going for a walk. I will say good-by to you."

"Oh no, don't. I came down to talk to you. First I have to say I'm sorry. I was rude, wasn't I? And you were very cool . . . but then you have to be, don't you? It's what one expects of the English."

"I am half French," I said.

"That accounts for the spirit in you. I saw you were really angry. It was only your voice that was cold. Inside you were angry, now weren't you?"

"I was naturally surprised that a girl of your obvious education could be so impolite to a guest in your father's house."

"But you weren't a guest, remember. You were there under . . ."

"There is no point in continuing this conversation. I accept your apology, and now I will leave you."

"But I came down specially to talk to you."

"But I came down to walk."

"Why shouldn't we walk together?"

"I did not invite you to accompany me."

"Well, my father didn't invite you to Gaillard, did he, but you came." She added hastily: "And I'm glad you came . . . so perhaps you'll be glad if I come with you."

She was trying to make amends and it was not for me to be churlish, so I smiled.

"You're prettier when you smile," she said. "Well," she put her head on one side, "not exactly pretty. But you look younger."

"We all look more pleasant when we smile. It is something you might remember."

Her laughter was high and quite spontaneous. I found myself joining in and laughing at myself. She was pleased and so was I to have her company; for I was almost as interested in people as I was in pictures. Father had called it idle curiosity—but it was strong in me and perhaps I had been wrong to have suppressed it.

Now I was eager for Geneviève's company. I had seen her once in a mood and now as a lively but extremely curious girl; but who was I to criticize curiosity who had more than my fair share of it?

"So," she said, "we'll go for a walk together, and I will show you what you want to see."

"Thank you. That will be very pleasant."

She laughed again. "I hope you will enjoy being here, Miss. Suppose I talk to you in English, will you speak slowly so that I can understand?"

"Certainly."

"And not laugh if I say something silly?"

"Certainly I shall not laugh. I admire your desire to improve your English."

She was smiling again, and I knew that she was thinking how like a governess I was.

"I am not very good," she said. "They are all afraid of me."

"I don't think they are afraid of you. They are perhaps distressed—and disgusted—by the unbecoming way in which you sometimes behave."

This amused her but she was serious almost immediately.

"Were you afraid of your father?" she asked, lapsing into French. I sensed that because she was interested in the subject she must speak in the language easier to her.

"No," I replied. "I was in awe of him perhaps."

"What's the difference?"

"One can respect people, admire them, look up to them, fear to offend them. It is not the same as being afraid of them."

"Let's go on talking in French. This conversation is too interesting for English."

She is afraid of her father, I thought. What sort of man is he to inspire fear in her? She was an odd child—wayward, perhaps violent; and he was to blame, of course. But what of the mother—what part had she played in this strange child's upbringing?

"So you weren't really afraid of your father?"

"No. Are you afraid of yours?"

She didn't answer, but I noticed that a haunted expression had come into her eyes.

I said quickly: "And . . . your mother?"

She turned to me then: "I will take you to my mother."

"What?"

"I said I would take you to her."

"She is in the *château*?"

"I know where she is. I'll take you to her. Will you come?"

"Why yes. Certainly. I shall be delighted to meet her."

"Very well. Come on."

She went ahead of me. Her dark hair was neatly tied back with a blue ribbon and perhaps it was the way of dressing it which so changed her appearance. Her head was set arrogantly on sloping shoulders; her neck was long and graceful. I thought: She will be a beautiful woman.

I wondered whether the Comtesse was like her; then I began rehearsing what I would say to her. I must put my case clearly to her. Perhaps she as a woman would feel less prejudiced against my work.

Geneviève halted and came to walk beside me. "I'm two different people, am I not?"

39

"What do you mean?"

"There are two sides to my character."

"We all have many sides to our character."

"But mine is different. Other people's characters are all of a piece. I am two distinct people."

"Who told you this?"

"Nounou. She says I'm a Gemini—that means I have two different faces. My birthday is in June."

"This is a fantasy. Everyone who is born in June is not like you."

"It is not fantasy. You saw how horrid I was yesterday. That was the bad me. Today I'm different. I'm good. I said I was sorry, didn't I?"

"I hope you *were* sorry."

"I said I was, and I shouldn't have said it if I wasn't."

"Then when you are being foolish, remember that you'll be sorry afterwards and don't be foolish."

"Yes," she said, "you should be a governess. They always make everything sound so easy. I can't help being horrid. I just am."

"Everyone can help the way he or she behaves."

"It's in the stars. It's fate. You can't go against fate."

Now I saw where the trouble lay. This temperamental girl was in the hands of a silly old woman and another who was half scared out of her wits; in addition there was the father who terrified her. But there was the mother, of course. It would be interesting to meet her.

Perhaps she, too, was in awe of the Comte. Most assuredly this was so, since everyone else was. I pictured her a gentle creature, afraid to go against him. He was becoming more and more of a monster with every fresh piece of information.

"You can be exactly as you wish to be," I said. "It is absurd to tell yourself you have two characters and then try to live up to the unpleasant one."

"I don't try. It just happens."

"Well, you must see that it doesn't happen."

Even as I spoke I despised myself. It was always so easy to solve other people's troubles. She was young and at times seemed childish for her age. If we could become friends I might be able to help her.

"I am eager to meet your mother," I said. She did not answer but ran on ahead of me.

I followed her through the trees, but she was more fleet than I and not so encumbered by her skirts. I lifted mine and ran but I lost sight of her.

I stood still. The trees were thicker here, and I was in a small copse. I was not sure which way I had entered it, and as I had no idea in which direction Geneviève had gone I felt suddenly lost. It was one of those moments such as I had experienced in the gallery when I had been unable to open the door. A strange feeling as though panic were knocking, gently as yet, on my mind.

How absurd to feel so in broad daylight! The girl was tricking me. She had not changed. She had deluded me into thinking that she was sorry; her conversation had almost amounted to a cry for help—and it was all a game, a pretense.

Then I heard her calling: "Miss! Miss, where are you? This way."

"I'm coming," I said and went in the direction of her voice.

She appeared among the trees. "I thought I'd lost you." She took my hand as though she feared I would escape from her, and we went on until after a short time the trees were less thick and then stopped abruptly. Before us was an open space in which the grasses grew long. I saw at once that the monuments erected there were to the dead and guessed we were in the graveyard of the de la Talles.

I understood. Her mother was dead. She was going to show me where she was buried. And she called this introducing me to her mother.

I felt shocked and a little alarmed. She was indeed a strange girl.

"All the de la Talles come here when they die," she said solemnly. "But I often come here too."

"Your mother is dead?"

"Come, I'll show you where she is."

She drew me through the long grass to an ornate monument. It was like a small house, and on top of it was a beautifully sculptured group of angels holding a large marble book on which was engraved the name of the person who was buried there.

"Look," she said, "there's her name."

I looked. The name on the book was Françoise, Comtesse de la Talle, aged thirty years. I looked at the date. It was three years ago.

So the girl had been eleven years old when her mother died.

"I come down often," she said, "to be with her. I talk to her. I like it. It's so quiet."

"You shouldn't come," I said gently. "Not alone."

"I like to come alone. But I wanted you to meet her."

I don't know what prompted me to say it but I blurted out: "Does your father come?"

"He never does. He wouldn't want to be with her. He didn't want to before. So why should he now?"

"How can you know what he would like?"

"Oh, I do know. Besides, it's because he wanted her to be here that she's here now. He always gets what he wants, you know. He didn't want her."

"I don't think you understand."

"Oh yes, I do." Her eyes flashed. "It's you who don't understand. How could you? You've only just come. I know he didn't want her. That was why he murdered her."

I could find nothing to say. I could only look at the girl in horror. But she seemed unaware of me as now she laid her hands lovingly on those marble slabs.

The stillness all round me; the warmth of the sun; the sight of those mausoleums which housed the bones of long dead de la Talles. It was macabre; it was fantastic. My instincts warned me to get away from the house; but even as I stood there I knew that I would stay if I could and that there was more to fascinate me in Château Gaillard than the paintings I loved.

❧ 2 ❧

It was my second day at the Château Gaillard. I had not been able to sleep during the night, mainly because the scene in the graveyard had so startled me that I could not get it out of my mind.

We had walked slowly back to the *château* and I had told her that she must not say such things of her father; she had listened to me quietly and made no comment; but I would never forget the quiet certainty in her voice when she had said: "He murdered her."

It was gossip, of course. Where had she heard it? It must be from someone in the house. Could it be the nurse? Poor child! How terrible for her! All my animosity towards her had disappeared. I felt I wanted to know more of her life, what her mother had been like, how those terrible suspicions had been planted in her mind.

But the matter made me very uneasy.

I had eaten a lonely dinner in my room and had gone through the notes I had made; then I tried to read a novel. The evening seemed long; and I wondered whether this was the life I should be expected to lead if I was allowed to stay on. In other great houses we had had our meals with the managers of the estates and sometimes with the family themselves. I had never before felt so lonely when working. But of course I must remember that I was not yet accepted; this was necessarily a period of waiting.

I went to the gallery and spent all the morning examining the pictures, assessing darkening of pigment, failing of paint, which we called "chalking," and other deteriorations such as cracks in the paint which had caught the dust and grime. I tried to work out what materials I should need beyond those which I had brought with me, and I planned

43

to ask Philippe de la Talle if I could look at some of the other pictures in the *château*, particularly some of the murals I had noticed.

I returned to my room for lunch and afterwards went out. I had made up my mind that today I should have a look at the surrounding country and perhaps the town.

All about me lay the vineyards, and I took the road through them although it led away from the town. I would look at the town tomorrow. I imagined what activity there must be during the harvest and wished that I had been here earlier to see it. Next year . . . I thought, and then laughed at myself. Did I really think I should be here next year?

I had come to several buildings and beyond them I saw a house of red brick with the inevitable shutters at all the windows—green in this case. They added a charm to the house which I realized must be about one hundred and fifty years old—built, I guessed, some fifty years or so before the Revolution. I could not resist the temptation of going a little nearer to examine it.

There was a lime tree in front of the house, and as I came near a high, shrill voice called: "Hello, Miss." Not Mademoiselle, as might have been expected, but Miss, pronounced *Mees,* which told me of course that whoever was calling was aware of my identity.

"Hello," I answered, but looking over the iron gates I could see no one.

I heard a chuckle and looking up saw a boy swinging in the tree like a monkey. He took a sudden leap and was beside me. "Hello, Miss. I'm Yves Bastide."

"How do you do?"

"This is Margot. Margot, come down and don't be silly."

"I am not silly."

The girl wriggled out of the branches and slid perilously down the trunk to the ground. She was slightly smaller than the boy.

"We live there," he told me.

The girl nodded, her eyes bright and inquisitive.

"It's a very pleasant house."

"We all live in it . . . *all* of us."

"That must be very nice for all of you."

"Yves! Margot!" called a voice from the house.

"We've got Miss, Gran'mère."

"Then invite her to come in and remember your manners."

44

"Miss," said Yves with a little bow, "will you come in to see Gran'-mère?"

"I should be pleased to." I smiled at the girl, who gave me a pretty curtsy. How different, I thought, from Geneviève.

The boy ran forward to open the wrought-iron gates and gravely he bowed as he held them for me to pass through. The girl walked beside me up the path between the bushes calling: "We're here, Gran'mère."

I stepped into a large hall and from an open door a voice called: "Bring the English lady in here, my children."

In a rocking chair sat an old woman; her face was brown and wrinkled, her plentiful white hair piled high on her head; her eyes were bright and very dark; her heavy lids fell like hoods over them; her thin veined hands, smudged with brown patches which at home were called "the flowers of death," gripped the arms of her rocking chair.

She smiled at me almost eagerly, as though she had been expecting my coming and welcomed it.

"You will forgive my not rising, Mademoiselle," she said. "My limbs are so stiff some days it takes me all of the morning to get out of my chair and all of the afternoon to get back into it."

"Please stay where you are." I took the extended hand and shook it. "It is kind of you to invite me in."

The children had taken a stand on either side of her chair and were regarding me intently and proudly as though I was something rather rare which they had discovered.

I smiled. "You seem to know me. I'm afraid you have the advantage."

"Yves, a chair for Mademoiselle."

He sprang to get one for me and carefully set it down facing the old lady.

"You will soon hear of us, Mademoiselle. Everyone knows the Bas-tides."

I settled in the chair. "How did you know *me?*" I asked.

"Mademoiselle, news travels quickly round the neighborhood. We heard that you had arrived and hoped that you would call on us. You see we are so much a part of the *château*. This house was built for a Bastide, Mademoiselle. There have been Bastides in it ever since. Before that the family lived on the estates because Bastides were always the winegrowers. It is said there would never have been Gaillard wine if there had never been Bastides."

"I see. The vines belong to you."

The lids came down over her eyes and she laughed aloud. "Like everything else in this place the vines belong to Monsieur le Comte. This is his land. This house is his. Everything is his. We are his work people, and although we say that without the Bastides there would be no Gaillard wine, we mean that the wine produced here would not be worthy of the name."

"I have always thought how interesting it must be to watch the wine-growing process . . . I mean, to see the grapes appear and ripen and be made into wine."

"Ah, Mademoiselle, it is the most interesting thing in the world . . . to us Bastides."

"I should like to see it."

"I hope you will stay with us long enough to." She turned to the children: "Go and find your brother, my children. And your sister and your father, too. Tell them we have a visitor."

"Please . . . you mustn't disturb them on my account."

"They would be very disappointed if they knew you had called and they had missed you."

The children ran away. I said how charming they were and that their manners were delightful. She nodded, well pleased; and I knew that she understood why I had made such a comment. I could only be comparing them with Geneviève.

"At this time of the day," she explained, "there is not so much activity out of doors. My grandson, who is in charge now, will be in the cellars; his father, who cannot work out of doors since his accident, will be helping him, and my granddaughter Gabrielle will be working in the office."

"You have a large family, and all engaged in the wine-growing business."

She nodded. "It is the family tradition. When they are old enough Yves and Margot will join the rest of the family."

"How pleasant that must be, and the whole family live together in this lovely house! Please tell me about them."

"There is my son Armand, the father of the children. Jean Pierre is the eldest of them and he is twenty-eight—he'll be twenty-nine soon. He manages everything now. Then there is Gabrielle, who is nineteen

46

—a gap of ten years, you see, between the two. I thought Jean Pierre would be the only one all those years and then suddenly Gabrielle was born. Then another gap and Yves came and after that Margot. There's only a year between those two. It was too soon and their mother was too old for childbearing."

"She is . . . ?"

She nodded. "That was a bad time. Armand, and Jacques, one of the workers, were in the cart when the horses bolted. They were both injured. Armand's wife, poor girl, thought he would die, and I suppose it all seemed too much for her. She caught the fever and died, leaving little Margot . . . only ten days old."

"How very sad."

"The bad times pass, Mademoiselle. It is eight years ago. My son is well enough to work; my grandson is a good boy and really head of the family now. He became a man when it was necessary to shoulder responsibilities. But that is life, is it not?" She smiled at me. "I talk too much of the Bastides. I will weary you."

"Indeed you do not. It is all very interesting."

"But your work must be so much more so. How do you find it at the *château?*"

"I have only been there a very short time."

"You are going to find the work interesting?"

"I don't know if I am going to do the work. Everything depends on . . ."

"On Monsieur le Comte. Naturally." She looked at me and shook her head. "He is not an easy man."

"He is unpredictable?"

She lifted her shoulders. "He was expecting a man. We were all expecting a man. The servants talked of the Englishman who was coming. You cannot keep secrets in Gaillard, Mademoiselle. At least most of us can't. My son says I talk too much. He, poor boy, talks little. The death of his wife changed him, Mademoiselle, changed him sadly."

She was alert, listening, and I heard the sound of horse's hoofs. A proud smile touched her face, changing it subtly. "That," she said, "will be Jean Pierre."

In a few moments he stood in the doorway. He was of medium height, with hair of a lightish brown—bleached, I imagined, by the sun, his dark eyes narrowed to slits as he smiled and his skin was tanned almost to copper color. There was about him an air of immense vitality.

"Jean Pierre!" said the old woman. "This is Mademoiselle from the *château*."

He came towards me, smiling, as though, like the rest of the family, he was delighted to see me. He bowed ceremoniously.

"Welcome to Gaillard, Mademoiselle. It is kind of you to call on us."

"It was not exactly a call. Your young brother and sister saw me passing and invited me in."

"Good for them! I hope this will be the first of many visits." He drew up a chair and sat down. "What do you think of the *château?*"

"It's a fine example of fifteenth-century architecture. I have not had much opportunity so far of studying it but I think it has characteristics similar to those of Langeais and Loches."

He laughed. "You know more of our country's treasures than we do, Mademoiselle, I'll swear."

"I don't suppose that is so, but the more one learns the more one realizes how much more there is to learn. For me it is pictures and houses, for you . . . the grape."

Jean Pierre laughed. He had spontaneous laughter, which was attractive. "What a difference! The spiritual and the material!"

"I think it must be exciting—as I was saying to Madame Bastide—to plant the vines, to tend the grapes, to watch over them and then to make them into wine."

"It's a matter of hazards," said Jean Pierre.

"So is everything."

"You have no idea, Mademoiselle, the torments we suffer. Will there be a frost to kill the shoots? Will the grapes be sour because the weather has been too cool? Each day the vines must be examined for mildew, black rot, and all the pests. So many pests have one ambition and that is to spoil the grape harvest. Not until the harvest is gathered in are we safe—and then you should see how happy we are."

"I hope I shall."

He looked startled. "You have started work at the *château*, Mademoiselle?"

"Scarcely. I am not yet accepted. I have to await . . ."

"The decision of Monsieur le Comte," put in Madame Bastide.

"It is natural, I suppose," I said, moved rather unaccountably by a desire to defend him. "One could say I had come under false pretenses. They were expecting my father and I did not tell them that he was dead and that I proposed to take over his commitments. Everything depends on Monsieur le Comte."

"Everything always depends on Monsieur le Comte," said Madame Bastide resignedly.

"Which," added Jean Pierre with his sunny smile, "Mademoiselle will say is natural since the *château* belongs to him, the pictures on which she plans to work belong to him, the grapes belong to him . . . in a sense we all belong to him."

"The way you talk it would seem we were back before the Revolution," murmured Madame Bastide.

Jean Pierre was looking at me. "Here, Mademoiselle, little has changed through the years. The *château* stands guarding the town and the surrounding country as it did through the centuries. It retains its old character and we whose forefathers depended on its bounty still depend upon it. There has been little change in Gaillard. That is how Monsieur le Comte de la Talle would have it, so that is how it is."

"I have a feeling that he is not greatly loved by those who depend on him."

"Perhaps only those who love to depend, love those they depend on. The independent ones always rebel."

I was a little mystified by this conversation. There was clearly strong feeling concerning the Comte in this household, but I was becoming more and more anxious to learn everything I could about this man on whom *my* fate depended, so I said: "Well, at the moment, I'm on sufferance, awaiting his return."

"Monsieur Philippe would not dare give a decision for fear of offending the Comte," said Jean Pierre.

"He is much in awe of his cousin?"

"More than most. If the Comte does not marry, Philippe could be the heir, for the de la Talles follow the old royalty of France and the Salic law which applied to the Valois and the Bourbons is for the de la Talles as well. But, like everything else, it rests with the Comte. As long as some male heir inherits he could pass over his cousin for some other relative. Sometimes I think Gaillard is mistaken for the Versailles of Louis XIV."

"I imagine the Comte to be young . . . at least not old. Why should he not marry again?"

"It is said that the idea is distasteful to him."

"I should have thought a man of his family pride would have wanted a son—for he is undoubtedly proud."

"He is the proudest man in France."

At that moment the children returned with Gabrielle and their father, Armand. Gabrielle Bastide was strikingly lovely. She was dark like the rest of the family, but her eyes were not brown but a deep shade of blue and those eyes almost made of her a beauty. She had a sweet expression and was more subdued than her brother.

I was explaining to them that I had had a French mother, which accounted for my fluency in their language, when a bell began to ring so suddenly that I was startled.

"It is the maid summoning the children for *goûter*," said Madame Bastide.

"I will go now," I said. "It has been so pleasant. I hope we shall meet again."

But Madame Bastide would not hear of my going. I must, she said, stay to try some of the wine.

Bread with layers of chocolate between it for the children, and for us little cakes and wine were brought in. We talked of the vines, pictures, and life in the neighborhood. I was told I must visit the church and the old *hôtel de ville*; and most of all I must come back and visit the Bastides. I must look in whenever I was passing. Both Jean Pierre and his father—who said very little—would be delighted to show me anything I wished to see.

The children were sent out to play when they had finished their bread and chocolate and the conversation turned once more to the *château*. Perhaps it was the wine—to which I, certainly, was unaccustomed, particularly at that hour of the day—but I grew more indiscreet than I would normally have been.

I was saying: "Geneviève is a strange girl. Not in the least like Yves and Margot. They are so spontaneous, so natural, normal, happy children. Perhaps the *château* is not a good environment for a child to grow up in." I was speaking recklessly and I didn't care. I had to find out more about the *château* and most of all the Comte.

"Poor child!" said Madame Bastide.

"Yes," I went on, "but I believe it is three years since her mother died, and that is time for one so young to have recovered."

There was silence, then Jean Pierre said: "If Mademoiselle Lawson is long at the *château* she will soon learn." He turned to me. "The Comtesse died of an overdose of laudanum."

I thought of the girl in the graveyard and I blurted out: "Not . . . murder!"

"They called it suicide," said Jean Pierre.

"Ah," put in Madame Bastide, "the Comtesse was a beautiful woman." And with that she returned to the subject of the vineyards. We talked of the great calamity which had hit most of the vineyards in France a few years ago when the vine louse had attacked the vines, and because Jean Pierre loved the vineyards so devotedly when he spoke of them he made everyone share his enthusiasm. I could picture the horror when the vine louse was discovered to be attached to the roots of the vine; I could feel the intense tragedy to all those concerned when they had to face the problem of whether or not to flood the vineyards.

"There was disaster throughout France at that time," he said. "That was less than ten years ago. Is that not so, Father?"

His father nodded.

"It has been a slow climb back to prosperity, but it's coming. Gaillard suffered less than most."

When I rose to go, Jean Pierre said he would walk back with me. Although there was no danger of my losing my way, I was glad of his company for I found the Bastides warm and friendly—a quality I had come to treasure. It occurred to me that when I was with them I myself became a different person from the cool and authoritative woman I showed to the people of the *château*. I was like a chameleon changing my color to fit in with the landscape. But it was done without thought, so it was absolutely natural. I had never before realized how automatically I put on my defensive armor, but it was very pleasant to be in company where I did not need it.

As we came out of the gate and took the road to the *château* I asked: "The Comte . . . is he really so terrifying?"

"He is an autocrat . . . one of the old aristocrats. His word is law."

"He has had tragedy in his life."

"I believe you are sorry for him. When you meet him you'll see that pity is the last thing he would need."

"You said that they called his wife's death suicide . . ." I began.

He interrupted me swiftly. "We do not even speak of such things."

"But . . ."

"But," he added, "we keep them in our minds."

The *château* loomed before us; it looked immense, impregnable. I thought of all the dark secrets it could be keeping and felt a shiver run down my spine.

"Please don't bother to come any further," I said. "I am sure I am keeping you from your work."

He stood a few paces from me and bowed. I smiled and turned towards the castle.

I went to bed early that night to make up for the previous night's lack of sleep. I dozed, and my dreams were hazy. It was strange, because at home I rarely dreamed. This was muddled dreaming of the Bastides, of cellars containing bottles of wine, and through these dreams flitted a vague faceless shape whom I knew to be the dead Comtesse. Sometimes I felt her presence without seeing her; it was as though she were behind me whispering a warning, "Go away. Don't you become involved in this strange household." Then again she would be jeering at me. Yet I was not afraid of her. There was another shady shape to strike terror into me. Monsieur le Comte. I heard the words as though from a long way; then growing so loud that it was like someone shouting in my ears.

I awoke startled. Someone *was* shouting. There were voices below and scurrying footsteps along the corridor. The *château* was waking up although it was not morning. In fact the candle I hastily lighted showed me my watch lying on the table and this told me it was only just after eleven.

I knew what was happening. It was what everyone was waiting for and dreading.

The Comte had come home.

I lay sleepless, wondering what the morning would bring.

The *château* was quiet when I awoke at my usual time. Briskly I rose and rang for my hot water. It came promptly. The maid looked different, I told myself. She was uneasy. So the Comte had his effect even on the humblest servants.

"You would like your *petit déjeuner* as usual, Mademoiselle?"

I looked surprised and said: "But of course, please."

I guessed they were all talking about me, asking themselves what my fate would be. I looked round the room. Perhaps I shall never sleep here again, I thought. Then I was unhappy thinking of leaving the *château*, never really knowing these people who had taken such a hold on my imagination. I wanted to know more of Geneviève, to try to understand her. I wanted to see what effect on Philippe de la Talle his cousin's return would have. I wanted to know how far Nounou was responsible for the waywardness of her charge. I should have liked to hear what had happened to Mademoiselle Dubois before she had come to the *château*. Then of course there were the Bastides. I wanted to sit in that cozy room and talk about the vines and the *château*. But most of all I wanted to meet the Comte—not just once and briefly to receive my dismissal, but to learn more of a man who, it seemed generally believed, had been responsible for the death of his wife, even if he had not actually administered the poison dose.

My breakfast came and I felt too excited for food, but I was determined none of them should say that I was so frightened that I had been unable to eat, so I drank two cups of coffee as usual and ate my twist of hot bread. Then I went along to the gallery.

It was not easy to work. I had already prepared an estimate which Philippe de la Talle had said would be given to the Comte on his return. He had smiled at me when I gave it to him and, glancing through it, had remarked that it looked like the work of an expert. I was sure he was hoping it would please the Comte—partly, I imagined, to justify his having allowed me to stay; but there was an element of kindness in him, I was sure, which made him want me to have the job because I had betrayed how badly I needed it. I summed him up as a man who would be kind, unless being so made too many demands upon him.

I imagined the Comte's receiving my estimate, hearing that a woman had come instead of a man. But I could not picture him clearly. All I could imagine was a haughty man in white wig and crown. It was a picture I had seen either of Louis XIV or XV. The King . . . the King of the Castle.

I had a notepad with me and tried to jot down a few points which I had passed over on my previous examination. If he will let me stay, I told myself, I shall become so absorbed in the work that he can have murdered twenty wives for all I care.

There was one painting in the gallery which had particularly caught my attention. It was a portrait of a woman. The costume placed it in the eighteenth century—mid- or perhaps a little later. It interested me not because of the excellence of the work—there were better pictures in the gallery—but because, although it was of a later date than most of them, it was in a greater state of deterioration. The varnish was very dark and the whole surface was mottled as though it suffered from a skin disease. It looked to me as though it had been exposed to the weather.

I was contemplating this picture when I heard a movement behind me. I swung round to find that a man had entered the gallery and was standing there watching. I felt my heart pound and my legs tremble. I knew at once that I was at last face to face with the Comte de la Talle.

"It is Mademoiselle Lawson, of course," he said. Even his voice was unusual—deep, cold.

"You are the Comte de la Talle?"

He bowed. He did not come towards me. His eyes surveyed me across the gallery, and his manner was as cool as his voice. I noticed that he was tallish, and I was struck by his leanness. There was a slight resemblance to Philippe; but there was none of Philippe's femininity in this man. He was darker than his cousin; his cheekbones were high and this gave his face the pointed look which seemed almost satanic. His eyes were very dark—sometimes they could seem almost black, I discovered later, depending on his mood; they were deeply set and his lids were heavy; his aquiline nose gave to his face the look of haughtiness; his mouth was mobile; it changed according to the man he was. But at this time I knew only one man—the arrogant King of the Castle on whom my fate depended.

He wore a black riding coat with a velvet collar and above his white cravat his face was pale, even cruel.

"My cousin has told me of your coming." He advanced towards me now. He walked as a king might have walked through the hall of mirrors.

I had regained my poise very quickly. There was nothing like haughtiness to bring out my bristling armor.

"I am glad you have returned, Monsieur le Comte," I said, "for I have been waiting several days to know whether you wish me to stay and do the work."

"It must have been tiresome for you to be uncertain whether or not you were wasting your time."

"I have found the gallery very interesting, I assure you, so it will not have been an unpleasant way of wasting time."

"It is a pity," he said, "that you did not tell us of your father's death. It would have saved so much trouble."

So I was to go. I felt angry because I was so miserable. Back to London, I thought. I should have to find a lodging. And how could I afford to live until I discovered a post? I looked down the years and saw myself becoming more and more like Mademoiselle Dubois. What nonsense! As if I ever should! I could go to Cousin Jane. Never, never!

I hated him in that moment because I believed he guessed the thoughts which were passing through my mind. He would know that a woman as independent as I must have been desperate to have come in the first place, and he was enjoying tormenting me. How she must have hated him—that wife of his! Perhaps she killed herself to get away from him. I should not be surprised if that were the answer.

"I did not realize that you were so old-fashioned in France," I said with a touch of venom. "At home I have done this work with my father. No one minded because I was a woman. But as you have different notions here there is nothing more to be said."

"I disagree. There is a great deal to be said."

"Then," I said, lifting my eyes to his face, "perhaps you will begin to say it."

"Mademoiselle Lawson, you would like to restore these pictures, would you not?"

"It is my profession to restore paintings and the more in need of repair they are, the more interesting the task becomes."

"And you find mine in that need?"

"You must know that some of these pictures are in poor condition. I was examining this one when I realized you had come in. What kind of treatment could it have had to be in that state?"

"Pray, Mademoiselle Lawson, do not look at me so sternly. I am not responsible for the state of the picture."

"Oh? I presumed it had been some time in your possession. You see, there is a failing in the paint. It is chalky. Obviously it has been ill-treated."

A smile twisted his mouth and his face changed. There might have been a glimmer of amusement there now.

"How vehement you are! You might be fighting for the rights of man rather than for the preservation of paint on canvas."

"When would you wish me to leave?"

"Not until we have talked, at least."

"Since you find you cannot employ a woman I do not think we should have anything to talk about."

"You are very impulsive, Mademoiselle Lawson. Now I should have thought that was a characteristic a restorer of old paintings could well do without. I have not said I would not employ a woman. That was your suggestion."

"I can see that you disapprove of my being here. That is enough."

"Did you expect approval of your . . . deception?"

"Monsieur le Comte," I said, "I worked with my father. I took over his commissions. You had previously approached him to come here. I thought the arrangement still stood, I see no deception in that."

"Then you must have been surprised by the astonishment you caused."

I replied shortly: "It would be difficult to do delicate work of this nature in an atmosphere of disapproval."

"That I can well understand."

"Therefore . . ."

"Therefore?" he repeated.

"I could leave today if I could be taken to the main line station. I understand there is only one morning train from the Gaillard halt."

"How thoughtful of you to look into such arrangements. But I must repeat, Mademoiselle Lawson, you are too impulsive. You must understand my uneasiness. And if you will forgive my saying so, you do not look old enough to have had a great deal of experience in skilled work of this nature."

"I have worked with my father for years. There are some who grow old and never acquire the skill. It is a feeling in oneself for the work, an understanding, a love of painting that is born in one."

"You are poetical as well as an artist, I see. But at . . . er . . . thirty or so . . . one would necessarily not have had a lifetime's experience."

"I am twenty-eight," I retorted hotly; and I saw at once that I had fallen into the trap. He had determined to bring me off the pedestal on which I was trying to take a firm stand and show me that I was after all an ordinary woman who couldn't bear to be thought older than she was.

He raised his eyebrows; he was finding the interview amusing. I saw that I had betrayed my desperate situation and the streak of cruelty in him made him want to prolong the indecision, to torment me for as long as possible.

For the first time since I had set out on this adventure I lost my control. I said: "There is no point in continuing. I realize that you have decided I cannot do this work because I am a woman. Well, Monsieur, I leave you with your prejudices. So I will go either today or tomorrow."

For a few seconds he looked at me in mock bewilderment, but as I moved towards the door, he was swiftly beside me.

"Mademoiselle, you have not understood. Perhaps your knowledge of French is not as expert as your knowledge of painting."

Once more I rose to the bait. "My mother was French. I have understood perfectly every word you have said."

"Then I am to blame for my lack of lucidity. I have no wish that you shall go . . . just yet."

"Your manner suggests that you are not prepared to trust me."

"Your own assumption, Mademoiselle, I do assure you."

"Then you mean you wish me to stay?"

He pretended to hesitate. "If I may say so without offense, I should like you to undergo a little . . . test. Oh please, Mademoiselle, do not accuse me of prejudice against your sex. I am prepared to believe that there may be brilliant women in the world. I am impressed by what you tell me of your understanding and love of painting. I am also interested in the estimates of damage and the cost of repairing the pictures you have examined. It is all very clear and reasonable."

I was afraid that my eyes had begun to shine with hope and so would betray my excitement. If, I told myself, he realized how very eagerly I desired this commission he might continue baiting me.

He *had* seen. "I was going to suggest . . . but then you may have decided that you would prefer to leave today or tomorrow."

"I have come a long way, Monsieur le Comte. Naturally I should prefer to stay and carry out the work—providing it could be done in a congenial atmosphere. What were you going to suggest?"

"That you restore one of the pictures and if that is satisfactorily accomplished you continue with the rest."

I was happy in that moment. I should have been relieved, of course, for I was certain of my capabilities. The immediate future was taken care of. No ignoble return to London! No Cousin Jane! But it was more than that. An inexplicable feeling of joy, anticipation, excitement. I could not explain. I was certain that I could pass this test and that meant a long stay at the castle. This wonderful old place would be my home for months to come. I could explore it, as well as its treasures. I could continue my friendship with the Bastides. I could indulge my curiosity concerning the inhabitants of the *château*.

I was insatiably curious. I had known this since my father had pointed it out to me—and deplored this trait; but I could not stop myself wanting to know what went on behind the façade people showed the world. To discover this was like removing the film of decay from an old painting; and to learn what the Comte was like would be revealing a living picture.

"This proposition seems to appeal to you."

So once more I had betrayed my feelings, something I prided myself on rarely doing. But perhaps he was particularly perceptive.

"It seems a very fair one," I said.

"Then it's agreed." He held out his hand. "We will shake on it. An old English custom, I believe. You, Mademoiselle, have been kind enough to discuss the problem in French; we will seal the bargain in English."

As he held my hand his dark eyes looked into mine and I felt decidedly uncomfortable. I felt suddenly innocent, unworldly, and that was, I was sure, how he intended I should feel.

I withdrew my hand with a hauteur which I trusted hid my embarrassment. "Which picture would you select for the . . . test?" I asked.

"What of the one you were examining when I came in?"

"That would be excellent. It is more in need of restoration than anything in the gallery."

We walked over to it and stood side by side, examining it.

"It has been very badly treated," I said severely. I was now on firm ground. "It is not very old. A hundred and fifty years at most and yet . . ."

"An ancestress of mine."

"It is a pity she was subjected to such treatment."

"A great pity. But there was a time in France when people like her were submitted to even greater indignity."

"I should say that this picture has probably been exposed to the weather. Even the color of her gown is faded, though alizarin is usually stable. I can't see in this light the true color of the stones about her neck. You see how darkened they have become. The same with the bracelet and the earrings."

"Green," he said. "I can tell you that. They are emeralds."

"It would be a colorful picture when restored. That dress as it must have been when it was painted, and the emeralds."

"It will be interesting to see what it looks like when you have finished with it."

"I shall start at once."

"You have all you require?"

"For a beginning. I will go to my room for what I need and get down to work immediately."

"I can see you are all eagerness and I am delaying you."

I did not deny this and he stood aside for me as I passed triumphantly from the gallery. I felt I had come satisfactorily through my first encounter with the Comte.

What a happy morning I spent working in the gallery! No one disturbed me. I had returned with my tools to find that two of the menservants had taken the picture from the wall. They asked if there was anything I needed. I told them I would ring if there was. They looked at me with some respect. They would go back to the servants' quarters, I know, and spread the news that the Comte had given his permission for me to stay.

I had put on a brown linen coat over my dress, and I looked very businesslike. Oddly enough, as soon as I put on that coat I felt competent. I wished I had been wearing it during my meeting with the Comte.

I settled down to study the condition of the paint. Before I attempted to remove the varnish I must assess the tightness of the paint to the ground. It was clear that there was more discoloration here than from the ordinary accumulation of dust and grime. I had often found that before using a resin on varnish it was wise to wash carefully with soap and water. It took me a long time to decide on this course, but eventually I did.

I was surprised when a maid knocked on the door to remind me that it was time for *déjeuner*. This I took in my room and, as it was my practice never to work after lunch, I slipped out of the *château* and walked to the Maison Bastide. It seemed only courteous to tell them what had happened since they had shown such interest in whether or not I stayed.

The old lady was in her rocking chair and delighted to see me. The children, she told me, were having lessons with Monsieur le Curé; Armand, Jean Pierre, and Gabrielle were working; but it was a great pleasure to see me.

I seated myself beside her and said: "I have seen the Comte."

"I heard he was back at the *château*."

"I am to restore a picture and if it is a success I am to complete the work. I have already started; it is a portrait of one of his ancestors. A lady in a red dress and stones which at the moment are the color of mud. The Comte says they are emeralds."

"Emeralds," she said. "They could be the Gaillard emeralds."

"Family heirlooms?"

"They were . . . once upon a time."

"And no longer so?"

"Lost. I think during the Revolution."

"I suppose the *château* passed out of the hands of the family then?"

"Not exactly. We are far from Paris, and there was less trouble here. But the *château* was overrun."

"It seems to have survived fairly well."

"Yes. It's a story that's been handed down to us. They were forcing their way in. Perhaps you have seen the chapel? It is in the oldest part of the castle. You will notice that over the door on the outer wall there is broken masonry. Once a statue of St. Geneviève stood there high over the door. The revolutionaries were bent on desecrating the chapel. Fortunately for Château Gaillard they tried to pull down St. Geneviève first; they were drunk on *château* wine when they attached ropes about the figure, but it was heavier than they thought and it collapsed on them and killed three of them. They took it for an omen. It was said afterwards that St. Geneviève saved Gaillard."

"So that is why Geneviève is so called?"

"There have always been Genevièves in the family; and although the Comte of the day went to the guillotine, his son, who was a baby then, was cared for and in time went back to the *château*. This is a story we Bastides like to tell. We were for the People—for liberty, fraternity, and equality, against the aristocrats, but we kept the baby Comte here in this house and looked after him till it was all over. My husband's father used to tell me about it. He was a year or so older than the young Comte."

"So your family history is close to theirs."

"Very close."

"And the present Comte . . . he is your friend?"

"The de la Talles were never friends of the Bastides," she said proudly. "Only patrons. They don't alter . . . and nor do we."

She changed the subject, and after a while I left and went back to the *château*. I was eager to continue with my work.

During the afternoon one of the servants came to the gallery to tell me that Monsieur le Comte would be pleased if I joined the family for dinner that night. They dined at eight o'clock, and as it would be such a small party it would be in one of the smaller dining rooms. The maid said that she would take me there if I would be ready at five minutes to eight.

I felt too bewildered to work after that. The maid had spoken to me with respect, and this could only mean one thing: not only was I considered worthy to restore his pictures, but of even greater honor, I was to dine in his company.

I wondered what I should wear. I had only three dresses suitable for evening, none of them new. One was brown silk with coffee-colored lace, the second very severe black velvet with a ruffle of white lace at the throat, and the third gray cotton with a lavender silk stripe. I decided at once on the black velvet.

I could not work by artificial light, so as soon as the daylight faded I went to my room. I took out the dress and looked at it. Velvet fortunately did not age but the cut was by no means fashionable. I held it up to myself and looked at my reflection. My cheeks were faintly pink, my eyes reflecting the black velvet looked dark, and a strand of hair had escaped from the coil. Disgusted with my silliness, I put down the dress and was adjusting my hair when there was a knock at the door.

Mademoiselle Dubois entered. She looked at me disbelievingly and then stammered: "Mademoiselle Lawson, is it true that you have been invited to dine with the family?"

"Yes. Does it surprise you?"

"I have never been asked to dine with the family."

I looked at her and was not surprised. "I daresay they want to discuss the paintings with me. It's easier to talk over the dinner table."

"The Comte and his cousin, you mean?"

"Yes. I suppose so."

"I think you should be warned that the Comte has not a good reputation where a woman is concerned."

I stared at her. "He doesn't regard me as a woman!" I retorted. "I'm here to restore his paintings."

"They say that he is callous and in spite of that some find him irresistible."

"My dear Mademoiselle Dubois, I have never yet found any man irresistible and don't intend to start at my time of life."

"Well, you are not all that old."

Not all that old! Did she too think I was thirty?

She saw that I was annoyed and hurried on deprecatingly. "There was that poor unfortunate lady—his wife. The rumors one hears are . . . quite shocking. It's terrifying, isn't it, to think that we are under the same roof with a man like that."

"I don't think either of us need be afraid," I said.

She came close to me. "I lock my door at nights . . . while he is in the house. You should do the same. And I should be very careful . . . tonight. It might be that he wants to amuse himself while he's here with someone in the house. You can never be sure."

"I will be careful," I said to placate and get rid of her.

As I dressed, I wondered about her. Did she in the quiet of her room dream erotic dreams of an enamored Comte's attempts to seduce her? I was certain that she was in as little danger of such a fate as I was.

I washed and put on the velvet gown. I coiled my hair high on my head using many pins to make sure no strands escaped. I put on a brooch of my mother's—simple but charming, consisting of a number of small turquoises set in seed pearls. I was ready a full ten minutes before the maid knocked on the door to take me to the dining room.

We went into the seventeenth-century wing of the *château*—the latest addition—to a large vaulted chamber, a dining hall, in which I imagined guests were entertained. It would have been absurd for a small party to sit at such a table and I was not surprised when I was led on to a small room—small that is by Gaillard standards—leading off this dining hall. It was a pleasant room; there were midnight-blue velvet curtains at the windows—mullioned, I imagined, and different from the embrasures in the thick walls which narrowed to slits and while providing the utmost protection from outside, excluded the light. At each end of the marble mantelpiece stood a candelabrum in which candles burned. There was a similar one in the center of a table which was laid for dinner.

Philippe and Geneviève were already there. They were both subdued. Geneviève wore a dress of gray silk with a lace collar; her hair was tied behind her back with a pink silk bow, and she looked almost demure and quite unlike the girl I had met previously. Philippe in evening clothes was even more elegant than on our first meeting; and he seemed genuinely pleased to see me there.

He smiled pleasantly. "Good evening, Mademoiselle Lawson." I returned the greeting and it was almost as though there was a friendly conspiracy between us.

Geneviève was bobbing an uneasy curtsy.

"I daresay you have had a busy day in the gallery," said Philippe.

I replied that I had and was making preparations. It was necessary to test so many things before one attempted the delicate work of restoration.

"It must be quite fascinating," he said. "I am sure you will be successful."

I was sure he meant it, but all the time he was talking to me I was aware that he was listening for the arrival of the Comte.

He came precisely at eight, and we took our places at the table—the Comte at its head, I on his right, Geneviève on his left, and Philippe opposite him. The soup was served without delay while the Comte asked me how I was progressing in the gallery.

I repeated what I had said to Philippe about my start on the pictures, but he expressed more interest, whether because he was concerned for his pictures or whether he was making an attempt to be polite I was not sure.

I told him that I had decided that the picture should first be washed with soap and water so that any surface grime should be removed.

He regarded me with an amused glint in his eyes and said: "I have heard of that. The water has to stand in a special pot and the soap made during the dark of moon."

"We are no longer ruled by such superstitions," I replied.

"You are not superstitious then, Mademoiselle?"

"Not more than most people of today."

"That could be a good deal. But I am sure you are too practical for such fancies; and that is as well while you stay in this place. We have had people here"—his eyes turned to Geneviève who seemed to shrink into her chair—"governesses who had refused to stay. Some of them declared the *château* was haunted; some gave no reason but silently departed. Something here was intolerable . . . either my *château* or my daughter."

There was a cool distaste in his eyes as they rested on Geneviève and I felt my resentment rising. He was the sort of man who must have a victim. He had baited me in the gallery; now it was Geneviève's turn. In my case it was different. I had come under false pretenses and I was able to take care of myself. But a child . . . for Geneviève was little more . . . and a nervous, highly-strung one at that! And yet what had he said? Very little. The venom was in his manner. It was not unexpected either. Geneviève was afraid of him. So was Philippe. So was everyone in the place.

"If one were superstitious," I said, feeling I had to come to Geneviève's rescue, "it would be very easy for one's fancies to grow in a place like this. I have stayed in some very ancient houses with my father yet I have never encountered a single ghost."

"English ghosts would perhaps be more restrained than French ones? They would not appear without an invitation, which means they would only visit the fearful. But then, perhaps I am wrong."

I flushed. "They would surely take their code of manners from the days in which they lived and etiquette in France was always more rigid than in England."

"You are right, of course, Mademoiselle Lawson. The English would be far more likely to come uninvited. Therefore you are safe in this *château* . . . provided you do not invite strange company."

Philippe was listening intently; Geneviève with some awe. For me, I think, because I dared engage in conversation with her father.

Fish had replaced the soup and the Comte lifted his glass to me. "I trust you will like the wine, Mademoiselle Lawson. It is our own vintage. Are you a connoisseur of wines as well as of pictures?"

"It is a subject about which I know very little."

"You will hear a great deal about it while you are here. Often it is the main topic of conversation. I trust you will not find it tiresome."

"I am sure I shall find it most interesting. It is always pleasant to learn."

I saw the smile at the corner of his mouth. Governess! I thought. Certainly if I ever had to take up that profession I should have the right demeanor for it.

Philippe spoke rather hesitantly: "What picture are you starting on, Mademoiselle Lawson?"

"A portrait, painted last century—in the middle, I should think. I place it about 1740."

"You see, Cousin," said the Comte, "Mademoiselle Lawson is an expert. She loves pictures. She chided me for neglecting them as though I were a parent who had failed in his duty."

Geneviève looked down at her plate in embarrassment. The Comte turned to her. "You should take advantage of Mademoiselle Lawson's presence here. She could teach you enthusiasm."

"Yes, Papa," said Geneviève.

"And," he went on, "if you can persuade her to talk to you in English, you might be able to speak that language intelligibly. You should try to persuade Mademoiselle Lawson when she is not engaged with her pictures, to tell you about England and the English. You could learn from their less rigid etiquette. It might give you confidence and er . . . aplomb."

"We have already spoken together in English," I said. "Geneviève has a good vocabulary. Pronunciation is always a problem until one has conversed freely with natives. But it comes in time."

Again spoken like a governess! I thought; and I knew he was thinking the same. But I had done my best to support Geneviève and defy him. My dislike was growing with every moment.

"It is an excellent opportunity for you, Geneviève. Do you ride, Mademoiselle Lawson?"

"Yes. I am fond of riding."

"There are horses in the stables. One of the grooms would advise you which was your most suitable mount. Geneviève rides too . . . a little. You might ride together. The present governess is too timid. Geneviève, you could show Mademoiselle Lawson the countryside."

"Yes, Papa."

"Our country is not very attractive, I fear. The wine-growing land rarely is. But if you ride out a little way I am sure you will find something to please you."

"You are very kind. I should like to ride."

He waved a hand, and Philippe, no doubt feeling that it was time he made an effort in the conversation, took the subject back to pictures.

I talked about the portrait I was working on. I explained one or two details and made them rather technical in the hope of confusing the Comte. He listened gravely with a faint smile lurking at the corners of his mouth. It was disconcerting to suspect that he knew what was going on in my mind. If this were so, he would know that I disliked him, and oddly enough this seemed to add to his interest in me.

"I am certain," I was saying, "that although this is far from a masterpiece, the artist had a mastery of color. I can see this already. I am sure the color of the gown will be startling, and the emeralds restored to the color the artist intended will be magnificent."

"Emeralds . . ." said Philippe.

The Comte looked at him. "Oh yes, this is the picture in which they are seen in all their glory. It will be interesting to see them . . . if only on canvas."

"That," murmured Philippe, "is the only chance we shall have of seeing them."

"Who knows?" said the Comte. He turned to me. "Philippe is very interested in our emeralds."

"Aren't we all?" retorted Philippe with unusual boldness.

"We should be if we could lay our hands on them."

Geneviève said in a high, excited voice: "They must be somewhere. Nounou says they are in the *château*. If we could find them . . . oh, wouldn't it be exciting!"

"That old nurse of yours is sure to be right," said the Comte with sarcasm. "And I do agree that it would be *exciting* to find them . . .

apart from the fact that the discovery would add considerably to the family's fortunes."

"Indeed!" said Philippe, his eyes glowing.

"Do you think they are in the *château?*" I asked.

Philippe said eagerly: "They have never been discovered elsewhere, and stones like that would be recognized. They could not be disposed of easily."

"My dear Philippe," said the Comte. "You forget the time when they were lost. A hundred years ago, Mademoiselle Lawson, such stones could have been broken up, sold separately and forgotten. The markets must have been flooded with stones which had been stolen from the mansions of France by those who had little understanding of their value. It is almost certain that this was the fate of the Gaillard emeralds. The *canaille* who ransacked our houses and stole our treasures had no appreciation of what they took." The momentary anger which had shown in his eyes faded and he turned to me. "Ah, Mademoiselle Lawson, how fortunate that you did not live in those days. How would you have endured to see great paintings desecrated, thrown out of windows to lie neglected and exposed to the weather . . . to collect what is it . . . Bloom?"

"It is tragic that so much that was beautiful was lost." I turned to Philippe: "You were telling me about the emeralds?"

"They were in the family for years," he said. "They were worth . . . it is difficult to say for values have changed so much. They were priceless. They were kept in our strong room at the *château*. Yet they were lost at the time of the Revolution. No one knew what had become of them. But the belief has always been that they are somewhere in the *château*."

"Periodically there are treasure hunts," said the Comte. "Someone has a theory and there is a great deal of excitement. We look. We dig. We attempt to discover hidden places in the *château* that have not been opened for years. This produces a great deal of activity but never any emeralds."

"Papa," cried Geneviève, "couldn't we have a treasure hunt now?"

The pheasant had been brought in. It was excellent but I scarcely tasted it. I found the conversation all-absorbing. I had been in a state of exultation all day because I was going to stay here.

"You have so impressed my daughter, Mademoiselle Lawson," said the Comte, "that she thinks you will succeed where others have failed. You want a renewed search, Geneviève, because you feel that now Mademoiselle Lawson is here she cannot fail?"

"No," said Geneviève, "I didn't think that. I just want to look for the emeralds."

"How ungracious you are! Forgive her, Mademoiselle Lawson. And Geneviève, I suggest that you show Mademoiselle Lawson the *château*." He turned to me: "You have not yet explored it, I am sure, and with your lively and most intelligent curiosity you will want to. I believe your father understood architecture as you do pictures and that you worked with him. Why, who knows, you might discover the hiding place which has baffled us for a hundred years."

"I should be interested to see the *château*," I admitted, "and if Geneviève will show me I shall be delighted."

Geneviève did not look at me, and the Comte frowned at her. I said quickly: "We will make an appointment if that is agreeable to you, Geneviève?"

She looked at her father and then at me. "Tomorrow morning?" she said.

"I am working in the morning, but tomorrow afternoon I should be most happy to come."

"Very well," she mumbled.

"I am sure it will be a profitable excursion for you, Geneviève," said the Comte.

Through the soufflé we talked of the neighborhood—mostly of the vineyards. I felt I had made great progress. I had dined with the family, something poor Mademoiselle Dubois had never achieved; I had been given permission to ride—I had brought my old riding habit with me hopefully; I was to be shown over the *château* the next day; and I had achieved some sort of relationship with the Comte, although I was not sure what sort.

I was rather pleased when I could retire to my room, but before I left the Comte said that there was a book in the library which I might like to see.

"My father had a man down here to write it," he explained. "He was extremely interested in the history of our family. The book was written and printed. It is years since I read it, but I do believe it would interest you."

I said that I was sure it would and I should be delighted to see it.

"I will have it sent to you," he told me.

I took my leave of the company when Geneviève did, and we left the men together. She conducted me to my room and bade me a cool good night.

I had not been long in my room when there was a knock on the door and a maid entered with the book.

"Monsieur le Comte said you wanted this," she told me.

She went out leaving me standing with the book in my hand. It was a slim volume, and there were some line drawings of the castle. I was sure I should find it absorbing, but at the moment my mind was full of the evening's events.

I did not want to go to bed, for my mind was too stimulated for sleep, and my thoughts were dominated by the Comte. I had expected him to be unusual. After all he was a man surrounded by mystery. His daughter was afraid of him; I was not sure about his cousin but I suspected he was too. The Comte was a man who liked those about him to fear him, and yet despised them for doing it. That was the conclusion I had come to. I had noted the exasperation those two had aroused in him and yet by his manner he had added to their fear. I wondered what his life had been like with the woman who had been unfortunate enough to marry him. Had she cowered from his contempt? How had he ill-treated her? It was not easy to think of him indulging in physical violence . . . and yet how could I be sure of anything where he was concerned? I scarcely knew him . . . yet.

The last word excited me. I had to admit it. For how did he think of me? Scarcely at all. He had looked me over, had decided to give me the job, and that could well be the end of his interest. Why had I been invited to dine with the family? So that he could look more intently at a human specimen who interested him vaguely? Because there was nothing else of interest at the castle? Dining alone with Philippe and Geneviève would be somewhat boring. I had defied him—not altogether successfully, for he was too clever not to see through my defense—and because I was bold it had amused him to submit me to further examination, to attempt to deflate me.

He was a sadist. That was my conclusion. He was responsible for his wife's death, for even if he had not administered the dose he had driven

69

her to take it. Poor woman! What must her life have been? How wretched could a woman be to be driven to take her life? Poor Geneviève, who was her daughter! I must try to understand that girl, somehow make a friend of her. I felt she was a lost child wandering through a maze, growing increasingly more afraid that she would never find a way out.

And I, who prided myself on being a practical woman, could grow quite fanciful in this place, where strange events must have happened over centuries, where a woman so recently had died unhappily.

To drive this man out of my thoughts I tried to think of another. How different was the open face of Jean Pierre Bastide!

Then suddenly I began to smile. It was strange that I who had never been interested in a man since I had loved Charles years ago had now found two who were constantly in my thoughts.

How foolish! I admonished myself. What have either of them to do with you?

I picked up the book the Comte had given me and began to read.

The castle had been built in the year 1405, and there was still much of the original structure standing. The two wings which flanked the old building had been added later, they were well over a hundred feet tall, and the cylindrical forts gave them added solidity. Comparisons were drawn to the royal *château* of Loches and it seemed that life in Château Gaillard was conducted in much the same manner as it was in Loches; for in Gaillard the de la Talles ruled as kings. Here they had their dungeons in which they imprisoned their enemies. In the most ancient part of the building there was one of the most perfect examples of the *oubliette*.

When these dungeons had been examined by the writer of the book, cages had been discovered similar to those in Loches, small hollows cut out of stone in which there was not room for a man to stand up; in these, human beings had been chained and left to die by fifteenth, sixteenth and seventeenth century de la Talles in the same way as Louis XI had dealt with his enemies. One man, left to die in the *oubliette*, had attempted to cut his way to freedom and had succeeded in boring a passage which had brought him out to one of the cages in the dungeons where he had died in frustrated despair.

I read on, fascinated not only by the descriptions of the *château* but by the history of the family.

Often during the centuries the family had been in conflict with the kings; more often they had stood beside them. One of the women of the house had been a mistress of Louis XV before she married into the family and it was this King who had presented her with an emerald necklace of great value. It was considered no dishonor to be a mistress of the King and the de la Talle who had married her when she left the royal service had sought to vie with the King's generosity and had presented his wife with an emerald bracelet made up of priceless stones to match those of the necklace. But a bracelet was less valuable than a necklace; so there had been a tiara of emeralds and two emerald rings, a brooch, and a girdle all set with emeralds, as proof that de la Talles could stand equal with royalty. Thus the famous de la Talle emeralds had come into being.

The book confirmed what I already knew, that the emeralds had been lost during the Revolution. Until then they had been kept with other treasures in the strong room in the gun gallery to which no one but the master of the house had the key or even knew where the key was hidden. So it had been until the Terror broke out all over France.

It was late but I could not stop reading, and I had come to the chapter headed "The de la Talles and the Revolution."

Lothair de la Talle, the Comte at that time, was a young man of thirty; he had married a few years before that fatal year and was called to Paris for the meeting of the States General. He never returned to the castle; he was one of the first whose blood was spilled on the guillotine. His wife Marie Louise, twenty-two years old and pregnant, remained in the *château* with the old Comtesse, Lothair's mother. I pictured it clearly; the hot days of July; the news being brought to that young woman of her husband's death; her grief for her husband, her fears for the child soon to be born. I imagined her at the highest window of the highest tower, straining her eyes over the countryside; wondering if the revolutionaries would come marching her way; asking herself how long the people of the district would allow her to live in peace.

All through the sultry days she must have waited, afraid to go into the little town, watchful of the work people who toiled in the vineyards, of the servants who doubtless grew a little less subservient with the passing of each day. I pictured the proud old Comtesse, desperately trying to preserve the old ways, and what those two brave women must have suffered during those terrible days.

Few escaped the Terror—and eventually it reached the Château Gaillard. A band of revolutionaries were marching on the *château,* waving their banners, singing the new song from the south. The workers left the vineyard; from the little cottages of the town ran the women and children. The stall holders and the shopkeepers spilled into the square. The aristocrats had had their day. They were the masters now.

I shivered as I read how the young Comtesse had left the castle and sheltered in a nearby house. I knew what house it was; I knew which family had taken her in. Had I not heard that their family history was entwined. They were never friends though, only patrons. I could clearly remember Madame Bastide's proud looks when she had said that.

So Madame Bastide, who must have been Jean Pierre's great-grandmother, had sheltered the Comtesse. She had ruled her household so that even the men had not dared disobey her. They were with the revolutionaries preparing to pillage the castle while she hid the Comtesse in her house and forbade them all to whisper outside the house a word of what was happening.

The old Comtesse refused to leave the *château.* She had lived there; she would die there. And she went into the chapel there to await death at the hands of the rebels. Her name was Geneviève and she prayed to St. Geneviève for help. She heard the rough shouting and coarse laughter as the mob broke into the castle; she knew they were tearing down the paintings and the tapestries, throwing them from the windows to their comrades.

And there were those who came to the chapel. But before they entered they sought to tear down the statue of St. Geneviève which had been set up over the door. They climbed up to it, but they could not move it. Inflamed with wine, they called to their comrades. Before they continued to pillage the *château* they must break down the statue.

At the altar the old Comtesse continued to pray to St. Geneviève while the shouting grew louder, and every moment she expected the rabble to break into the chapel and kill her.

Ropes were brought; to the drunken strains of the "Marseillaise" and "Ça Ira" they worked. She heard the great shout that went up. "Heave,

72

comrades . . . all together!" And then the crash, the screams . . . and the terrible silence.

The *château* was out of danger; St. Geneviève lay broken at the door of the chapel, but beneath her lay the bodies of three dead men; she had saved the *château*, for superstitious, fearful, in spite of their professed ungodliness, the revolutionaries slunk away. A few bold ones had tried to rally the mob but it was useless. Many of them came from the surrounding district and they had lived their lives under the shadow of the de la Talles. They feared them now as they had in the past. They had one wish and that was to turn their backs on Château Gaillard.

The old Comtesse came out of the chapel when all was silent. She looked at the broken statue and, kneeling beside it, gave thanks to her patron saint. Then she went into the *château* and with the help of one servant attempted to set it to rights. There she lived alone for some years, caring for the young Comte who was stealthily brought back to his home. His mother had died in giving birth to him, which was not surprising considering all that she had suffered before his birth and the fact that Madame Bastide had been afraid to call the midwife to her. There they lived for years in the *château*—the old Comtesse, the young child and one servant; until the times changed, the Revolution passed and life at the *château* began to slip back into the old ways. Servants came back; repairs were made; the vineyards became prosperous. But although the strong room in which they had been kept was untouched, the emeralds had disappeared and were lost to the family from that time.

I closed the book. I was so tired that I was soon asleep.

❀ 3 ❀

I spent the next morning in the gallery. I was half expecting a visit from the Comte, after the interest he had shown the night before, but he did not come.

I had lunch in my room as usual, and when I had finished there was a knock on my door and Geneviève came in.

Her hair was neatly tied behind her back and she looked subdued as she had last night at dinner. It occurred to me that her father's being in the house had a marked effect upon her.

First we mounted the staircase in the polygonal tower and reached the summit of the building. In the tower she pointed out to me the surrounding country speaking in slow, rather painful English, as the Comte had suggested. I believed that although at times she hated and feared him, she had a desire to win his respect.

"Mademoiselle, can you see a tower right away to the south? That is where my grandfather lives."

"It is not very far."

"It is nearly twelve *kilomètres*. You can see it today only because the air is so clear."

"Do you visit him often?"

She was silent, looking at me suspiciously. I said: "It is not so very far."

"I go sometimes," she said. "Papa does not go. Please do not tell him."

"He would not wish you to go?"

"He has not said so." Her voice was faintly bitter. "He doesn't say much to me, you know. Please promise not to tell him."

"Why should I tell him?"

"Because he talks to you."

74

"My dear Geneviève, I have met him only twice. Naturally he talks about his paintings to me. He is concerned for them. He is not likely to speak to me of other things."

"He doesn't usually talk to people . . . who come to work here."

"They probably don't come to restore his paintings."

"I think he was interested in *you*, Mademoiselle."

"He was concerned as to what I should do to his works of art. Now, look at this vaulted ceiling. Notice the shape of the arched door. That enables you to place it within a hundred years or so." Actually I wanted to talk about her father, to ask how he usually behaved to people in the house; I wanted to know why he would not wish her to visit her grandfather.

"You speak too fast, Mademoiselle, I cannot follow."

We descended the staircase and when we had reached the bottom, she said in French: "Now you have been to the top you must see the lower part. Did you know that we had dungeons in the *château*, Mademoiselle?"

"Yes, your father sent me a book which had been written by an ancestor of yours. It gave a very good idea of what the *château* contained."

"We used to keep our prisoners here, Mademoiselle. If anyone offended a Comte de la Talle he was put into the dungeons. My mother told me. She took me there once and showed me. She said that you didn't have to be in a dungeon though to be imprisoned. She said stone walls and chains were one way of keeping prisoners; there were others."

I looked at her sharply, but her eyes were wide and innocent and the demure look was still on her face.

"In the royal *châteaux* there were dungeons . . . *oubliettes* they called them, because people were sent into them and forgotten. They are the prisons of the forgotten. Did you know, Mademoiselle, that the only way into these prisons was through trap doors which could not be easily seen from above?"

"Yes. I have read of these places. The victim was made to stand unsuspectingly on the trap door which was opened by pressing a lever in another part of the room; suddenly the floor opened beneath him and he would fall down."

"Down into the *oubliette*. It is a long drop. I've seen it. Perhaps his leg would be broken and there would be no one to help him; he would lie there forgotten with the bones of others who had gone before him. Mademoiselle, are you afraid of ghosts?"

"Of course not."

"Most of the servants are. They won't go into the room above the *oubliette* . . . at least they won't go alone. They say at night there are noises in the *oubliette* . . . queer groaning noises. Are you sure you want to see it?"

"My dear Geneviève, I have stayed in some of the most haunted houses in England."

"Then you are safe. Papa said, didn't he, that French ghosts would be more polite than English ones and only come when expected. If you aren't frightened and don't believe in them you wouldn't be expecting them, would you? That was what he meant."

How she remembered his words! I thought then: This child needs more than discipline. She needs affection. It was three years since her mother had died. How she must have missed it since then with such a father!

"Mademoiselle, you are sure you are not afraid of the *oubliette?*"

"Quite sure."

"It is not as it was," she said almost regretfully. "They cleared out a lot of bones and horrid things a long time ago when there was a search for the emeralds. It was my grandfather who did that, and of course the first place you would look for them would be in the *oubliette*, wouldn't it? They didn't find them though, so they weren't there. They say they were taken away, but I think they're here. I wish Papa would have a treasure hunt again. Wouldn't that be fun?"

"I expect thorough searches have been made. From what I have read it seems certain that they were stolen by the revolutionaries who broke into the *château*."

"But then they didn't break into the strong room did they? And yet the emeralds were gone."

"Perhaps the emeralds were sold before the Revolution. Perhaps they hadn't been in the *château* for years. I'm merely guessing. But suppose one of your ancestors needed money and sold them. He—or she—might not have told anyone of this. Who can say?"

She looked at me with surprise. Then she said triumphantly: "Have you told my father that?"

"I'm sure the idea has occurred to him. It's one obvious solution."

"But the woman in the picture you are working on is wearing them. They must have been in the family then."

"They could have been imitation."

"Mademoiselle, no de la Talle would wear imitation jewels."

I smiled and then gave a little exclamation of pleasure for we had come to a narrow and uneven staircase. "This leads underground, Mademoiselle. There are eighty steps. I've counted them. Can you manage? Hold the rope banister."

I did so and followed her down; the staircase became spiral and narrow, so there was only room for us to go in single file.

"Can't you feel the cold, Mademoiselle?" There was a note of excitement in her voice. "Oh, imagine being brought down here knowing that you might never come up again. We are now down below the level of the moat. This is where we used to keep people who had offended us."

Having passed down the eighty steps we were confronted by a heavy oak door studded with iron; words had been carved on it and they stood out clearly and ironically.

"Entrez, Messieurs, Mesdames,
chez votre maître le Comte de la Talle."

"You are thinking it a pleasant welcome, Mademoiselle?" She was smiling at me slyly and it was as though another girl peeped out from behind that demure expression.

I shuddered.

She came close to me and whispered: "But it is all over now, Mademoiselle. This is no longer *chez nous*. We never entertain here now. Come along in. Look at these holes in the walls. They are called *cages*. Look at the chains. We used to chain them here and give them bread and water now and then. They never lived long though. You see, it is dark even now, but with the door shut there is no light at all . . . no light . . . no air. Next time we come we must bring candles . . . or a lantern would be better. The air is so close. If I had brought a light I could have shown you the writing on the walls. Some of them scratched prayers to the saints and the Holy Mother. Some of them scratched what revenge they would take on the de la Talles."

"It's unhealthy down here," I said, looking at the fungoid growth on the slimy walls. "And as you say we can see little without a light."

"The *oubliette* is on the other side of the wall. Come on. I will show you. The *oubliette* is even more haunted than this place, Mademoiselle, because there were the truly forgotten ones."

She smiled secretly and led the way up the stairs. Throwing open a door she announced: "This is now the gun gallery."

I stepped inside and saw the guns of all shapes and sizes ranged about the walls. The ceiling was vaulted and supported by stone pillars; the floor appeared to be of flagged stone and was covered in places by rugs. There were the same stone window seats which were in my bedroom and the alcoves narrowing to a slit letting in a little light. I had to admit to myself, although I would not to Geneviève, that there was something chillingly forbidding about this chamber. It had not been altered for hundreds of years and I could imagine the unsuspecting victim coming into the room. There was one chair, so ornately carved that it was almost like a throne. I wondered that such a piece of furniture was left in a room like this. It was a large wooden chair, and the carving on the back was of the *fleurs-de-lis* and arms of the de la Talle family. I pictured the man who would sit there—and naturally I pictured the present Comte—talking to his victim and then suddenly the pressing of the lever which would release the spring of the trap door; the agonizing scream, or the moment of silent terror as the victim realized what was happening to him as the floor opened and he fell down to join those who had gone before him, never again to see the light of day, to join the forgotten.

"Help me with the chair, Mademoiselle," said Geneviève. "The spring is under it."

Together we pushed aside the thronelike chair and Geneviève rolled up the rug. "There," she went on. "I press here . . . and look . . . see . . . it's happening."

There was a groaning, squeaking sound and it was as though a large square hole had appeared in the floor.

"In the old days it happened quickly and noiselessly. Look down there, Mademoiselle. You can't see much, can you? But there is a rope ladder. It's kept in the cupboard here. Twice a year some of the menservants go down there, to clean it, I suppose. Of course it's all right now. No bones, Mademoiselle, no moldering bodies. There are only ghosts . . . and you don't believe in them."

She had brought out the rope ladder, hung it on two hooks, which had evidently been fixed for it beneath the floorboards, and let it fall.

"There, Mademoiselle, are you coming down with me?" She started to descend, laughing up at me. "I know you're not afraid."

She reached the floor, and I followed her.

We were in a small chamber; a little light penetrated from the open trap door and there was just enough to show me the piteous engravings on the walls.

"Look at those openings in the walls. They were for a purpose. The prisoners thought there was a way out through them. There's a sort of maze in which you can lose yourself; you see they would think that if they could find the way through those passages they would be free. They only lead back to the *oubliette*. It's called exquisite torture."

"That's interesting," I said. "I have never heard of that. This must be unique."

"Do you want to examine it, Mademoiselle? I knew you would, because you are not afraid, are you? You are so brave, and you don't believe in ghosts."

I went to the opening in the wall and took a few steps into the darkness. I touched the cold wall and it took me some seconds to realize that this did not lead anywhere. It was merely an alcove cut into the thickness of the wall.

I turned and heard a low chuckle. Geneviève had ascended the ladder and was pulling it up.

"You love the past, Mademoiselle," she said. "Well, this is like it. The de la Talles do still leave their victims to perish in their *oubliettes*."

"Geneviève!" I cried shrilly.

She laughed. "You're a liar," she retorted shrilly. "But perhaps you don't know it. Now is the time to find out whether you're afraid of ghosts!"

The trap door shut with a bang. For the moment the darkness seemed intense, and then my eyes grew accustomed to the dimness. It was some more seconds before the horror of my position began to dawn on me.

The girl had planned this last night when her father had suggested she should show me the *château*. After a while she would release me. All I had to do was keep a hold on my dignity, to refuse to admit even to myself the rising panic and wait until I was free.

"Geneviève!" I called. "Open that trap door immediately."

I knew that my voice could not be heard. The walls were thick, so were the slabs over my head. What would be the point of an *oubliette* where the screams of the victims could be heard? The very description implied what happened to those who were incarcerated here. Forgotten!

I had been foolish to trust her. I had had a glimpse of her nature when I had first seen her; yet I had allowed myself to be deceived by her apparent docility. Suppose she was more than mischievous? Suppose she was wicked?

With sudden horror I asked myself what would happen when I was missed. But when should I be missed? Not until dinner time when either a tray would be brought to my room or I should be summoned to dine at the family table. And then . . . Should I have to wait in this gruesome place all those hours?

Another thought occurred to me. What if she went to my room, hid my things, making it seem that I had left? She might even forge a note explaining that I had gone because I was not pleased with my reception . . . because I no longer cared to do the work.

Was she capable of that?

She could be—the daughter of a murderer!

Was that fair? I knew scarcely anything of the mystery surrounding the Comte's wife—all I knew was that there was a mystery. But this girl was strange; she was wild; I now believed she was capable of anything.

In those first moments of near panic I understood a little of what those victims must have felt when they found themselves in this terrible place. But I could not compare myself with them. They would have fallen, damaging their limbs; I had at least descended by the ladder. I was the victim of a joke; they of revenge. It was quite different. Soon the trap door would open, the girl's head would appear. I must be very stern with her, at the same time showing no sign of panic and above all retaining my dignity.

I sat on the floor, leaning against the cold stone wall, and looked up at the trap door. I tried to see the time by the watch pinned to my blouse. I could not do so, but the minutes were ticking away. It was useless to pretend I was not frightened. A sense of terrible doom impregnated the place; the air was close; I felt stifled; and I knew that I, who had always prided myself on my calmness, was near to panic.

Why had I come to the *château?* How much better to have tried to find a respectable post as a governess to which I should have been so well fitted! How much better to have gone to Cousin Jane, to have nursed her, waited on her, read to her, listened to her a hundred times a day reminding me that I was a poor relation!

I wanted a chance to live quietly, without excitement, I should not mind as long as I could live. How often had I said I would rather be dead than live a life of servitude—and I had thought I meant it. Now I was ready to barter independence, a life of interest . . . anything for the chance of remaining alive. I would never have thought it possible until this moment. How much did I know of myself? Could it be that the armor I put on to face the world deceived me as much as it did others?

I was trying to think of anything which would turn my thoughts from this terrible place in which it seemed to me tortured minds and bodies of those who had suffered had left something behind them.

"Do you believe in ghosts, Mademoiselle?"

Not in the broad skeptical daylight when I am within easy reach of my fellow human beings. In a dark *oubliette* into which I had been tricked and left . . . I did not know.

"Geneviève!" I called. And the note of panic in my voice frightened me.

I stood up and paced up and down. I called again and again until my voice was hoarse. I sat down and tried to be calm; then I paced up and down again. I found myself looking furtively over my shoulder. I began to tell myself that I was watched. I kept my eyes on the opening in the wall which I could just make out and which Geneviève had said was a maze and I knew to be a dark alcove . . . but I was expecting someone . . . something to emerge.

I was afraid that I was going to sob or scream. I tried to take a grip on myself by saying aloud that I would find a way out, although I knew there was no way. I sat down again and tried to shut out the gloom by covering my face with my hands.

I started up in dismay. There was a sound. I put my hand to my mouth automatically to suppress the scream. I fixed my eyes on that dark aperture.

A voice said: "Mademoiselle!" And the place had lightened. I gave a great sob of joy and relief. The trap door was open, and the gray, frightened face of Nounou was looking down at me.

"Mademoiselle, are you all right?"

"Yes . . . yes . . ." I had run to look up at her.

"I will get the ladder," she said.

It seemed a long time before she came back, but she had the ladder. I grasped it and stumbled up, so eager to reach the top that I almost fell.

Her frightened eyes searched my face. "That naughty girl! Oh dear, I don't know what will become of us all. You look so pale . . . so *distrait*."

"Who would not, shut in that place! I'm forgetting to thank you for coming. I can't tell you how . . ."

"Mademoiselle, will you come to my room? I will give you some good strong coffee. I would like to talk to you, too, if you will allow me."

"It is good of you. But where is Geneviève?"

"You are angry, naturally. But I can explain."

"Explain! What is there to explain? Did she tell you what she had done?"

The nurse shook her head. "Please come to my room. It is easy to talk there. Please, I must speak to you. I want you to understand. Besides, it was a terrible ordeal. You are shocked. Who would not be?" She slipped her arm through mine. "Come, Mademoiselle, it is best for you."

Still feeling dazed, I allowed myself to be led away from that dreadful room which I was sure I should never willingly enter again. She had the soothing manner of one who has spent a lifetime looking after the helpless, and in my present mood her gentle authority was what I needed.

I did not notice where she was leading me but when she threw open a door to show a small and cozy room I realized that we were in one of the newer wings.

"Now you must lie down. Here on this sofa. So much more restful than sitting."

"This isn't necessary."

"Forgive me, Mademoiselle, it is very necessary. I am going to make you some coffee." There was an open fire in her grate and on a hob a kettle was singing. "Good hot strong coffee. It will help you to feel better. My poor Mademoiselle, it has been terrible for you!"

"How did you know what had happened?"

She turned to the fire and busied herself with the coffee.

"Geneviève came back by herself. I saw by her face . . ."

"You guessed?"

"It happened before. There was one of the governesses. Not like you at all . . . a pretty young lady—a little brazen perhaps . . . Geneviève did the same thing to her. It was soon after her mother died . . . not long afterwards."

"So she shut her governess in the *oubliette* as she did me. How long did *she* stay there?"

"Longer than you did. You see, as she was the first, I didn't find out until some time. Poor young lady, she was fainting with fear. She refused to stay in the *château* after that . . . and that was the end of her as far as we were concerned."

"You mean that girl makes a habit of this?"

"Only twice. Please, Mademoiselle, do not excite yourself. It is bad for you after what happened."

"I want to see her. I shall make her understand . . ."

I realized that the reason I was so angry was because I had been near to panic and was ashamed of myself, disappointed and surprised. I had always believed myself to be so self-reliant and it was as though I had removed a film from a painting and found something unsuspected beneath. And here was another discovery, I was doing that which I had so often condemned in others—turning my anger on someone because I was angry with myself. Of course Geneviève had behaved abominably —but it was my own conduct that was upsetting me now.

Nounou came and stood beside the sofa, clasping her hands together and looking down at me.

"It is not easy for her, Mademoiselle. A girl like her to lose her mother. I have tried to do my best."

"She was devoted to her mother?"

"Passionately. Poor child, it was a terrible shock to her. She has never recovered from it. I trust you will remember that."

"She is undisciplined," I said. "Her behavior on the first occasion we met was intolerable and now this . . . I suppose I should have been left there indefinitely if you had not discovered what she had done."

"No. She only wanted to frighten you, perhaps because you seemed so well able to take care of yourself and she, poor child, is so definitely not."

"Tell me," I said, "why is she so strange?"

She smiled with relief. "That is what I want to do, Mademoiselle, to tell you."

"I should like to understand what makes her act as she does."

"And when you do, Mademoiselle, you will forgive her. You will not tell her father what has happened this afternoon? You will not mention it to anyone?"

I was unsure. I said promptly: "I certainly intend to speak to Geneviève about it."

"But to no one else, I beg of you. Her father would be very angry and she dreads his anger."

"Wouldn't it be good for her to realize the wickedness of what she did? We shouldn't pat her on the back and tell her nothing matters because you came and rescued me."

"No, speak to her if you wish, but I must talk to you first. There are things I want to tell you."

She turned away and busied herself at the table.

"About," she said slowly, "her mother's death."

I waited for her to go on. She could not have been more eager to tell me than I was to hear. But she would not speak until she had made the coffee. She left the brown jug to stand and came back to the couch.

"It was terrible . . . *that* to happen to a young girl of eleven. She was the one who found her dead."

"Yes," I agreed, "that would be terrible."

"She used to go in and see her mother first thing in the morning. Imagine a young girl going in and finding that!"

I nodded. "But it was three years ago and terrible as it was it does not excuse her for locking me in that place."

"She has never been the same since. She changed afterwards. There were these fits of naughtiness in which she seemed to delight. It is because she misses her mother's love; because she is afraid . . ."

"Of her father?"

"So you have seen that. At the same time there were the questions and inquiries. It was so bad for her. The whole household believed that he had done it. He had his mistress . . ."

84

"I see. The marriage was unhappy. Did he love his wife when they were first married?"

"Mademoiselle, he could only love himself."

"And did she love him?"

"You have seen how he frightens Geneviève. Françoise was afraid too."

"Was *she* in love with *him* when she married him?"

"You know how marriages are arranged between such families. But perhaps it is not so in England. In France among our noble families marriages are always arranged by the parents. Isn't it so in England?"

"Not to the same extent. Families are apt to disapprove of a choice, but I do not think the rules are so rigid."

She shrugged her shoulders. "Here it is so, Mademoiselle. And Françoise was betrothed to Lothair de la Talle when they were in their teens."

"Lothair . . ." I repeated.

"Monsieur le Comte. It is a family name, Mademoiselle. There have always been Lothairs in the family."

"It is a king's name," I said. "That is why." She looked puzzled, and I said quickly: "I'm sorry. Pray go on."

"The Comte had his mistress as Frenchmen do. No doubt he was more fond of her than of his affianced bride, but she was not suitable to be his wife, and so my Françoise married him."

"You were her nurse too?"

"I came to her when she was three days old, and was with her till the end."

"And now Geneviève has taken her place in your affections?"

"I trust to be with her always as I was with her mother. When it happened I couldn't believe it. Why should it have happened to my Françoise? Why should she have taken her own life? It was unlike her."

"Perhaps she was unhappy."

"She did not hope for the impossible."

"Did she know of his mistress?"

"Mademoiselle, in France these things are accepted. She was resigned. She feared him; and I fancied she was glad of those visits to Paris. When he was there . . . he was not in the *château*."

"It does not sound to me like a happy marriage."

"She accepted it."

"And yet . . . she died."

"She did not kill herself." The old woman put her hands over her eyes and whispered as though to herself: "No, she did *not* kill herself."

"But wasn't that the verdict?"

She turned on me almost fiercely. "What other verdict could there be . . . except murder?"

"I heard it was an overdose of laudanum. How did she get it?"

"She often had toothache. I had the laudanum in my little cupboard, and I used to give it to her. It soothed the toothache and sent her to sleep."

"Perhaps she accidentally took too much."

"She did not mean to kill herself. I am sure of it. But that was what they said. They had to . . . hadn't they . . . for the sake of Monsieur le Comte?"

"Nounou," I said, "are you trying to tell me that the Comte murdered his wife?"

She stared at me as though startled. "You cannot say I said that, Mademoiselle. I said no such thing. You are putting words into my mouth."

"But if she did not kill herself . . . then someone must have."

She turned to the table and poured out two cups of coffee.

"Drink this, Mademoiselle, and you will feel better. You are overwrought."

I could have told her that in spite of my recent unpleasant experience I was less overwrought than she, but I wanted to glean as much as I could, and I realized that I was more likely to do so from her than from anyone else.

She gave me the cup and then drew a chair up to the sofa and sat down beside me.

"Mademoiselle, I want you to understand what a cruel thing this was which happened to my little Geneviève. I want you to forgive her . . . to help her."

"Help her? *I*?"

"Yes, you can. If you will forgive her. If you will please not tell her father . . ."

"She is afraid of him. I sensed that."

Nounou nodded. "He paid attention to you at dinner. She told me. And in a different way he paid attention to the pretty young governess.

86

Do please understand. It is something to do with her mother's death. It brings it back to her. You see, there is gossip, and she knew that there was another woman."

"Does she hate her father?"

"It is a strange relationship, Mademoiselle. He is so aloof. Sometimes she might not be there for all the notice he takes of her. At others he seems to take a delight in taunting her. It's as though he dislikes her, as though he's disappointed in her. If he would show her a little affection . . ." She lifted her shoulders. "He is a strange, hard man, Mademoiselle, and since the scandals he has become more so."

"Perhaps he does not know what is said of him. Who would dare tell him of these rumors?"

"No one. But he is aware. He has been different since her death. He is no monk, Mademoiselle, but he seems to have a contempt for women. Sometimes I think he is a most unhappy man."

Perhaps, I thought, it is not very good taste to discuss the master of the house with one of his servants; but I was avidly curious and could not have stopped myself had I wanted to. This was something else I was discovering about myself. I refused to listen to my conscience.

"I wonder he has not married again," I said. "Surely a man in his position would want a son."

"I do not think he will marry again, Mademoiselle. It is for that reason that he sent for Monsieur Philippe."

"So he *sent* for Philippe?"

"Not long ago. I daresay Monsieur Philippe will be expected to marry and his son will have everything."

"I find that very hard to understand."

"Monsieur le Comte *is* hard to understand, Mademoiselle. I have heard that he lives very gaily in Paris. Here he is much alone. He is melancholy and seems to take pleasure only in the discomfort of everyone else."

"What a charming man!" I said scornfully.

"Ah, life is not easy at the *château*. And most difficult of all for Geneviève." She laid her hand on mine; it was cold. I knew in that moment how dearly she loved her charge and how anxious she was. "There is nothing wrong with her," she insisted. "These tantrums of hers . . . she will grow out of them. There was nothing wrong with her mother. A gentler, sweeter girl it would be difficult to find."

"Don't worry," I said, "I shall not mention what happened to her father nor to anyone. But I think I should speak to her."

Nounou's face cleared. "Yes, you speak to her . . . and if you should be in conversation with Monsieur le Comte . . . and could tell him . . . say how clever she is at speaking English . . . how gentle she is . . . how calm . . ."

"Her English would quickly improve, I'm sure. But I could scarcely call her calm."

"Because it is said her mother took her own life, people are inclined to say she is highly strung."

I thought she certainly was but did not say so. Oddly enough Nounou had brought me here to soothe me and I was ending by soothing her.

"Françoise was the most natural normal little girl you could have met." She set down her cup and going to the other side of the room returned with a wooden box inlaid with mother-of-pearl.

"I keep some of her things in here. I look at them sometimes to remind me. She was such a good child. Her governesses were delighted with her. I often tell Geneviève how good she was."

She opened the box and took out a book bound in red leather. "She pressed her flowers in this. She was fond of flowers. She'd roam through the fields gathering them. And she would pick some from the gardens. There, look at that forget-me-not. You see this handkerchief? She did that for me. Such pretty embroidery. She would embroider for me for Christmas and *fête* days and she'd always hide it when I came near to keep it a surprise. Such a good quiet girl. Girls like that don't take their lives. She was good and she was religious too. She had a way of saying her prayers that would make your heart ache; she used to decorate the chapel here herself. She would have thought it a sin to take her life."

"Did she have brothers and sisters?"

"No, she was an only child. Her mother was . . . not strong; I nursed her too. She died when Françoise was nine years old, and Françoise was eighteen when she herself married."

"And she was quite happy to marry?"

"I do not think she knew what marriage meant. I remember the night of the *diner contrat*. You understand, Mademoiselle? Perhaps you do not have this in England? But here in France when two people are to marry, there are the contracts to be talked of and agreed on; and when this is done there is the *diner contrat*—the dinner at the bride's house, and there she dines with her family and the bridegroom and some members of his family, and afterwards the contracts are signed. She was very happy then, I think. She would be the Comtesse de la Talle and the de la Talles are the most important family—and the richest—for miles. It was a good match, an achievement. Then there was the civil marriage and after that the marriage in church."

"And after that she was less happy?"

"Ah, life cannot be all that a young girl dreams, Mademoiselle."

"Particularly married to the Comte de la Talle."

"As you have said, Mademoiselle." She held out the box to me. "But you see what a sweet girl she was, her pleasures so simple. It was a shock to her to marry a man like the Comte."

"The sort of shock many young girls have to face."

"You speak truth, Mademoiselle. She used to write in her little books, she called them. She liked to keep an account of the things that happened. I keep the little books." She went to a cupboard, unlocked it with a key which dangled from a bunch at her waist, and took out a small notebook. "This is the first. See how good her handwriting is."

I opened the book and read:

"May 1st. Prayers with Papa and the servants. I repeated the collect to him and he said I had made progress. I went to the kitchen and watched Marie baking the bread. She gave me a piece of sugar cake and said not to tell because she was not supposed to be baking sugar cake."

"A sort of diary," I commented.

"She was so young. Not more than seven. How many of seven can write as well? Let me get you more coffee, Mademoiselle. Look at the book. I often read it. It brings her back to me."

I turned the pages, glancing at the large, childish handwriting.

"I think I will make a tray cloth for Nounou. It will take a long time but if it is not finished in time for her birthday she can have it for Christmas."

"Papa talked to me today after prayers. He said I must always be good and try to forget myself."

"I saw Mama today. She did not know who I was. Papa talked to me afterwards and said that she might not be with us much longer."

"I have blue silks for the tray cloth. I will find some pink as well. Nounou nearly saw it today. That was very exciting."

"I heard Papa praying in his room yesterday. He called me in and made me pray with him. Kneeling hurts my knees, but Papa is so good he does not notice."

"Papa said he will show me his greatest treasure on my next birthday. I shall be eight. I do wonder what it is."

"I wish there were children to play with. Marie said that in the house where she used to work there were nine. All those brothers and sisters would be nice. There would be one who was my special one."

"Marie made a cake for my birthday. I went to the kitchen to watch her make it."

"I thought Papa's treasure would be pearls and rubies but it is only an old robe with a hood. It's black and smells fusty after being shut up. Papa said I must not mistake the shadow for the substance."

Nounou was standing over me. "It's rather sad," I said. "She was a lonely child."

"But good. You can learn that. That brings her to life. She had a sweet temper. And it comes through, doesn't it? She accepts things as they are . . . do you know what I mean?"

"Yes, I think I know."

"Not the sort, you see, to take her own life. There was nothing hysterical about her. And really Geneviève is the same . . . at heart."

I was silent, sipping the coffee she had brought to me. I felt drawn towards her because of the deep devotion she had felt to the mother and daughter. I sensed in a way that she was trying to win me to her point of view.

In that case I should be frank with her.

"I think I ought to tell you," I said, "that on the first day I was here Geneviève took me to see her mother's grave."

"She often goes there," said Nounou quickly, lights of fear darting to her eyes.

"She did it in a peculiar way. She said she was taking me to see her mother . . . and I thought that I was going to be taken to a living woman."

Nounou nodded, her eyes averted.

"Then she said that her father had murdered her mother."

Nounou's face wrinkled in fear.

She laid her hand on my arm. "But you understand, don't you? The shock of finding her . . . her own mother. And then the gossip. It was *natural*, wasn't it?"

"I shouldn't like to think it was natural for a child to accuse her father of murdering her mother."

"The shock . . ." she repeated. "She needs *help,* Mademoiselle. Think of this household. The death . . . the whispers in the *château* . . . the gossip outside. I know that you are a *sensible* woman. I know that you will want to do all you can."

The hands were clutching at my arm; the lips moved as though mouthing words that she dared not say.

She was a frightened woman and because of my recent experience at the hands of her charge she was asking my help.

I said cautiously: "It would certainly have been a great shock. She must be treated with care. Her father does not seem to realize this."

Nounou's face twisted in lines of bitterness. She hates him, I thought. She hates him for what he is doing to his daughter . . . and what he did to his wife.

"But *we* realize it," said Nounou. I was touched and I put out my hand and pressed hers.

It was as though we made a pact then. Her face brightened and she said, "We've let our coffee get cold. I'll make some more."

And there in that little room I knew that I was being caught up in the life of the *château.*

❧ 4 ❧

I told myself it was not my affair to assess whether or not the master of the house was a murderer, but to discover how much restoration the paintings needed and what methods should be used to produce the best results; and during the weeks that followed I became absorbed in my work.

Guests came to the *château*, which meant that I was not invited to dinner. I was not really displeased about this, as the Comte's attitude towards me disturbed me. I felt that he was almost hoping that I would fail. I feared that he might undermine my confidence, and while I was occupied in my delicate task I had to believe it would be a complete success.

But after leaving me alone for a few days he came to the gallery one morning while I was at work.

"Oh dear, Mademoiselle Lawson," he exclaimed as he looked at the picture before me. "What *are* you doing?"

I was startled, for the picture had been reacting perfectly to my treatment, and I felt the color rush to my cheeks. I was about to protest angrily when he went on: "You are going to restore such color to this painting that you will remind us all over again of those tiresome emeralds."

He was amused to see my relief that he had not implied criticism of my work.

I said sharply, to hide my embarrassment: "Then you are becoming convinced that a woman might have some ability?"

"I always suspected you had great ability. Who but a woman of character and determination would have come to us in the first place, eager to defend what is—I am sure misguidedly—called the weaker sex?"

"My only wish is to do a good job."

"If all the militant females in the past had had your good sense, what a lot of trouble might have been saved!"

"I hope I shall be able to save you trouble, for I can assure you that had these paintings been neglected much longer . . ."

"I am aware of it. That was why I decided to ask your father here. Alas, he could not come. But in his place we have his daughter. How fortunate we are!"

I turned to the painting, but I was afraid to touch it. I dared not make a false move. Work such as this needed complete absorption.

He came and stood close to me, and although he pretended to be studying the picture, I believe he was watching me.

"It seems so interesting," he said. "You must explain to me."

"I have carried out one or two tests, and naturally, before beginning, I have made sure that I am using what, in my opinion, is the best treatment."

"And what is the best treatment?" His eyes were fixed on my face and again I felt the uncomfortable color in my cheeks.

"I'm using a mild alcohol solvent. It wouldn't be active on a hardened layer of oil paint, but this paint has been mixed with a soft resin . . ."

"How clever of you!"

"It is part of my work."

"At which you are such an expert."

"Are you convinced of that then?" My voice sounded a little too eager and I felt my lips harden to counteract the effect my remark may have had.

"You are in the process of convincing me. You like this picture, Mademoiselle Lawson?"

"It's interesting. It's not one of your best. It doesn't compare, of course, with the Fragonards or Bouchers. But I think the artist was a master of color. The alizarin is beautiful. He is daring in his use of color. His brush strokes are a little harsh, but . . ." I trailed off because I sensed he was laughing at me. "I'm afraid I become rather boring when I talk about paintings."

"You are too self-critical, Mademoiselle Lawson."

I! Self-critical! It was the first time anyone had ever told me that. And yet I knew it was true. I knew that I was like a hedgehog, putting out my prickles in self-defense. So I had betrayed myself.

"You will soon have restored this picture," he went on.

"And then I shall know whether you have decided if I am worthy to be given this commission."

"I'm sure you have no doubt what the verdict will be," he answered and, smiling, left me.

A few days later the picture was finished, and he came to pass judgment. He stood for some seconds frowning at it, and I felt my spirits sinking although before he had come in I had felt pleased with my work, knowing I had done a good job. The colors were startling, and the fabric of the gown and the artist's facility with handling his paint reminded me of Gainsborough. All this had been hidden when I had started the work; now it was revealed.

And he stood there looking dismayed.

"So," I said, "you are not pleased?"

He shook his head.

"Monsieur le Comte, I don't know what you expect, but I assure you that anyone who *understands* painting . . ."

He turned his attention from the picture to me; he had raised those proud eyebrows very slightly; his mouth was curved in a smile which belied the astonishment his eyes were trying to convey.

". . . as you do," he finished for me. "Ah yes, if I possessed that talent, I should cry: 'This is a miracle. That which was hidden has now been shown to us in all its glory!' It's true. It's magnificent. But I'm still thinking of those emeralds. You have no idea what trouble they have caused us. Now, due to you, Mademoiselle Lawson, there will be new treasure hunts. There will be new speculations."

I knew that he was teasing me and I told myself fiercely that he had been hoping I should fail. Now he was reluctant to admit that I had succeeded admirably and as he couldn't deny it, was talking about his emeralds.

It was typical of the man, I told myself; and then quickly added a reminder that whatever he was, was no concern of mine. *He* was of no importance to me; I was only interested in his paintings.

"And as far as the picture is concerned you have no complaints?" I asked coolly.

"You live up to your credentials."

"Then you will wish me to continue with the rest of the paintings?"

An expression I did not understand flickered across his face. "I should be very disappointed if you did not."

I felt radiant. I had won.

But my triumph was not complete, for as he stood there smiling at me, I knew he was reminding me how well aware he was of my doubts and fears and everything I had sought to hide.

Neither of us had noticed that Geneviève had come into the gallery, and as she did not make her presence known she could have been there for some seconds watching us.

The Comte saw her first. "What do you want, Geneviève?" he asked.

"I . . . I came to see how Mademoiselle Lawson was getting on with the picture."

"Then come and see."

She came, looking sullen, as she so often did in company.

"There!" he said. "Is it not a revelation?"

She did not answer.

"Mademoiselle Lawson expects to be complimented on her work. You remember what the picture was like before."

"No, I don't."

"Such lack of artistic appreciation! You must try to persuade Mademoiselle Lawson to teach you to understand pictures while she is with us."

"So . . . she is going to stay?"

His voice changed suddenly. It was almost caressing. "I hope," he said, "for a long time. Because you see there are so many in the *château* who need her attentions."

Geneviève gave me a swift glance; her eyes were hard; they looked like black stones. She turned to the picture and said: "Perhaps if she is so clever she will find the emeralds for us."

"You see, Mademoiselle Lawson, it is exactly as I said."

"They certainly look magnificent," I replied.

"No doubt due to the artist's . . . er . . . facility with paint?"

I cared nothing for his mockery, nor for the brooding resentment of his daughter. It was these beautiful paintings which were my concern, and the fact that they were now shrouded in the fog of neglect only made my project the more exciting.

Even in that moment he knew what I was thinking, for he bowed and said: "I will leave you, Mademoiselle Lawson. I can see you are eager to be alone . . . with the pictures." He signed to Geneviève to go with him; and when they had gone I stood there in the gallery and let my eyes revel first in one and then in another.

I had rarely been so excited in my life.

Now that I was staying at the *château* to complete the work I decided to take advantage of the Comte's offer and make use of the stables, which would enable me to see more of the country. I had already explored the little town; had drunk coffee in the *pâtisserie,* chatting with the genial but inquisitive proprietress who was pleased to welcome anyone from the *château*. She had talked with reverence but sly knowingness of Monsieur le Comte, with respectful contempt of Monsieur Philippe and with pity for Mademoiselle Geneviève. And Mademoiselle was there to clean the pictures! Well, well, that was very interesting, that was, and she hoped Mademoiselle would come again and next time perhaps take a little of the *gâteau de la maison* which was highly thought of in Gaillard.

I had wandered through the market and had seen the glances in my direction; I had visited the ancient *hôtel de ville* and the church.

So the prospect of going farther afield was pleasant, and I was particularly pleased that I was expected at the stables.

A suitable mount, named Bonhomme, was found for me, and we approved of each other from the beginning.

I was surprised and pleased when Geneviève asked me if she could accompany me one morning. She was in one of her demure moods, and as we rode I asked her why she had been so foolish as to shut me in the *oubliette*.

"Well, you weren't afraid, so you said, and I didn't think it would hurt you."

"It was a stupid thing to do. Suppose Nounou hadn't found out!"

"I should have rescued you after a while."

"After a while! Do you know some people might have died of fright?"

"Died!" she said fearfully. "No one dies of being shut up."

"Some nervous people might have died of fright."

"But *you* never would." She regarded me intently. "You didn't tell my father. I thought you might . . . as you and he are so friendly."

She rode on a little way in advance, and when we returned to the stables she said casually: "I'm not allowed to ride alone. I always have to take one of the grooms with me. There was no one to ride with me this morning, so I shouldn't have had a ride if you hadn't come with me."

"I'm glad to have been of service," I replied coolly.

I met Philippe when I was in the gardens, and I fancied he knew I was there and had come out purposely to talk to me.

"Congratulations," he said. "I've been looking at the picture. The difference is remarkable. It's hardly recognizable."

I glowed with pleasure. How different, I thought, from the Comte. He is genuinely pleased.

"I'm so glad you think so."

"Who could help thinking so! It's miraculous. I'm delighted . . . not only that the picture is a success but that you've proved you could do it."

"How kind of you!"

"I'm afraid I was rather ungracious when you arrived. I was so taken by surprise and not sure what would be expected of me."

"You were not ungracious, and I can well understand your surprise."

"You see, this was my cousin's affair, and naturally I wanted to do what he would wish."

"Naturally. And it is good of you to take such an interest."

He wrinkled his brow. "I feel a kind of responsibility . . ." he began. "I hope that you will not regret coming here."

"Indeed no. The work is proving to be most interesting."

"Oh yes . . . yes . . . the work."

He began to speak rather hurriedly of the gardens and insisted on showing me the sculptural decorations which had been done by Le-Brun soon after he had completed the frescoes in the Hall of Mirrors at Versailles.

"Fortunately they escaped at the time of the Revolution," he explained; and I sensed his reverence for everything connected with the *château*. I liked him for it—also for his gracious apology for anything he might have said to hurt me during our first interview and his obvious pleasure in the fact that I had succeeded.

My days had formed themselves into a pattern. I was in the gallery early and worked steadily all through the morning. After lunch I usually went out, returning before dusk, which, at this time of the year, was soon after four o'clock. Then I would occupy myself with mixing solutions or reading notes of past experiments which filled my time until dinner. Sometimes I took this alone in my room, but on several occasions Mademoiselle Dubois had asked me to dine in her room. I could not refuse these invitations, although I wanted to; I listened to her life history: how she was the daughter of a lawyer, brought up not to work, how her father had been let down through a partner, how he had died of a broken heart, and how she, being penniless, had been obliged to become a governess. Told in her self-pitying way the story seemed incredibly dull, and I made up my mind not to inflict boredom on her by telling her my own.

After dinner I would read one of the books I had found in the library, for Philippe had told me that the Comte would be pleased if I made use of anything I wanted there.

As the days passed through that November, I was on the periphery of the *château* life, aware of it yet not aware of it, just as I heard the music in my room—conscious of it, yet only now and then did I know what was being played.

One day when I had left the *château* on Bonhomme I met Jean Pierre on horseback. He greeted me with customary gaiety and asked whether I was going to call on his family. I told him I was.

"Ride with me first over to the St. Vallient vineyard and then we will go back together."

I had never been St. Vallient way and agreed. I always enjoyed his company, and the Bastide household never seemed the same without him. He had a vitality and gaiety which appealed to me.

We talked of Christmas which would soon be with us.

"You will spend the day with us, Mademoiselle?" he asked.

"Is that a formal invitation?"

"You know that I am never formal. It is just a heartfelt wish on behalf of the family that you will honor us."

I remarked that I should be delighted and it was good of them to want me.

"The motives are entirely selfish, Mademoiselle." With one of those quick gestures which were characteristic of him he leaned towards me and touched my arm. I met his warm glance unwaveringly, telling myself that his manner of making me feel I was important to him was merely the natural courtesy Frenchmen showed automatically towards all women.

"I shall tell you nothing of our Christmas celebrations now," he said. "It must all be a surprise to you."

When we reached the St. Vallient vineyards I was introduced to Monsieur Durand, who was in charge of them. His wife brought out wine and little cakes, which were delicious, and Jean Pierre and Monsieur Durand discussed the quality of the wine. Then Monsieur Durand took Jean Pierre off to talk business while his wife was left to look after me.

She knew a great deal about me, for clearly the affairs of the *château* were the pivot round which gossip revolved. What did I think of the *château*, the Comte? I gave guarded answers and she evidently thought she would glean little from me, so she talked of her own affairs, how anxious she was on Monsieur Durand's behalf because he was too old to continue with his work.

"The anxieties! Each year it is the same, and since the big trouble ten years ago, it has not been good here at St. Vallient. Monsieur Jean Pierre is a wizard. The *château* wine is becoming as good as it ever was. I trust soon that Monsieur le Comte will allow my husband to retire."

"Must he await permission from Monsieur le Comte?"

"Indeed yes, Mademoiselle. Monsieur le Comte will give him his cottage. How I long for that day! I will keep a few chickens and a cow . . . perhaps two; and that will be the best for my husband. It is too much for an old man. How can he, when he is no longer young, fight all the hazards? Who but the good God can say when the frost is coming to destroy the vines? And when the summers are too humid there are always pests. The spring frosts are the worst though. The day will be fine and then the frost comes like a thief in the night to rob us of our grapes. And if there is not enough sun, then the grapes are sour. It is a life for a young man . . . such as Monsieur Jean Pierre."

"I hope then that you will soon be allowed to retire."

"It is all in the hands of God, Mademoiselle."

"Or perhaps," I suggested, "Monsieur le Comte."

She lifted her hands as though to say that was the same thing.

After a while Jean Pierre returned, and we left St. Vallient.

We talked of the Durands, and he said that the poor old man had had his day and it was time he retired.

"I was hearing how he had to wait for the Comte's decision."

"Oh yes," replied Jean Pierre. "Everything here depends on him."

"You resent it?"

"The days of despotic rulers are supposed to have ended."

"You could always break away. He could not prevent you."

"Leave our home?"

"If you hate him so much . . ."

"Did I give that impression?"

"When you speak of him, your voice hardens and there is a look in your eyes . . ."

"It is nothing. I am a proud man, perhaps too proud. This place is my home as much as his. My family has been here through centuries just as his has. The only difference is that his lived in the *château*. But we were all brought up in the shadow of the *château,* and this is our home . . . just as it is his."

"I understand that."

"If I do not like the Comte I am merely in the fashion. What does he care for this place? He is hardly ever here. He prefers his mansion in Paris. He does not deign to notice us. We are not worthy of his attention. But I would never let him drive me from my home. I work for him because I must and I try not to see him or think of him. You will feel the same. I expect you already do."

He began to sing suddenly; he had a pleasant tenor voice which vibrated with emotion.

> *"Qui sont-ils, les gens qui sont riches?*
> *Sont-ils plus que moi qui n'ai rien?*
> *Je cours, je vas, je vir, je viens;*
> *Je n'ai pas peur de perd' ma fortune.*
> *Je cours, je vas, je vir, je viens,*
> *Pas peur-de perdre mon bien."*

He finished and smiled at me, waiting for my comments.

"I like that," I said.

"I am so pleased; so do I."

He was looking at me so intently that I lightly touched my horse's flank. Bonhomme broke into a gallop. Jean Pierre was close behind me; and so we returned to Gaillard.

As we passed the vineyard I saw the Comte. He could only have come from the vineyard buildings. He inclined his head in greeting when he saw us. "You wished to see me, Monsieur le Comte?" asked Jean Pierre.

"Another time will do," answered the Comte, and rode on.

"Should you have been there when he called?" I asked.

"No. He knew I was going to St. Vallient. It was on his instructions that I went."

He was puzzled, but as we passed the buildings on the way to the Bastide house Gabrielle came out. Her cheeks were flushed and she looked very pretty.

"Gabrielle," called Jean Pierre. "Here is Mademoiselle Lawson."

She smiled at me rather absently, I thought.

"The Comte called, I see," said Jean Pierre. His manner had changed also. "What did he want?"

"To look at some figures . . . that was all. He will call another time to see you."

Jean Pierre wrinkled his brows and he kept looking at his sister.

Madame Bastide welcomed me as warmly as ever, but I noticed all the time I was there how absent-minded Gabrielle was and that even Jean Pierre was subdued.

While I was working in the gallery next morning the Comte looked in.

"And how is the work progressing?" he asked.

"Satisfactorily, I think," I answered.

He looked quizzically at the picture on which I was working. I pointed out the surface coating which was brittle and discolored and said that I had come to the conclusion that the varnish was responsible for the buckling of the paint.

"I'm sure you're right," he said lightly. "I am glad too that you don't spend all your time working."

I thought he was referring to the fact that he had seen me riding on the previous day when I might have been working in the gallery, and

I retorted hotly: "My father always said that it was not wise to work after luncheon. The work demands great concentration, and after having worked all the morning one is possibly not as alert as one should be."

"You looked surprisingly alert when we met yesterday."

"Alert?" I repeated the word foolishly.

"At least," he went on, "as though the amenities we have to offer are as interesting outside the *château* as in."

"You mean the horse? You did say I might ride if I had the opportunity."

"I am delighted that you are able to find opportunities . . . and friends with whom to share them."

I was startled. Surely he could not object to my being friendly with Jean Pierre.

"It is kind of you to take an interest in how I spend my leisure time."

"Well, you know I happen to have a great regard for . . . my pictures."

We walked round the gallery, studying them, but I fancied he was not doing so with real attention; and I believed he was critical of my riding —not with Jean Pierre, but riding when I might have been working. The idea made me indignant. I had quoted an estimate for the work, but of course if I completed it quickly I would cease to live at the *château* and so cease to be a burden on the household.

I blurted out: "If you are not satisfied with the speed at which I am working . . ."

He spun round as though delighted and smiled at me across the distance which separated us. "What gave you such an idea, Mademoiselle Lawson?"

"I thought . . . I imagined . . ."

His head was slightly on one side. He was discovering traits in my character of which I myself had not been aware. He was saying: See how quickly you take offense! Why? Because you feel yourself to be vulnerable . . . very vulnerable?

"Then," I went on lamely, "you are satisfied with what I am doing?"

"Immensely so, Mademoiselle Lawson."

I turned back to my work and he continued to walk round the gallery. I was not looking when he went out and shut the door quietly behind him.

I could not work comfortably for the rest of that morning.

Geneviève came running after me when I was on my way to the stables.

"Mademoiselle, will you ride over to Carrefour with me?"

"Carrefour?"

"My grandfather's house. If you won't come I shall have to take one of the grooms. I'm going to see my grandfather. I'm sure he'd like to meet you."

If I had been inclined to refuse such an ungracious invitation the mention of her grandfather decided me.

Through Nounou's conversation and the little notebooks which Françoise had written I had a clear picture of a neat little girl with her innocent secrets and her charming ways. Now the opportunity to meet that little girl's father and to see the house which formed a background to the life portrayed in those notebooks was irresistible.

Geneviève sat her horse with the ease of one who had been in the saddle from early childhood. Occasionally she pointed out landmarks to me and at one spot pulled up so that we could look back at the *château*.

It was an impressive sight seen from this distance; here one could get a better conception of the symmetry of those ancient embattled walls, the massive buttresses, the cylindrical towers and the sharp conical points which rose from the roofs. There it stood in the midst of the vineyards; I could see the church spire and the *hôtel de ville* standing guard over the houses of the little town.

"You like it?" asked Geneviève.

"I think it's a lovely sight."

"It all belongs to Papa, but it never will to me. I should have been a son. Then Papa would have been pleased with me."

"If you are good and well mannered he will be pleased with you," I replied sententiously.

She looked at me with the scorn I felt I deserved. "Really, Mademoiselle, you do talk just like a governess. They always say things they don't mean. They tell you you should do this . . . but they don't always do it themselves." She looked at me sideways, laughing to herself. "Oh, I don't mean Esquilles. She would never do anything. But there are some . . ."

I remembered suddenly the governess whom she had shut in the *oubliette* and I did not pursue the conversation.

She touched her horse's flanks and galloped ahead of me, a charming picture with her hair flying out from under her riding hat. I came up beside her.

"If Papa had had a son we need not have Cousin Philippe here. That would have been pleasant."

"I am sure he is always kind to you."

She gave me a sidelong glance.

"At one time I was going to marry him."

"Oh . . . I see. And not now."

She shook her head. "I don't care. You don't imagine I should want to marry Philippe, do you?"

"He is considerably older than you."

"Fourteen years . . . just double."

"But I suppose as you grew older the disparity would not seem so great."

"Well, Papa decided against it. Tell me, why do you think he did that, Mademoiselle? You know so much."

"I assure you I know nothing of your father's intentions. I know nothing of your father . . ." I was surprised at the heat in which I had spoken for it was quite uncalled for.

"So you don't know everything! I'll tell you something. Philippe was very angry when he knew Papa wouldn't let him marry me."

She tossed her head and smiled complacently so I retorted: "Perhaps he does not know *you* very well."

That made her laugh. "It's nothing to do with me really," she admitted. "It's being Papa's daughter. No, when my mother was . . . when my mother died, Papa changed his mind. He changed a great deal then. I think he wanted to insult Philippe."

"Why should he want to insult Philippe?"

"Oh . . . just because it amuses him. He hates people."

"I am sure that is not the truth. People don't hate . . . indiscriminately . . . without reason."

"My father is not like ordinary people." She spoke almost proudly—her voice unconsciously vibrating with hatred, a queer inverted hatred which was touched with respect.

"We are all different," I said quickly.

Her laughter was high-pitched, and I noticed that it took on this quality when she talked of her father.

"He hates me," she went on, "I am like my mother, you see. Nounou says I grow more like her every day. I remind him of her."

"You have listened to too much gossip."

"Perhaps *you* haven't listened to enough."

"Listening to gossip is not a very admirable way of spending the time."

That made her laugh again. "All I can say, Miss, is that you don't always spend your time admirably."

I felt myself flush with that annoyance which a home truth inspires.

She pointed at me. "You love to gossip, Miss. Never mind. I like you for it. I couldn't *bear* you if you were as good and proper as you make out to be."

"Why don't you speak to your father naturally . . . not as though you're afraid of him," I said.

"But everybody's afraid of him."

"I am not."

"Really, Miss?"

"Why should I be? If he doesn't like my work he can say so and I should go away and never see him again."

"Yes, it might be easy for you. My mother was afraid of him . . . terribly afraid of him."

"Did she tell you so?"

"Not in words, but I knew. And you know what happened to her."

I said: "Isn't it time we went on? We shan't be back before dark if we dally like this."

She looked at me pleadingly for a moment and then said: "Yes, but do you think when people die . . . not like ordinary people die but when they are . . . Do you think that some people don't rest in their graves? Do you think they come back looking for . . . ."

I said sharply: "Geneviève, what are you saying?"

"Miss," she said, and it was like a cry for help, "sometimes at night I wake up startled and I think I hear noises in the *château*."

"My dear Geneviève, everyone awakes startled now and then. It's usually a bad dream."

"Footsteps . . . tapping . . . I hear it. I do. I *do*. And I lie there shivering . . . expecting to see . . ."

"Your mother?"

This girl was frightened; she was stretching out to me for help. It was no use telling her she was speaking nonsense, that there were no ghosts. That would not help her at all because she would think it was merely grown-up talk to soothe the children.

I said: "Listen, Geneviève, suppose there are ghosts, suppose your mother did come back?"

She nodded, her eyes enormous with interest.

"She loved you, didn't she?"

I saw her hands tighten on the reins. "Oh yes, she loved me . . . no one loved me like she did."

"She would never have hurt you, would she? Do you think that now she is dead she would have changed towards you?"

I saw the relaxed expression; I was pleased with myself. I had found the comfort she so desperately needed.

I went on: "When you were a child she looked after you; if she saw you about to fall she would rush to pick you up, wouldn't she?" She nodded. "Why should she change towards you because she is dead? I think what you hear is creaking boards in a very old house, the rattling of doors, windows . . . anything like that. There could be mice . . . But just suppose there are ghosts. Don't you think your mother would be there to *protect* you from harm?"

"Yes," she said, her eyes shining. "Yes, she would. She loved me."

"Remember that if you awake startled in the night."

"Oh yes," she said. "I will."

I was pleased and felt that to continue the conversation might spoil the effect I had made, so I moved on, and in a short while we were cantering side by side.

We did not speak again until we reached Maison Carrefour.

It was an old house standing back from the crossroads. A thick stone wall surrounded it, but the elaborately wrought-iron gates were open. We went through these gates and under a wide archway and were in an inner courtyard. There were green shutters at the windows, and I was immediately conscious of a deep silence. I had imagined the home of the bright little girl who had recorded her daily life in her notebooks to be different from this.

Geneviève glanced at me quickly to guess my reactions, but I hoped I betrayed nothing.

We left our horses in the stables and Geneviève led me to a door. She lifted the heavy knocker and I heard the sound reverberating through the lower part of the house. There was silence; then came the shuffle of footsteps, and a manservant appeared.

"Good day, Maurice," said Geneviève. "Mademoiselle Lawson has come with me today."

The courtesies exchanged we were in the hall, the floor of which was covered with mosaic tiles.

"How is my grandfather today, Maurice?" asked Geneviève.

"Much the same, Mademoiselle. I will see if he is ready."

The manservant disappeared for a few moments before he came back to the hall and said that his master would see us now.

There was no fire in the room, and the chill struck me as I entered. At one time it must have been beautiful, for it was perfectly proportioned. The ceiling was carved and there was an inscription on it which I couldn't see clearly except that it was in medieval French; the closed shutters kept out all but the minimum of light and the room was austerely furnished. In a wheelchair sat an old man. He startled me, for he was more like a corpse than a living human being; his eyes were sunken in his cadaverous face and his eyes were too brilliant. In his hands he held a book which he had closed as we entered. He was wearing a brown dressing gown tied with a brown cord.

"Grandfather," said Geneviève, "I have come to see you."

"My child," he answered in a surprisingly firm voice, and held out a thin white hand on which blue veins stood out.

"And," went on Geneviève, "I have brought Mademoiselle Lawson, who has come from England and is cleaning my father's pictures."

The eyes, which were all that seemed alive about him, were trying to probe my mind.

"Mademoiselle Lawson, you will forgive my not rising. I can do so only with great difficulty and the help of my servants. I am pleased you have come with my granddaughter. Geneviève, bring a chair for Mademoiselle Lawson . . . and for yourself."

"Yes, Grandfather."

We sat before him. He was charmingly courteous; he asked me about my work, expressed great interest and said that Geneviève must show me his collection. Some of them might be in need of restoration. The thought of living, even temporarily in such a house as this, depressed me. For all its mystery the *château* was alive. Alive! That was it. This was like a house of the dead.

Now and then he addressed Geneviève, and I noticed how his eyes rested on her. He had given me his polite attention but the intentness of his scrutiny of her surprised me. He cares deeply for her, I thought. Why should she think herself unloved—for I had come to the conclusion that this was one of the main reasons for her bad behavior—when she had such a doting grandparent.

He wanted to hear what she was doing, how she was progressing with her lessons. I was surprised that he spoke of Mademoiselle Dubois as though he knew her intimately, while I had gathered from Geneviève that he had never actually met her. Nounou he knew well of course, for she had once been part of this household, and he spoke of her as though she were an old friend.

"How is Nounou, Geneviève? I trust you are kind to her. Remember she is a good soul. Simple, perhaps, but she does her best. She always did. And she is good to you. Always remember that and treat her kindly, Geneviève."

"Yes, Grandfather."

"I hope you don't grow impatient with her."

"Not often, Grandfather."

"Sometimes?" He was alert, uneasy.

"Well, only a little. I just say: 'You are a silly old woman.'"

"That's unkind. Did you pray afterwards to the saints for forgiveness?"

"Yes, Grandfather."

"It is no use asking for forgiveness if you commit the same sin immediately afterwards. Guard your temper, Geneviève. And if you are ever tempted to do foolish things, remember the pain that causes."

I wondered how much he knew of the wildness of his granddaughter and whether Nounou paid him visits and told him. Did he know that she had shut me in the *oubliette*?

He sent for wine and the biscuits which were usually served with it. These were brought by an old woman whom I guessed to be one of the Labisses. She wore a white cap on her gray hair and somewhat morosely set down the wine without a word. Geneviève murmured a greeting and the woman bobbed a curtsy and went out.

While we were drinking the wine the old man said: "I had heard that the pictures were to be restored, but I did not expect a lady to do them."

I explained about my father's death and that I was completing his commitments.

"There was a little consternation at first," I said, "but the Comte seems pleased with my work."

I saw his lips tighten and his hand clench on the rug.

"So . . . he is pleased with you." His voice and his whole expression changed. I saw that Geneviève was sitting on the edge of her chair nervously watching her grandfather.

"At least he implies that he is, by allowing me to continue with the pictures," I said.

"I hope," he began, and his voice sank and I did not catch the rest of the sentence.

"I beg your pardon."

He shook his head. The mention of the Comte's name had evidently upset him. So here was another who hated that man. What was it in him that inspired such fear and such hatred? Conversation became uneasy after that and Geneviève, seeking to escape, asked if she might show me the grounds.

We left the main hall and went through several passages until we came to a stone-floored kitchen; she took me through this to a garden.

"Your grandfather is pleased to see you," I commented. "I believe he would like you to come often to see him."

"He doesn't notice. He forgets. He is very old and hasn't been the same since . . . his stroke. His mind isn't clear."

"Does your father know you come?"

"He doesn't ask."

"You mean he never comes here?"

"He hasn't been since my mother died. Grandfather wouldn't want him, would he? Can you imagine my father here?"

"No," I answered truthfully.

I looked back at the house and saw the curtains in an upper room move. We were being watched. Geneviève followed my gaze. "That's Madame Labisse. She's wondering who you are. She doesn't like it the way it is now; she would like to go back to the old days. Then she was parlormaid and Labisse was footman. I don't know what they are now. They wouldn't stay except for the fact that Grandfather has left them a legacy provided they're in his service when he dies."

"It's a strange household," I said.

"That's because Grandfather is only half alive. He has been like this for three years. The doctor says he cannot live for many more years—so I suppose the Labisses think it worth while."

Three years, I thought. That was the time of Françoise's death. Was he so affected that he had had a stroke? If he loved her as he obviously did his granddaughter, I could understand it.

"I know what you're thinking," cried Geneviève. "You're thinking that that was the time my mother died. Grandfather had his stroke a week before she died. Wasn't it strange . . . everyone was expecting him to die, but she was the one."

How strange! She had died of an overdose of laudanum a week after her father had a stroke. Had it affected her so much that she had taken her life?

Geneviève had turned back to the house and I walked silently beside her. There was a door in the wall and she quickly passed through it holding it for me to do the same. We were in a small cobbled court-yard; it was very quiet here. Geneviève walked across the cobbles and I followed, feeling as though I were joining in a conspiracy.

We were standing in a dark lobby.

"Where is this?" I asked, but she put a hand to her lips.

"I want to show you something."

She crossed the lobby and led the way to a door which she pushed open. It was a room bare of everything but a pallet bed and a *prie-dieu* and a wooden chest. The floor was of stone flags, and there were no rugs or carpets.

"Grandfather's favorite room," she said.

"It's like a monk's cell," I said.

She nodded delightedly. She looked about her furtively and opened the chest.

"Geneviève," I said, "you have no right . . ."

But curiosity would not let me resist looking at what lay there. I thought in astonishment: It's a hair shirt. There was something else that made me shudder. A whip!

Geneviève let the lid of the chest fall.

"What do you think of this house, Mademoiselle?" she asked. "It is as interesting as the *château,* don't you think?"

"It is time we left," I said. "We must say good-by to your grandfather."

She was silent all the way home. As for myself, I could not get that strange house out of my thoughts. It was like something that clings to the memory after a nightmare.

The guests who had been staying at the castle left, and I was immediately aware of the change. I became less aloof from the life of the place. For instance, when I was leaving the gallery one morning I came face to face with the Comte.

He said: "Now that all the visitors have gone, you should dine with us now and then, Mademoiselle Lawson. *En famille,* you understand? I am sure you could enlighten us all on your favorite subject. Would you care to do so?"

I replied that it would be a pleasure.

"Well, join us tonight," he said.

I felt elated as I went to my room. My encounters with him were always stimulating although often they left me tingling with rage. I took my black velvet dress and laid it on my bed, and while I was doing this there was a knock on my door and Geneviève came in.

"Are you going out to dinner tonight?" she asked.

"No, I'm dining with you."

"You look pleased. Did Papa ask you?"

"It is a pleasure to receive an invitation when they are rather rare."

She stroked the velvet thoughtfully. "I like velvet," she said.

"I was just going to the gallery," I told her. "Did you want to see me about something?"

"No, I only wanted to see you."

"You can come to the gallery with me."

"No, I don't want to."

I went alone to the gallery and was there until it was time to change for dinner. I sent for hot water and washed in the *ruelle* in an absurd but happy state of expectation. But when I came to put on my dress I stared at it in horror. I could not believe what I saw. When I had laid it out it had been ready to slip on; now the skirt hung in jagged and uneven strips. Someone had ripped it from waist to hem; the bodice, too, had been slashed across.

I picked it up and stared at it in bewilderment and dismay.

"It's not possible," I said aloud. Then I went to the bell rope and pulled.

Josette came hurrying to me. "Why, Mademoiselle . . ."

As I held out the dress to her she clapped her hands over her mouth to stop the exclamation.

"What does it mean?" I demanded.

"Oh . . . but it's wicked. Oh, but *why?*"

"I can't understand it," I began.

"I didn't do it, Mademoiselle. I swear I didn't do it. I only came to bring the hot water. It must have been done then."

"I didn't think for a moment you did it, Josette. But I'm going to find out who did."

She ran out crying almost hysterically: "I didn't do it. I didn't do it. I won't be blamed."

And I stood in my room staring at the ruined dress. Then I went to my wardrobe and took out the gray with the lavender stripe. I had only just hooked it up when Josette appeared dramatically waving a pair of scissors.

"I knew who'd done it," she announced. "I went to the schoolroom and found these . . . just where she'd laid them down. Look, Mademoiselle, pieces of velvet are still in them. See these little bits. They're velvet."

I knew, as I had known almost as soon as I had seen the ruined dress. Geneviève. But why had she done this? Did she hate me so much?

I went along to Geneviève's room. She was sitting on her bed staring blankly before her while Nounou was pacing up and down crying.

"Why did you do it?" I asked.

"Because I wanted to."

Nounou stood still staring at us.

"You behave like a baby. You don't think before you act, do you?"

"Yes, I do. I thought I'd like to do it, so when you went to the gallery, I went for my scissors."

"And now you're sorry?"

"I'm not."

"I am. I haven't many dresses."

"You might wear it all cut up. It might be becoming. I'm sure some people would think so." She began to laugh helplessly, and I could see that she was near to tears.

"Stop it," I commanded. "It's a foolish way to behave."

"It's the way to cut up a dress. Whish! You should have heard the scissors. It was lovely." She went on laughing and Nounou put a hand to her shoulder only to have it shaken off.

I left them; it was useless to try to reason with her while she was in that mood.

The dinner to which I had looked forward was an uncomfortable meal. I was conscious all the time of Geneviève, who had appeared, sullen and silent. She was watching me furtively all through the meal, waiting, I knew, for me to betray her to her father.

I talked a little, mostly about the pictures and the *château,* but I felt I was being rather dull and disappointing to the Comte, who had wanted perhaps to provoke spirited answers to his teasing manner.

I was glad to escape to my room immediately the meal was over. I was turning over in my mind what I should do. I should have to reason with Geneviève; I should have to explain to her that she could not find lasting pleasure in behaving as she did.

It was while I was meditating about this that Mademoiselle Dubois came to my room.

"I must talk to you," she said. "What a commotion!"

"You've heard about my dress?"

"The whole household knows of it. Josette went to the *sommelier* and he went to the Comte. Mademoiselle Geneviève has played too many tricks."

"And so . . . he knows."

She regarded me slyly. "Yes . . . he knows."

"And Geneviève?"

"She's in her room, cowering behind Nounou's skirts. She'll be punished and she deserves it."

"I can't think why she takes a delight in doing such things."

"Mischief! Malice! She's jealous of your being asked to dine with the family and the Comte taking such an interest."

"Naturally he would be interested in his pictures."

She tittered. "I've always been careful. Of course when I came here I had no idea what sort of place it was. A *comte* . . . a *château* . . . it sounds wonderful. But when I heard those terrible stories, I was quite terrified. I was ready to pack my bags and go. But I decided to give it a chance, though I saw how dangerous it was. A man like the Comte, for instance . . ."

"I should not think you would be in any danger from him."

"A man whose wife died like that! You are rather innocent, Mademoiselle Lawson. As a matter of fact I had to leave my last post because of the unwelcome attentions of the master of the house."

She had grown quite pink with, I told myself cynically, the exertion of imagining herself desirable. I am sure all the near seductions she talked of had only taken place in her imagination.

"How awkward for you," I said.

"When I came here I knew I had to take special care in view of the Comte's reputation. There will always be scandal surrounding him."

"There will always be scandal where there are those to make it," I put in.

I disliked her for so many things; for her enjoyment of others' discomfort, for her stupid simpering suggestions that she was a *femme fatale*; and irrationally for her long nose which made her look like a shrew mouse. Poor woman, as if she could help her appearance! But the meanness of her soul was in her face that night and I disliked her. I told myself I hated those who stood in judgment on others.

I was glad when she had gone. My thoughts were occupied by Geneviève. Our relationship had suffered a big setback, and I was disappointed. The loss of my dress troubled me little compared with the absence of the confidence I had felt I was beginning to inspire. And oddly enough, in spite of what she had done, I felt a new tenderness towards her. Poor child! She was in need of care; and she was groping blindly, trying to call attention to herself, I was sure. I wanted to understand her; I wanted to help her. It occurred to me that she received very little help and understanding in this house—despised and rejected by her father, spoiled by her nurse. Something should be done, I was sure. It was not often that I acted on impulse, but I did then.

I went to the library and knocked at the door. There was no answer, so I went in and pulled the bell rope. When one of the menservants appeared, I asked if he would take a message to the Comte, as I wished to speak to him.

Only when I saw the surprise in the man's face was I aware of the greatness of my temerity, but I still felt that the need to act was so urgent that I didn't care. On reflection, I expected him to return and say that the Comte was too busy to see me and perhaps a meeting could be arranged the next day, but to my surprise when the door opened it was to admit the Comte.

"Mademoiselle Lawson, you sent for me?"

I flushed at the irony. "I wished to speak to you, Monsieur le Comte."

He frowned. "This disgraceful affair of the dress. I must apologize for my daughter's behavior."

"I have not come for an apology."

"You are very forgiving."

"Oh, I was angry when I saw the dress."

"Naturally. You will be recompensed, and Geneviève shall make you an apology."

"That is not what I want."

The puzzled expression on his face might have been feigned. He gave the impression, as he so often did, of knowing exactly what was going on in my mind.

"Then perhaps you will tell me why you . . . summoned me here?"

"I did not summon you. I asked if you would see me here."

"Well, I am here. You were very quiet during dinner. It was no doubt due to this foolish affair, and you were being discreet, displaying national *sang-froid* and hiding the indignation you felt towards my daughter. But now the secret is out and you no longer have any need to fear you are telling tales. And so . . . you have something to say to me."

"I wanted to talk about Geneviève. Perhaps it is presumptuous of me . . ." I paused for a reassurance that this was not so, but it did not come.

"Please go on," was all he said.

"I am concerned about her."

He signed for me to be seated and sat opposite me. As he opened his eyes wider and sat back in his chair, folding his hands with the carved jade signet ring on his little finger, I could believe all the rumors I had heard of him. The aquiline nose, the proud set of the head on the shoulders, the enigmatic mouth, and the eyes whose expression was unfathomable belonged to a man who was born to rule; a man who believed in his divine right to have his own way and found it natural to remove anything or anyone who stood in his path.

"Yes, Monsieur le Comte," I went on, "I am concerned for your daughter. Why do you think she did this?"

"She will no doubt explain."

"How can she? She doesn't even know herself. She has suffered a terrible ordeal."

Was it my imagination or did he seem to grow a little more alert?

"What ordeal was this?" he asked.

"I mean . . . the death of her mother."

His gaze met mine, steady, implacable, arrogant.

"That was several years ago."

"But she found her mother dead."

"I see that you have been well informed of the family's history."

I stood up suddenly. I took a step towards him. He immediately rose—although I was tall, he was considerably taller than I—and looked down at me. I tried to read the expression in those deep-set eyes.

"She is lonely," I said. "Don't you see? Please don't be harsh with her. If you would only be kind to her. . . . If only . . ."

He was no longer looking at me; a faintly bored expression had come into his face.

"Why, Mademoiselle Lawson," he said, "I thought you had come here to restore our pictures, not ourselves."

I felt defeated.

I said: "I'm sorry. I shouldn't have come. I should have known it was useless."

He led the way to the door; he opened it and bowed his head slightly as I went through.

I went back to my room wondering what I had done.

The next morning I went to the gallery to work as usual, expecting a summons from the Comte because I was certain that he would not allow such interference to pass. I had wakened often during the night to recall that scene, exaggerating it to such an extent that it was as though the devil himself had sat opposite me in that chair watching me through heavy-lidded eyes.

Lunch was brought up as usual. While I was eating it, Nounou came up. She looked very old and tired and I guessed she had scarcely slept all night.

"Monsieur le Comte has been in the schoolroom all the morning," she burst out. "I can't think what it means. He has been looking at all the exercise books and asking questions. Poor Geneviève is almost hysterical with fright." She looked at me fearfully and added: "It's so unlike him. But he has asked this that and the other and says he thinks she is quite ignorant. Poor Mademoiselle Dubois is almost in a state of collapse."

"No doubt he feels it is time he took some notice of his daughter."

"I don't know what it means, Miss. I wish I did."

I went for a walk taking a road which neither passed the Bastides' house nor led into the town. I did not want to meet anyone; I merely wanted to be alone to think about Geneviève and her father.

When I returned to the *château* it was to find Nounou in my room waiting for me.

"Mademoiselle Dubois has gone," she announced.

"What?" I cried.

"Monsieur le Comte just gave her her salary in lieu of notice."

I was shaken. "Oh . . . poor woman! Where will she go? It seems so . . . ruthless."

"The Comte makes up his mind quickly," said Nounou, "and then he acts."

"I suppose there will be a new governess, now."

"I do not know what will happen, Miss."

"And Geneviève, how is she?"

"She never had any respect for Mademoiselle Dubois . . . and to tell the truth nor did I. She is afraid though."

After Nounou had gone, I sat in my room wondering what would happen next. And what of myself? He could not call me inefficient. The work on the pictures was progressing very satisfactorily; but people were dismissed for other failings. Insolence for one thing. And I had dared summon him to his own library, to criticize his treatment of his daughter. Now I came to consider it calmly, I had to admit that it would be understandable if I received my orders to go. As for the pictures, he could find someone to continue with the work. I was by no means indispensable.

Then, of course, there was the affair of the dress. I had been the loser, but every time he saw me he would remember what his daughter had done—and remember, moreover, that I had had too close a glimpse into his family's secrets.

Geneviève came to my room and uttered a sullen apology which I knew she did not mean. I was too depressed to say much to her.

When I was hanging up my things for the night I looked for the dress, which I had thrown into the wardrobe. It was no longer there. I was surprised and wondered whether Geneviève had removed it, but I decided to say nothing about its disappearance.

I was working in the gallery when the summons came.

"Monsieur le Comte would like to see you in the library, Mademoiselle Lawson."

"Very well," I said. "I will be there in a few moments." I picked up the sable brush I had been using and studied it thoughtfully. It is my turn now, I thought.

The door shut and I gave myself a few seconds in which to compose myself. Whatever happened I should pretend indifference. At least he would not be able to say I was incompetent.

I braced myself to go to the library. I thrust my hands into the pockets of the brown linen coat I was wearing, for fear they might tremble and betray my agitation. I wished my heart would not beat so fast; it might be obvious. I was glad my thick matte skin did not flush easily; but I guessed my eyes would be brighter than usual.

Without any outward show of haste I went to the library. As I approached the door I touched my hair and was reminded that it was probably untidy as it often became when I was working. All to the good. I did not want him to think I had prepared myself for the interview.

I knocked at the door.

"Please come in." His voice was soft, inviting, but I did not trust his gentleness.

"Ah, Mademoiselle Lawson."

He was smiling at me intently, mischievously. What sort of a mood was this?

"Please sit down."

He took me to a chair which faced the window, so that the light was full on my face, and seated himself in shadow. I felt it was an unfair advantage.

"When we last met you were kind enough to express an interest in my daughter," he said.

"I am very interested in her."

"So good of you, particularly as you came here to restore the pictures. One would imagine you had little time to spare for that which did not concern your work."

Now it was coming. I was not progressing fast enough. I was not giving satisfaction. This afternoon I would be speeding on my way from the *château* just as yesterday poor Mademoiselle Dubois had gone.

A horrible depression came over me. I could not bear to go. I should be more wretched than I had ever been in my life. I should never forget the *château*. I should be tormented by memories all my life. I wanted so much to know the truth about the *château* . . . about the Comte himself—whether he was such a monster as most people seemed to think him. Had he always been as he was now? If not, what had made him so?

Did he know what I was thinking? He had paused and was watching me intently.

"I don't know what you will think of my proposition, Mademoiselle Lawson, but one thing I do know is that you will be absolutely frank."

"I shall try to be."

"My dear Mademoiselle Lawson, you do not have to *try*. You are so naturally. It is an admirable characteristic and, may I say, one which I greatly admire."

"You are very kind. Please tell me of this . . . proposition."

"I feel my daughter's education has been neglected. Governesses are a problem. How many of them take the posts because they have a vocation? Very few. Most take them because, having been brought up to do nothing, they suddenly find themselves in a position where they have to do something. It is not a good motive for undertaking this most important occupation. In your profession it is necessary to have a gift. You are an artist . . ."

"Oh no . . . I would not claim . . ."

"An artist *manqué*," he finished, and I sensed his mockery.

"Perhaps," I said coolly.

"You see how different from these poor dejected ladies who come to teach our children! I have decided to send my daughter to school. You were gracious enough to offer an opinion as to her well-being. Please give me that candid opinion on this."

"I think it could be an excellent idea, but it would depend on the school."

He waved his hand. "This is no place for a highly strung child. Do you agree? It is for antiquarians, those whose passion is architecture, paintings . . . and those who are imbued with the old traditions—antiquated too, you might say."

He had read my thoughts. He knew that I saw him as the autocrat, the upholder of the divine right of the nobility. He was telling me so.

I said: "I suppose you are right."

"I know I am. I have chosen a school in England for Geneviève."

"Oh!"

"You seem surprised. Surely you believe that the best schools are in England?"

Here was mockery again and I said rather too warmly: "That could be possible."

"Exactly. There she would not only learn to speak the language but to acquire that excellent *sang-froid* with which you, Mademoiselle, are so lavishly endowed."

"Thank you. But she would be far from her home."

"A home in which, as you pointed out to me, she is not particularly happy."

"But she could be. She is capable of great affection."

He changed the subject. "You work during the mornings in the gallery, but not in the afternoons. I'm glad that you are making use of the stables."

I thought: He has been watching me. He knows how I spend my time. I believed I knew what was coming. He was going to send me away as he had Mademoiselle Dubois. My impertinence was as distasteful to him as her incompetence.

I wondered whether he had submitted her to an interview like this. He was a man who liked to hunt his prey before the kill. I remembered that thought occurring to me once before in this library.

"Monsieur le Comte," I said, "if you are not satisfied with the work I have done, please tell me. I will prepare to leave at once."

"Mademoiselle Lawson, you are very hasty. I am pleased to discover at least this flaw in you, because it prevents you from being perfect. Perfection is so dull. I did not say I was displeased with your work. In fact I find your work excellent. Some time I shall come to you in the gallery and ask you to show me how you get such excellent results. Let me tell you what I have in mind. If my daughter is to go to England she must have a good knowledge of the language. I do not propose that she shall go immediately. Perhaps not for another year. In the meantime she will take lessons from the Curé. He will be at least as good as the governess who has just left us. Indeed he must be, for he couldn't be worse. But it is her English about which I am most concerned. Until the spring you will be in the gallery only during the mornings. That leaves you some free time. I was wondering whether you would undertake to teach Geneviève English when you are not engaged on the pictures. I am sure she would profit greatly from such an arrangement."

I was so overcome by my emotion that I could not speak.

He went on quickly: "I do not mean, that you would confine yourself to a schoolroom, but that you and she should ride together . . . walk together. . . . She knows the fundamentals of grammar. At least I hope so. It is practice in conversation that she needs, and of course to acquire a reasonably good accent. You understand what I mean?"

"Yes, I understand."

"You would of course be reimbursed. That is a matter which you could discuss with my steward. Now what do you say?"

"I . . . I accept with pleasure."

"That is excellent." He had stood up and was holding out his hand. I put mine in his. He gripped it firmly and shook it.

I was so happy. The thought occurred to me that I had rarely been as happy in my life.

It was a week later when, entering my bedroom, I found a large cardboard box on my bed. I thought there had been a mistake until I saw my name on it; and at the foot of the label was an address in Paris.

I opened the box.

Green velvet in a rich jewel color. Emerald green velvet! I took it out of the box. It was an evening gown, simply cut but exquisite.

Certainly there must be some mistake. All the same I held it against me and went to the mirror. My shining eyes reflected the color so that they seemed to match the velvet. It was beautiful. Why had it come to me?

I laid it reverently on my bed and examined the box. There I found a parcel wrapped in tissue paper and when I unrolled this, there was my old black velvet. I understood, before I read the card that fell out. I saw the crest which I had begun to know well, and on the card was written: *"I trust this will replace the one which was spoilt. If it is not what you need, we must try again. Lothair de la Talle."*

I went to the bed; I picked up the dress; I held it against me; I hugged it. In fact I behaved like a foolish girl. And all the time my other self, the one I was always trying to be, was saying: Ridiculous! You can't accept it. And the real Me, the one who only appeared now and then but was there all the time lying in wait to betray me, was saying: It's the most beautiful dress. Every time you put it on you will feel excited. Why, in such a dress you could be an attractive woman.

Then I laid the dress on the bed and said: "I shall go to him at once and tell him that I cannot dream of accepting it."

I tried to compose my features into a severe mold, but I kept thinking of his coming into my room—or sending someone—to find the ruined black velvet, sending it to Paris with the order: "Make a gown to these measurements. Make the finest gown you have ever made."

How stupid I was! What was happening to me?

I had better see him so that the dress could be sent back to Paris without delay.

I went down to the library. Perhaps he was expecting me, for he may have known that the dress had arrived. As if he would care *when* the dress arrived. He had merely decided it should be given to me as recompense and then forgotten all about it.

He was there.

"I must speak to you," I said, and as always, because I was embarrassed, I sounded arrogant. He noticed it, for a smile briefly touched his lips and the amused glint leaped into his eyes.

"Please sit down, Mademoiselle Lawson. You are agitated."

I was immediately at a disadvantage because the last thing I wanted was to betray my feelings, which I did not entirely understand myself. It was unlike me to be so excited about clothes.

"By no means," I said. "I have merely come to thank you for sending me the dress to replace mine and to tell you that I cannot accept it."

"So it has arrived. Does it not fit then?"

"I . . . cannot say. I have not tried it. There was no need for you to have sent for it."

"Forgive my disagreement, but in my opinion there was every need."

"But no. It was a very old dress. I had had it for years, and this one is, er . . ."

"I see that you do not like it."

"That is not the point at issue." Again the severity in my voice made him smile.

"Really? What *is* the point at issue?"

"That I cannot dream of accepting the dress."

"Why not?"

"Because it is not necessary."

"Now come, Mademoiselle Lawson, be frank and say that you consider accepting a . . . garment from me is improper—if that is what you mean."

"I think no such thing. Why should I?"

Again he made that entirely French gesture which implied anything one wished it to. "I do not know. I do not imagine for one moment that I could understand what goes on in *your* mind. I was merely trying to find some reason why having had an article ruined in this house you could not accept a replacement."

"This is a *dress* . . ."

"Why should a dress be different from any other object?"

"This is a purely personal thing."

"Ah! Purely personal! If I had destroyed one of your solutions, would you not have allowed me to replace it? Or is it really because this is a dress . . . something you would wear . . . something intimate, shall we say?"

I could not look at him; there was a warmth in his expression which disturbed me.

I turned away from his gaze and said: "There was no need for the gown to be replaced. In any case the green velvet is far more valuable than the one for which it was meant to compensate me."

"Value is difficult to assess. The black dress was clearly more valuable to *you,* since you were distressed to have lost it and are reluctant to accept this one."

"I think you willfully misunderstand."

He came to me swiftly and laid a hand on my shoulder. "Mademoiselle Lawson," he said gently, "it will displease me if you refuse to accept this dress. Your own was destroyed by a member of my family and I wish to replace it. Will you please accept it?"

"Since you put it that way . . ."

His hand fell from my shoulder, but he was still standing close. I felt uneasy yet indescribably happy.

"Then you will. You are very generous, Mademoiselle Lawson."

"It is you who are generous. There was no need . . ."

"I repeat there was every need."

"To replace it so extravagantly," I finished.

He laughed suddenly and I realized I had never heard him laugh like that before. There was no bitterness, no mockery.

"I hope," he said, "that one day I shall be allowed to see you wearing it."

"I have very few occasions for wearing such a dress."

"But since it is such an *extravagant* dress, perhaps those occasions should be created."

"I do not see how that can be," I replied, my voice growing colder as my hidden emotions grew greater. "I can only say it was unnecessary, but good of you. I will accept the dress and thank you for your generosity."

I moved to the door but he was there before me, opening it, inclining his head so that I could not see his expression.

As I went up to my room my emotions were overwhelming. If I had been wise I should have analyzed them. I should have been wise, but of course I wasn't.

5

My interest in the Comte and his affairs added such a zest to my life that each morning I would awaken with a feeling of expectation, telling myself that this very day might be the one when I would learn something new, begin to understand him more, and perhaps find the clue which would tell me whether he was a murderer or a much maligned man.

Then, without warning, he went to Paris, and I heard that he would return just before Christmas when there would be guests at the *château*. I shall find myself on the edge of affairs, I thought, looking in from outside.

I took on my new duties with enthusiasm, and I was rather pleased to find that Geneviève by no means resented me but was in fact eager to learn English. The prospect of going to school was a terrifying one, but it was too far in the future to be a real menace. She would ask me questions about England when we went for our rides and we even found some amusement in our English conversations. She was taking lessons with the Curé and although none shared her lessons, she often saw the Bastide children on their way to the Curé's house. I believed it was good for her to mix with the other children.

One morning while I was in the gallery, Philippe came in. When the Comte was not at the castle he seemed to take on a new stature. Now he looked like a pale shadow of his cousin, but having been made more and more aware of the Comte's virility, I was struck afresh by the weakness—almost effeminacy—of Philippe.

But his smile was very friendly as he asked how the work was progressing.

"You are skillful," he commented when I showed him.

"It is care that is needed as much as skill."

"And expert knowledge." He was standing before the picture I had restored. "One has the feeling that one could put out a hand and touch those emeralds," he said.

"The skill of the painter, not the restorer."

He continued to gaze wistfully at the picture and once more I sensed his deep love for the *château* and everything connected with it. That was how I should feel were I a member of such a family.

Turning suddenly and catching my eyes upon him, he looked faintly embarrassed, as though he were wondering whether he should say what was in his mind. Then he said quickly: "Mademoiselle Lawson, are you happy here?"

"Happy? I find the work very satisfying."

"The work, yes. I know how you feel about that. I was thinking of"— he made a gesture with his hand—"the atmosphere here . . . the family." I looked surprised and he went on: "There was that unfortunate affair of the dress."

"It is all forgotten now." I wondered whether my face betrayed my pleasure as I thought of the green dress.

"In a household like this one . . ." he stopped as though he did not know how to go on. "If you found it intolerable here . . ." he went on hurriedly, "if you wished to leave . . ."

"To leave!"

"I meant if it became difficult. My cousin might . . . er . . ." He abandoned what he had been going to say, but I knew he was thinking, as I was, of the green velvet dress and the fact that the Comte had given it to me. He saw something significant in that. But it was evidently too dangerous to discuss. How he feared his cousin! He smiled brightly. "A friend of mine has a fine collection of pictures and some are in need of restoration. They could keep you busy for a long time, I have no doubt."

"It will be a long time before I finish here."

"My friend, Monsieur de la Monelle, needs his pictures restored immediately. I thought that if you were unhappy here . . . or you felt you would like to get away . . ."

"I have no wish to leave this work."

He looked alarmed, fearful that he had said too much. "It was only a suggestion."

"You are very kind to be so concerned."

His smile was very charming. "I feel responsible. On that first occasion I could have sent you away."

"But you didn't. I appreciate that."

"Perhaps it would have been better."

"Oh no! I find the work here absorbing."

"It's a wonderful old place." He spoke almost eagerly. "But it is not the happiest of households and, in view of what happened in the past . . . my cousin's wife died, you know, in rather mysterious circumstances."

"I have heard that."

"And my cousin can be rather ruthless in getting what he wants. I shouldn't have said that. He has been good to me. I am here . . . it is now my home . . . thanks to him. It is only that I have this feeling of responsibility towards you and I would like you to know that if you did need my help . . . Mademoiselle Lawson, I hope you will say nothing of this to my cousin."

"I understand. I shan't mention it."

"But please bear in mind. If my cousin . . . if you should feel you ought to get away, please come to me."

He went to one of the paintings and asked questions about it, but I did not think he was paying attention to the answers.

When his eyes met mine they were rather shy, diffident, but very warm. He was certainly anxious on my behalf and I understood that he was warning me about the Comte.

I felt I had a good friend in the *château*.

Christmas was almost upon us. Geneviève and I were riding every day and there was a marked improvement in her English. I told her of our Christmases in England and how we brought in the holly and mistletoe; how we kissed under the mistletoe; how everyone had to have a stir at the Christmas puddings and what a great day it was when they were boiling and we hauled out the tiny basin with the "taster" in it. What an important moment that was when we each had our spoonful, for the taster was an indication of what the whole boiling of puddings would be.

"My grandmother was alive then," I said. "That was my mother's mother. She was French and had to learn all our customs, but she took to them very quickly and she would never have dreamt of giving up any of them."

"Tell me some more, Miss," begged Geneviève.

So I told her how I used to sit on a high stool beside my mother and help stone the raisins and peel the almonds.

"I used to eat them whenever I could."

That amused Geneviève. "Oh, Miss, fancy *your* being a little girl once."

I told her about waking on Christmas morning to find my stocking filled.

"*We* put our shoes by the fireplace . . . at least some people do. I don't."

"Why don't you?"

"Nounou would be the only one to remember. And you can't have one pair of shoes; you want a lot, otherwise it's no fun."

"You tell me."

"Well, you put your shoes round the fireplace on Christmas Eve when you come in from Midnight Mass and then you go to bed. In the morning, the little presents are inside your shoe and the big ones round it. We did it when my mother was alive."

"And then you stopped?"

She nodded.

"It's a nice custom."

"*Your* mother died," she said. "How did she die?"

"She was ill for a long time. I nursed her."

"You were grown up then?"

"Yes, I suppose you would call it that."

"Oh, Miss. I believe you were *always* grown up."

We called in at the Bastides' on our way back to the *château*. I had encouraged this because I felt that she should meet people outside the *château*, particularly children, and although Yves and Margot were younger than she was and Gabrielle older, at least they were nearer her age than anyone else she knew.

There was excitement in that household because of the nearness of Christmas—whispering in corners and hinting at secrets.

Yves and Margot were busy making the *crèche*. Geneviève watched them with interest and, while I talked to Madame Bastide, went over to join them.

"The children are so excited," said Madame Bastide. "It is always so. Margot tells us every morning how many hours it is until Christmas Day."

We watched them arrange the brown paper to look like rocks. Yves took out his painting set and painted moss on it, and Margot started to color the stable brown. On the floor lay the little sheep which they had made themselves and which they would set up on the rocks. I watched Geneviève. She was quite fascinated.

She looked into the cradle. "It's empty," she said, rather scornfully.

"Of course it's empty! Jesus isn't born yet," retorted Yves.

"It is a miracle," Margot told her. "We go to bed on Christmas Eve . . ."

"After we put our shoes round the fire . . ." added Yves.

"Yes, we do that . . . and the cradle is empty and then . . . on Christmas morning when we get up to look, the little Jesus is lying in it."

Geneviève was silent.

After a while she said: "Can I do something?"

"Yes," replied Yves. "We want more shepherds' crooks. Do you know how to make them?"

"No," she said humbly.

"Margot will show you."

I watched the two girls, their heads close together, and I said to myself: This is what she needs.

Madame Bastide followed my gaze. She said: "And you think Monsieur le Comte will allow this? You think he will agree to this friendship between our children and his daughter?"

I said: "I have never seen her so . . . relaxed, so unconscious of herself."

"Ah, but Monsieur le Comte will not wish his daughter to be carefree. He wants her to be the grand lady of the *château*."

"This companionship is what she needs. You have invited me to join you on Christmas Day. May I bring her with me? She has talked about Christmas so wistfully."

"You think it will be permitted?"

"We can try," I said.

"But Monsieur le Comte . . . ?"

"I will answer to him," I replied boldly.

A few days before Christmas the Comte returned to the *château*. I had expected that he would seek me out to discover either how his daughter or his paintings were progressing but he did no such thing. This was probably because he was thinking of the guests who would soon be arriving.

There would be fifteen people, I heard from Nounou. Not so many as usually came, but entertaining was rather a delicate matter when there was no lady of the house.

I was out riding with Geneviève the day before Christmas Eve when we met a party of riders from the *château*. The Comte rode at the head of them, and beside him was a beautiful young woman. She wore a high black riding hat swathed with gray and there was a gray cravat at her throat. The masculinity of her riding habit served to accentuate her femininity, and I noticed at once how bright was her hair, how delicate her features. She was like a piece of china from the collection in the blue drawing room which I had seen once or twice. Such women always made me feel even taller than I was, even more plain.

"Here is my daughter," said the Comte, greeting us almost affectionately.

We pulled up, the four of us, for the rest of the party were some way behind.

"With her governess?" added the beautiful creature.

"Certainly not. This is Miss Lawson from England who is restoring our pictures."

I saw the blue eyes take on a coolly appraising expression.

"Geneviève, you will have met Mademoiselle de la Monelle."

Mademoiselle de la Monelle! I had heard the name before.

"Yes, Papa," said Geneviève. "Good day, Mademoiselle."

"Mademoiselle Lawson, Mademoiselle de la Monelle."

We greeted each other.

"Pictures must be quite fascinating," she said.

I knew then. This was the name of the people whom Philippe had mentioned as having pictures to be restored.

"Miss Lawson thinks so." And to us, so cutting short the encounter: "Were you returning?"

We said we were and rode on.

"Would you say she was beautiful?" asked Geneviève.

"What was that?"

"You're not listening," accused Geneviève and repeated the question.

"I should think most people would."

"I said you, Miss. Do you think so?"

"She has a type of good looks which most people admire."

"Well, *I* don't like her."

"I hope you won't take your scissors to *her* room, because if you did anything like that there would be trouble . . . not only for you but for others. Have you thought of what has happened to poor Mademoiselle Dubois?"

"She was a silly old woman."

"That's no reason for being unkind to her."

She laughed rather slyly. "Well, you came out of that affair well, didn't you? It's a lovely dress my father gave you. I don't suppose you ever had a dress like that in your life before. So you see I really did you a good turn."

"I don't agree. It was an embarrassing situation for us all."

"Poor old Esquilles! It wasn't fair really. She didn't want to go. You wouldn't want to go either."

"No, I shouldn't. I'm very interested in my work."

"And in us?"

"Certainly I hope to see you more fluent in your English than you are." Then I relented and said: "No, I should not want to leave you, Geneviève."

She smiled, but almost immediately the malicious look came into her face. "Nor my father," she said. "But I don't think he will be taking much notice of you now, Miss. Did you see the way he looked at *her?*"

"At her?"

"You know who I mean. Mademoiselle de la Monelle. And she *is* beautiful."

She rode on and looked over her shoulder at me, laughing.

I touched Bonhomme's flanks and broke into a gallop. Geneviève was beside me.

I could not get Mademoiselle de la Monelle's beautiful face out of my mind and both Geneviève and I were silent as we rode back to the *château.*

The next day I came face to face with the Comte on my way to the gallery. I thought as he was no doubt preoccupied with his guests he would merely greet me and pass on, but he paused.

"And how is my daughter progressing with her English?"

"Very well. I think you will be pleased."

"I knew you would be an excellent teacher."

Did I look so much like a governess? I wondered.

"She is interested and that is a great help. She is happier now."

"Happier?"

"Yes, haven't you noticed?"

He shook his head. "But I accept your word."

"There is always a reason why young people want to destroy things . . . without reason. Do you agree with me?"

"I am sure you are right."

"I think she feels the loss of her mother deeply, and misses the fun that most children have."

He did not flinch at the mention of his dead wife.

"Fun, Mademoiselle Lawson?" he repeated.

"She has been telling me how they used to put their shoes in front of the fire on Christmas Eve . . . rather wistfully I thought."

"Isn't she rather old for that sort of thing?"

"I don't think one is ever too old."

"You surprise me."

"It's a pleasant custom," I insisted. "We have decided that we will follow it this Christmas and . . . perhaps you will be surprised by my presumption but . . ."

"You have ceased to surprise me."

"I thought that you might put your present with the others. That would delight her."

"You think that by finding a gift in a shoe instead of shall we say at the dinner table, my daughter is less likely to play childish tricks?"

I sighed. "Monsieur le Comte, I see I *have* been presumptuous. I'm sorry."

I passed quickly on and he did not attempt to stop me.

I went to the gallery, but I could not work. I felt too disturbed. I had two images in my mind: the proud innocent man showing a defiant face to the world and . . . the callous murderer.

Which was the true one? I wished I knew! But then what concern was it of mine? I was concerned with the pictures, not the man.

On Christmas Eve we all went to the midnight service in the old Gaillard church. The Comte sat in the first of the pews reserved for the *château* family with Geneviève beside him and the guests in the pews immediately behind. Farther back I sat with Nounou; and as the servants were all there the *château* pews were full.

I saw the Bastide family in their best clothes, Madame all in black and Gabrielle looking very pretty in gray. There was the young man with her whom I had seen now and then about the vineyard; he was Jacques, who had been with Armand Bastide at the time of the accident; I knew him by the scar on his left cheek.

Yves and Margot could scarcely keep still; Margot was no doubt counting the minutes now instead of the hours.

I saw that Geneviève was watching them, and I guessed that she was wishing that instead of going back to the *château* she was going to the Bastides' house that she might join in the fun which only children can give to Christmas.

I was glad I had announced that I was going to put my shoes by the schoolroom fire and suggested that she do the same. It could not but be a quiet little party when compared with the frivolity which would take place on Christmas morning round the Bastide fireplace, but still, it would be better than nothing; and I had been surprised by Geneviève's enthusiasm. After all, she had never been used to a large family; and when her mother had been alive it must have been the three of them—Geneviève, Françoise, Nounou and perhaps the governess of the time. And what of the Comte? Surely when his wife was alive and his daughter young he would have joined the Christmas customs.

The nursery quarters were not far from my own and consisted of four rooms adjoining each other. There was first the schoolroom, lofty with a vaulted ceiling and embrasures with the stone window seat benches which were a feature of the *château*. In it was a huge fireplace large enough, as Nounou had said, to roast an ox. To one side of it was an enormous pewter caldron which was always full of logs. There were three doors which led from this room—one was Geneviève's bedroom; one Nounou's; and the other was reserved for the governess.

Into the schoolroom we solemnly went after we returned from church and there we laid our shoes before the dying fire.

Geneviève went to bed and, when we guessed she was asleep, Nounou and I laid out gifts in the shoes. I had a scarf of scarlet silk for Geneviève which I thought could be used as a cravat. It would be most becoming to her dark coloring and useful for riding. For Nounou I had what Madame Latière at the *pâtisserie* had assured me were her favorite sweets, a kind of cushion made of rum and butter in a very charming box. Nounou and I pretended not to see our own gifts, said good night and went back to our rooms.

I was awakened early next morning by Geneviève.

"Look, Miss. Look!" she cried.

I sat up, startled, and then remembered that it was Christmas morning.

"The scarf is lovely. Thank you, Miss." She was wearing it over her dressing gown. "And Nounou has given me handkerchiefs . . . all beautifully embroidered. And there is too . . . oh, Miss, I haven't opened it. It's from Papa. It says so. Read it."

I was sitting up in bed as excited as she was.

"It was by my shoe with the others, Miss."

"Oh," I cried. "That's wonderful!"

"He hasn't done it for years. I wonder why this year . . ."

"Never mind. Let's see what it is."

It was a pearl pendant on a slender gold chain. "Oh, it's lovely," I cried.

"Fancy!" she said. "He put it there."

"You're pleased with it?"

She could not speak; she nodded.

"Put it on," I said, and helped her fasten it.

She went to the looking glass and studied herself. Then she came back to the bed and, picking up my scarf, which she had taken off to put the pendant on, she laid it across her shoulders.

"Happy Christmas, Miss," she said gaily.

I thought it was going to be one.

She insisted that I go into the schoolroom. "Nounou's not up yet. She can have hers later. Now, Miss, do look at yours." I picked up Geneviève's parcel. It was a book about the castle and the neighborhood. She watched me delightedly while I opened it.

"How I shall enjoy that!" I cried. "So you knew how fascinated I was."

"Yes, you show it, Miss. And you do like old houses so much, don't you? But you mustn't start reading it now."

"Oh, Geneviève, thank you. It was good of you to think of me."

She said: "Look. You've got a tray cloth from Nounou. I know who did that. My mother. Nounou's got a whole boxful of them."

The handkerchiefs; the tray cloth . . . they were all the work of Françoise! I wondered that Nounou had parted with them.

"And there's something else for you, Miss." I had seen the parcel, and a wild thought had come into my head which, while quite crazy, was so exciting that I was afraid to pick up the parcel for fear of almost certain disappointment.

"Open it! Open it!" commanded Geneviève. I did and found an exquisite miniature set with pearls. It portrayed a woman holding a spaniel in her arms. The head of the dog was just visible and I knew by the hair style of the woman that it had been painted some hundred and fifty years ago.

"Do you like it?" cried Geneviève. "Who gave it?"

"It's beautiful but too valuable. I . . ."

Geneviève picked up a note which had fallen from the parcel. On it was written: *"You will recognize the lady whom you have so expertly cleaned. She would probably be as grateful to you as I am, so it seems fitting that you should have this. I had intended to give it to you when I came across it the other day, but since you like our old customs it is here in your shoe. Lothair de la Talle."*

"It's Papa!" cried Geneviève excitedly.

"Yes. He's pleased with my work on the pictures and this is his appreciation."

"Oh . . . but in your shoe! Who would have thought . . ."

"Well, he must have thought that while he was putting your pendant in your shoe he could put this in mine."

Geneviève was laughing uncontrollably.

I said: "This is the lady on the portrait with the emeralds. That is why he has given it to me."

"You like it, Miss? You *do* like it?"

"Well, it is a very beautiful miniature."

I handled it lovingly, noting the exquisite coloring and the lovely setting of pearls. I had never possessed anything so beautiful.

Nounou appeared. "Such a noise!" she said. "It woke me. Happy Christmas."

"Happy Christmas, Nounou."

"Just look what Papa has given me, Nounou. And in my shoe."

"In your shoe?"

"Oh wake up, Nounou. You're half asleep. It's Christmas morning. Look at your presents. If you don't open them I will. Open mine first."

Geneviève had bought her a primrose-colored apron which Nounou declared was just what she wanted; then she expressed her pleasure over my bonbons. The Comte had not forgotten her either; there was a large fleecy woolen shawl in a shade of dark blue.

Nounou was puzzled. "From Monsieur le Comte . . . but why?"

"Doesn't he usually remember Christmas?" I asked.

"Oh yes, he remembers. The vineyard workers all have their turkeys and the indoor servants have gifts of money. The steward gives them out. It has always been the custom."

"Show her what you've got, Miss."

I held out the miniature.

"Oh!" said Nounou and for a moment she looked at me blankly; then I saw the speculation in her eyes.

I was responsible for this giving of presents, Nounou was thinking. I knew it; and I was glad.

But Nounou was disturbed.

6

In the morning Geneviève and I walked to the Bastides'. Madame Bastide hot from the kitchen came out to greet us waving a ladle; Gabrielle looked over her shoulder, for her services were also needed in the kitchen from which a delicious smell was coming. Yves and Margot dashed at Geneviève and told her what they had found in their shoes; I was glad she could tell them what she had found in hers; I noticed with what pleasure she displayed her gifts. She went to the *crèche* and called out in delight as she peered into the cradle.

"He's here!" she cried.

"Of course," retorted Yves. "What did you expect? It's Christmas morning."

Jean Pierre came in with a load of logs and his face lit up with pleasure.

"This is a great day when *château* people sit down at our table."

"Geneviève could scarcely wait for this," I told him.

"And you?"

"I too have looked forward to it."

"Then, we must see that you are not disappointed."

Nor were we. It was a gay occasion; the table which Gabrielle had decorated so charmingly with feathery evergreens was overcrowded that day, for Jacques and his mother had joined the party. She was an invalid and it was touching to see how tender Jacques was to her; and with Madame Bastide, her son, and four grandchildren besides Geneviève and myself we made a sizable party, kept merry by the excitement of the children.

Madame Bastide sat at the head of the table and her son opposite her. I was on Madame Bastide's right hand, Geneviève on that of her son.

We were the guests of honor and here, as in the *château*, etiquette was observed.

The children chattered all the time, and I was glad to see that Geneviève was listening intently and occasionally joining in. Yves would not allow her to be shy. I was certain that it was company such as this that she needed, for she seemed happier than I had ever seen her before. About her neck was her pendant. I guessed she would never want to take it off and would perhaps sleep in it.

Madame Bastide carved the turkey, which was stuffed with chestnuts and served with a *purée* of mushrooms. It was quite delicious, but the great moment was when a large cake was brought in to the delighted shrieks of the children.

"Who will get it? Who will get it?" chanted Yves. "Who'll be King for the day?"

"It might be a Queen," Margot reminded him.

"It'll be a King. What's the good of a Queen?"

"If a Queen has the crown she can rule . . ."

"Be silent, children," scolded Madame Bastide. "Does Mademoiselle Lawson know of this old custom?"

Jean Pierre was smiling at me across the table. "You see that cake," he said.

"Of course she sees it," cried Yves.

"It's big enough," added Gabrielle.

"Well," went on Jean Pierre, "inside it is a crown—a tiny crown. Now the cake is going to be cut into ten pieces—one for each, and all the cake must be eaten . . . and with care . . ."

"You might have the crown," shrieked Yves.

"With care," went on Jean Pierre, "for someone round this table is going to find the crown in the cake."

"And when it is found?"

"King for the day," shouted Yves.

"Or Queen for the day," added Margot.

"They wear the crown?" I asked.

"It's too little," Gabrielle told me. "But . . ."

"Better than that. The one who gets the crown is King—or, as Margot says, Queen—for the day," explained Jean Pierre. "It means that he . . . or she . . . rules the household. What he"—he smiled at Margot—"or she . . . says is law."

138

"For the whole of the day!" cried Margot.

"If I get it," said Yves, "you can't think what I'll do!"

"What?" demanded Margot.

But he was too overcome by mirth to tell, and everyone was impatient for the cutting of the cake.

There was a tense silence while Madame Bastide plunged in the knife; the cake was cut, and Gabrielle stood up to take the plate and hand it round. I was watching Geneviève, delighted to see how she could join in the simple fun.

There was no sound as we started to eat—only the ticking of the clock and the crackle of logs in the fireplace.

Then suddenly there was a shout and Jean Pierre was holding up the little gold-colored crown.

"Jean Pierre has it! Jean Pierre has it!" sang out the children.

"Call me Your Majesty when you address me," retorted Jean Pierre with mock dignity. "I order my coronation to take place without delay."

Gabrielle went out of the room and returned carrying, on a cushion, a metal crown decorated with tinsel. The children wriggled on the seats with delight, and Geneviève watched round-eyed.

"Who does Your Majesty command should crown you?" asked Gabrielle.

Jean Pierre pretended to survey us all regally; then his eyes fell on me. I glanced towards Geneviève and he understood the message at once.

"Mademoiselle Geneviève de la Talle step forward," he said.

Geneviève leaped to her feet, her cheeks pink, her eyes shining.

"You have to put the crown on his head," Yves told her.

So Geneviève walked solemnly to the cushion which Gabrielle held and, taking the crown, put it on Jean Pierre's head.

"Now you kneel and kiss his hand," commanded Yves, "and swear to serve the King."

I was watching Jean Pierre sitting back in his chair, the crown on his head, while Geneviève kneeled at his feet on the cushion on which Gabrielle had carried the crown. His expression was one of complete triumph. He certainly played the part well.

Yves broke up the solemn proceedings by demanding what was His Majesty's first command. Jean Pierre thought for a while and then he looked at Geneviève and me and said: "That we dispense with formality. Everyone here is commanded to call everyone else by their Christian names."

I saw Gabrielle look at me apprehensively, so I smiled and said: "Mine is Dallas. I hope you can all say it."

They all repeated it with the accent on the last syllable and there was laughter from the children as I corrected each one in turn.

"Is it a well-known English name?" asked Jacques.

"Like Jean Pierre and Yves in France?" added Yves.

"By no means. It's entirely my own, and there's a reason for it. My father was Daniel, my mother Alice. Before I was born he wanted a girl; she wanted a boy; he wanted it named after my mother, she after him. Then I appeared . . . and they merged their names and made Dallas."

This delighted the children, who started a game of linking names to see who could get the most amusing.

And immediately we were on Christian-name terms and it was extraordinary how that broke down all formality.

Jean Pierre sat back, his crown on his head like a benevolent monarch, and yet now and then I thought I could see a trace of arrogance which reminded me of the Comte.

He caught me watching him and laughed.

He said to me: "It is good of you, Dallas, to join in our games."

And for some absurd reason I was relieved to find he referred to this as a game.

When the Bastides' maid came to put up the shutters I was reminded how the time was flying. It had been such a pleasant afternoon; we had played games, miming and guessing all under the command of Jean Pierre; we had danced, for Armand Bastide's contribution to the jollity had been to play the violin.

There was only one time as good as Christmas, Margot confided in me as she taught me how to dance the "Sautière Charentaise," and that was grape harvest . . . but she didn't think even that was quite as good for there weren't the presents and the tree and King for a day.

"Grape harvest is really for the grownups," added Yves sagely. "Christmas is ours."

I was delighted to see Geneviève throw herself so wholeheartedly into the playing of games. I could see that she wanted the afternoon to go on and on; but I knew that we should return to the *château*. Even now our absence would have been noticed, and I did not know what reaction there would be.

I told Madame Bastide that we must most regretfully be leaving, and she signaled to Jean Pierre.

"My subjects wish to speak with me?" he said, his warm brown eyes twinkling first at me, then at Geneviève.

"We have to go," I explained. "We'll slip away . . . quietly. Then they won't notice that we've gone."

"Impossible! They'll all be desolate. I don't know whether I shan't have to exercise my royal prerogative . . ."

"We'll go now. I hate taking Geneviève away. She has had such a wonderful time."

"I will accompany you to the *château*."

"Oh, there is no need . . ."

"No need . . . when it's growing dark! I shall insist. You know I can . . ." His eyes were a little wistful. "Only for today it is true but I must make the most of my hour of power."

We were all rather silent during the walk back to the *château* and when we reached the drawbridge, Jean Pierre halted and said: "There! You are safely home."

He took my hand in one of his and Geneviève's in the other. He kissed them both; and still held them. Then to my surprise he drew me towards him and kissed my cheek; and immediately did the same to Geneviève.

We were startled, both of us, but he was smiling.

"The King can do no wrong," he reminded us. "Tomorrow I shall be plain Jean Pierre Bastide, but today I am King of my little castle."

I laughed and, taking Geneviève's arm, said: "Well, thank you, and good day."

He bowed and we went across the drawbridge into the castle.

Nounou was waiting for us, a little anxious.

"Monsieur le Comte came to the schoolroom. He asked where you were, and I had to tell him."

"Of course," I said, my heart beginning to beat fast.

"You see, you were not here for *déjeuner*."

"There is no need to keep anything secret," I replied.

"He wishes to see you when you return."

"Both of us?" said Geneviève and I thought how she had changed from the excited girl who had joined in the Bastides' games.

"No, only Mademoiselle Lawson. He will be in the library until six o'clock. You would just catch him, Miss."

"I will go to him at once," I said; and I went out leaving Nounou and Geneviève together.

He was there reading and when I entered he languidly, almost reluctantly, laid aside his book.

"You wished to see me?" I asked.

"Please sit down, Mademoiselle Lawson."

"I must thank you for the miniature. It is quite lovely."

He bowed his head. "I thought you would appreciate it. You recognized her, of course."

"Yes. The likeness is there. I feel you have been too generous."

"Can one be too generous?"

"It was kind of you to put the gifts in the shoes."

"You had made my duty plain to me." He smiled and looked down at his hands. "You have had a pleasant visit?"

"We have been at the Maison Bastide. I think it excellent for Geneviève to be with young people." I spoke defiantly.

"I am sure you are right."

"She enjoyed the games . . . the Christmas festivities . . . the simplicity of it all. I hope you do not disapprove."

He lifted his shoulders and spread his hands in a gesture which might have meant anything.

"Geneviève should join us for dinner tonight," he said.

"I am sure she will enjoy that."

"I don't suppose we can vie with the *bonhomie,* the *camaraderie,* you enjoyed earlier in the day, but you too must join us . . . if you wish, Mademoiselle Lawson."

"Thank you."

He inclined his head to indicate that the interview was over; I rose and he followed me to the door which he held open for me.

"Geneviève was delighted with your gift," I told him. "I wish you could have seen her face when she took off the wrappings."

He smiled and I was very happy. I had expected a reprimand and instead had been given an invitation.

This was a wonderful Christmas.

This was my first opportunity to wear the new dress. As I put it on I felt excited—strangely expectant, as though the fact that I was wearing a dress he had chosen for me made a different woman of me.

But of course he hadn't chosen it. He had merely asked the Paris house to send a dress to fit a woman who had worn the black velvet. Yet the color was the most becoming I could have worn. Was that chance? Or had he suggested it? My eyes looked brilliantly green and my hair was the color of polished chestnuts. I believed I was almost attractive in that dress.

It was in a mood of exhilaration that I started down the stairs, and as I did so I came face to face with Mademoiselle de la Monelle. She looked enchanting in a gown of lavender chiffon trimmed with green satin bows; her fair hair was worn in curls held high with a clip of pearls and some glistening coils falling over her long slender neck. She looked at me in some bewilderment as though she were trying to remember where we had met before. I imagined I looked very different in this gown than in my shabby riding habit.

"I'm Dallas Lawson," I said. "I'm restoring the pictures."

"You are joining us?" There was a cold surprise in her voice which I found offensive.

"On the Comte's invitation," I replied as coolly.

"Is that so?"

"Indeed yes."

Her eyes were taking in the details of my dress, assessing its cost; it seemed to surprise her as much as the Comte's invitation.

She turned and went on ahead of me. The gesture seemed to imply that even if the Comte was so eccentric as to invite someone who was working for him to mingle with his friends, *she* did not wish to know me.

The guests were gathered in one of the smaller rooms near the banqueting hall. The Comte was already deep in conversation with Mademoiselle de la Monelle and was unaware of my entrance, but Philippe made his way towards me. I fancied he knew that I might be feeling a little uneasy and had been waiting for me. Another example of his kindness.

"May I say how elegant you look."

"Thank you. I wanted to ask you whether the Mademoiselle de la Monelle who is here is a member of the family whose collection of paintings you mentioned."

"Why . . . er . . . yes. Her father is here too. But I hope you won't mention this to my cousin."

"Of course not. In any case I think it would be very unlikely that I should leave the *château* to go to her home."

"You may think that now, but . . . if at any time . . ."

"Yes, I will remember it."

Geneviève came over to us. She was wearing a dress of pink silk and looked rather sullen—scarcely a hint of the girl who had crowned the King for the day a short while ago.

At that moment dinner was announced and we went into the banqueting hall, where the glittering table was lit by candelabra placed at intervals.

I was seated next to an elderly gentleman who was interested in pictures and we talked together. I supposed I had been put there to entertain him. Turkey was served with chestnuts and truffles, but I did not enjoy it as I had that at the Bastides'—perhaps because I was so conscious of Mademoiselle de la Monelle seated next to the Comte, who seemed absorbed in her animated conversation.

How foolish I was to think I was attractive because I was wearing a beautiful dress! How much more than foolish to imagine that he who had known many charming women would be aware of me when he was in the company of this one. Then I heard him mention my name—

"Mademoiselle Lawson has to answer for this."

I looked up and met his eyes, and I did not know whether he was displeased with me or merely amused.

I fancied he had disapproved of my taking his daughter to eat Christmas dinner with his work people, that he knew I was aware of this, and that he wanted me to be in doubt of what form his disapproval would take.

Mademoiselle de la Monelle was looking at me too. Her eyes, I thought, are ice blue, cold and calculating. She was irritated because I, for the second time this evening, had been brought to her notice.

"Yes, Mademoiselle Lawson," went on the Comte. "Last night we were looking at the picture and your work on my ancestress was greatly admired. She has lived under a cloud for so many years. Now she has emerged, so have her emeralds. It's those emeralds . . ."

"Every so often interest in them is revived," said Philippe.

"And, Mademoiselle Lawson, *you* have started the new revival." He was looking at me in mock exasperation.

"And you don't wish for one?" I asked.

"Who knows? One of these new outbursts of interest may result in their discovery. Last night when the pictures were examined someone suggested a treasure hunt and the cry went up. So a treasure hunt there has to be. You must join in, of course."

Mademoiselle de la Monelle laid a hand on his arm. "I shall be terrified to wander about this place . . . alone."

Someone replied that he very much doubted she would be allowed to do that; and there was laughter in which the Comte joined.

Then he was looking at me again, the laughter still in his eyes. "A mock treasure hunt. You'll hear about it later. We're going to start soon because we don't know how long it will last. Gautier has been preparing the clues all morning."

It was an hour or so later when the treasure hunt started. Clues had been written on pieces of paper and hidden at certain places all over the *château*. Everyone was presented with the first clue from which they had to work out from the cryptic message where to go for the second; if they found the right place they would discover a little pile of papers there from which they would take one on which the next clue would be written; obviously the one who solved the final clue first would be the winner.

There was a great deal of chatter and exclamations of horror while they read their clues. Several of the guests went off in pairs. I could see neither the Comte, Philippe, nor Geneviève, and I felt as though I were in a household of strangers. No one approached me. Perhaps they wondered why a woman who was merely in the *château* to work for the Comte should have been asked to join the party. I supposed that had I lived in France I should have gone home for Christmas; did the fact that I was here brand me as someone with nowhere to go?

I saw a young man and woman slip out hand in hand, and it occurred to me that the object of a game like this was not so much to solve the clues but to give opportunities for flirtation.

I turned my attention to the clue and read:

"Go to do homage and drink if you are thirsty."

After a few seconds reflection that seemed simple. To do homage was to court and in the courtyard was a well.

I made my way through the loggia to the courtyard and sure enough there on the parapet round the well was a large stone under which the clues had been put. I took one out and hurried back into the castle. I looked at the next clue which took me to the top of the tower. The castle had been especially lighted for this occasion, and on the walls candles glowed in branches of three.

By the time I had discovered three of the clues I became excited by the game, and I found myself playing it with a great determination, for there is something fascinating about a treasure hunt—even a game, especially when it is played in an ancient *château*. And although this was a game there had been other more serious hunts. How they must have searched for those emeralds!

The sixth clue took me down to dungeons where I had only once been before with Geneviève. The stairs were lighted so I did not think I had been mistaken in imagining I should find the clue somewhere down there.

Down the narrow stairs I went clinging to the rope. I was in the dungeons. No, it couldn't be there—there were no lights. Gautier would not have set a clue in this gruesome place.

I was about to mount the stairs when I heard voices just above.

"But Lothair . . . my dear."

I stepped back into the darkness, although there was no need to, for they were not coming down the stairs.

I heard the Comte's voice, warm as I had never heard it before. "I shall have to be content to have you here . . . always."

"Have you thought what it will be like for me . . . living under the same roof?"

I should not have stood there, but I could not decide what I should do. To mount the stairs and confront them would embarrass us all. Perhaps they would go away and never know that I had overheard them. The woman was Mademoiselle de la Monelle, and she was speaking to the Comte as though he were her lover.

"My dear Claude, you will be happier this way."

"If it could be you . . . instead of Philippe."

"You wouldn't be happy. You would never feel safe."

"Do you imagine I should think you were going to murder me!"

"You don't understand. The scandal would be revived. You can't imagine how unpleasant it would be. It would be a canker to destroy everything. I have vowed never to marry again."

"So you would have me go through this farce with Philippe . . ."

"It will be better for you. Now we must go back. But not together . . ."

"Lothair . . . just one moment."

There was a short silence during which I imagined their embrace. Then I heard the footfalls growing fainter, and I felt most desolately alone in the darkness.

I remounted the steps, no longer thinking of the clues. I knew that the Comte and Mademoiselle de la Monelle were lovers—or in love—and that he would not marry her. A man who had been suspected of murdering his first wife would be watched with suspicion if he took a second. It would be a delicate situation which only a strong-minded woman who loved him devotedly could handle. I did not think Mademoiselle de la Monelle fitted into that category. Perhaps he knew it too, for he was shrewd and I imagined that his head would always command his heart. So, if my inference was right, he had devised a scheme for marrying her to Philippe and keeping her in the house. It was cynical; but then, so was he. It was, I told myself bitterly, typical of the man. Through the ages kings had found complaisant husbands for their mistresses because they could not—or would not—marry them themselves.

I was disgusted. I wished that I had never come to the *château*. If I could escape . . . take the way out Philippe had offered and go to the home of Mademoiselle de la Monelle . . . as if I should escape that way? And how strange that it should have been to *her* home he had suggested sending me! There was only one retreat . . . home to England. I played with the idea, knowing very well I would not leave the *château* until I was forced to.

And what concern of yours are the murky love affairs of a dissolute French *comte*? I asked myself. None whatever.

And to prove it, I took a fresh look at the clue. It led me, instead of to the dungeons, to the gun gallery in which was the *oubliette*. I hoped I should not have to descend the ladder; surely Gautier would not have laid a clue there. I was right. I found what I wanted on the window seat; and when I read what was written on the paper I was told to report to the banqueting hall with all the clues for that would take me to the end of the treasure hunt.

When I arrived there it was to find Gautier seated at a table drinking a glass of wine.

When he saw me he stood up and cried: "Don't tell me you've found them all, Mademoiselle Lawson!"

I said I thought I had and gave them to him.

"Well," he said, "you're the first in."

"Perhaps," I said, thinking of the Comte and Mademoiselle de la Monelle, "the others didn't try very hard."

"Well now, all you have to do is to go to the cabinet there for the treasure."

I went to it, opened the drawer he indicated and found a cardboard box about two inches square.

"That's it," he said. "There'll be a ceremonial presentation."

He picked up a brass bell and began to ring it.

It was the signal that the hunt was over and everyone should return to the hall.

It took some time for them all to assemble; I noticed that some were flushed and a little ruffled. The Comte, however, arrived looking as cool as ever; he came in alone and I noticed that Mademoiselle de la Monelle was with Philippe.

The Comte smiled when he knew that I was the winner, and I fancied he was amused.

"Of course," commented Philippe with a friendly smile, "Mademoiselle Lawson had an unfair advantage. She's an expert on old houses."

"Here is the treasure," said the Comte, opening the box to disclose a brooch—a green stone on a slender gold bar.

One of the women cried: "It looks like an emerald."

"All the treasure hunts in this *château* are for emeralds. Didn't I tell you?" replied the Comte.

He took it from the box and said, "Allow me, Mademoiselle Lawson." And he pinned it on my dress.

"Thank you . . ." I murmured.

"Rather thank your skill. I don't think anyone else found more than three of Gautier's clues."

Someone said: "Had we known the prize was an emerald we might have tried harder. Why didn't you warn us, Lothair?"

Several of them came up to admire the brooch, among them Claude de la Monelle. I could sense her indignation. Her white fingers touched the brooch quickly.

"It really is an emerald!" she murmured. And as she turned away she added: "Mademoiselle Lawson is a very clever woman, I am sure."

"Oh no," I replied quickly. "It was merely because I played the game."

She turned back and for a moment our eyes met. Then she laughed and went to stand close to the Comte.

Musicians appeared and took their places on a dais. I watched Philippe and Mademoiselle de la Monelle lead the dance. Others fell in, but no one approached me, and I felt suddenly so desolate that I wanted nothing so much as to slip away. This I did as quickly as possible and made my way up to my room.

I unpinned the brooch and looked at it. Then I took out the miniature and thought of that moment when I had unwrapped it and seen who had sent it. How much happier I had been then than when he had pinned the emerald brooch on my dress! As my eyes fell on those white hands with the jade signet ring, I had imagined them caressing Mademoiselle de la Monelle while they planned that she should marry Philippe because he, Lothair, the Comte de la Talle, had no wish to marry again.

There was no doubt that he saw himself as a king in his own world. He commanded and others obeyed; and no matter how cynical the proposal he put to those whom he considered to be his subjects, they were expected to obey.

How could I possibly make excuses for such a man?

Yet it had been such a happy Christmas until I had overheard that conversation.

I undressed thoughtfully and lay in bed listening to the far-off music. Down there they would be dancing and no one would miss me. How foolish I had been to indulge in daydreams in which I had deceived myself into believing that I was of some importance to the Comte. This night had shown me how preposterous that was. I didn't belong here. I had not understood there were such men in the world as the Comte de la Talle. But I was beginning to. Tonight I had learned a great deal.

Now I must be reasonable, sensible. I tried not to think of the Comte and his mistress and another picture came into my mind: Jean Pierre with the crown on his head—King for a day.

I thought of his complacent expression, the pleasure he had taken in his temporary power.

All men, I thought, would be kings in their own castles.

And with that I fell into a sleep, but in my dreams I was disturbed and I was aware of a great shadow hanging over me which I knew was the hopeless future, but I covered up my eyes and refused to see it.

❧ 7 ❧

On the first day of the New Year Geneviève told me that she was going to ride over to Maison Carrefour to see her grandfather and wanted me to accompany her.

I thought it would be interesting to see the old house again, so I readily agreed.

"When my mother was alive," Geneviève told me, "we always went to see Grandfather on New Year's Day. All children in France do the same."

"It's a nice custom."

"Cake and chocolate are brought for the children while the grownups drink wine and eat wine cakes. Then the children play the piano or the violin to show how they are getting on. Sometimes they have to recite."

"Are you going to do this?"

"No, I shall have to say my catechism, though. My grandfather likes prayers better than the piano or the violin."

I wondered how she felt about the visits to that strange house, and couldn't resist asking: "You like going?"

She frowned and looked puzzled. "I don't know. I want to go and then . . . when I'm there, sometimes I feel as though I can't bear it any more. I want to run out . . . right away and never go there again. My mother used to talk of it so much that I sometimes feel I've lived there myself. I don't know whether I want to go or not, Miss."

When we reached the house Maurice let us in and took us to the old man who looked more feeble than when I had last seen him.

"You know what day it is, Grandfather?" asked Geneviève.

And when he did not answer, she put her lips to his ear and said:

"New Year's Day! So I've come to see you. Mademoiselle Lawson is here, too."

He caught my name and nodded. "Good of you to come. You will excuse my not rising . . ."

We sat down near him. Yes, he had changed. There was a complete lack of serenity in his eyes; they looked like those of a lost man who is trying hard to find his way through a jungle. I guessed what he was searching for was memory.

"Shall I ring the bell," asked Geneviève. "We are rather hungry. I should like my cakes and chocolate, and I'm sure Mademoiselle Lawson is thirsty."

He did not answer so she rang the bell. Maurice appeared and she ordered what she wanted.

"Grandfather is not so well today," she said to Maurice.

"He has his bad days, Mademoiselle Geneviève."

"I don't think he knows what today is." Geneviève sighed and sat down. "Grandfather," she went on, "we had a treasure hunt on Christmas night at the *château* and Mademoiselle Lawson won."

"The only treasure is in Heaven," he said.

"Oh yes, Grandfather, but while you're waiting for that it's nice to find some on earth."

He looked puzzled. "You say your prayers?"

"Night and morning," she answered.

"It is not enough. You, my child, must pray more earnestly than most. You have need of help. You were born in sin . . ."

"Yes, Grandfather, I know we all are but I do say my prayers. Nounou makes me."

"Ah, the good Nounou! Always be kind to Nounou; she is a good soul."

"She wouldn't let me forget my prayers, Grandfather."

Maurice returned with wine, cakes, and chocolate.

"Thank you, Maurice," said Geneviève. "I will serve them. Grandfather," she continued, "on Christmas Day Mademoiselle Lawson and I went to a party, and they had a *crèche* and a cake with a crown in it. I wish you had had lots of sons and daughters, then their children would have been my cousins. They would all be here today and we could have had a cake with a crown in it."

He didn't follow what she was saying and had turned his gaze on me. I tried to make some sort of conversation but I could only think of that cell-like room and the chest which contained the whip and hair shirt.

He was a fanatic—that much was obvious. But why had he become so? And what sort of life had Françoise led here? Why had she died when he had had a stroke? Was it because she could not endure to live without him? Without this man—this wild-eyed cadaverous fanatic in this gloomy house with its cell and chest . . . when she was married to the Comte and the *château* was her home!

Everyone may not think that such a glorious fate as you do . . .

I checked my thoughts. What had made me think such a thing? A glorious fate . . . when one who had suffered it—yes, suffered was the word . . . had killed herself.

But why . . . why? What had started as idle curiosity was becoming a burning desire to know. Yet, I quickly told myself, there is nothing unusual in this. This passionate interest in the affairs of others was inherent. I had this curiosity to know how people's minds worked just as I cared deeply why a painter had used such a subject, why he had portrayed it in such a way, what had been behind his interpretation, his use of color and mood.

The old man could not take his eyes from me. "I can't see you very well," he said. "Could you come closer?"

I drew my chair close to him.

"It was wrong," he whispered, "quite wrong."

He was talking to himself and I glanced at Geneviève, who was busily selecting a piece of chocolate from the dish Maurice had brought.

"Françoise must not know," he said.

I knew his mind was wandering then and that I had been right when I had thought he was not so well as when we had last seen him.

He peered at me. "Yes, you do look well today. Quite."

"Thank you, I feel well."

"It was a mistake. . . . It was my cross and I was not strong enough to carry it."

I was silent, wondering whether we ought to call Maurice.

He did not take his eyes from my face and drew himself back in his chair as though he were afraid of me; as he moved, the rug about him slipped and I caught it and wrapped it about him. He recoiled and shouted: "Go away. Leave me. You know my burden, Honorine."

I said: "Call Maurice." And Geneviève ran from the room.

The old man had gripped my wrist; I felt his nails in my skin. "You are not to blame," he said. "The sin is mine. It is my burden. I carry it to my grave. . . . Why are you not . . . ? Why did I . . . ? Oh, the tragedy . . . Françoise . . . little Françoise. Go away. Keep away from me. Honorine, why do you tempt me?"

Maurice came hurrying into the room. He took the rug and wrapped it round the old man and said over his shoulder: "Slip outside. It would be better."

So Geneviève and I went out of the room while Maurice took the crucifix which was hanging about the old man's neck and put it into his hands.

"That was . . . frightening," I said.

"Were you very frightened, Miss?" asked Geneviève, almost pleased.

"He was wandering in his mind."

"He often does. After all he's very old."

"We shouldn't have come."

"That's what Papa says."

"You mean he forbids it?"

"Not exactly, because he isn't told when I'm coming. But if he knew he would have."

"Then . . ."

"Grandfather was my mother's father. Papa doesn't like him for that reason. After all he didn't like my mother, did he?"

As we rode back to the *château*, I said to Geneviève: "He thought I was someone else. Once or twice he called me Honorine."

"She was my mother's mother."

"He seemed . . . afraid of her."

Geneviève was thoughtful. "It's odd that my grandfather should be afraid of anyone."

I thought then that the lives we led in the *château* were in some mysterious way intricately linked with the dead.

I couldn't resist talking to Nounou about our visit to Carrefour.

She shook her head. "Geneviève shouldn't go," she said. "It's better not."

"She wanted to go because of the New Year custom of visiting grandparents."

"Customs are good in some families—not in others."

"They are not observed much in this family," I suggested.

"Oh, customs are for the poor. They make something to live for."

"I think rich and poor enjoy them. But I wish we hadn't gone. Geneviève's grandfather was wandering in his mind, and it was not pleasant."

"Mademoiselle Geneviève should wait until he sends for her. She shouldn't pay these surprise calls."

"He must have been very different when you were there . . . when Françoise was a child, I mean."

"He was always a strict man. With himself and others. He should have been a monk."

"Perhaps he thought so. I have seen that cell-like place where I imagined he slept at one time."

Nounou nodded again. "Such a man should never have married," she said. "But Françoise didn't know what was going on. I tried to make it all natural for her . . ."

"What was going on?" I asked.

She shot a sharp look at me. "He wasn't cut out to be a father. He wanted the house run like a . . . monastery."

"And her mother . . . Honorine."

Nounou turned away. "She was an invalid."

"No," I said, "not a happy childhood for poor Françoise . . . a father a fanatic, a mother an invalid."

"*I* saw that she was happy."

"Yes, she sounds happy with her embroidery and piano lessons. . . . She writes about them as though she enjoys them. When her mother died . . ."

"Yes?" said Nounou sharply.

"Was she very unhappy?"

Nounou rose and from a drawer took another of those little notebooks.

"Read it," she said.

I opened it. She had been for a walk. She had had her music lesson. She had embroidered the altar cloth she was working on; she had had lessons with her governess. The orderly life of an ordinary little girl.

And then came the entry:

"Papa came to the schoolroom this morning when we were doing history. He looked very sad and said: 'I have news for you, Françoise. You have no mother now!' I felt I ought to cry but I couldn't. And Papa looked at me so sadly and sternly. 'Your mother has been ill for a long time and could never have been well. This is God's answer to our prayers.' I had not prayed that she should die, I said; and he replied that God worked in a mysterious way. We had prayed for my mother and this was a happy release. 'Her troubles are over now,' he said. And he went out of the schoolroom."

"Papa has been sitting in the death chamber for two days and nights. He has not left it and I have been there too to pay my respects to the dead. I knelt by the bed for a long time and I cried bitterly. I thought it was because Maman was dead, but it was really because my knees hurt and I didn't like being there. Papa prays all the time; and it is all about forgiveness for his sins. I was frightened for if he is so sinful what about the rest of us who don't pray half as much as he does?"

"Maman wears a nightdress in her coffin. Papa says she is now at peace. All the servants have been in to pay their last respects. Papa stays there and prays all the time for forgiveness."

"Today was the funeral. It was a magnificent sight. The horses wore plumes and sable trappings. I walked with Papa at the head of the procession with a black veil all over my face and the new black frock which Nounou sat up all night to finish. I cried when we came out of the church and stood beside the hearse while the orator told everyone that Maman had been a saint. It seemed dreadful that such a good person should die."

"It is quiet in the house. Papa is in his cell. I know he is praying because when I stood outside the door I could hear him. He prays for forgiveness, that his great sin may die with him, that he alone shall suffer. I think he is asking God not to be too hard on Maman when she gets to heaven and that whatever the Great Sin was, it was his fault not hers."

I finished reading and looked up at Nounou.

"What is this Great Sin? Did you ever discover?"

"He was a man who saw sin in laughter."

"I wonder he married. I wonder he didn't go into a monastery and live his life there."

Nounou would only lift her shoulders.

The Comte went to Paris in the New Year, and Philippe accompanied him. I was progressing with my work and now had several pictures to show for it. It was tremendously exhilarating to see their original beauty. It gave me great pleasure merely to look at them and to remember how little by little those glowing colors had emerged when they had been released from the grime of years. But this was more than a return to beauty; it was my own vindication.

Yet each day I would awake with the definite feeling that I ought to leave the *château*. It was almost like an inner warning: make some excuse and get away!

But I had never enjoyed work as I did this; and I had never found a house which intrigued me as Château Gaillard did.

January was exceptionally cold and there was a great deal of activity in the vineyards, where it was feared the frosts would kill the vines. Geneviève and I often stopped during our rides or walks to watch the workers. Sometimes we called in at the Bastides', and on one occasion Jean Pierre took us down to the cellars and showed us the casks of wine which were maturing and explained to us the processes through which the wine had to pass.

Geneviève said that the deep cellars reminded her of the *oubliette* in the *château* to which Jean Pierre remarked that nothing was forgotten here. He showed us how the light was admitted through small apertures in order to regulate the temperature; he warned us that no plants or flowers must be brought down here, as they give something to the wine which would spoil the taste.

"How old are these cellars?" Geneviève wanted to know.

"They've been here as long as there was wine here . . . and that's hundreds of years ago."

"And while they looked after their wine and made sure the temperature was all right," commented Geneviève, "they were putting people into the dungeons and leaving them to freeze and starve to death."

"Wine being more important to your noble ancestors than their enemies, naturally."

"And all those years ago it was the Bastides who made the wine."

"And there was one Bastide who earned the honor of becoming an enemy of your noble ancestors. His bones lie in the *château*."

"Oh, Jean Pierre! Where?"

"In the *oubliette*. He was insolent to the Comte de la Talle, was called before him and never seen again. He went to the *château*, but he never came out. Imagine him. Called before the Comte. 'Come in, Bastide. Now what is this trouble you are making?' The bold Bastide tries to explain, falsely believing that he is as good as his masters; and then Monsieur le Comte moves his foot and the ground opens . . . down goes the insolent Bastide where others have gone before him. To freeze to death, to starve to death . . . to die of the wounds he receives in the fall. What does it matter? He is no longer a nuisance to Monsieur le Comte."

"You still sound resentful," I said in surprise.

"Oh no. There was the Revolution. Then it was the turn of the Bastides."

He was not talking seriously, for almost immediately he was laughing.

The weather changed suddenly, and the vines were no longer in acute danger, although, Jean Pierre told us, the spring frosts could be the most dangerous enemy to the grape of all because they could strike unexpectedly.

Those days stand out as the peaceful days. There were happy little incidents which I remember vividly. Geneviève and I were often together; our friendship was growing slowly but steadily. I made no attempt to force it, for although I was growing closer to her, there were times when she seemed a stranger to me. She had been right when she had said she had two personalities. Sometimes I found her watching me almost slyly; at others she was naïvely affectionate.

I thought constantly of the Comte and when he was absent once again I started to build up a picture of him which common sense warned me was not true. I remembered his tolerance in giving me a chance to prove my ability, and his generosity, when he found he had been wrong to doubt me, in admitting it by giving me the miniature. Then he had put the presents in the shoes which showed a desire to make his daughter happy. I was sure he had been pleased that I had won the emerald brooch. Why? Simply because he wanted me to have something of value that would be a little nest egg for the future.

I shivered, contemplating that future. I could not stay indefinitely at the *château*. I had restored a number of the pictures in the gallery and those were the ones I had been employed to deal with. The work would not last forever. Yet in this pleasant dream world in which I lived during those weeks, it was firmly fixed in my mind that I should be at the *château* for a long time to come.

Some people find it easy to believe things are what they want them to be. I had never been like that . . . until now, preferring always to face the truth, priding myself on my good sense. I had changed since I had come here; and oddly enough I would not look deep enough into my mind to discover why.

Mardi Gras was the time for Carnival, and Geneviève was as excited as Yves and Margot, who showed her how to make paper flowers and masks; and because I thought it was good for her to join in these activities we rode into the little town on one of the Bastides' carts, and behind our grotesque masks we pelted each other with paper flowers.

We were present in the square when they hung the Carnival Man from the mock gibbet and we actually danced in the crowd.

Geneviève was ecstatic when we returned to the castle.

"I've often heard of Mardi Gras," she declared, "but I never knew it was such fun."

"I hope," I said, "that your father would not have objected to your being there."

"We shall never know," she answered mischievously, "because we're not going to tell him, are we, Miss?"

"If he asked we should certainly tell him," I retorted.

"He never would. He's not interested in us, Miss."

Was she a little resentful? Perhaps, but she cared less about his neglect than she had once. And Nounou raised no objections as long as wherever Geneviève went I was with her. She seemed to have a faith in me which I found flattering.

And when I took her into the town Jean Pierre had been with us. It was he who suggested these jaunts; he delighted in them; and Geneviève enjoyed his company. No harm could come to Geneviève while she was with the Bastides, I assured myself.

It was during the first week of Lent that the Comte and Philippe returned to the *château*.

The news spread rapidly throughout the household and in the town.

Philippe was betrothed. He was going to marry Mademoiselle Claude de la Monelle.

The Comte came to me in the gallery where I was working. It was a lovely sunny morning, and now that the days were longer I was spending more time in the gallery. The brightness made more obvious my work of restoration, and he studied the pictures with pleasure.

"Excellent, Mademoiselle Lawson," he murmured; and his eyes were on me, dark with the expression which always set me wondering.

"And what's this operation?" he asked.

I explained to him that the painting on which I was working had been badly damaged and that layers of paint were missing. I was filling them with gesso putty and afterwards I should retouch with paint.

"You are an artist, Mademoiselle Lawson."

"As you once remarked . . . an artist *manqué*."

"And you have forgiven though not forgotten that unkind observation?"

"One does not have to forgive others for speaking the truth."

"How strong-minded you are. We as well as our pictures have need of you."

He had taken a step nearer to me and his eyes were still fixed on my face. It could not be with admiration? I knew what I looked like. My brown coat had never been becoming; my hair had a habit of escaping from its pins, and I was always unaware of it until something happened to make me; my hands were stained with the materials I used. It was certainly not my appearance which interested him.

It was the way in which philanderers behaved to all women, of course. The thought spoilt my pleasure in the moment and I tried to push it away.

I said: "You need have no fear. I shall use a paint which is easily soluble in case it should have to be removed. Colors ground in synthetic resin are, you know."

"I did not know," he replied.

"It is so. You see when these pictures were painted, artists mixed their own paints. They and they alone knew the secrets . . . and each painter had his own method. That is what makes the old masters unique. It's so difficult to copy them."

He bowed his head.

"Retouching is a delicate operation," I went on. "Naturally a restorer should not attempt to add his ideas to an original."

He was amused, realizing perhaps that I was talking to hide my embarrassment. Then he said suddenly: "I can see that could be disastrous. It would be like trying to make a person what you thought he should be. Instead of which you should help to bring out the good . . . subdue the evil."

"I was thinking only of painting. It is the only subject on which I could speak with some knowledge."

"And your enthusiasm when you speak of it proclaims you an expert. Tell me, how is my daughter progressing with her English?"

"She is making excellent progress."

"And you do not find teaching her and the care of the pictures too much for you?"

I smiled. "I enjoy them both so much."

"I'm glad that we can provide you with so much pleasure. I thought you might find our country life dull."

"By no means. I have to thank you for allowing me the use of your stables."

"Something else you enjoy?"

"Very much."

"Life here at the *château* has been much quieter than in the past." He looked over my head and added coldly: "After my wife's death we did not entertain as we used to, and we have never gone back to the old ways. It will probably be different now that my cousin is to be married and his wife will be mistress of the *château*."

"Until," I said impulsively, "you yourself marry."

I was sure I detected bitterness in his voice as he said: "What makes you imagine I should do so?"

I felt I had been guilty of tactlessness and I said in self-defense: "It seems perhaps natural that you should . . . in time."

"I thought that you knew the circumstances of my wife's death, Mademoiselle Lawson?"

"I have heard . . . talk," I replied, feeling like a woman who has put one foot in a quagmire and must withdraw quickly before she is completely submerged.

"Ah," he said, "*talk!* There are people who believe I murdered my wife."

"I am sure you would not be affected by such nonsense."

"You are embarrassed?" He was smiling, taunting me now. "That shows me that you do not think it is necessarily nonsense. You think me capable of the darkest deeds. Admit it."

My heart had begun to beat uncomfortably fast. "You are joking, of course," I said.

"This is what we expect of the English, Mademoiselle Lawson. This is unpleasant, so we will not discuss it." His eyes were angry suddenly. "No, we will not discuss it; better to continue to believe in the victim's guilt."

I was startled. "You are quite wrong," I said quietly.

He had recovered his calm as quickly as he had lost it. "And you, Mademoiselle Lawson, are admirable. You understand though that, in the circumstances, I should never marry again. But you are surprised that I should discuss my views on marriage with you?"

"I'll admit I am."

"But then you are such a sympathetic listener. I do not mean sympathetic in the usual sentimental sense. I mean that you betray such calm good sense, such frankness, and these qualities have lured me to the indiscretion of discussing my private affairs with you."

"I am not sure whether I should thank you for your compliments or apologize for luring you to indiscretion."

"You mean that as you do everything—or almost everything—you say. That is why I am going to ask you a question, Miss Lawson. Will you give me a frank answer?"

"I will try to."

"Well, here it is: Do you think I murdered my wife?"

I was startled; his heavy lids half hid his eyes, but I knew he was watching me intently, and for a few significant seconds I did not answer.

"Thank you," he said.

"I have not answered yet."

"But you have. You wanted time to find a tactful answer. I did not ask for tact. I wanted truth."

"You must allow me to speak, having asked my opinion."

"Well?"

"I do not believe for one moment that you gave your wife a dose of poison, but . . ."

"But . . ."

"Perhaps you . . . disappointed her . . . perhaps you did not make her happy. I mean perhaps she was unhappy being married to you and rather than continue so she took her life."

He was looking at me with a twisted smile on his lips. I sensed in him then a deep unhappiness and there came to me an overwhelming desire to make him happy. It was absurd, but it was there, and I could not deny it. I believed that I had seen a little of the man beneath that exterior of arrogance and indifference to others.

It was almost as though he read my thoughts for his expression hardened as he replied: "Now you see, Mademoiselle Lawson, why I have no desire to marry; you think I am obliquely guilty, and you being such a wise young woman are no doubt right."

"You are thinking me foolish, tactless, *gauche* . . . everything that you most dislike."

"I find you . . . refreshing, Mademoiselle Lawson. You know that. But I believe you have a saying in your country, 'Give a dog a bad name and hang him.' Is that so?" I nodded. "Well, here you see that dog with his bad name. A bad name is one of the easiest things to live up to. There! In exchange for the lesson you gave me on restoring pictures I have given you one on family history. What I set out to tell you was that, as soon as Easter is over, my cousin and I will leave for Paris. There is no reason why Philippe's marriage should be delayed. He and I will attend the *diner contrat* at the bride's house, and after that there will be the ceremonies. The honeymoon will follow, and when they return to the *château* we shall do a little more entertaining."

How could he talk so calmly of this matter? When I considered his part in it, I felt angry with him for behaving so and with myself for so easily forgetting his faults and being ready to accept him on his own terms, one might say, every time he presented himself to me in a new light.

He went on: "We shall give a ball as soon as they return. The new Madame de la Talle will expect it. Then two nights later we shall have a ball for everyone connected with the *château* . . . the vine-workers, the servants, everyone. It is an old custom when the heir of the *château* marries. I hope you will attend both these ceremonies."

"I shall be delighted to join in with the workers, but I am not sure that Madame de la Talle would wish me to be a guest at her ball."

"I wish it, and if I invite you she will welcome you. You are not sure of that? My dear Miss Lawson, I am the master of the house. Only my death can alter that."

"I am sure of it," I answered, "but I came here to work and am not prepared for grand functions."

"But I am sure you will adjust yourself to the unexpected. I must not detain you further. I see you are waiting to return to your work."

With that he left me—bewildered, excited, and with the faint warning that I was sinking lower into a quicksand from which every day it was becoming more difficult to escape. Did he know this? Was his conversation meant to convey a warning?

The Comte and Philippe left for Paris the day after Good Friday; and on Monday I went to call on the Bastides, where I found Yves and Margot playing in the garden. They called out to me to come and see the Easter eggs which they had found on Sunday—some in the house, some in the outhouses; there were as many as they found last year.

"Perhaps you don't know, Miss," said Margot, "that the bells all go to Rome for the benediction and on the way they drop eggs for the children to find."

I admitted I had never heard that before.

"Then don't you have Easter eggs in England?" asked Yves.

"Yes . . . but just as presents."

"These are presents too," he told me. "The bells don't really drop them. But we find them, you see. Would you like one?"

I said I would like to take one for Geneviève, who would be pleased to hear that they had found it.

The egg was carefully wrapped up and solemnly presented to me, and I told them I had come to see their mother.

Glances were exchanged and Yves said: "She's gone out . . ."

"With Gabrielle," added Margot.

"Then I'll see her some other day. Is anything wrong?"

They lifted their shoulders to indicate ignorance, so I said good-by and continued my walk.

This took me to the river and there I saw their maidservant Jeanne with a *brouette* of clothes. She was beating them with a piece of wood as she washed them in the river.

"Good afternoon, Jeanne," I said.

"Good afternoon, Miss."

"I've been to the house. But I've missed Madame Bastide."

"She has gone into the town."

"It's so rarely that she is out at this time of day."

Jeanne nodded and grimaced at her stick.

"I hope all is well, Miss."

"Have you reason to think it isn't?"

"I have a daughter of my own."

I was puzzled and wondered whether I had been mistaken in the *patois*.

"You mean Mademoiselle Gabrielle . . ."

"Madame is most distressed and I know that she has taken Mademoiselle Gabrielle to the doctor." She spread her hands. "I pray to the saints that there is nothing wrong, but when the blood is hot, Mademoiselle, these things will happen."

I could not believe what she was hinting, so I said: "I hope Mademoiselle Gabrielle has nothing contagious."

I left her smiling to herself at what she thought was my innocence.

I felt very anxious though on behalf of the Bastides and on my way back I called at the house.

Madame Bastide was at home; she received me, her face stony with bewilderment and grief.

"Perhaps I've called at the wrong time," I said. "I'll go, unless there is anything I can do."

"No," she said. "Don't go. This is not a matter which can be kept secret for long . . . and I know you are discreet. Sit down, Dallas."

She herself sat heavily and leaning her arm on the table covered her face with one hand.

I waited in embarrassment, and after a few minutes when I believed she was contemplating how much to tell me she lowered her hand and said, "That this should have happened in our family!"

"Is it Gabrielle?" I asked.

She nodded.

"Where is she?"

She jerked her head to the ceiling. "In her room. She's stubborn. She won't say a word."

"She's ill?"

"Ill. I'd rather she were. I'd rather anything . . . but this."

"Can nothing be done?"

"She won't tell us. She won't say who it is. I never believed this could be. She was never a girl to go gadding about it. She's always been so quiet."

"Perhaps it can all be worked out."

"I hope so. I dread what Jean Pierre will say when he hears. He's so proud. He'll be so angry with her."

"Poor Gabrielle!" I murmured.

"Poor Gabrielle! I wouldn't have believed it. And not a word until I found out and then . . . I saw how frightened she was, so I guessed I was right. I thought she'd been looking peaky lately; worried . . . never joining in with the family; and then we were getting the washing ready this morning, and she fainted. I was pretty certain then, so down to the doctor we went and he confirmed what I feared."

"And she refused to tell you the name of her lover?"

Madame Bastide nodded. "That's what worries me. If it was one of the young men . . . well, we'd not like it but we could put it to rights. But as she won't say, I'm afraid. . . . Why should she be afraid to tell us if it could all be put right? That's what I want to know. It looks as if it's someone who can't do the right thing."

I asked if I could make some coffee, and to my surprise she allowed me to. She sat at the table staring blankly before her and when I had made it I asked if I could take a cup up to Gabrielle.

Permission given, I carried the cup upstairs and when I knocked at the door, Gabrielle said: "It's no use, Grand'mère." So I opened the door and went in, holding the cup of steaming coffee.

"You . . . Dallas!"

"I've brought you this. I thought you might like it."

She lay and looked at me with leaden eyes.

I pressed her hand. Poor Gabrielle, her position was that of thousands of girls, and to each it is like a new and personal tragedy.

"Is there anything we can do?" I asked.

She shook her head.

"You can't marry and . . ."

She shook her head more violently and turned it away so that I could not see her face.

166

"Is he . . . married already?"

She closed her lips tightly and refused to answer.

"Well, in that case, he can't marry you and you'll just have to try and be as brave as possible."

"They're going to hate me," she said. "All of them. . . . It won't be the same again."

"That's not true," I said. "They're shocked . . . they're hurt . . . but they'll grow away from that and when the child comes they'll love it."

She smiled at me wanly. "You always want to make things right, Dallas, people as well as pictures. There's nothing you can do though. I've made my bed, as they say, and I'm the one that's got to lie on it."

"Someone else should be with you in this trouble."

But she was stubborn and would not tell anything.

I went sadly back to the *château* remembering that happy table on Christmas Day and thinking how suddenly how alarmingly life could change. There was no security in happiness.

The Comte did not return to the *château* immediately after the wedding. Philippe and his bride had gone to Italy for their honeymoon, and I wondered whether the Comte had found someone with whom to amuse himself now that he had so cynically handed Claude to Philippe.

That, I told myself angrily, was the most reasonable explanation of his absence.

He did not return until it was almost time for Claude and Philippe to come home, and even then he made no attempt to see me alone. I asked myself whether he sensed my disapproval. As if he would care for that! Still, he might decide that I was being even more presumptuous than usual.

I was very disappointed for I had been hoping to talk to him again and I was dreading the time when Philippe and his wife returned. I was certain that Claude already disliked me and I imagined she was the sort of woman who would make no secret of her dislike. Perhaps it would be necessary to take up Philippe's offer to find me other employment. In spite of my growing apprehension, the thought of leaving the *château* was distinctly depressing.

After the three weeks' honeymoon they returned, and on the very day following her arrival, I had an encounter with Claude and discovered how deeply she disliked me.

I was coming from the gallery when we met.

"I should have thought you would have finished the work by now," she said. "I remember how well advanced you were at Christmas time."

"Restoring pictures is a very exacting task. And the collection in the gallery has been sadly neglected."

"But I thought it would present little difficulty to *such* an expert."

"There are always difficulties and a great deal of patience is required."

"Which is why you need such concentration and cannot work all day?"

So she had noticed my method! And was she hinting that I was wasting time in order to prolong my stay at the castle?

I said warmly: "You can be assured, Madame de la Talle, that I shall finish the pictures as quickly as possible."

She bowed her head. "It is a pity that they could not have been completed in time for the ball which we are giving to our friends. I expect you, like the rest of the household, are looking forward to the *second* ball."

She swept past me before I had time to answer. She was clearly indicating that she would not expect to see me at the first. I wanted to cry out: "But the Comte has already invited me. And he is still the master of the house!"

I went to my room and looked at the green velvet dress. Why shouldn't I go? *He* had asked me and he would expect me. What a triumph to be welcomed by him under the haughty nose of the new Madame de la Talle.

But by the night of the ball I had changed my mind. He had not found an opportunity of being with me. Did I really think that he would take my side against hers?

I went to bed early on the night of the ball. I could hear the music now and then from the ballroom as I lay trying to read but actually picturing the brilliant scene. On the dais the musicians would be playing behind the banks of carnations which I had seen the gardeners arranging during the day. I pictured the Comte's opening the ball with his cousin's wife. I imagined myself in my green dress with the emerald brooch I had won at the treasure hunt pinned to it. Then I began thinking of the emeralds in the portrait and myself wearing them. I should look like a comtesse.

I gave a snort of laughter and picked up my book. But I found it difficult to concentrate. I thought of the voices I had heard from the top of the staircase which led to the dungeons, and I wondered whether those two were together now. Were they congratulating each other on their cleverness in arranging this marriage which brought her under his roof?

What an explosive situation! What would come out of it? It was small wonder that scandal surrounded the Comte. Had he been as reckless in his treatment of his wife?

I heard footsteps in the corridor outside my room. I listened. They had stopped outside my door. Someone was standing there. I could distinctly hear the sound of breathing.

I sat up in bed, my eyes fixed on the door; then suddenly the handle turned.

"Geneviève!" I cried. "You startled me."

"I'm sorry. I've been standing outside wondering whether you were asleep."

She came and sat on the bed. Her blue silk ball dress was charming but her expression sullen.

"It's a hateful ball," she said.

"Why?"

"*Aunt* Claude!" she said. "She's not my aunt. She's the wife of Cousin Philippe."

"Speak in English," I said.

"I can't when I'm angry. I have to think too much and I can't be angry and think at the same time."

"Then perhaps it would be an even better idea if you spoke English."

"Oh, Miss, you sound just like old Esquilles. To think that woman is going to live here . . ."

"Why do you dislike her so?"

"I don't dislike her. I hate her."

"What has she done to you?"

"She's come here to live."

"It's a large castle. There's plenty of room."

"If she would stay in one place all the time I wouldn't mind because then I shouldn't have to go where she was."

"Please, please, Geneviève, don't plan to shut her in the *oubliette*."

"Nounou would get her out so that wouldn't be any good."

"Why have you turned against her? She's very pretty."

"That's the trouble. I don't like pretty people. I like them plain, like you, Miss."

"What a charming compliment."

"They spoil things."

"She's hardly been here long enough to spoil anything."

"She will though. You see. My mother didn't like pretty women either. They spoiled it for her."

"You can't know anything about that."

"I do, I tell you. She used to cry. And then they'd quarrel. They quarreled quietly. I always think quiet quarrels are worse than noisy ones. Papa just says cruel things quietly and that makes them more cruel. He says them as though they amuse him . . . as though people amuse him because they're so stupid. He thought she was stupid. It made her very unhappy."

"Geneviève, I don't think you should go on brooding on what happened so long ago, and you don't really know very much about it."

"I know that he killed her, don't I?"

"You know no such thing."

"They say she killed herself. But she didn't. She wouldn't have left me all alone."

I laid my hand over hers. "Don't think about it," I begged.

"But you have to think about what's happening in your own home! It's because of what happened that Papa hasn't got a wife. That's why Philippe's had to get married. If I had been a son it would have been different. Papa doesn't like me because I'm not a son."

"I'm sure you imagine your father doesn't like you."

"I don't like you much when you pretend. You're like all grown-up people. When they don't want to answer they pretend they don't know what you're talking about. I think my father killed my mother and she comes back from the grave to have her revenge on him."

"What nonsense!"

"She walks about the *château* at night with the other ghosts from the *oubliette*. I've heard them, so it's no use your saying they're not there."

"Next time you hear them, come and tell me."

"Shall I, Miss? I haven't heard them for a long time. I'm not frightened, because my mother wouldn't let them hurt me. Remember you told me that?"

"Let me know when you hear them next."

"Do you think we could go and look for them, Miss?"

"I don't know. We would listen first."

She leaned towards me and cried: "It's a promise."

At the *château* there was talk of little else but the ball for the servants and the vine-workers, and preparations went on with more feverish activity than for those given by the Comte for his friends. There was chattering in courtyards and corridors and the servants were obviously humored during that day.

I wore my green dress for the occasion. I felt the need for confidence. I dressed my hair high on my head, and the effect was pleasing.

I was thinking a great deal about Gabrielle Bastide and wondering whether she had come to any decision.

Boulanger, the *sommelier,* was the master of ceremonies, and he received everyone in the banqueting hall of the castle. There was to be a buffet supper during the evening and the newly married pair, together with the Comte and Geneviève, would appear when the ball was in progress. They would slip in, so I was told, unceremoniously, and dance with a few of the company; and then Boulanger would—as if by chance —discover their presence and propose the health of the newly married couple which would be drunk by all in the best *château* wine.

The Bastide family had already arrived by the time I joined the ball. Gabrielle was with them, looking very pretty, although melancholy, in a dress of pale blue which I guessed she had made herself, for I had heard that she was very good with her needle.

Madame Bastide had come on the arm of her son, Armand; and she took an early opportunity of whispering to me that Jean Pierre did not yet know; they hoped to have discovered the name of the man and have arranged a marriage by the time he did.

This was a hint to me to say nothing; and I wondered whether she was regretting having confided in me, which she had no doubt done because I happened to be at hand when she was suffering from the first shock of the news.

Jean Pierre sought me out and we danced together to the tune of the "Sautière Charentaise," which I had heard before in the Bastide house and to which the words Jean Pierre had once sung to me were set.

He sang them softly as we danced:

"*Qui sont-ils les gens qui sont riches . . .*"

"You see," he said, "even here, in all this splendor, I can still sing those words. This is a great occasion for us humble folk. It is not often that we have an opportunity of dancing in the *château* ballroom."

"Is it any better than dancing in your own home? I did enjoy Christmas Day so much—and so did Geneviève. In fact, I am sure she preferred your celebrations to those of the *château*."

"She is a strange girl, that one."

"I loved to see her so happy."

He smiled at me warmly, and I kept thinking of Gabrielle coming in with the crown on the cushion and later when he had kissed us as a privilege due to the King for the day.

"She has been happier since you came here, perhaps," he added. "She is not the only one."

"You flatter me."

"Truth is not flattery, Dallas."

"In that case I am pleased to know I am so popular."

He pressed my hand lightly. "Inevitably so," he assured me. "Ah, look . . . the great ones are with us. I do declare, Monsieur le Comte has his eyes on us. Perhaps he is looking for you as the one who, not being as humble as his servants or those who work in his vineyards, is a most suitable partner."

"I am sure he thinks no such thing."

"You are hot in his defense."

"I am quite cool and he has no need of my defense."

"We shall see. Shall we have a little bet—you and I? I will say that the first one he dances with will be you."

"I never gamble."

The music had stopped. "As if by chance," murmured Jean Pierre, "Monsieur Boulanger has given the discreet sign. Stop dancing! The great are among us." He led me to a chair, and I sat down. Philippe and Claude had separated from the Comte, who was coming in my direction. The music struck up again. I turned my head towards the musicians, expecting every moment to see him standing there, for I, like Jean Pierre, had thought he would choose to dance with me.

I was astonished to see him dance past with Gabrielle.

I turned to Jean Pierre with a laugh.

"I rather regret I do not gamble."

Jean Pierre was looking after the Comte and his sister with a puzzled look.

"And I regret," he said, turning to me, "that you will have to be content with the master of the vineyard instead of the master of the castle."

"I am delighted to do so," I replied lightly.

As we danced I saw Claude with Boulanger and Philippe with Madame Duval, who was the head of the female staff. I supposed the Comte had chosen Gabrielle as the member of the Bastide family who were the head of the vineyards. It would all, I assured myself, have been worked out with the precision of court protocol.

When the dance was over, Boulanger made his speech, and the health of Philippe and Claude was drunk by everyone present. After that the musicians played what I learned was the "Marche pour Noce" and this was led by Philippe and Claude.

It was then that the Comte approached me.

In spite of my determination to remain aloof, I felt my cheeks flush slightly as he took my hand lightly and asked for the pleasure of the dance.

I said: "I am not sure that I know the dance. This seems to be something indigenous to France."

"No more than the *noce* itself, and you cannot pretend, Mademoiselle Lawson, that we are the only nation who marry."

"I had no intention of doing so. But this dance is unknown to me."

"Did you dance much in England?"

"Not often. I rarely had the opportunity."

"A pity. I was never much of a dancer myself, but I suspect you would dance well as you do everything else, if you had the will to. You should seize every opportunity . . . even if you are not eager to mingle with the company. You did not accept my invitation to the ball. I wondered why."

"I thought I explained that I had not come prepared to attend grand functions."

"But I had hoped that as I expressed my special desire that you would be there, you would have come."

"I did not think that my absence would have been noticed."

"It was . . . and regretted."

"Then I am sorry."

"You do not appear to be."

"I meant that I am sorry to have caused regret—not to have missed the ball."

"That is good of you, Mademoiselle Lawson. It shows a pleasant concern for the feelings of others, which is always so comforting."

Geneviève danced past with Jean Pierre. She was laughing up at him; I saw that the Comte had noticed this.

"My daughter is like you, Mademoiselle Lawson; she prefers certain entertainments to others."

"No doubt this seems a trifle gayer than the more grand occasion."

"How can you know that when you weren't there?"

"It was a suggestion—not a statement of fact."

"I might have known. You are always so meticulous. You must give me another lesson in restoration. I was fascinated by the last. You will find me visiting you in the gallery one morning."

"That will be a pleasure."

"Will it?"

I looked into those strange hooded eyes and said: "Yes, it will be."

The dance was over and he could not dance with me again; that would be to invite comment. Not more than once with each member of the household; and after six dances he would be free to go, so Jean Pierre told me. It was the custom. He, Philippe, Claude, and Geneviève would perform their duty and one by one slip away—not all together; that would appear too formal, and informality was the order of the day; but the Comte would go first and the others choose their time.

It was as he said. I noticed the Comte slip away quietly. After that I had no great wish to stay.

I was dancing with Monsieur Boulanger when I saw Gabrielle leave the ballroom. There was something about the manner of her going which aroused my suspicions. She gave a quick look round, pretended to examine the tapestry on the wall, and then another quick look, and she was out of the door.

For one second I had glimpsed her desperate expression, and I was afraid of what she might be going to do.

I had to make sure; so as soon as the music stopped and I could escape from my partner I took an opportunity of slipping out too.

I had no idea where she had gone. I wondered what a desperate girl would do. Throw herself down from the top of the castle? Drown herself in the old well in the courtyard?

As I stood outside the ballroom, I realized the unlikeliness of either. If Gabrielle was going to commit suicide why should she choose the castle, unless of course there was some reason . . . and what reason could she have?

I knew of one which I would not accept. But while my mind rejected it, my footsteps by some instinct led me towards the library where I had had my interviews with the Comte.

I wanted very much to be able to laugh at the notion which had come into my head.

I reached the library. I could hear the sound of voices and I knew whose they were. Gabrielle's breathless . . . rising to hysteria. The Comte's low yet resonant.

I turned and went to my room. I had no desire to go back to the ballroom. No desire for anything but to be alone.

A few days later I went to call at Maison Bastide where Madame Bastide received me with pleasure, and I could see that she was feeling much better than she had when I had last been in the house.

"The news is good. Gabrielle is going to be married."

"Oh, I am so pleased."

Madame Bastide smiled at me. "I knew you would be," she said. "You have made our trouble yours."

My relief was obvious. I was laughing at myself. (You fool, you suspicious fool, why do you always believe the worst of him!)

"Please tell me," I begged. "I am so happy about this and I can see you are."

"Well," said Madame Bastide, "in time people will know it was a hasty marriage . . . but these things happen. They have forestalled their marriage vows as so many young people do, but they will confess and be shriven. And they will not bring a bastard into the world. It is the children who suffer."

"Yes, of course. And when will Gabrielle be married?"

"In three weeks. It is wonderful, for Jacques is now able to marry. That was the trouble. He could not support a wife and a mother and knowing this Gabrielle had not told him of her condition. But Monsieur le Comte will make everything right."

"Monsieur le Comte!"

"Yes. He has given Jacques charge of the St. Vallient vineyard. For a long time Monsieur Durand has been too old. He is now to have his cottage on the estate and Jacques will take over St. Vallient. But for Monsieur le Comte it would have been difficult for them to marry."

"I see," I said slowly.

Gabrielle was married, and although there was a good deal of gossip, which I heard on my expeditions to the little town and in the *château* and vineyard district, these comments were always whispered with a shrug of the shoulders. Such affairs provided the excitement of a week or two and none could be sure when their own families would be plunged into a similar situation. Gabrielle would marry and if the baby arrived a little early, well, babies had a habit of doing that the whole world over.

Jacques Faillard was lucky to have secured St. Vallient just at the time when he wanted to marry and settle down.

The wedding was celebrated at the Maison Bastide with all that Madame Bastide considered essential in spite of the fact that there had been little time to prepare. The Comte, so I heard, had been good to his workers and had given the couple a handsome wedding present which would buy the furniture they needed; and as they were taking over some of the Durands' pieces, because naturally the old couple couldn't fit them into a small cottage, they could settle in at once.

The change in Gabrielle was astonishing. Serenity replaced fear and she looked prettier than ever. When I went over to St. Vallient to see her and Jacques' old mother she made me very welcome. There was so much I should have liked to ask her but I could not, of course; I wanted to tell her that I did not want to know merely to satisfy an idle curiosity.

When I left she asked me to look in again when I was riding that way and I promised to do so.

It was four or five weeks after the wedding. We were now well into the spring, and the climbing stems of the vines were beginning to grow fast. There was continual activity out of doors which would continue until harvest.

Geneviève was with me but our relationship was no longer as harmonious as it had been. The presence of Claude in the *château* affected her adversely, and I was continually on tenterhooks, wondering what turn it would take. I had felt I was making some progress with her; and now it was as though I had achieved a false brightness on a picture by using a solution which could only give a temporary effect and might even be injurious to the paint.

I said: "Shall we call on Gabrielle?"

"I don't mind."

"Oh well, if you are not eager, I'll go alone."

She shrugged her shoulders but continued to ride beside me.

"She's going to have a baby," she said.

"That," I replied, "will make her and her husband very happy."

"It will arrive a little too soon, though, and everyone is talking about it."

"Everyone! I know many who are not. You really shouldn't exaggerate. And why are you not speaking in English?"

"I'm tired of speaking in English. It's such a tiresome language." She laughed. "It was a marriage of convenience. I've heard that said."

"All marriages should be convenient."

That made her laugh again. Then she said: "Good-by, Miss. I'm not coming. I might embarrass you by talking indelicately . . . or even looking. You never know."

She spurred her horse and turned away. I was about to follow her because she was not supposed to be riding about the countryside alone. But she had the start of me and had disappeared into a small copse.

It was less than a minute later when I heard the shot.

"Geneviève!" I called. As I galloped towards the copse, I heard her scream. The branches of the trees caught at me as though to impede me—and I called again: "Geneviève, where are you? What's happened?"

She was sobbing: "Oh, Miss . . . Miss . . ."

I went in the direction of her voice. I found her; she had dismounted, and her horse was standing patiently by.

"What's happening . . ." I began; and then I saw the Comte lying on the grass, his horse beside him. There was blood all over his riding jacket.

"He . . . he's been . . . killed," stammered Geneviève.

I leaped to the ground and knelt beside him. A terrible fear came to me then.

"Geneviève," I said, "go quickly for help. St. Vallient is nearest. Send someone for a doctor."

She acted promptly.

Those next minutes are hazy in my mind. I listened to the thudding of hoofbeats as Geneviève reached the road and galloped off.

"Lothair . . ." I murmured, saying his unusual name for the first time and saying it aloud. "It can't be. I couldn't bear it. I could bear anything but that you should die."

I noticed the short thick lashes; the hoodlike lids drawn like shutters taking away the light from his life . . . from mine forevermore.

Such thoughts come and go while one's hands are more practical. I lifted his hand and a wild exultation came to me for I felt the pulse although it was feeble.

"Not . . . dead," I whispered. "Oh thank God . . . thank God." I heard the sob in my voice and was aware of a wild happiness surging through me.

I unbuttoned the jacket. If he had been shot through the heart as I had imagined, there should have been a bullet hole. I could find none. He was not bleeding.

Quite suddenly the truth dawned on me. He had not been shot. The blood came from the horse lying beside him.

I took off my jacket and rolled it into a pillow to support his head, and I fancied I saw the color warm in his face; his eyelids flickered.

I heard myself saying: "You're alive . . . *alive*. . . . Thank God."

I was praying silently that help would come soon. I was praying that no harm had come to him. I knelt there, my eyes upon his face, my lips silently moving.

Then the heavy lids flickered; they lifted and his eyes were on me. I saw the faint lift of his lips as I bent towards him.

I felt my own lips tremble; the emotion of the last minutes was unbearable—the fear replaced by sudden hope which in itself must be tinged with fear.

"You will be all right," I said.

He closed his eyes, and I knelt there waiting.

✿ 8 ✿

The Comte was suffering from nothing more than concussion and bruises. It was his horse that had been shot. The accident was discussed for days in the *château*, the vineyards and the town. There was an inquiry, but the identity of the one who had fired the shot was not brought to light, for the bullet was one which could have come from a hundred guns in the neighborhood. The Comte could remember little of the incident. He could only say that he had been riding in the copse, had ducked to pass under a tree and the next thing he knew was that he was being put on a stretcher. It was believed that ducking had probably saved his life for the bullet had ricocheted, hit the branch of a tree and then struck through the horse's head. It had all happened in less than a second; the horse had fallen and the Comte had been thrown into unconsciousness.

I was happy during the days that followed. I knew it was an uneasy situation, but only one thing mattered: he was alive.

Because I had always been sensible, even during those days of exquisite relief, I asked myself what the future held. What had happened to me that I had allowed a man to become so important to me? In the first place, it was hardly likely that he could have a similar interest in me; and if he did his reputation was such that any sensible woman would avoid him. And had I not prided myself on being a sensible woman?

But there was nothing in my life in those days but blissful relief.

I walked down to the *pâtisserie* in the market square. I often went there during my afternoon walks and had a cup of coffee.

Madame Latière, the proprietress, welcomed me; she was always happy to see someone from the *château,* and when she brought my coffee she could make excuses to stand and talk to me.

On this occasion she plunged quickly into the topic of the day.

"A mercy, Mademoiselle. I hear Monsieur le Comte is unharmed. His saint was watching over him that day."

"Yes, he was fortunate."

"A terrible thing, Mademoiselle. Our woods aren't safe, it seems. And they haven't caught the one who did it."

I shook my head.

"I've told Latière not to ride through *those* woods. I shouldn't like to see him on a stretcher. Though Latière's a good man, Mademoiselle. He hasn't an enemy in the place."

I stirred my coffee uneasily.

She flicked a *serviette* over the table absently. "Ah, Monsieur le Comte. He is *galant—vert galant.* My grandfather often talked of the Comte of his day. No girl in the neighborhood safe . . . but he always found a husband if there was trouble and believe me, they didn't suffer for it. We've a saying here that in Gaillard you often come across *château* features. Handed down through the generations. Oh well, there's human nature for you."

"What a change in the vineyards in these last weeks," I said. "I'm told that if the weather stays warm and sunny this will be a good year."

"A good harvest." She laughed. "That will make up to Monsieur le Comte for what has happened in the woods, eh?"

"I hope so."

"Well, it's a warning, would you not say so, Mademoiselle? He'll not ride in those woods for a while, I'll swear."

"Perhaps not," I said uneasily; and, finishing my coffee, rose to go.

"*Au revoir,* Mademoiselle," said Madame Latière rather wistfully. I think she had hoped for more gossip.

I couldn't resist going over to see Gabrielle the very next day. She had changed since I had last seen her; her manner was nervous, but when I complimented her on her new house, which was looking charming, she was pleased.

"It is more than I dared hope," she said.

"And you are feeling well?"

"Yes, I have seen Mademoiselle Carré; she is the midwife, you know.

She is satisfied and now it is only a matter of waiting. *Maman,* Jacques'
mother, is always at hand and so good to me."

"Do you want a girl or a boy?"

"A boy, I think. Everyone likes the first to be a boy."

I pictured him playing in the garden—a small sturdy little fellow.
Would he have *château* features?

"And Jacques?"

She blushed.

"Oh, he is happy, very happy."

"How fortunate that . . . it all worked out so well."

"Monsieur le Comte is very kind."

"Everybody doesn't think so. At least the one who took a shot at
him didn't."

She clenched her hands together. "You think it was deliberate. You
don't think . . ."

"He had a lucky escape. It must have been a shock to you when it
happened . . . so near here."

As soon as I had said that I was ashamed of myself, for I knew that
if there could be any foundation for my suspicion about the Comte and
Gabrielle I must be hurting her deeply; but this was not my desire
to probe into other people's motives; this was a need to be reassured.
Had Madame Latière been hinting that the Comte had his reasons for
helping Gabrielle to marry? Who else would be thinking the same? I
had to know whether the Comte was the father of her child.

But she did not resent what I had said and that made me happy, for
she did not seem to grasp the implication which, I was sure, had she
been guilty she would immediately have done.

She said: "Yes, it was a great shock. Fortunately Jacques wasn't far
away and he got the man with the stretcher."

Still, I had to pursue my investigation. "Do you think the Comte has
enemies about here?"

"Oh, it was an accident," she said quickly.

"Well," I added, "he wasn't hurt much."

"I'm so thankful." There were tears in her eyes. I wondered whether
they were tears of gratitude or something that went deeper.

A few days later I was walking in the gardens when I came face to
face with the Comte. I was in the middle terrace with its ornamental
gardens and parterres separated from each other by boxwood hedges,

and wandering into one of these I found him sitting on a stone bench overlooking a small lily pond in which the goldfish were visible.

The sun was hot in the enclosed garden and at first I thought he was asleep. I stood looking at the scene for a few seconds and then was about to go away when he called to me: "Mademoiselle Lawson."

"I hope I am not disturbing you."

"It's the pleasantest of disturbances. Do come and sit down for a while."

I went to the seat and sat beside him.

"I've never really thanked you for your prompt action in the woods."

"I'm afraid I did nothing praiseworthy."

"You acted with commendable promptitude."

"I only did what anyone would in the circumstances. Are you feeling recovered now?"

"Absolutely. Apart from certain strained muscles. I am told that in a week or so all that will pass. In the meantime I hobble round with my stick."

I looked at his hands with the jade signet ring on the little finger which curled about the ivory-topped walking stick. He wore no wedding ring as was the custom for men in France. I wondered whether he was just naturally flouting conventions or whether that was significant.

He glanced at me and said: "You look . . . so contented, Mademoiselle Lawson."

I was startled. I wondered how much of my feelings I had divulged. It was so important that I betray nothing now that I had something to hide.

"This setting," I said quickly. "The warm sun . . . the flowers, the fountain . . . it's all so beautiful. Who wouldn't be contented in such a garden? What is the statue in the middle of the pond?"

"It's Perseus rescuing Andromeda. Rather a pleasant piece of work. You must take a close look at it. It was done about two hundred years ago by a sculptor whom one of my ancestors brought to the *château*. It would appeal to you particularly."

"Why particularly?"

"I think of you as a female Perseus rescuing art from the dragon of decay, age, vandalism and so on."

"That's a very poetic fancy. You surprise me."

"I'm not such a Philistine as you imagine. When you have given me a few more lessons in the gallery I shall become quite knowledgeable. You will see."

"I am sure you will have no wish to acquire knowledge which would be of no use to you."

"I always understood that all knowledge was useful."

"Some more than others, and as one can't acquire it all, it might be a waste of time to clutter the mind with that which is of no practical use . . . at the expense of so much that is." He lifted his shoulders and smiled. And I went on: "It could be useful to know who caused the accident in the woods."

"You think so?"

"Of course. What if it were repeated?"

"Well then there might be a more unfortunate outcome . . . or fortunate, of course. It depends on which way you look at it."

"I find your attitude extraordinary. You don't seem to care that someone who intended to murder you is not discovered."

"How? My dear Mademoiselle Lawson, there have been numerous inquiries. It is not so easy to identify a bullet as you imagine. There is a gun in almost every cottage. Hares abound in the neighborhood, and they do some damage. They are good in the pot, and shooting of them has never been discouraged."

"Then if someone was shooting a hare why shouldn't they come forward and say so?"

"What! When they shot my horse instead."

"So someone was shooting in the woods and the bullet hit the tree and then killed the horse. Wouldn't that person with the gun have been aware of you in the woods?"

"Let us say he . . . or she . . . was not."

"So you accept the theory that it was an accident?"

"Why not, since it's a reasonable theory?"

"It's a comfortable theory, but I should not have thought you were a man to accept a theory because it was comfortable."

"Perhaps when you know me better you will change your mind." He was smiling at me. "It is so pleasant here. I hope you had no other plans. If not, will you stay and talk awhile? Then I will take you to the pond and you can have a closer look at Perseus. It's really a little masterpiece. The look of determination on his face is quite extraordinary. He is determined of course to slay his monster. Now talk to me about the pictures. How are they progressing? You are such a worker. In a short time you will have finished work in the gallery and we shall have our pictures looking as they did when they were first painted. It's fascinating, Mademoiselle Lawson."

I talked of the pictures, and after a while we looked at the statues. Then we returned to the *château* together.

Our progress through the terraces was necessarily slow; and as we went into the *château* I fancied that I saw a movement at the schoolroom window. I wondered who was watching us—Nounou or Geneviève?

Suddenly interest in the Comte's accident waned because the vines were in danger. They were now growing rapidly towards the peak at which they would arrive in early summer when the black measles scare arose.

The news spread through the town and the *château*.

I went over to see Madame Bastide to hear what was happening; she was as disturbed as she had been over Gabrielle's trouble.

As we sat drinking coffee together she told me what damage black measles could do. If it wasn't kept down the whole crop could be contaminated—perhaps not only this year but for years to come.

Jean Pierre and his father were working half the night. The vines had to be sprayed with a sodium arsenite spray and too much of such a solution could be harmful, too little could fail to destroy the pest.

"That is life," said Madame Bastide with a philosophical shrug, and proceeded to tell me once more of the great calamity when the vine louse had destroyed vines all over the country.

"Years it took us to bring prosperity back to the vines," she declared. "And every year there are these troubles . . . if it is not the black measles it is the grape leaf hopper or the root worm. Ah, Dallas, who would be a vinegrower?"

"Yet when the harvest is safely gathered in what a joy it must be."

"You are right." Her eyes shone at the thought. "You should see us then. That is a time when we go wild with joy."

"And if there hadn't been continual danger you couldn't feel quite so gay."

"It is true. There is no time in Gaillard like the harvest . . . and to enjoy we must first suffer."

I asked how Gabrielle was getting on.

"She is very happy. And to think it was Jacques all the time."

"Were you surprised?"

"Oh, I don't know. They were children together . . . always good friends. Perhaps one does not see the change coming. The girl is suddenly the woman, the boy the man; and there is nature waiting for them. Yes, I was surprised that it should be Jacques, though I should have known she was in love. She has been so absent-minded lately. Ah well, there it is. Everything is settled happily now. Jacques will do well at St. Vallient. Now of course he will be working as we are here for these pests spread fast. It would be bad luck if one struck St. Vallient just as Jacques has taken over."

"It was good of the Comte to offer Jacques St. Vallient at this time," I said. "It was just at the right moment."

"Sometimes the good God gives us evidence of his loving care."

I walked thoughtfully back to the *château*. Of course, I assured myself, Gabrielle had spoken to the Comte of her predicament, and because she was pregnant by Jacques who was unable to support both a wife and his mother, the Comte had given Jacques St. Vallient. The Durands were too old to manage it now in any case. Naturally that was what had happened.

I was changing. I was becoming adept at believing what I wanted to.

Behind her simplicity Nounou was a shrewd woman. I think she understood my growing feelings for the Comte. She had some affection for me, I believed, because I had had what she considered a good effect on Geneviève. She was the dedicated nurse, and the only matters of importance were those which touched her charges. Thus she must have been when Françoise was alive.

She was pleased when I called in at her private room, which I did fairly frequently; she would always have the coffee waiting for me, and we would sit and talk together—almost always of Geneviève and Françoise.

At this time when the whole district was worrying about black measles, Nounou's one concern was the fretfulness of Geneviève; her room seemed to be the one place where the vines were not discussed.

"I'm afraid she does not like Monsieur Philippe's wife," said Nounou, peering at me anxiously from under her heavy brows. "She never liked a woman in the house since . . ."

I would not meet her eye; I did not want Nounou to tell me what I already knew about the Comte and Claude.

I said briskly: "It is a long time since her mother died. She must grow away from it."

"If she had had a brother it would have been different. But now the Comte has brought Monsieur Philippe here and has married him to that woman . . ." I knew she had seen me chatting with the Comte in the gardens and was warning me.

"I daresay Philippe was eager to marry," I said. "Otherwise why should he? You talk as though . . ."

"I talk of what I know. The Comte will never marry. He dislikes women."

"I have heard rumors that he is rather fond of them."

"Fond! Oh no, Miss." She spoke bitterly. "He was never fond of anyone. A man can amuse himself with what he despises, and if he has a certain nature the more contemptuous he is, the more amusement he gets, if you follow me. Oh well, it's no concern of ours, you're thinking, and you're right. But I expect you'll soon be leaving us and forgetting all about us."

"I haven't looked so far ahead as that."

"I thought you hadn't." She smiled dreamily. "The *château* is a little kingdom of its own. I can't imagine living anywhere else . . . yet I only came here when Françoise did."

"It must be very different from Carrefour."

"Everything's different here."

Remembering the gloomy mansion which had been Françoise's home I said: "Françoise must have been very happy when she first came."

"Françoise wasn't ever happy here. He didn't care for her, you see." She looked at me earnestly. "It's not in him to care for anyone . . . only to use people. He uses everyone—his workers, who produce the wine . . . and us here in the *château*."

I said indignantly: "But isn't it always so? One can't expect one man to work a vineyard himself. Everyone has servants . . ."

"You did not understand me, Miss. How could you? I say he did not love my Françoise. It was an arranged marriage. Well, so are most in their station, but good comes from these marriages. Some are the better for being arranged, but not this one. Françoise was there because his family thought her a suitable wife; she was there to provide the family. As long as she did that he cared nothing for her. But she . . . she was young and sensitive . . . she did not understand. So . . . she died. The Comte is a strange man, Miss. Do not mistake that."

"He is . . . unusual."

She looked at me sadly and she said: "I wish I could show you how she was before . . . and after. I wish you could have known her."

"I wish it too."

"There are the little books she used to write in."

"Yes, they give me an idea of what she was like."

"She was always writing in them and when she was unhappy they were a great pleasure to her. Sometimes she would read them aloud to me. 'Do you remember this, Nounou?' she would say; and we'd laugh together. At Carrefour she was an innocent young girl. But when she married the Comte, she had to learn so much and learn quickly. How to be the mistress of a *château* . . . but that was not all."

"How did she feel when she first came here?" My eyes strayed to the cupboard in which Nounou kept her treasures. There was the box containing the pieces of embroidery which Françoise had given her for her birthdays, and there were those revealing notebooks which contained the story of Françoise's life. I wanted to read about the Comte's wooing; I wanted to know Françoise, not as the young girl living her secluded life in Carrefour with her strict father and her doting Nounou, but as the wife of the man who had begun to dominate my life.

"When she was happy she did not write in her little books," said Nounou. "And when she first came here there were so many excitements . . . so much to do. Even I saw little of her."

"So she *was* happy at first."

"She was a child. She believed in life . . . in people. She had been told she was fortunate, and she believed it. She was told that she would be happy . . . and she believed that too."

"And when did she start to be unhappy?"

Nounou spread her hands and looked down at them as though she expected to find the answer there.

"She soon began to understand life was not as she had imagined it would be. And then she was going to have Geneviève and she had something to dream of. That was a disappointment, for everyone hoped for a son."

"Did she confide in you, Nounou?"

"Before her marriage she would tell me everything."

"And not afterwards?"

Nounou shook her head. "It was only when I read . . ." she nodded to the cupboard, "that I understood. She was not such a child. She understood much . . . and she suffered."

"Do you mean he was unkind to her?"

Nounou's mouth hardened. "She needed to be loved," she said.

"And she loved him?"

"She was terrified of him."

I was startled by her vehemence. "Why?" I asked. Her mouth trembled and she turned away. I saw from her expression that she was looking into the past. Then suddenly her mood changed and she said slowly: "She was fascinated by him . . . at first. It's a way he has with some women."

She seemed to come to a decision, for she stood up suddenly and went to the cupboard and taking the key which was always kept dangling at her waist she opened it.

I saw the notebooks all neatly stacked together. She selected one.

"Read about it," she said. "Take it away and read about it. But don't let anyone else see it . . . and bring it back safely to me."

I knew I should refuse; I felt I was prying not only into her private life but into his. But I couldn't; I had to know.

Nounou was worried on my account. She believed that the Comte was to some extent interested in me. She was telling me in this oblique way that the man who had brought his mistress into the house and married her to his cousin, was also a murderer. She was telling me that if I allowed myself to become involved with such a man I too could be in danger. In what way, she could not say. But she was warning me all the same.

I took the book back to my room. I could scarcely wait to read it; and as I read I was disappointed. I had expected dramatic revelations.

There were the entries not unlike those I had read before. She had her own little plot in the garden where she grew her own flowers. It was such a pleasure to grow flowers.

"I want Geneviève to love them as I do."

"My first roses. I cut them and kept them in a vase in my bedroom. Nounou says flowers should not be kept in your bedroom at night because they take all the air which you need. I told her it was nonsense but to please her I let her take them out."

Reading through those pages I searched in vain for his name. It was not until almost at the end of the book that he was mentioned.

"Lothair returned from Paris today. Sometimes I think he despises me. I know I am not clever like the people he meets in Paris. I must really try harder to learn something about the things he is interested in. Politics and history, literature and pictures. I wish I did not find them so dull."

"We all went riding today—Lothair, Geneviève and myself. He was watching Geneviève. I was terrified that she would take a toss. She was so nervous."

"Lothair has gone away. I am not sure where but I expect to Paris. He did not tell me."

The account of her daily life went on. It was uneventful but she seemed satisfied with it. The *kermesse* which was given in the *château* grounds seemed to delight her. All the vineyard workers, the servants and the townsfolk had attended.

"I made ten lavender sachets—satin and silk—and they were all bought. Nounou said that we could have sold double the number if I had had time to make them. Geneviève was at the stall with me. We did very well."

"Geneviève and I had the young children at the château today. We are teaching them their catechism. I want Geneviève to understand what her duty is as daughter of the château. We talked about it afterwards, and it was so peaceful. I love the evenings when they begin to darken and Nounou comes to draw the curtains and light the lamps. I reminded her how I had always liked that part of the day at Carrefour when she would come and close the shutters . . . just before it was dark, so that we never really saw the darkness. I told her this. And she said, 'You are full of fancies, cabbage.' She has not called me 'cabbage' since before my marriage."

"I went to Carrefour today. Papa was pleased to see me. He says that Lothair should build a church for the poor and I must persuade him to do this."

"I spoke to Lothair about the church. He asked me why they wanted another church when they had one in the town. I told him that Papa thought that if they had a church close to the vineyard they could go in and worship at any hour of the day. It was for the good of their souls. Lothair said they had to concern themselves during working hours with the good of the grape. I don't know what Papa will say when I see him again. He will dislike Lothair more than ever."

"Papa says Lothair should dismiss Jean Lapin because he is an atheist. He says that by continuing to employ him Lothair is condoning his sin and Lapin should be sent away and his family with him. When I told Lothair he laughed and said he would decide who should work for him and Lapin's opinions were no concern of his, still less of my father's. Sometimes I think Lothair dislikes Papa so much that he wishes he had never married me. And I know Papa wishes I had never married Lothair."

"I went to Carrefour today. Papa took me to his bedroom and made me kneel and pray with him. I dream about Papa's bedroom. It is like a prison. It is so cold kneeling on the stone flags that I feel cramped long afterwards. How can he sleep on such a hard pallet made of nothing but straw. The crucifix on the wall is the only brightness there; there is nothing else but the pallet and prie-dieu in the room. Papa talked after we had prayed. I felt wicked . . . sinful."

"Lothair came back today, and I am afraid. I felt I should scream if he came near me. He said: 'What is the matter with you?' And I could not tell him how frightened I was of him. He went out of the room. I believe he was very angry. I think Lothair is beginning to hate me. I am so different from the women he likes . . . the women I believe he is with in Paris. I picture them in diaphanous gowns, laughing and drinking wine . . . abandoned women . . . gay and amorous. It is horrible."

"I was frightened last night. I thought he was coming to my room. I heard his footsteps outside. He stopped at the door and waited. I thought I should scream aloud in terror . . . but then he went away."

I had come to the last entry in the book.

What did it mean? Why had Françoise been so frightened of her husband? And why had Nounou shown me that book? If she wanted me to know the story of Françoise's life why did she not give them all to me? I knew there were others there. Could it be that Nounou, through those books which revealed the secrets of Françoise's life, knew the secret of her death? And was it for this reason that she was warning me to leave the *château*?

I took the book back to Nounou the next day.

"Why did you give me this one to read?" I asked.

"You said you wanted to know her."

"I feel I know her less than ever. Have you other books? Did she go on writing right until the time of her death?"

"She did not write so much after she wrote that one. I used to say to her: 'Françoise *chérie*, why don't you write in your little notebooks?' And she would say: 'There is nothing to write now, Nounou.' And when I said 'Nonsense!' she scolded me, and said I wanted to pry. It was the first time she'd said that. I knew she was afraid to write down what she felt."

"But why was she afraid?"

"Don't we all have thoughts which we would not wish to be known?"

"You mean she did not want her husband to know that she was afraid of him?" She was silent and I went on: "Why was she afraid of him? You know, Nounou?"

She pursed her lips tightly together as though nothing on earth would make her speak.

But I knew that there was some dark secret; and I believed that had she not thought that I was of some use to Geneviève she would have told me to leave the *château* because she feared for me. But I knew that she would sacrifice me willingly for the sake of Geneviève.

She knew something about the Comte which she was trying to tell me. Did she know that he had murdered his wife?

The desire to know was becoming an obsession. But it was more than a desire to know; it was a desperate need to prove him innocent.

We were riding, when Geneviève, speaking in her rather slow English, told me that she had heard from Esquilles.

"Such an important person she seems to have become, Miss. I will show you her letter."

"I am so pleased that she is happily settled."

"Yes, she is companion to Madame de la Condère, and Madame de la Condère is very appreciative. They live in a fine mansion, not as ancient as ours but much more *comme il faut*. Madame de la Condère gives card parties and old Esquilles often joins them to make up the number. It gives her an opportunity of mixing in the society to which by rights she should belong."

"Well, all's well that ends well."

"And, Miss, you will be glad to hear that Madame de la Condère has a nephew who is a very charming man and he is always very agreeable to Esquilles. I must show you her letter. She is so coy when she writes of him. I do believe she has hopes of becoming Madame Nephew before long."

"Well, I'm very pleased. I have thought about her now and then. She was so suddenly dismissed, and it was all due to your naughtiness."

"She mentions Papa. She says how grateful she is to him for finding her such a congenial situation."

"He . . . found it?"

"Of course. He arranged for her to go to Madame de la Condère. He wouldn't just have turned her out. Or would he?"

"No," I said firmly. "He wouldn't turn her out."

That was a very happy morning.

The atmosphere lightened considerably during the next weeks. The black measles had been defeated and there was rejoicing throughout the vineyards and the towns which depended on their prosperity.

Invitations came to the *château* for the family to a wedding of a distant connection. The Comte said he was too bruised to go—he continued to walk with a stick—and that Philippe and his wife must represent their branch of the family.

I knew that Claude was resentful and hated the idea of going and leaving the Comte at the *château*. I was in one of the small walled gardens when she walked past with the Comte. We did not see each other but I heard their voices—hers quite distinctly for it was high-pitched and very audible when she was angry.

"They'll expect *you!*"

"They'll understand. You and Philippe will explain about my accident."

"Accident! A few bruises!" He said something which I did not hear and she went on: "Lothair . . . *please!*"

"My dear, I shall stay here."

"You don't listen to me now. You seem as if . . ."

His voice was low, almost soothing and by the time he had finished speaking they were out of earshot. There was no doubt of the relationship which existed between them, I thought sadly.

But to Paris went Claude and Philippe, and I thrust aside my doubts and fears and prepared to enjoy Claude's absence.

The days were long and full of sunshine. The vines were in bloom. Each day I rose with a feeling of anticipation. I had never been so happy in my life; yet I knew that my happiness was about as dependable as an April day. I could make some alarming discovery; I could be sent away. In a moment the skies could darken and the sun be completely blotted out. All the more reason to bask in it while it was there.

As soon as Philippe and Claude had left, the Comte's visits to the gallery had become more frequent. Sometimes I fancied he was escaping from something, searching and longing to discover. There were times when I caught a glimpse of a different man behind his teasing smiles. I even had the idea that he enjoyed our interviews as much as I did.

When he left me I would come to my senses and laugh at myself asking: How far are you prepared to delude yourself?

There was a simple explanation of what was happening: There was no one at the *château* to amuse him; therefore he found me and my earnestness for my work diverting. I must remember that.

But he *was* interested in painting, and knowledgeable too. I recalled that pathetic entry in Françoise's diary. She must try to learn something of the things which interested him. Poor frightened little Françoise! Why had she been afraid?

There were times when his face would darken with a cynicism which I imagined could be alarming to a meek and simple woman. There might even be a touch of sadism, as though he delighted in mockery and the discomfort it brought to others. But to me those expressions of his were like a film which something in his life had laid over his true nature—just as lack of care will spoil a picture. I believed that as a picture could be restored to its original beauty, so could a character. But there must be understanding of pictures, a confident yet humble approach, even an ability to paint before one attempted to restore. How much more careful one must be before attempting to restore a human being!

I was arrogant. Governessy, as Geneviève would say. Did I really think that because I could bring its old glory back to a painting I could change a man?

But I was obsessed by my desire to know him, to probe beneath that often sardonic mask, to change the expression of the mouth from a certain bitter disillusion. But before I could attempt this . . . I must know my subject.

How had he felt towards the woman whom he had married? He had ruined her life. Had she ruined his? How could one know when the past was engulfed in secrecy?

The days when I did not see him were empty; and those encounters which seemed so short left me elated and exhilarated by a happiness I had never in my life known before.

We talked of pictures; of the *château*; of the history of the place and the days of the *château's* glory during the reigns of the fourteenth and fifteenth Louis. "Then there was the change. Nothing was ever the same again, Mademoiselle Lawson. Some saw it coming years before. '*Après moi le déluge*,' said Louis XV. And *déluge* there was, with his successor going to the guillotine and taking so many of our people with him. My own great great-grandfather was one of them. We were fortunate not to lose our estates. Had we been nearer Paris we should have done so. But you read about the miracle of St. Geneviève and how she saved us from disaster." His tone lightened. "You are thinking that perhaps we were not worth saving."

"I was thinking no such thing. As a matter of fact I think it's a pity when estates have to pass out of families. How interesting to trace one's family back hundreds of years."

"Perhaps the Revolution did some good. If they had not stormed the *château* and damaged these pictures, we should not have needed your services."

I shrugged my shoulders. "If the pictures had not been damaged, they would not have needed restoration certainly. They might have needed cleaning . . ."

"But you might not have come here, Miss Lawson. Think of that."

"I am sure the Revolution was a greater catastrophe than that would have been."

He laughed; and he was different then. I caught a glimpse of the lighthearted person through the mask. It was a wonderful moment.

I joined him and Geneviève for dinner each night during the absence of Philippe and Claude. The conversation was animated between us, and Geneviève would look on in a kind of bewilderment; but attempts to draw her in were not very successful. She, like her mother, seemed to be afraid of him.

Then, one evening when we went down to dinner, he was not there. He had left no message that he would not be in, but after we had waited for twenty minutes, dinner was served and we ate alone.

I felt very uneasy. I kept picturing him lying hurt—or worse—in the woods. If someone had tried to kill him and failed, wasn't it plausible that they should have another attempt?

I tried to eat, tried to disguise my anxiety, which Geneviève did not share, and I was glad when I could go to my room to be alone.

I walked up and down; I sat at my window; I could not rest. There was a mad moment when I thought of going to the stables and taking a horse to look for him. How could I do so at night, and what right had I to concern myself in his affairs?

Of course, I reminded myself, the Comte who had been such a gracious companion to me had been the invalid. He had been recuperating from his accident, and while he was confined to the *château* found me a substitute for his friends.

Why hadn't I seen it?

It was daylight before I slept—and when the maid brought my breakfast to my room I looked at her in surreptitious anxiety to see if she had heard any terrible news. But she was as placid as ever.

I went down to the gallery feeling tired and strained and in no mood to work; but I had told myself that if anything had happened I should have heard by now.

I had not been there very long when he came into the gallery. I started when I saw him and he looked at me strangely.

I said without thinking: "Oh . . . are you all right then?"

His face was expressionless, but he regarded me intently.

"I'm sorry I missed seeing you at dinner last night," he said.

"Oh . . . yes. I . . . wondered . . . ?"

What was the matter with me? I was stammering like the foolish girls I so despised.

He continued to look at me, and I was certain he had detected the signs of sleeplessness. What a fool I had been! Did I expect him to explain to me when he went out visiting his friends? Of course he would go out. He had only confined himself to the *château* because of his accident.

"I believe," he said, "you were concerned for my safety." Did he know the state of my feelings as well as—or perhaps better than—I knew them myself? "Tell me, did you imagine me shot through the heart . . . no, the head, because I believe you secretly think, Mademoiselle Lawson, that I have a stone where my heart should be. An advantage in a way. A bullet can't pierce a stone."

I knew it was no use denying my concern, so I tacitly admitted it in my reply. "If you had been shot once it seemed plausible to imagine that it might happen again."

"It would be too coincidental, don't you think? A man shooting a hare happens to shoot my horse. It's the sort of thing that could only happen once in a lifetime. And you are expecting it twice in a few weeks."

"The hare theory might not be the true one."

He sat down on the sofa beneath the picture of his ancestress in emeralds and regarded me on my stool. "Are you comfortable there, Mademoiselle Lawson?"

"Thank you." I could feel animation coming back into my body; everything was gay again. I had only one fear now. Was I betraying myself?

"We've talked about pictures, old castles, old families, revolutions, yet never about ourselves," he said almost gently.

"I am sure those subjects are more interesting than I personally could be."

"Do you really think that?"

I shrugged my shoulders—a habit I had learned from those about me. It was a good substitute for the answer expected to a difficult question.

"All I know is that your father died and you took his place."

"There is little else to know. Mine has been a life like many others of my class and circumstances."

"You never married. I wonder why."

"I might reply as the English milkmaid, 'Nobody asked me, sir, she said.'"

"That I find extraordinary. I am sure you would make an excellent wife for some fortunate man. Just imagine how useful you would be. His pictures would always be in perfect condition."

"What if he had none?"

"I am sure you would very quickly remedy that omission."

I did not like the light turn of the conversation. I fancied he was making fun of me; and it was a subject about which, in view of my new emotions, I did not care to be mocked.

"I am surprised that you should be an advocate for marriage." As soon as I had spoken I wished I hadn't. I flushed and stammered: "I'm sorry . . ."

He smiled, the mockery gone.

"And I'm not surprised that you are surprised. Tell me, what does D. stand for? Miss D. Lawson. I should like to know. It is such an unusual name."

I explained that my father had been Daniel and my mother Alice.

"Dallas," he repeated my name. "You smile?"

"It's the way in which you say it . . . with the accent on the last syllable. We put it on the first."

He tried it out again, smiling at me. "*Dal*las. *Dal*las." He made me feel that he liked saying it.

"You yourself have an unusual name."

"It's been used by my family for years . . . since the first King of the Franks. We have to be royal, you see. We throw in an occasional Louis, a Charles, an Henri. But we must have our Lothairs. Now let me tell you how wrongly *you* pronounce my name."

I said it and he laughed and made me say it again.

"Very good, *Dal*las," he said. "But then everything you do you do well."

I told him about my parents and how I had helped Father in his work. Somehow it came through that they had dominated my life and kept me from marriage. He mentioned this.

"Perhaps it was better so," he said. "Those who don't marry often regret the omission; but those who do so, often regret far more bitterly. They long to go back in time and not do what they did. Well, that's life, isn't it?"

"That may be so."

"Take myself. I was married when I was twenty to a young woman who was chosen for me. It is so in our families you know."

"Yes."

"These marriages are often successful."

"And yours was?" My voice was almost a whisper.

He did not answer, and I said quickly: "I'm sorry. I am being impertinent."

"No. You should know."

I wondered why, and my heart began to beat uncomfortably.

"No, the marriage was not a success. I think I am incapable of being a good husband."

"Surely a man could be . . . if he wanted to."

"Mademoiselle Lawson, how could a man who is selfish, intolerant, impatient, and promiscuous be a good husband?"

"Simply by ceasing to be selfish, intolerant, and so on."

"And you believe that one can turn off these unpleasant qualities like a tap?"

"I think one can try to subdue them."

He laughed suddenly and I felt foolish.

"I amuse you?" I said coolly. "You asked an opinion and I gave it."

"It's absolutely true, of course. I could imagine you subduing such unpleasant characteristics if only I could so far stretch my imagination as to picture you possessing them. You know how disastrously my marriage ended."

I nodded.

"My experiences as a husband have convinced me that I should abandon that role forever."

"Perhaps you are wise to make such a decision."

"I was sure you would agree."

I knew what he meant. If what he suspected was true and I had allowed my feelings for him to become too deep, I should be warned.

I felt humiliated and wounded and I said briskly: "I am very interested in some of the wall surfaces I have noticed about the *château*.

It has occurred to me that there might be some murals hidden beneath the lime-wash."

"Oh?" he said; and I thought he was not paying attention to what I said.

"I remember my father's making a miraculous discovery on the walls of an ancient mansion in Northumberland. It was a wonderful painting, which had been hidden for centuries. I feel certain that there must be similar discoveries here."

"Discoveries?" he repeated. "Yes?"

What was he thinking of? That stormy married life with Françoise? But had it been stormy? Deeply unhappy, entirely unsatisfactory since he had determined never to run the risk of such an experience again.

I was aware of an intense passion engulfing me. I thought: What could I do? How could I leave this and go back . . . to England . . . back to a new life where there was no *château* full of secrets, no Comte whom I longed to restore to happiness.

"I should like to have a closer look at those walls," I went on.

He said almost fiercely as though denying everything that had gone before: "Dallas, my *château* and myself are at your disposal."

9

A few days later Philippe and Claude returned from Paris, and the intimacy which had grown between the Comte and myself seemed as though it had never been.

Claude and he often rode together. Philippe was not so fond of being in the saddle. Sometimes I watched them from the window of my room, laughing and talking together; and I remembered that conversation I had heard between them on the night of the ball.

Well, now she was married to Philippe and her home was in the *château*. She was mistress of it—although not the Comte's wife.

I soon became aware of her rule. It was the day after her return and about fifteen minutes before dinner when there was a knock on my door. I was surprised to see the maid with my tray, for during the absence of Philippe and Claude I had taken this meal in the dining room and had already changed into my brown silk in preparation for doing so.

When the maid set the food out on the little table I asked who had told her to bring it.

"Madame ordered it. Boulanger sent Jeanne to change the table because she had laid a place for you. Madame said that you would be taking your meals in your own room. Boulanger said in the kitchens how was he to know? You had been dining with Monsieur le Comte and Mademoiselle Geneviève. Well, those were Madame's orders."

I felt my eyes blazing with anger, which I managed to hide from the maid.

I pictured their going in to dinner. I imagined his looking round for me and his consternation when I was not there.

"And where is Mademoiselle Lawson?"

"I have told them to take up her tray. She cannot expect to eat at table with us. After all, she is not a guest; she is employed to work here."

I saw his face darken with contempt for her and . . . regard for me. "What nonsense. Boulanger, another place, please. And go at once to Mademoiselle Lawson's room and tell her that I am looking forward to her presence at dinner."

I waited. The food on the tray was getting cold.

It did not happen as I had hoped. There was no message.

Now if ever I should see what a fool I was. This woman was his mistress. He had married her to Philippe so that she could be at the *château* without arousing scandal, because he was wise enough to see that he could afford no more scandal since even kings in their castles had to be a little careful.

As for me—I was the odd Englishwoman who was so intense about her work and to whom it was amusing to talk for a time when one was indisposed and confined to the *château*.

Naturally her presence was not needed when Claude was at hand. Moreover, Claude was the mistress of the *château*.

Startled out of my sleep, I awoke in terror, for someone was in my room, standing there at the bottom of my bed.

"Miss." Geneviève glided towards me, a lighted candle in her hand.

"I heard the tapping, Miss. Only a few minutes ago. You said to come and tell you."

"Geneviève . . ." I sat up in bed, my teeth chattering. I must have had a nightmare in those seconds before waking.

"What's the time?"

"One o'clock. It woke me up. Tap . . . tap . . . and I was frightened and you said we'd go and see . . . together."

I put my feet into slippers and hastily put on my dressing gown.

"I expect you imagined it, Geneviève."

She shook her head. "It's like it was before. Tap . . . tap . . . as though someone is trying to let you know where they are."

"Where?"

"Come to my room. I can hear it there."

I followed her through the *château* to the nursery, which was in the oldest part of the house.

I said: "Have you awakened Nounou?"

She shook her head. "Nounou never wakes once she's asleep. She says once she gets off she sleeps the sleep of the dead."

We went into Geneviève's room and listened. There was silence.

"Wait a minute, Miss," she pleaded. "It stops and goes on."

"From what direction?"

"I don't know. . . . Down below, I think."

The dungeons were immediately below this part of the *château*. Geneviève would know that, and to a girl of her imagination this fact might have given her ideas.

"It'll come again soon, I know it will," said Geneviève. "There! I thought I heard . . ."

We sat tense, listening; a bird gave its call from the lime trees.

"It's an owl," I said.

"Of course it is. Do you think I don't know that! There!"

Then I heard it. Tap tap. Softly then louder.

"It's below," I said.

"Miss . . . you said you wouldn't be afraid."

"We'll go and see if we can find out what's happening."

I took the candle from her and led the way down the staircase to the lower floors.

Geneviève's belief in my courage gave me that quality. I should have been very uneasy walking about the *château* alone like this at night.

We had reached the door of the gun gallery and paused there listening. Distinctly we heard a sound. I was not sure what it was, but I felt the goose pimples rising on my flesh. Geneviève gripped my arm and in the candlelight I saw her startled eyes. She was about to speak but I shook my head.

Then came the sound again.

It was from the dungeons below.

There was nothing I wanted so much as to turn and go back to my room; I was sure Geneviève felt the same; but because she did not expect such behavior from me I could not tell her that I, too, was afraid, that it was all very well to be bold by daylight and quite another matter in the dungeons of an old *château* at dead of night.

She pointed down the stone spiral staircase, and, holding up my long skirts with the same hand as that which grasped the candle, for

I needed the other to grip the rope banister, I led the way down the stairs.

Geneviève behind me, suddenly lurched forward. It was fortunate that she fell against me, thus preventing herself from tripping down the stairs. She gave a little scream and immediately clapped her hands to her mouth.

"It's all right," she whispered. "I tripped over my dressing gown."

"For heaven's sake, hold it up."

She nodded, and for a few seconds we stood there on that spiral staircase trying to steady ourselves; my heart was leaping about uncomfortably and I knew Geneviève's was doing the same. I believed that in a moment she would be saying: "Let's go back. There's nothing here." And I would be willing enough.

But some persistent faith in my invincibility prevented her from speaking.

Now there was absolute silence everywhere. I leaned against the stone wall and could feel the coldness through my clothes in contrast to Geneviève's hot hand which was gripping my arm. She did not look at me.

This was absurd, I thought. What was I doing wandering about the *château* at night? Suppose the Comte should discover me? What a fool I should look! I should go straight back to my room now and in the morning report the sounds I had heard during the night. But Geneviève would think I was afraid if I did that. She would not be wrong either. If I did not go on now she would lose that respect for me which I believe was what gave me some authority over her; and if I were to help her overcome the demons in her which forced her to strange acts, I must retain that authority.

I gathered my skirts higher, descended the staircase, and, when I reached the bottom, pushed open the iron-studded door to the dungeons. The dark cavern yawned ahead of us, and the sight of it made me more reluctant than ever to go on.

"This is where the sound comes from," I whispered.

"Oh . . . Miss . . . I can't go in there."

"It's only the old cages."

Geneviève was tugging on my arm. "Let's go back, Miss."

It would be folly to go walking down there with only the light of the candle to guide us. The floor was uneven, and Geneviève's near fall on the stairs was a warning. How much more dangerous it would be down here! This was what I told myself. But the truth was that the cold eeriness of the place was so repellent that all my instincts called out to me to go back.

I lifted the candle high. I saw the damp walls, the fungoid growth, the darkness going on unendingly, it seemed. I could see one or two of the cages with the great chains which had held men and women prisoners of the de la Talles.

I said: "Is anyone there?"

My voice echoed uncannily. Geneviève pressed her body against me, and I could feel her shaking.

I said: "There's no one here, Geneviève."

She was only too ready to admit it. "Let's go, Miss."

I said: "We'll come and have a look in daylight."

"Oh, yes . . . yes . . ."

She had seized my hand and was pulling me. I wanted to turn and hurry from the place, but in those seconds I was conscious of a horrible fascination. I could easily believe that somewhere in the darkness, someone was watching me . . . luring me onwards . . . further into the darkness to some sort of doom.

"Miss . . . come on."

The feeling had passed, and I turned. As Geneviève went before me up the staircase, I felt as though my feet were made of lead and I could scarcely lift them; I almost fancied I heard a footstep behind me. It was as though icy hands were laid on me pulling me back into the gloom. It was all imagination; my throat was constricted so that I could scarcely breathe, my heart a great weight in my chest. The candle dipped erratically and for one second of horror I was afraid it was going out. I felt we should never reach the top of that stairway. The ascent could not have taken more than a minute or so, but it seemed like ten. I stood breathless at the top of the stairs . . . outside the room in which was the *oubliette*.

"Come on, Miss," said Geneviève, her teeth chattering. "I'm cold."

We climbed the stairs.

"Miss," said Geneviève, "can I stay in your room for tonight?"

"Of course."

"I . . . I might disturb Nounou if I went back."

I did not point out that Nounou was never disturbed; I knew that she too had shared my fear and was afraid to sleep alone.

I lay awake for a long time, going over every minute of that nocturnal adventure.

Fear of the unknown, I told myself, was an inheritance from our savage forbears. What had I feared in the dungeons? Ghosts of the past? Something that did not exist outside a childish imagination?

Yet when I did sleep my dreams were haunted by the sound of tapping. I dreamed of a young woman who could not rest because she had died violently. She wanted to return to explain to me exactly how she had died.

Tap! Tap!

I started up in bed. It was the maid with my breakfast.

Geneviève must have awakened early, for she was no longer in my room.

The next afternoon I went down to the dungeons alone. I had intended to ask Geneviève to accompany me, but she was nowhere to be found, and as I was a little ashamed of my terror of the night before, I wanted to show myself that there was nothing to fear.

Nevertheless, I had heard Geneviève's tapping sound and I should like to discover what that was.

It was a sunny day—and how different everything looked in sunshine! Even the old staircase, in the light which came through one of the long narrow slits in the wall was not in complete darkness. It looked gloomy, of course, but different from the light of one small candle.

I reached the entrance to the dungeons and stood staring into the gloom. Even on one of the lightest days of the year it was not easy to see, but after I had stood peering there for a short while my eyes grew accustomed to the dimness. I could make out the outline of several of those horrible little openings which were called the cages, and as I stepped farther into the dungeon, the heavy door closed behind me and I could not suppress a little scream for a dark shadow loomed up behind me and a hand caught my arm.

"Mademoiselle Lawson!"

I gasped. The Comte was standing behind me.

"I . . ." I began. "You startled me."

"It was foolish of me. How dark it is with the door shut." Still he did not open it. I was conscious of him very close to me.

"I wondered who was here," he said. "I might have known it would be you. You are so interested in the *château*. So naturally you love to explore . . . and a gruesome place like this would be particularly attractive."

He had laid a hand on my shoulder. If I had wanted to protest at that moment, I should have been unable to; I was filled with fear—the more frightening because I did not know what I feared.

His voice sounded close to my ear. "What did you hope to discover, Mademoiselle Lawson?"

"I hardly know. Geneviève heard noises and last night we came down to investigate. I said we would come back by daylight."

"So she is coming too?"

"She may."

He laughed.

"Noises?" he said. "What noises?"

"A tapping sound. Geneviève has mentioned it before. She came to my room because I was interested and I had said that if she heard it again we would investigate."

"You can guess what it is," he said. "Some death-watch beetle settling down to a banquet off the old *château*. We've had them before."

"Oh . . . I see."

"It would have occurred to you, of course. You must have encountered him in some of your stately homes of England."

"Of course. But these stone walls . . ."

"There's plenty of wood in the place." He drew away from me and, going to the door, threw it open. Now I could see more clearly, the miserable caves, the dreadful rings and chains . . . and the Comte, looking pale, I thought, and his expression more veiled even than usual. "If we have some beetle in the place it means trouble." He grimaced and lifted his shoulders.

"You will have this investigated?"

"In time," he said. "After the grape harvest perhaps. It takes those wretches a long time to tap this place away. It was only ten years ago that it was overhauled. There shouldn't be much trouble."

"You suspected it?" I asked. "Is that why you were investigating?"

"No," he said. "I saw you turn down the staircase and followed. I thought perhaps you had made a discovery."

"A discovery? What sort of discovery?"

"Uncovered some work of art. You remember you were telling me?"

"Down here?"

"One would never be sure where the treasure lay, would one?"

"No, I suppose not."

"At the moment," he said, "we will say nothing of the tapping. I don't want Gautier to hear. He'll be all for getting the experts in right away. We must wait until after the harvest. You've no idea, Mademoiselle Lawson, although you will when you see for yourself, what feverish excitement there is when the grapes ripen. We could not have workmen in the *château* at such a time."

"May I tell Geneviève what your answer to her tapping is?"

"Yes, do tell her. Tell her to go to sleep and not listen for it."

"I will," I said.

We mounted the stairs together, and, as usual in his company, my feelings were mixed. I felt as though I had been caught prying and on the other hand I was elated to be talking to him again.

I explained to Geneviève when we went riding together the next day.

"Beetles!" she cried. "Why, they're almost as bad as ghosts."

"Nonsense," I laughed. "They're tangible creatures and they can be destroyed."

"If not, they destroy houses. Ugh! I don't like the thought of our having beetles. And what are they tapping for?"

"They tap on the wood with their heads to attract their mates."

That made Geneviève laugh, and we became rather gay. I saw that she was relieved.

It was a lovely day. There had been heavy intermittent showers all the morning and the grass and trees smelt wonderfully fresh.

The grapes which had been severely pruned so that about ninety per cent of the growth had been cut away, were looking fine and healthy. Only the best remained, and they would have plenty of room to absorb the sunshine to make them sweet and give a real *château* wine.

Geneviève said suddenly, "I wish you came to dinner, Miss."

"Thank you, Geneviève," I said, "but I cannot come uninvited, and in any case I am perfectly content with a tray in my room."

"Papa and you used to talk together."

"Naturally."

She laughed.

"I wish *she* hadn't come here. I don't like her. I don't think she likes me either."

"You are referring to your Aunt Claude?"

"You know to whom I'm referring and she's not my aunt."

"It's easier to call her so."

"Why? She's not much older than I am. They seem to forget I'm grown up. Let's go to the Maison Bastide and see what they're doing."

Her face, which had been set in discontented lines when she had talked of Claude, changed at the prospect of going to the Bastides', and as I was afraid of these sudden moods of hers, I was very willing to turn Bonhomme in the direction of their house.

We found Yves and Margot in the garden. They carried baskets on their arms and were bent double examining the front path as they sang in their thin, childish voices, now and then shouting to each other.

We tied our horses to the post, and Geneviève ran to them asking what they were doing.

"Don't you know?" demanded Margot, who was at this stage of her young life inclined to think those who did not know what she knew were excessively ignorant.

"Snails!" cried Geneviève.

Yves looked up at her, grinning, and held out his basket to show her. In it lay several snails.

"We're going to have a feast!" he told her.

He stood up and began to dance, singing:

> "C'était un petit bonhomme luron
> C'était un petit bonhomme
> Qui allait a Montbron . . ."

He squealed: "Look at this one. He'll never go to Montbron. Come on *mon petit bonhomme.*" He grinned at Geneviève. "We're going to have a feast of snails. The rain has brought them out. Get a basket and come and help."

"Where?" asked Geneviève.

"Oh, Jeanne will give you one."

Geneviève ran off to the back of the house and round to the kitchen where Jeanne was busy preparing some *pot-au-feu;* and I thought how she changed when she came to this house.

Yves rocked on his haunches.

"You must come and join in the feast, Miss Dallas," he said.

"Not for two weeks," shrilled Margot.

"We keep them for two weeks and then they're served with garlic and parsley." Yves smoothed his hands over his stomach reminiscently. "Delicious!"

Then he began to hum his *escargot* song to himself, while Geneviève came back with a basket and I went into the house to talk to Madame Bastide.

Two weeks later, when the snails the children had collected were ready to be eaten, Geneviève and I were invited to the Maison Bastide. Their habit of making a celebration out of simple occasions was an endearing one and was for the benefit of the children. I thought what an excellent idea it was, because Geneviève was always happier at such times, and when she was happier her conduct improved. She really seemed as if she wanted to please.

But as we rode over we met Claude, who appeared to be coming from the vineyards. I saw her before she saw us; her face was flushed and there was an air of absorption about her; I was struck afresh by her beauty. However, when she saw us her expression changed.

She asked where we were going and I told her we had been invited to the Bastides'.

When she rode on, Geneviève said: "I believe she would have liked to forbid us to go. She thinks she is mistress here, but she's only Philippe's wife. She behaves as though . . ."

Her eyes narrowed, and I thought: She is less innocent than we have believed. She *knows* of the relationship between this woman and her father.

I said nothing, and we rode on until we came to the Maison Bastide. Yves and Margot were waiting for us and greeted us vociferously.

It was the first time I had tasted snails, and they all laughed at my reluctance. I am sure they were delicious, but I could not eat them with the same enthusiasm as the rest of the party.

The children talked of snails and how they asked their saints to send the rain to bring them out, while Geneviève listened eagerly to all they said. She was shouting as loudly as the others and joining in when they sang the *escargot* song.

Jean Pierre came in the middle of it. I had seen less of him lately, for he had been so busy in the vineyards. He greeted me with his usual gallantry, and I noticed with some alarm the change in Geneviève when he entered. She seemed to throw off her childishness, and it was apparent to me that she listened eagerly to everything he said.

"Come and sit next to me, Jean Pierre," she cried, and without hesitation he drew a chair to the table and wedged it in between her and Margot.

They talked of snails, and Jean Pierre sang to them in his rich tenor voice while Geneviève watched him, a dreamy expression in her eyes.

Jean Pierre caught my glance and immediately turned his attention to me. Geneviève burst out: "We've got beetles in the *château*. I wouldn't mind if they were snails. Do snails ever come indoors? Do they ever tap with their shells?"

She was making a desperate bid for his attention, and she had it.

"Beetles in the *château*?" he asked.

"Yes, they tap. Miss and I went down to see in the night, didn't we, Miss? Right down into the dungeons we went. I was scared. Miss wasn't. Nothing would scare you, Miss, would it?"

"Certainly not beetles," I said.

"But we didn't know it was beetles till Papa told you."

"Beetles in the *château*," repeated Jean Pierre. "Death-watch? That's set Monsieur le Comte in a panic, I'll swear."

"I have never yet seen him in a panic and he certainly was not over this."

"Oh, Miss," cried Geneviève, "wasn't it awful . . . down there in the dungeon and we only had the candle. I was certain someone was there . . . watching us. I felt it, Miss. I did really." The children were listening with round-eyed attention, and Geneviève could not resist the temptation to focus the interest on herself. "I heard a noise . . ." she went on. "I knew there was a ghost down there. Someone who had been kept a prisoner and had died and whose soul couldn't rest . . ."

I could see that she was getting too excited. There was a rising hysteria in her. I caught Jean Pierre's eye, and he nodded.

"Well," he cried, "who is going to dance the 'March of the Escargots?' It is only fitting that having feasted off them we should dance in their honor. Come, Mademoiselle Geneviève. We will lead the dance."

Geneviève sprang up with alacrity, her face flushed, her eyes shining, and putting her hand in Jean Pierre's, she danced round the room.

We left the Maison Bastide about four o'clock. As we entered the *château* one of the maids came running to me and told me that Madame de la Talle wished to see me in her boudoir as soon as possible.

I did not wait to change but went to her in my riding habit.

I knocked on her bedroom door and heard her voice, rather muffled, bidding me enter. I did so. There was no sign of her in the elaborately furnished room with its four-poster bed hung with peacock blue silk hangings.

I noticed an open door, and through it she called to me: "In here, Mademoiselle Lawson."

Her boudoir was a room about half the size of her bedroom. It was fitted with a large mirror, hip bath, dressing table, chairs, and sofa and contained an overpowering smell of scent. She herself was reclining on the sofa wrapped in a pale blue silk robe, her yellow hair falling about her shoulders. I hated admitting it to myself but she looked very beautiful and seductive.

She regarded one bare foot which was thrust out from the blue robe. "Oh, Mademoiselle Lawson, you've just come in. You've been to the Bastides'?"

"Yes," I said.

"Of course," she went on, "we have no objection to your friendship with the Bastides."

I looked puzzled, and she added with a smile: "Certainly not. *They* make our wine; *you* clean our pictures."

"I don't see the connection."

"I am sure you will, Mademoiselle Lawson, if you consider it. I am thinking of Geneviève. I am sure Monsieur le Comte would not wish her to be on terms of such . . . intimate friendship with . . . his servants." I was about to protest when she went on quickly, and there was almost a gentle note in her voice as though she were trying to make this as easy as possible for me: "Perhaps we protect our young girls more here than you do in England. We feel it unwise to allow them to mix too freely with those not in their social class. It could in some circumstances lead to . . . complications. I am sure you understand."

"Are you suggesting that I should prevent Geneviève's calling at the Bastides' house?"

"You do agree that it is unwise?"

"I think you give me credit for carrying more weight than I do. I am sure I could not prevent her doing what she wished. I can only ask her to come to you so that you can make your wishes known to her."

"But you accompany her to these people. It is due to your influence . . ."

"I am sure I could not stop her. I will tell her you wish to speak to her."

And with that, I left her.

I had retired to my room that night and was in bed but not asleep when the disturbance started.

I heard shrill screams of fear and anger and, putting on my dressing gown, went into the corridor. I could hear someone calling out in protest. Then I heard Philippe's voice.

As I stood at the door of my room hesitating what to do, one of the maids came running by.

"What's wrong?" I cried.

"Snails in Madame's bed."

I went back to my room and sat down thoughtfully. So this was Geneviève's answer. She had taken the reprimand demurely enough, or so it had seemed—while she planned her revenge. There would be trouble about this.

I went along to her room and knocked lightly on the door. There was no answer so I went in to find her lying on her back, pretending to be asleep.

"It's no use," I said.

So she opened one eye and laughed at me.

"Did you hear the shouting, Miss?"

"Everyone must have heard it."

"Imagine her face when she saw them!"

"It's not really very funny, Geneviève."

"Poor Miss. I'm always sorry for people who have no sense of humor."

"And I'm sorry for people who play senseless pranks for which they alone will have to suffer. What do you think is going to be the outcome of this?"

"She is going to learn to mind her own affairs and not pry into mine."

"It might not turn out as you think."

"Oh, stop it! You're as bad as she is. She is trying to stop my going to see Jean Pierre and the rest of them. She won't, I tell you."

"If your father forbids it . . ."

She stuck out her lower lip. "Nobody is going to forbid me to see Jean Pierre . . . and the rest of them."

"The way to deal with this is not to play schoolgirl tricks with snails."

"Oh, isn't it? Didn't you hear her shout? I'll bet she was terrified. Just serves her right."

"You don't imagine that she will let this pass?"

"She can do what she likes. I'm going to do what I like."

I could see that it was no use talking to her, so I left her. But I was growing alarmed; not only by her foolish behavior, which I was sure would only result in her disadvantage, but by the fact of her growing obsession with Jean Pierre.

I was in the gallery next morning when Claude came in. She was dressed in dark blue riding habit and wore a blue bowler riding hat. Beneath it her eyes were deep blue; I knew she was very angry and trying to hide it.

"There was a disgraceful scene last night," she said. "Perhaps you heard."

"I heard something."

"Geneviève's manners are deplorable. It is not to be wondered at, considering the company she keeps."

I raised my eyebrows.

"And I think, Mademoiselle Lawson, that you are in some ways to blame. You will agree that it is since you came here that she has become so friendly with the winegrowers."

"That friendship has nothing to do with her bad manners. They were deplorable when I arrived."

"I am convinced that your influence is not a good one, Mademoiselle Lawson, and for that reason I am asking you to leave."

"To leave!"

"Yes, it's by far the best way. I shall see that you are paid what is due to you and my husband may help you to find other work. But I don't want any arguments. I should like you to be out of the *château* within two hours."

"But this is absurd. I haven't finished my work."

"We will get someone to take it over."

"You don't understand. I use my own methods. I can't leave this picture until it's finished."

"I am mistress here, Mademoiselle Lawson, and I am asking you to leave."

How sure she was of herself! Had she reason to be? Had she so much influence with him? Had she but to ask favors for them to be granted? She was clearly of that opinion. She had complete confidence that the Comte would deny her nothing.

"I am employed by the Comte," I reminded her.

Her lips curled. "Very well. You shall receive your orders from him."

I was conscious of a cold fear. There must be a strong reason for that absolute assurance. Perhaps she had already discussed me with the Comte. Perhaps she had already asked for my dismissal and he, being eager to indulge her, had granted this wish. I tried to hide my apprehension as I followed her to the library.

She threw open the door and cried: "Lothair!"

"Claude," he said, "my dear?"

He had risen from his chair and was coming towards us when he saw me. For half a second he was taken aback. Then he bowed his head in acknowledgment of my presence.

"Lothair," she said, "I have told Mademoiselle Lawson that she cannot remain. She refuses to take her dismissal from me, so I have brought her to you so that you can tell her."

"Tell her?" he asked, looking from her angry face to my scornful one. I was conscious in that moment how beautiful she was. Anger had put a deep flush in her cheeks which accentuated the blue of her eyes, the whiteness of her perfectly shaped teeth.

"Geneviève put snails in my bed. It was horrible."

"My God!" he murmured under his breath. "What pleasure does she get from playing these foolish tricks?"

"She thinks it is very amusing. Her manners are appalling. What can be expected . . . did you know that her dearest friends are the Bastides?"

"I did not know," said the Comte.

"Well, I can assure you it is so. She is constantly there. She tells me that she does not care for any of us here. We are not so pleasant, so amusing, so clever as her dear friend Jean Pierre Bastide. Yes, he is her dearest friend, although she adores the whole family. The Bastides! You know what they are."

"The best winegrowers in the district," said the Comte.

"The girl scuttled into a hasty marriage only a short while ago."

"Such scuttling is not such a rare occurrence in our district, Claude, I do assure you."

"And this wonderful Jean Pierre. He's a gay fellow—so I've heard. Are you going to allow your daughter to behave like a village girl who in a very short time will have to learn to, er . . . scuttle out of an unfortunate position?"

"You are becoming too excited, Claude. Geneviève shall not be allowed to do anything unbecoming. But how does this concern Mademoiselle Lawson?"

"She has fostered this friendship; she accompanies Geneviève to the Bastides'. She is their great friend. That is all very well. It is because she has introduced Geneviève into their circle that I say she must go."

"Go?" said the Comte. "But she hasn't finished the pictures. Moreover she has been talking to me about wall panels."

She went close to him, lifting those wonderful blue eyes to his face.

"Lothair," she said, "please listen to me. I am thinking of Geneviève."

He looked beyond her at me. "You do not say anything, Mademoiselle Lawson."

"I shall be sorry to leave the pictures unfinished."

"That is unthinkable."

"You mean . . . you are on her side?" demanded Claude.

"I mean that I can't see what good Mademoiselle Lawson's going could bring to Geneviève and I *can* see what harm it would bring to my pictures."

She stood back from him. For a moment I thought she was going to strike him; instead she looked as though she were about to burst into tears and turning walked out of the room.

"She is very angry with you," I said.

"With me? I thought it was with you."

"With both of us."

"Geneviève has behaved badly again."

"Yes, I fear so. It was because she was forbidden to go to the Bastides'."

"And you have taken her there?"

"Yes."

"You thought it wise?"

"At one time I thought it very wise. She misses the society of young people. A girl of her age should have friends. It is because she had none that she is so unpredictable . . . given to moods and tantrums, playing these tricks."

"I see, and it was an idea of yours to give her this companionship?"

"Yes. I have seen her very happy at the Bastides'."

"And you also?"

"Yes. I have enjoyed their company very much."

"Jean Pierre has a reputation for being . . . gallant."

"Who has not? Gallantry is as common in this part of your country as the grape." To be in his company made me reckless. I felt I had to discover what his feelings were towards me . . . and how they compared with what he felt for Claude. I said: "I've been thinking that perhaps it would be as well if I left. I could go in, say . . . two weeks. I think I could finish the pictures I have started on by that time. That would satisfy Madame de la Talle, and as Geneviève could scarcely go riding alone to the Bastides', this matter would be neatly settled."

"One cannot run one's life for the sake of neatness, Mademoiselle Lawson."

I laughed, and he laughed with me.

"Now please," he said, "no more talk of leaving us."

"But Madame de la Talle . . ."

"Leave me to deal with her."

He looked at me, and for one glorious moment it seemed as though the mask slipped from his face. He might have been telling me that he could no more bear to lose me than I could bear to go.

When I next saw Geneviève I noticed the sullen set of her lips.

She told me she hated everyone . . . the whole world. Chiefly she hated that woman who called herself Aunt Claude.

"She has forbidden me again to go the Maison Bastide, Miss. And this time Papa was with her. He said I must not go there without permission from him. That means never . . . because he'll never give it."

"He might. If . . ."

"No. She has told him not to, and he does what she tells him. It's strange to think of him doing what anyone tells him . . . but he does what she says."

"I'm sure he doesn't always."

"You don't know, Miss. Sometimes I think you don't know much about anything but speaking English and being a governess."

"Governesses at least have to know a good deal before they can teach."

"Don't try to change the subject, Miss. I hate everybody in this house, I tell you. One day I'll run away."

A few days later I met Jean Pierre. I was riding alone, for Geneviève had avoided me since her outburst.

He came galloping up to me, his expression one of extreme pleasure, as it always was when he saw me.

"Look at those grapes!" he cried. "Did you ever see the like? We shall have wine this year worthy of bottling with the *château* label. If nothing goes wrong," he added hastily, as though placating some god who might be listening and punish him for arrogance. "There's only one other season I remember when they were as good." His expression changed suddenly. "But I might not be here to see this harvest."

"What!"

"Hints so far. But Monsieur le Comte is looking for a good man to send to the Mermoz vineyard, and I am a very good man, so I'm told."

"Leave Gaillard! But how could you do that?"

"Simply by moving myself to Mermoz."

"It's impossible."

"With God and the Comte all things are possible." He was passionately angry suddenly. "Oh don't you see, Dallas, we are of no importance to Monsieur le Comte. We are pawns to be moved this way and that all for the benefit of the games he plays. He does not want me here, shall we say . . . well then, I am moved across the checkerboard to another place. I am a danger here . . . to Monsieur le Comte."

"A danger. How could you be?"

"How can a humble pawn threaten to put the King in check? That is the subtlety of the game. We do not see how we disturb or threaten the peace of mind of the great. But if we do for a moment we are whisked far away. Do you understand?"

"He was very kind to Gabrielle. He settled her in St. Vallient with Jacques."

"Oh, very kind . . ." murmured Jean Pierre.

"And why should he want *you* out of the way?"

"There could be several reasons. It may be because you and Geneviève have visited us."

"Madame de la Talle wanted to dismiss me because of it. In fact she appealed to the Comte."

"And he wouldn't hear of it?"

"He wants his pictures restored."

"Is that all, do you think? Dallas, be careful. He's a dangerous man."

"What do you mean?"

"Women are fascinated by danger, so they tell me. His wife, poor lady, was most unhappy. She was unwanted so she departed."

"What are you trying to tell me, Jean Pierre?"

"To take care," he said. "To take great care." He leaned towards me and taking my hand, kissed it. "It is important to me."

❧ 10 ❧

The atmosphere of the *château* had grown heavy with tension. Geneviève was sullen, and I wondered what was going on in her mind. As for Claude, she was angry and humiliated because the Comte had refused to comply with her wishes, and I sensed her brooding resentment against me. She read a significance in his championing of me—and so did I.

Philippe was uneasy. He came to me when I was in the gallery almost shyly, as though he did not want to be discovered there. I imagined that he was afraid of his wife as well as the Comte.

"I hear that you have had a disagreement with . . . my wife. I'm sorry about it. It's not that I wish you to go, Mademoiselle Lawson. But here in this house . . ." He lifted his shoulders.

"I feel I should finish what I have begun."

"And you will do so . . . soon?"

"Well, there is more to do yet."

"And when it is finished you can rely on me to help if I can . . . but if you should decide to go before, I could probably find you other similar work."

"I will remember."

He went away rather sadly, and I thought: He is a man who is all for peace. He has no spirit. Perhaps that is why he is here.

Yet strangely enough there was a similarity between him and the Comte; his voice was like the Comte's, his features too. Yet one was so positive, the other negative. Philippe must always have lived in the shadow of his rich and powerful relations. Perhaps that had made him the man he was—timidly seeking peace. But he had been kind to me from the first and I believed now that he wanted me to go because of the conflict between myself and his wife.

Perhaps he was right. Perhaps I should leave as soon as I had finished the picture on which I was working. No good could come of my staying here. The emotions the Comte aroused in me could only become more involved; the scars which separation must necessarily inflict would only be deeper.

I will go, I promised myself. And then, because in my heart I was determined not to leave, I began to look for the wall-painting which I suspected might be hidden under the lime-wash that covered the walls. I could become absorbed again in this work and forget the conflicts which swirled about me; and at the same time give myself an excuse for staying at the *château*.

The room I was particularly interested in was a small one leading from the gallery. There was a window facing north which gave an excellent light and from it I could look across the gentle slopes of vineyards in the direction of Paris.

I remembered how excited my father had been on the occasion when he had seen a wall rather similar to this. He had told me then how in many English mansions wall-paintings had been hidden under coats of lime-wash. They had been covered, he said, perhaps because they had been damaged or because the pictures had become no longer pleasing.

The removal of coats of lime-wash—and there could be several—was a delicate operation. I had watched my father perform it and had even helped him; I had a natural flair for this type of work. It is difficult to say, but perhaps it is an instinct—my father had it, and I seemed to have inherited it—but from the moment I had seen that wall I had been excited by it and I was ready to swear that the lime-wash was hiding something.

I set to work with a palette knife, but I could not loosen the outer coat and I could naturally use only the lightest touch; one careless move could ruin what might prove a very valuable painting.

I worked at this for an hour and a half. I knew that it was unwise to work longer, since the utmost concentration was needed, and during that time I had discovered nothing to substantiate my suspicion.

But the next day I was fortunate. I was able to flake away a small piece of lime-wash—no more than about one sixteenth of an inch, it was true, but I was certain on that second day that there was a picture on the wall.

This was indeed the wisest thing I could do for it took my mind from the rising emotional tension of the *château*.

I was working on the wall when Geneviève came into the gallery. "Miss!" she called. "Miss, where are you?"

"Here," I answered.

As she ran in I saw that she was distraught.

"It's a message from Carrefour, Miss. My grandfather is worse. He's asking for me. Come with me."

"Your father . . ."

"He is out . . . riding with *her*. Please, Miss, do come. Otherwise I'll have to go with the groom."

I stood up and said I would change quickly and see her in the stables in ten minutes' time.

"Don't be longer," she begged.

As we rode to Carrefour together she was silent; I knew that she dreaded these visits and yet was fascinated by them.

When we reached the house, Madame Labisse was in the hall waiting for us.

"Ah, Mademoiselle," she said, "I am glad you have come."

"He is very ill?" I asked.

"Another stroke. Maurice found him when he took his *petit déjeuner*. The doctor has been and it was then that I sent for Mademoiselle."

"Do you mean he's . . . dying?" asked Geneviève in a hollow voice.

"We cannot say, Mademoiselle Geneviève. He still lives, but he is very ill."

"May we go to him now?"

"Please come."

"You stay," said Geneviève to me.

We went into that room, which I had seen before. The old man was lying on the pallet, and Madame Labisse had made some attempt at comfort. She had put a coverlet over him and had placed a small table and chairs in the room. There was even a rug on the floor. But the bare walls decorated only by the crucifix and the *prie-dieu* in the corner preserved the appearance of a monk's cell.

He was lying back on the pillows—a pathetic sight, his eyes set in dark caverns and the flesh falling away from each side of his long nose. He looked like a bird of prey.

"It is Mademoiselle Geneviève, Monsieur," murmured Madame Labisse.

An expression flickered over his face so that I guessed he recognized her. His lips moved and his speech was slurred and muffled.

"Granddaughter . . ."

"Yes, Grandfather. I am here."

He nodded, and his eyes were on me. I did not believe he could see with the left one; it seemed dead, but the right was alive.

"Come closer," he said, and Geneviève moved nearer to the bed. But he was looking at me.

"He means you, Miss," whispered Geneviève. So we changed chairs and I took the one nearest him, which seemed to satisfy him.

"Françoise," he said. Then I understood, he was under the impression that I was Geneviève's mother.

"It is all right. Please don't worry," I said.

"Don't . . ." he muttered. "Careful. Watch . . ."

"Yes, yes," I said soothingly.

"Should never have married . . . that man. Knew it was . . . wrong . . ."

"It's all right," I assured him soothingly.

But his face was contorted.

"You must. . . . He must . . ."

"Oh, Miss," said Geneviève, "I can't bear it. I'll come back in a minute. He's rambling. He doesn't know I'm here. Must I stay?"

I shook my head and she went away leaving me in that strange room alone with the dying man. I sensed that he had noticed her disappearance and was relieved. He seemed to make a great effort.

"Françoise. . . . Keep away from him. Do not let him . . ."

He was straining every effort to make me understand; and I was trying to with all my might; for he was talking about the Comte and I felt that in this very room I might discover the secret of Françoise's death. And what I wanted more than anything in the world was to prove that her husband had had no part in it.

"Why?" I said. "Why keep away from him?"

"Such sin . . . such sin," he moaned.

"You must not distress yourself," I said.

"Come back here. . . . Leave the *château*. There is only doom and disaster there . . . for you."

The effort required for such a long speech seemed to have exhausted him. He closed his eyes, and I felt afraid and frustrated for I knew he could have told me so much.

He opened his eyes suddenly.

"Honorine, you're so beautiful. Our child . . . what will become of her? Oh, sin . . . sin."

Exhaustion overcame him. I thought he was dying. I went to the door to call Maurice.

"The end cannot be far off," said Maurice.

Labisse looked at me and nodded.

"Mademoiselle Geneviève should be here."

"I will go and bring her," I said, glad to escape from the room of death.

As I walked along the corridor I was conscious of the gloom. Death was close. I sensed it. But it was more than that. It was like a house from which all light had been excluded, a house in which it had been considered sinful to laugh and be happy. How could poor Françoise have been happy in such a house? How glad she must have been to escape to the castle!

I had reached a staircase and stood at the foot, looking up.

"Geneviève," I called softly.

There was no answer. On a landing was a window the light from which was almost shut out because the heavy curtains were half drawn across it. I imagined this was how they always were kept. I went to them and looked out at the overgrown garden. I tried to open the window, but could not do so. It must have been years since anyone had opened it.

I was hoping to see Geneviève in the garden and sign to her; but she was not there.

I called her name again; there was still no reply, so I started up the stairs.

The stillness of the house closed in on me. I wondered whether Geneviève was hiding in one of those rooms, keeping away from the sickroom because she hated the thought of death. It was like her to run away from what she found intolerable. Perhaps that was at the root of her trouble. I must make her see that if she was afraid of something it was better to look it straight in the face.

"Geneviève!" I called. "Where are you?"

I opened a door. It was a dark bedroom, the curtains half drawn as they were on the landing. I shut the door and opened another. This part of the house could not have been used for years.

There was another flight of stairs and this I guessed would lead to the nurseries, for these were usually at the top of the house.

In spite of what was happening in the room far below I was thinking also of the childhood of Françoise of which I had read in those notebooks which Nounou doled out one by one. It occurred to me then that Geneviève had probably listened to stories of her mother's childhood in this house and if she wanted to hide, where would she be more likely to come than to the nurseries?

I was certain that I should find her up here.

"Geneviève," I called more loudly than before. "Are you up here?"

No answer. Only a faint return of my own voice like a ghostly echo to mock me. If she was there, she was not going to let me know.

I opened the door. Before me was a room which, though lofty, was not large. There was a pallet on the floor, a table, a chair, a *priedieu* at one end and a crucifix on the wall. It was furnished as that room in which the old man now lay. But there was a difference about this room. Across the only window which was high in the wall were bars. The room was like a prison cell. I knew instinctively that it *was* a prison cell.

I felt an impulse to shut the door and hurry away; but curiosity was too strong. I entered the room. What was this house? I asked myself. Was it conducted like a monastery, a convent? I knew that Geneviève's grandfather regretted he had not become a monk. The "treasure" in the chest explained that—a monk's robe was his dearest possession. I had learned that from the first of Françoise's notebooks. And the whip? Had he scourged himself . . . or his wife and daughter?

And who had lived here? In this room someone had awakened every morning to that barred window; those bleak walls, to this austerity. Had he . . . or she . . . desired it? Or . . .

I noticed the scratching on the distempered walls. I looked closer. "Honorine," I read, "the prisoner."

So I was right. It was a prison. Here she had been detained against her will. She was like those people who had lived in the dungeons at the *château*.

I heard the sound of slow padding steps on the stairs. I stood very still, waiting. Those were not Geneviève's steps.

Someone was on the other side of the door. I heard distinctly the sound of breathing, and I went swiftly to the door and pulled it open.

The woman looked at me with wide incredulous eyes.

"Mademoiselle!" she cried.

"I was looking for Geneviève, Madame Labisse," I told her.

"I heard someone up here. I wondered . . . you are wanted downstairs. The end is very near."

"And Geneviève?"

"I believe she is hiding in the garden."

"It is understandable," I said. "The young do not wish to look on death. I thought I might find her in the nurseries, which I guessed would be up here."

"The nurseries are on the lower floor."

"And this . . . ?" I began.

"This was Mademoiselle Geneviève's grandmother's room."

I looked up at the barred window.

"I looked after her until she died," said Madame Labisse.

"She was very ill?"

Madame Labisse nodded coldly. I was too inquisitive, she seemed to be telling me. In the past she had not given secrets away, for she was paid well to keep them; and she was not going to jeopardize her future by betraying them now.

"Mademoiselle Geneviève is certainly not up here," she said; and turning she left the room. I had no alternative but to follow her.

She was right; Geneviève was hiding in the garden. It was only after her grandfather was dead that she returned to the house.

The family went over to Carrefour for the funeral, which was, I heard, carried out with the pomp usual on such occasions. I stayed behind. Nounou did not go either; she had one of her headaches, she said, and when she had one of them she was fit for nothing but her own bed. I guessed the occasion would have aroused too many painful memories for her.

Geneviève went over in the carriage with her father, Philippe, and Claude; and when they had left I went along to see Nounou.

I found her, as I expected, not in bed; and I asked if I could stay and talk with her awhile.

She replied that she would be glad of my company, so I made the coffee and we sat together.

The subject of Carrefour and the past was one which both fascinated and frightened her and she was half evasive, half eager.

"I don't think Geneviève wanted to go to the funeral," I said.

She shook her head. "I wish she need not have gone."

"But it was expected of her. She is growing up—scarcely a child any more. How do you think she is? Less inclined to tantrums? More calm?"

"She was always calm enough . . ." lied Nounou.

I looked at her sadly and she looked sadly back. I wanted to tell her that we should get nowhere by pretense.

"When I was last at the house I saw her grandmother's room. It was very strange. It was like a prison. And she felt it too."

"How can you know?" she demanded.

"Because she said so."

Her eyes were round with horror. "She . . . told you. . . . How . . ."

I shook my head. "She did not return from the dead if that's what you're thinking. She wrote on the wall that she was a prisoner. I saw it. 'Honorine, the prisoner.' Was she a prisoner? You would know. You were there."

"She was ill. She had to stay in her room."

"What a strange room for an invalid . . . right at the top of the house. It must have made a lot of work for the servants . . . carrying to her up there."

"You are very practical, Miss. You think of such things."

"I should think the servants thought of it, too. But why should she think of herself as a prisoner? Wasn't she allowed to go out?"

"She was ill."

"Invalids are not prisoners. Nounou, tell me about it. I feel it's important . . . to Geneviève perhaps."

"How could it be? What are you driving at, Miss?"

"To understand all is to know all, they say. I want to help Geneviève. I want to make her happy. She's had an unusual upbringing. That place where her mother lived and then this castle . . . and everything that happened. You must see that all that could affect a child . . . an impressionable, highly strung child. I want you to help me to help her."

"I would do anything in the world to help her."

"Please tell me all you know, Nounou."

"But I know nothing . . . nothing . . ."

"But Françoise wrote in her notebooks, didn't she? You haven't shown them all to me."

"She didn't intend anyone to see them."

"Nounou . . . there are others, aren't there . . . more revealing . . . ?"

She sighed and taking the key from the chain at her waist she unlocked her cupboard.

She selected a notebook and gave it to me. I noticed from where she took it. There was another there—the last in the line—and I hoped that she would give me that too. But she didn't.

"Take it away and read it," she said. "And bring it straight back to me. Promise you'll show no one else and bring it straight back."

I promised.

This was different. This was the woman in great fear. She was afraid of her husband. As I read I could not rid myself of the feeling that I was spying into the mind and heart of a dead woman. But he was concerned in this. What would he think of me if he knew what I was doing?

Yet I must read on. With every day I spent in the *château* it was becoming more and more important for me to know the truth.

"*I lay in bed last night praying that he would not come to me. Once I thought I heard his step, but it was only Nounou. She knows how I feel. She hovers . . . praying with me, I know. I am afraid of him. He knows it. He cannot understand why. Other women are so fond of him. Only I am afraid.*"

"*I saw Papa today. He looked at me as he often does, as though he would look deep into my mind, as though he is trying to discover every moment of my life . . . but mostly that. 'How is your husband?' he says to me. And I stammer and blush, for I know what he is thinking. He said: 'There are other women, I have heard.' And I did not*" answer. He seemed pleased that there were. 'The devil will take care of him for God will not,' he said. Yet he seems pleased that there are other women and I know why. Anything is preferable to my being sullied."

"Nounou prowls about. She is very frightened. I am so afraid of the nights. I find it so hard to get to sleep. Then I awake startled and fancy someone has come into the room. It's an unnatural marriage. I wish I were a little girl again playing in the nursery. The best time was before Papa showed me the treasure in the trunk . . . before Maman died. I wish I didn't have to grow up. But then of course I should never have had Geneviève."

"Geneviève flew into a passion today. It was because Nounou said she must stay indoors. She has a slight cold and Nounou was worried. She locked Nounou in her room and the poor creature waited patiently there until I went to find her. She didn't want to betray Geneviève. We were both frightened afterwards when we scolded Geneviève. She was so . . . wild and naughty. I said she reminded me of her grandmother and Nounou was so upset by her naughtiness."

"Nounou said, 'Never say that again, Françoise dear. Never, never.' I realized she meant what I had said of Geneviève's being like her grandmother."

"Last night I awoke in a fright. I thought Lothair had come into the room. I saw Papa during the day. He made me more frightened than usual, perhaps. It was a dream. It was not Lothair. Why should he come? He knows I hate his coming. He no longer tries to make me see life from his way. I know that is because he does not care for me. He is glad to escape. I am sure of it. But I dreamed he was there and it was a horrible nightmare, for I believed he would be cruel to me. But it was only a dream. Nounou came in. She had been lying awake listening, she said. I said, 'I can't sleep, Nounou. I'm frightened,' so she gave me some laudanum. She uses it for her headaches. She says it takes the pain away and makes her sleep. So I took it and I slept, and in the morning it all seemed like a nightmare . . . nothing more. He would never force himself on me now. He doesn't care enough. There are the others."

"I told Nounou I had a raging toothache, and she gave me laudanum. It is such a comfort to know that when I can't sleep there it is in the bottle waiting to help me."

"A sudden thought came to me today. It can't be true. But it could be. I wonder if it is. I am frightened that it might be . . . and yet in a way I'm not. I shan't tell anyone yet . . . certainly not Papa; he would be horrified. He loathes anything to do with it, although he is my father, which is strange, so it could not always have been so. I shan't tell Lothair . . . not until it is necessary. I shan't even tell Nounou. Not yet in any case. But she'll find out sooner or later. Well, I'll wait and see. I may be imagining it."

"Geneviève came in this morning a little late. She had overslept. I was quite frightened that something might have happened to her. When she came she just ran to me; she sobbed when we hugged each other and I couldn't calm her down. Dear Geneviève. I should love to tell her but not yet . . . oh no, not yet."

That was the end, and I had not discovered what I wanted to know; but there was one thing I had discovered—that the important notebook was the last one, the one I had seen in Nounou's cupboard. Why had she not given me that one?

I went back to her room. She was lying on the couch, her eyes closed.

"Nounou," I said, "what was it . . . the secret? What did it mean? What was she afraid of?"

She said: "I'm in such pain. You've no idea how these headaches affect me."

"I'm sorry. Is there anything I can do?"

"Nothing . . . there is nothing to be done but to keep quiet."

"There is the last book," I said. "The one she wrote in before she died. Perhaps the answer is in that book . . ."

"There is nothing," she said. "Will you draw the curtains? The light hurts me."

I laid the notebook on the table near her couch, drew the curtains and went out.

But I had to see that last notebook. I was sure it would give me some

229

clue as to what had really happened in the days before Françoise's death.

During the next day I made such a discovery that I almost forgot my desire to see the notebook. I had been working patiently on the suspected wall-painting, very cautiously flaking off pieces of lime-wash with a fine ivory paper-knife, when I uncovered . . . paint! My heart began to hammer with excitement, my fingers to tremble. I had to restrain the impulse to work on fervently. This I dared not do. I was far too excited and I could not trust myself. If it were true that I was on the point of discovering a wall-painting—and I believed this could well be—my hands must be absolutely steady; I should have to curb this wild excitement.

I stood a few paces back, my eyes fixed on that magic fraction of what I believed to be paint. There was a film over it which might be difficult to remove, so it was not easy to assess the color. But it was there . . . I was sure of it.

I did not want to say anything until I was sure what I was about to discover would be worthwhile.

During the next days I worked almost furtively, but as I revealed little by little I became more and more certain that I was about to expose a painting of some value.

I was determined that the first to hear of this should be the Comte; and in the middle of the morning I left my tools in the gallery and went along to the library in the hope of finding him. He was not there, and, as I had done on a previous occasion, I rang the bell and when the servant appeared I asked that Monsieur le Comte should be told that I wished to speak to him urgently in the library.

I was told that he had left for the stables a few moments before.

"Please go and tell him that I want to see him at once. It is most important."

When I was alone I wondered if I had been too impulsive. After all, perhaps he would think such an item of news could wait until a more propitious moment. It might be that he would not share my excitement. But he must, I told myself. After all the picture had been found in his house.

I heard his voice in the hall; and the door of the library was flung open and he stood there looking at me in some surprise. He was dressed for riding and had clearly come straight from the stables.

"What is it?" he asked; and in that moment I realized he was expecting to hear that something had happened to Geneviève.

"A most important discovery! Can you come and look at it now? There is a picture under the lime-wash after all . . . and I think there is no doubt that it is a valuable one."

"Oh," he said; and then his lips betrayed some amusement. "Of course I must come."

"I have interrupted something . . ."

"My dear Mademoiselle Lawson, such an important discovery must come before all else, I'm sure."

"Please come and see."

I led the way to that small room which led from the gallery, and there it was—just a small part exposed, but there was no doubt that it was a hand lying on velvet and on the fingers and at the wrist were jewels.

"It is a little somber at the moment but you can see it is in need of cleaning. It's a portrait, and you can tell by the way the paint has been put on . . . and the fold of that velvet . . . that a master has been at work."

"You mean, my dear Mademoiselle Lawson, that *you* can."

"Isn't it wonderful?" I said to him.

He looked into my face and smiling said: "Wonderful."

I felt vindicated. I was certain there had been something there under the lime-wash and all those hours of work were not in vain.

"There is very little so far . . ." he went on.

"Oh, but it's there. Now I have to make sure that I mustn't get too excited, which could mean impatient. I am longing to expose the rest, but I must go to work very carefully. I have to be sure not to damage it in any way."

He laid his hand on my shoulder. "I am very grateful to you."

"Perhaps now you are not sorry you decided to trust your pictures to a woman."

"I quickly learned that you are a woman to whom I would trust a great deal."

The pressure of his hand on my shoulder; the brilliance of those

231

hooded eyes, the joy of discovery were intoxicating. I thought recklessly: This is the happiest moment of my life.

"Lothair!" It was Claude standing there frowning at us. "What on earth has happened? You were there . . . and then you suddenly disappeared."

He dropped his hand and turned to her. "I had a message," he said. "An urgent message. Mademoiselle Lawson has made a miraculous discovery."

"What?" She came towards us and looked from him to me.

"A most miraculous discovery!" he repeated, looking at me.

"What is this all about?"

"Look!" said the Comte. "She has uncovered a painting . . . a valuable one apparently."

"That! It looks like a smudge of paint."

"You say that, Claude, because you do not see it with the artist's eye. Now Mademoiselle Lawson tells me that it is part of a portrait by an artist of great talent because of the way the paint is put on."

"You have forgotten that we are riding this morning."

"Such a discovery makes my forgetfulness excusable, don't you agree, Mademoiselle Lawson?"

"It is very rarely that such discoveries are made," I replied.

"We are late already," said Claude, without looking at me.

"You must tell me more some other time, Mademoiselle Lawson," said the Comte, as he followed her to the door; but as he reached it, he turned to smile at me. Claude saw the look which passed between us and I was aware of the intensity of her dislike. She had failed to get rid of me; that in itself must have been a great blow to her dignity for she had been so sure of her power. She would hate me for that. Why had she been so anxious for me to go? Could it be that she was actually jealous of me?

That thought was almost more intoxicating than anything else that had happened.

During the next few days I worked with an intensity that I knew to be dangerous; but by the end of three days I had uncovered more of the figure and, as each inch was exposed, I grew more and more certain that I was right in thinking that the painting was valuable.

One morning, however, I had a shock, for when I was working on one part of the lime-wash I uncovered something I could not understand. A letter emerged. There was writing on the wall. Something which might confirm the date of the painting? My hand was trembling. Perhaps I should have stopped work until I felt more calm, but that would be asking too much. I had uncovered the letters BLI. I worked carefully round them and I had *oubliez*, I could not give up. Before the morning was over, by working with great care I had the words *Ne m'oubliez pas*. Forget me not. I was certain too that they had been painted at a much later date than the portrait which was now half exposed.

It was something to show the Comte. He came to the room and we examined it together. He shared my excitement or made a good pretense of doing so.

The door opened behind me. I was smiling as I carefully pressed the edge of the knife to the border of the lime-wash. He is growing as excited by this discovery as I am and finding it difficult to keep away, I thought.

There was a deep silence in the room, and as I turned the smile must have faded quickly from my face, for it was not the Comte who stood there but Claude.

She gave me a half smile which seemed to cover a certain embarrassment. I could not understand this new mood.

"I heard you had uncovered some words," she said. "May I see?" She came close to the wall and peered at it murmuring: "*Ne m'oubliez pas.*" Then she turned to me, her eyes puzzled. "How did you know it was there?"

"It's an instinct perhaps."

"Mademoiselle Lawson . . ." She hesitated as though she found it difficult to say what was in her mind. "I'm afraid I've been rather hasty. The other day. . . . You see, I was alarmed for Geneviève."

"Yes, I understand."

"And I thought . . . I thought that the best thing . . ."

"Would be for me to go?"

"It wasn't only Geneviève."

I was taken aback. Was she going to confide in me? Was she going to tell me that she was jealous of the Comte's regard for me. Impossible!

233

"You may not believe me, but I was thinking of you, too. My husband has spoken to me of you. We both feel that . . ." She frowned and looked at me helplessly. "We feel you might want to get away."

"Why?"

"There could be reasons. I just wanted you to know that I've heard of a possibility . . . a really exciting one. Between us, my husband and I could probably arrange a brilliant opportunity for you. I know how interested you are in old buildings, and I daresay you would welcome the chance to examine in detail some of our old churches and abbeys. And of course the picture galleries."

"I should, of course, but . . ."

"Well, we have heard of a little project. A party of ladies are planning a tour to inspect the treasures of France. They want a guide—someone who has a deep knowledge of what they will see. Naturally they would not want a man to accompany them and so they thought that if there were such a lady who could conduct them and explain to them. . . . It's a unique chance. It would be well paid and I can assure you it would lead to excellent opportunities. It would enhance your reputation and I know give you an entry into many of our oldest families. You would be in great demand, for the ladies who wish to make this tour are all art fanciers and have collections of their own. It seems such an excellent opportunity."

I was amazed. She was certainly eager to be rid of me. Yes, indeed she must be jealous!

"It sounds a fascinating project," I said. "But this work . . ." I waved my hand towards the wall.

"You will finish it shortly. Consider this project. I really think you should."

She was like a different person. There was a new gentleness about her. I could almost believe that she was genuinely concerned for me. I thought of making a minute examination of the treasures of France; I thought of discussing these with people who were as interested in them as I was. She could not have offered a more dazzling bait.

"I can get more details for you," she said eagerly. "You will think about it, Mademoiselle Lawson?"

She hesitated again as though she would say more and, deciding against it, left me.

234

I was puzzled. She was either a jealous woman who was ready to go to great lengths to be rid of me, or she was warning me against the Comte. She might be implying: Be careful. See how he uses women. Myself . . . married to Philippe for *his* convenience; Gabrielle married to Jacques. What will happen to *you* if you stay here and let him govern your life for that little while it pleases him to do so?

But in my heart I believed she suspected the Comte had some regard for me and wanted me out of the way. It was an exhilarating thought. But . . . for how long? Then I thought of the proposition she had laid before me. It was one which an ambitious woman eager to advance in her profession would be foolish to reject. It was a chance which came once in a lifetime.

When I thought of that—and the possibilities the future held for me here in the *château,* I was tormented with doubts and fears and the hopes of wild, and what my good sense told me were hopeless, impossibilities.

I called on Gabrielle. She was noticeably pregnant, but she seemed very happy. We talked about the coming baby and she showed me the layette she was preparing.

I asked after Jacques and then she talked to me more frankly than she had before.

"Having a baby changes you. The things that seem important before no longer seem anything but trivial. The child is all-important. I can't understand now why I was so frightened. If I had told Jacques we could have arranged something. But I was so scared . . . and now it all seems so foolish."

"What does Jacques feel?"

"He scolds me for being so foolish. But I was afraid because we'd wanted to marry for so long and we knew we couldn't because we had his mother to support. We just could not have managed to live . . . the three of us."

How stupid I had been to suspect the Comte was the father of her child. How could she have been so radiantly happy if this had been the case.

"But for the Comte . . ." I said.

"Ah, but for the Comte!" She was smiling placidly.

"It seems strange to me that you could not tell Jacques but you could tell *him*."

Again that smile. "Oh no. He would understand. I knew it. Besides he was the one who could help . . . and he did. Jacques and I will always be grateful to him."

This meeting with Gabrielle did something to lift the indecision which Claude's offer had brought to me. I would not leave the *château* until it was absolutely necessary, no matter how dazzling the prospects laid before me.

Now I had two overwhelming interests: to uncover what lay beneath the lime-wash and to reveal the true character of the man who was beginning to mean so much—far too much—in my life.

The words "Forget me not" had been intriguing, and I was hoping to uncover more, but I did not. What I did uncover was the face of a dog which appeared to be crouching at the feet of the woman of whom the painting was going to prove a portrait. It was while I was working in this section that I discovered paint which I thought might be part of a later work. I suffered moments of horror because I knew it was a practice to cover old paintings with a layer of lime-wash and repaint on the new layer; in which case I might have destroyed a picture which had been painted over the one on which I was working.

I could only go on with what I had begun, and to my amazement, in an hour I had revealed that what seemed like a painting was something which had been added to the original picture—although at a later date.

It was extraordinary, and it grew more so, for the dog was revealed to be in a case which was the shape of a coffin; and beneath this were those words, "Forget me not."

I laid down my knife and looked at it. The dog was a spaniel like the one in the miniature which the Comte had given me at Christmas. I was certain that this was a portrait of the same woman—the subject of the first picture I had cleaned, of my miniature, and now the wall-painting.

I wanted to show this to the Comte, so I went to the library. Claude was there alone. She looked up hopefully when she saw me, and I realized immediately that she thought I had come to accept her offer.

"I was looking for the Comte," I said.

Her face hardened and the old dislike was visible. "Did you propose to *send* for him?"

"I thought he would be interested to look at the wall."

"When I see him I will tell him you sent for him."

I pretended not to see the mockery.

"Thank you," I said, and went back to my work.

But the Comte did not come.

Geneviève had a birthday in June which was celebrated by a dinner party at the *château*. I did not attend it although Geneviève had invited me. I made excuses, knowing full well that Claude, who was after all the hostess, had no desire for my presence.

Geneviève herself did not mind whether I went or not; nor it seemed, to my chagrin, did the Comte. It was a very lukewarm affair and Geneviève was almost sullen about it.

I had bought her a pair of gray gloves which she had admired in one of the town's shop windows, and she did say she was pleased with them, but she was in one of her gloomy moods, and I felt that it would have been better not to have celebrated a birthday in such circumstances.

The day after we went riding together, and I asked how she had enjoyed the party.

"I didn't," she declared. "It was hateful. What's the good of having a party when you don't invite the guests. I would have liked a real party . . . perhaps with a cake and a crown in it . . ."

"That's not a birthday custom."

"What does it matter? In any case there must be birthday customs. I expect Jean Pierre would know. I'll ask him."

"You know what your Aunt Claude feels about your friendship with the Bastides."

Fury broke out all over her face. "I tell you I shall choose my own friends. I'm grown up now. They'll have to realize it. I'm fifteen . . ."

"It's not really such a great age."

"You're just as bad as the rest of them."

For a few moments I saw her stormy profile before she broke into a gallop and was away. I tried to follow her but she was determined I shouldn't.

After a while I rode back to the *château* alone; I was very uneasy about Geneviève.

The hot days of July passed like a dream to me; August had come, and the grapes were just ripening in the sun. As I passed the vineyards one of the workers would usually comment on them. "A good harvest this year, Mademoiselle."

In the *pâtisserie* where now and then I took coffee and a slice of the *gâteau de la maison,* Madame Latière talked to me of the size of the grapes. They would be sweetened by all the sunshine they had had this year.

The harvest was almost upon us, and it seemed that the thoughts of all were on it. It was a kind of climax. I still had work to do on the wall-painting; and there were pictures still to be cleaned; but I could not stay indefinitely at the *château.* Was I being foolish to reject Claude's offer?

But I refused to think of leaving the *château;* I had lived in it for about ten months, but I felt that I had never truly been alive before I had come; and a life away from it seemed impossible, vague, no life at all. Nothing, however interesting, could compensate me if I went away.

Often I recalled the conversations which had taken place between us and asked myself if I had read something into them which did not exist; I was not sure whether the Comte had been mocking me, in truth telling me to mind my own business, or whether he had been telling me obliquely of his regard for me.

I threw myself into the life of the *château,* and when I heard of the annual *kermesse* I wanted to play my part.

It was Geneviève who told me.

"You ought to have a stall, Miss. What will you sell? You've never been to a *kermesse* before, have you?"

I told her that they occurred regularly in our villages and towns. I had made all sorts of things for our church bazaars and I imagined that a *kermesse* was not very different from these.

She wanted to hear about this and when I told her she was delighted, agreeing that I was very well acquainted with what went on at a *kermesse.*

I had a notion for painting flowers on cups and saucers and ash trays. And when I had completed a few and shown them to Geneviève, she laughed with pleasure. "But, Miss, that's wonderful. They've never had anything like it at our *kermesse* before." I painted enthusiastically—not only flowers but animals on mugs—little elephants, rabbits, and cats. Then I had the idea of painting names on the mugs. Geneviève would sit beside me telling me what names I should do. I did Yves and Margot, of course; and she named other children who would most certainly be at the *kermesse*.

"That's a certain sale," she cried. "They won't be able to resist buying mugs with their own names on. May I be at your stall? Trade will be so brisk you'll need an assistant."

I was very happy to see her so enthusiastic.

"Papa will be here for this *kermesse*," she told me. "I don't remember his being here for one before."

"Why was he not here?"

"Oh, he was always in Paris . . . or somewhere. He has been here more than ever before. I heard the servants talking about it. It is since his accident."

"Oh?" I said, attempting to appear unconcerned.

Perhaps, I reminded myself caustically, it is because Claude is here.

I talked of the *kermesse*; I thought of the *kermesse*; and I was delighted because Geneviève shared my excitement and recalled previous ones.

"This," I said, "must be the most successful of all."

"It will be, Miss. We have never had mugs with children's names on before. The money we make goes to the convent. I shall tell the Holy Mother that she has to be grateful to you, Miss."

"*Il ne faut pas vendre la peau de l'ours avant de l'avoir tué,*" I reminded her. And added in English: "We mustn't count our chickens before they're hatched."

She was smiling at me, thinking I knew that whatever the occasion I would always play the governess.

One afternoon when we were returning from our ride I had the idea of using the moat. I had never explored it before, so we went down there together. The grass was green and lush; and I suggested that it would be original to have the stalls there.

Geneviève thought it an excellent idea. "Everything should be different this time, Miss. We've never used the old moat before, but of course it's ideal. How warm it is down here!"

"It's sheltered from all the breezes," I said. "Can you imagine the stalls against the gray walls?"

"I'm sure it'll be fun. We will have it here. Do you feel shut in down here, Miss?"

I saw what she meant. It was so silent, and the tall gray walls of the *château* so close were overpowering.

We had walked all round the *château* and I was wondering whether my suggestion to have the stalls here on the uneven ground of the dried-up moat had not been rather hastily made, considering how much more comfortable one of the well-kept lawns would be, when I saw the cross. It was stuck in the earth close to the granite wall of the *château*, and I pointed it out to Geneviève.

She was on her hands and knees examining it and I joined her.

"There's some writing on it," she said.

We bent over to examine it.

I read out: "'Fidèle, 1747.' It's a grave," I added. "A dog's grave."

Geneviève raised her eyes to me. "All those years ago! Fancy."

"I believe he's the dog on my miniature."

"Oh yes, the one Papa gave you for Christmas. Fidèle! What a nice name."

"His mistress must have loved him to bury him like that . . . with a cross and his name and the date."

Geneviève nodded.

"Somehow," she said, "it makes a difference. It makes the moat a sort of graveyard."

I nodded.

"I don't think we would want to have the *kermesse* down there where poor Fidèle is buried."

I agreed. "And we should all be badly bitten, too. There are lots of unpleasant insects in this long grass."

We entered a door of the *château* and as the cool of those thick walls closed in on us, she said: "I'm glad we found poor Fidèle's grave though, Miss."

"Yes," I said, "so am I."

The day of the *kermesse* was hot and sunny. Marquees had been set up on one of the lawns and early in the morning the stall holders arrived to set out their wares. Geneviève worked with me to make ours gay; she had spread a white cloth over the counter and had decorated it most tastefully with leaves, and on this we set out our painted crockery.

It looked very charming, and I secretly agreed with Geneviève that ours was the most outstanding of all the stalls. Madame Latière from the *pâtisserie* was supplying refreshments in a tent; needlework figured largely in the goods for sale; there were flowers from the *château* gardens; cakes, vegetables, ornaments, and pieces of jewelry. Claude would rival us, Geneviève told me, because she would sell some of her clothes, and she had wardrobes full of them; of course everyone would want to wear her clothes, which they knew came from Paris.

The local musicians, led by Armand Bastide and his violin, would play intermittently all the afternoon, and when it was dusk the dancing would begin.

I was certainly proud of my mugs, and the first buyers were the Bastide children who shrieked delightedly when they found their own names, as though they were there by a coincidence; and as I provided plain mugs to be painted with any names which were not already on display, I was kept busy.

The *kermesse* was opened by the Comte—and this in itself made it a special occasion—for as I was told several times in the first half hour it was the first *kermesse* he had attended for years. "Not since the death of the Comtesse." This was significant, said some. It meant that the Comte had decided that life should be more normal at the *château*.

Nounou came by and insisted that I paint a mug with her name on it. I worked under a blue sunshade which spread itself over our stall; I was conscious of the hot sun, the smell of flowers, the jumble of voices and constant laughter, and I was very happy under that blue sunshade.

The Comte came by and stood watching me at work.

Geneviève said: "Oh, Papa, isn't she good at it? The quick way she does it. You must have one with your name on it."

"Yes, certainly I must," he agreed.

"Your name isn't here, Papa. You didn't do a Lothair, Miss?"

"No, I didn't think we should need one."

"You were wrong there, Mademoiselle Lawson."

"Yes," agreed Geneviève gleefully as though she, as much as her father, enjoyed seeing that I could make a mistake. "You were wrong there."

"It's a wrong which can quickly be remedied if the commission is serious," I retorted.

"It's very serious."

He leaned against the counter while I selected one of the plain mugs.

"Have you any preference for color?"

"Please choose for me. I am sure your taste is excellent."

I looked at him steadily. "Purple I think, purple and gold."

"Royal colors?" he asked.

"Most appropriate," I retaliated.

A little crowd had collected to watch me paint a mug for the Comte. There was a little whispering among the watchers.

I felt as though the blue umbrella sheltered me from all that was unpleasant. Yes, I was certainly happy on that afternoon.

There was his name in royal purple—the *i* dotted with a touch of gold paint, and a full stop after the name also in gold.

There was an exclamation of admiration from those who looked on, and somewhat deliriously I painted a gold *fleur-de-lis* below the name.

"There," I said. "Isn't that fitting?"

"You must pay for it, Papa."

"If Mademoiselle Lawson will name the price."

"A little more, I think, don't you, Miss, because after all it *is* a special one."

"A great deal more, I think."

"I am in your hands."

There was an exclamation of amazement as the Comte dropped his payment into the bowl Geneviève had placed on the counter. I was sure it meant that we should have the largest donation to the Convent.

Geneviève was pink with pleasure. I believe she was almost as happy as I was.

As the Comte moved on I saw Jean Pierre at my side. "I would like a mug," he said, "and a *fleur-de-lis* also."

"Please do one for him, Miss," pleaded Geneviève, smiling up at him.

So I did.

Then everyone was asking for *fleurs-de-lis* and mugs already sold were brought back.

"It will cost more for the *fleur-de-lis*," cried Geneviève in triumph.

And I painted and Geneviève grew pinker with pleasure, while Jean Pierre stood by smiling at us.

It had been a triumph. My mugs had earned more than any other stall. Everyone was talking about it.

And with the dusk the musicians began to play, and there was dancing on the lawn and in the hall for those who preferred it.

This was the way it always was, Geneviève told me, yet there had never been a *kermesse* like this one.

The Comte had disappeared. His duties did not extend beyond being present at the *kermesse*; Claude and Philippe had left too; I found myself wistfully looking for the Comte, hoping that he would return and seek me out.

Jean Pierre was at my side. "Well, what do you think of our rural pleasures?"

"That they are very much like the rural pleasures I have known all my life."

"I'm glad of that. Will you dance with me?"

"I shall be pleased to."

"Shall we go onto the lawn? It is so hot in here. It's much more pleasant to dance under the stars."

He took my hand and led me in the dreamy waltz which the musicians had started to play.

"Life here interests you," he said, and his lips were so close to my ear that he seemed to whisper. "But you cannot stay here forever. You have your own home . . ."

"I have no home. Only Cousin Jane is left."

"I do not think I like Cousin Jane."

"But why not?"

"Because you do not. I hear it in your voice."

"Do I betray my feelings so easily?"

"I understand you a little. I hope to understand you more, for we are good friends, aren't we?"

"I hope so."

"We have been very happy . . . my family and I . . . that you should treat us as friends. Please tell me, what shall you do when the work at the *château* is finished?"

"I shall leave here, of course. But it is not yet finished."

"And they are pleased with you . . . up at the *château*. That is obvious. Monsieur le Comte looked this afternoon as though he approved of . . . of you."

"Yes, I think he is pleased. I flatter myself that I have done good work on his pictures."

He nodded. "You must not leave us, Dallas," he said. "You must stay with us. We could not be happy if you went away . . . none of us. Myself especially."

"You are so kind . . ."

"I will always be kind to you . . . for the rest of our lives. I could never be happy again if you went away. I am asking you to stay here always . . . with me."

"Jean Pierre!"

"I want you to marry me. I want you to assure me that you will never leave me . . . never leave us. This is where you belong. Don't you know it, Dallas?"

I had stopped short and he had slipped his arm through mine to draw me into the shelter of one of the trees.

"This could not be," I said.

"Why not? Tell me why not."

"I am fond of you . . . I shall never forget your kindness to me when I first came here . . ."

"But, you are telling me, you do not love me?"

"I'm telling you that although I am fond of you I don't think I should make you a good wife."

"But you do like me, Dallas?"

"Of course."

"I knew it. And I will not ask you to say Yes or No now. Because it may be that you are not ready."

"Jean Pierre, you must understand that I . . ."

"I understand, my dearest."

"I don't think you do."

"I shall not press the matter, but you will not leave us. And you will stay as my wife . . . because you could not bear to leave us . . . and in time . . . in time, my Dallas . . . you will see."

He took my hand and kissed it quickly.

"Do not protest," he said. "You belong with us. And there can be no one else for you but me."

Geneviève's voice broke in on my disturbed thoughts.

"Oh, there you are, Miss. I was looking for you. Oh, Jean Pierre, you must dance with me. You promised you would."

He smiled at me; I saw the lift of the eyebrows—as expressive as that of the shoulders.

As I watched him dance away with Geneviève, I was vaguely apprehensive. For the first time in my life I had received a proposal of marriage. I was bewildered. I could never marry Jean Pierre. How could I when . . .

It was disconcerting, particularly as I had a feeling that he had spoken before he was ready to do so, that he had not meant to propose to me . . . yet. Then why? Was it because I had betrayed my feelings? Could it be that as he stood at my stall that afternoon, the Comte had betrayed his?

The joy had gone out of the day. I was glad when the dancing was over, when the "Marseillaise" had been played and the revelers went home and I to my room in the *château* to think of the past and grope blindly towards the future.

I found it difficult to work the next day, and I was afraid that I should damage the wall-painting if I continued in this absent-minded mood. So I accomplished little that morning, but my thoughts were busy. It seemed incredible that I, who since my abortive affair with Charles had never had a lover, should now be attractive to two men, one of whom had actually asked me to marry him. But it was the Comte's intentions that occupied my thoughts. He had looked younger, almost gay when he had stood by the stall yesterday. I was certain in that moment that he could be happy; and I believed that I was the one to make him so. What presumption! The most he could be thinking of was one of those light love affairs in which it seemed he indulged from time to time. No, I was sure that was not true.

After I had taken breakfast in my room, Geneviève burst in on me. She looked at least four years older because she had pinned up her long hair into a coil on the top of her head which made her taller and more graceful.

"Geneviève, what *have* you done?" I cried.

She burst into loud laughter. "Do you like it?"

"You look . . . older."

"That's what I want. I'm tired of being treated like a child."

"Who does treat you so?"

"Everybody. You, Nounou, Papa . . . Uncle Philippe, and his hateful Claude . . . just everybody. You haven't said whether you like it."

"I don't think it . . . suitable."

That made her laugh. "Well, I think it is, Miss, and that is how I shall wear it in future. I'm not a child any more. My grandmother married when she was only a year older."

I looked at her in astonishment. Her eyes were gleaming with excitement. She looked wild; and I felt very uneasy, but I could see it would be useless to talk to her.

I went along to see Nounou, and asked after her headaches. She said they had troubled her less during the last few days.

"I'm a little anxious about Geneviève," I told her. The startled look came into her eyes. "She's put her hair up. And she no longer looks like the child she is."

"She is growing up. Her mother was so different . . . always so gentle. She seemed a child even after Geneviève's birth."

"She said that her grandmother was married when she was sixteen . . . almost as though she were planning to do the same."

"It's her way," said Nounou.

And I realized that I had been rather intense about a perfectly ordinary matter. Lots of girls of fifteen were tired of being children: lots of them tried wearing their hair up, which was something most girls did on their seventeenth birthday.

But two days later I was not so sure, for Nounou came to me in some distress and told me that Geneviève, who had gone out riding alone that afternoon had not come home. It was then about five o'clock.

I said: "But surely one of the grooms was with her. She never goes riding alone."

"She did today."

"You saw her?"

"Yes, from my window. I could see she was in one of her moods, so I watched. She was galloping across the meadow and there was no one with her."

"But she knows she's not allowed . . ."

I looked at Nounou helplessly.

"She had been in this mood since the *kermesse*," sighed Nounou. "And I was so happy to see how interested she was. Then . . . she seemed to change."

"Oh, I expect she'll be back soon. I believe she just wants to prove to us that she's grown up."

I left her then and in our separate rooms we waited for Geneviève's return. I guessed that Nounou, like myself, was wondering what steps we should have to take if the girl had not returned within the next hour.

We were spared that, for half an hour or so after I had left Nounou, from my window I saw Geneviève coming into the castle.

I went to the schoolroom through which she would have to pass to her own bedroom, and as I entered Nounou came out of her room.

"She's back," I said.

Nounou nodded. "I saw her."

Shortly afterwards Geneviève came up.

She looked flushed and almost beautiful with her dark eyes brilliant. When she saw us waiting there she smiled mischievously at us and, taking off her hard riding hat, threw it on the schoolroom table.

Nounou was trembling, and I said: "We were anxious. You know you are not supposed to go riding alone."

"Really, Miss, that was long ago. I'm past that now."

"I didn't know it."

"You don't know everything—although you think you do."

I was deeply depressed, because the girl who stood before us, defying us, jeering at us, was no different from the one who had been so rude to me on my arrival. I had thought that we had made some progress, but I realized there had been no miracle. She was still the same creature of moods. Although occasionally she could be interested and pleasant, she was wild as ever when the desire to be so took possession of her.

"I am sure your father would be most displeased."

She turned on me angrily. "Then tell him. Tell him. You and he are such friends."

I said angrily: "You are being absurd. It is very unwise for you to ride alone."

She stood still, smiling secretly, and I wondered in that moment whether she had been alone. The thought was even more alarming.

Suddenly she swung round and faced us. "Listen," she said, "both of you. I shall do as I like. Nobody . . . just nobody . . . is going to stop me."

Then she picked up her hat from the table and went into her room slamming the door behind her.

Those were uneasy days. I had no wish to go to the Bastides', for I feared to meet Jean Pierre and I felt that the pleasant friendly relationship which I had always enjoyed would be spoilt. The Comte had gone up to Paris for a few days after the *kermesse*. Geneviève avoided me. I tried to throw myself even more wholeheartedly into work, and now that more of the wall-painting was emerging this helped my troubled mind.

I was working one morning when I looked up suddenly and found that I was not alone. This was an unpleasant habit of Claude's. She would come into a room noiselessly, and one would be startled to find her there.

She looked very pretty that morning, in a blue morning gown piped with burgundy-colored ribbon. I smelt the faint musk-rose scent she used.

"I hope I didn't startle you, Mademoiselle Lawson?" she said pleasantly.

"Of course not."

"I thought I would speak to you. I am growing more and more uneasy about Geneviève. She is becoming impossible. She was very rude to me and to my husband this morning. Her manners seem to have deteriorated lately."

"She is a child of moods, but she can be charming."

"I find her extremely ill-mannered and *gauche*. I hardly think any school would want her if she behaved like this. I noticed her behavior with the winegrower at the *kermesse*. In her present mood there could be trouble if she became too headstrong. She can no longer be called a child and I fear she might form associations which could be . . . dangerous."

I nodded, for I understood clearly what she meant. She was referring to Geneviève's obsession with Jean Pierre.

She moved closer to me. "If you could use your influence with her. If she knew we were concerned she would be all the more reckless. But I can see you realize the dangers . . ."

She was looking at me quizzically. I guessed she was thinking that if there should be trouble of the nature she was hinting at, I should in a

248

way be to blame. Wasn't I the one who had fostered this friendship? Geneviève had scarcely been aware of Jean Pierre before my friendship with the family.

I felt uneasy and a little guilty.

She went on: "Have you thought any more of that proposition I put to you the other day?"

"I feel I must finish my work here before I consider anything else."

"Don't leave it too long. I heard a little more about it yesterday. One of the party is thinking of starting an exclusive art school in Paris. I think there would be a very good opening there."

"It sounds almost too good to be true."

"It's a chance in a lifetime, I should imagine. But, of course, the decision will have to be made fairly soon."

She smiled at me almost apologetically and left.

She wanted me to go. That much was evident. Was she piqued because some of that attention which she felt should be hers was given to me by the Comte? It might be. But was she also genuinely concerned for Geneviève? This could be, I was ready to admit, a very real problem. Had I misjudged her?

I tried to work, but I could not put my mind to it. Was I being a fool to turn away from that chance of a lifetime for the sake of . . . for the sake of what?

I soon became convinced that Claude was really concerned about Geneviève. That was when I heard her in deep conversation with Jean Pierre in the copse in which the Comte had had his accident. I had been to see Gabrielle and was on my way back to the *château* and had taken the short cut through the copse, when I heard their voices. I did not know what was said and I wondered why they had chosen such a *rendezvous*. Then it occurred to me that the meeting might not have been arranged. They had met by chance, and Claude had decided to take the opportunity of telling Jean Pierre that she did not approve of Geneviève's friendship with him.

It was, after all, no concern of mine, and I turned hastily away. Skirting the copse, I rode back to the *château*. But the incident confirmed me in my opinion that Claude really was worried about Geneviève. And in my pride I had thought her main feeling was jealousy of the Comte's interest in me!

I tried to put all these disturbing matters out of my mind by concentrating on my work. The picture was growing—and there she was before me—the lady with the emeralds, for discolored as they were I could see by the shape of the ornaments that they were identical to those which I had seen on the first picture I had cleaned. The same face. This was the woman who had been the mistress of Louis XV and had started the emerald collection. In fact the picture was very like that other except that in this her dress was of blue velvet and in the other red, and in this one, of course, nestling against the blue velvet of her skirt was the spaniel. It was the inscription that puzzled me. "Forget me not." And now I had uncovered the dog in his glass coffin and saw there was something lying beside him. It had been a moment of excitement so great when I had uncovered that object that I almost forgot my personal dilemma.

Beside the dog in the glass coffin was something which looked like a key, at one end of which was an ornamental *fleur-de-lis*.

I was sure it was meant to convey something, for the lettering, the case in which the dog was enclosed, and the key, if key it was, were not part of a later painting; they had been put onto the original portrait of the woman and dog—and by a hand which could be called nothing more than that of an unskilled amateur.

As soon as the Comte returned to the *château* I should show him this.

The more I thought about the addition to the wall-painting the more significant it seemed. I tried to think of it exclusively; other thoughts were too painful. Geneviève avoided me. She went riding alone every afternoon, and no one prevented her. Nounou shut herself in her room and, I believe, reread the earlier diaries in a vain endeavor, I supposed, to relive the peaceful days with a more amenable charge.

I was worried about Geneviève and wondered if Claude was right and I was partly to blame.

I thought of our first meeting, how she had shut me in the *oubliette* and how even before that she had promised to introduce me to her mother and had taken me to her grave and there informed me that she had been murdered . . . by her father.

I suppose it was this memory which led me one afternoon to the graveyard of the de la Talles.

I went to that of Françoise and read her name once more on the open marble book, and then I looked for the grave of the lady in the portrait. She must be there.

I did not know her name, only that she was one of the Comtesses de la Talle but since she had been a mistress of Louis XV in her youth I guessed that the date of her death must be somewhere in the second half of the eighteenth century. Eventually I discovered a Marie Louise de la Talle, who had died in the year 1761. This would doubtless be the lady of the pictures, and as I approached the vault with its statues and decorations my foot touched something. I stared down incredulously, for what I saw was a cross similar to that which I had discovered in the moat. I bent down to look and I discovered that a date had been scratched on it. There were letters too. I knelt down. I could just read it. "Fidèle 1790."

The same name! Only the date was different. The dog had been buried in the moat in 1747. This dog had the same name and a different date. This Fidèle had died when the revolutionaries were marching on the *château*, when the young Comtesse had had to flee, not only for her own life but for that of the unborn child.

Surely there was something significant about this? I was deeply conscious of it as I stood there. Whoever had painted the coffinlike case about the dog and had written the words "Forget me not" on the picture was trying to convey something. What?

And here I had stumbled on this second grave of Fidèle, and the date was important. I knelt down and looked at the cross. Beneath the name Fidèle and the date, some words had been scratched.

"N'oubliez pas . . ." I made out, and my heart beat wild with excitement then, for the inscription was like that on the picture. *"N'oubliez pas ceux qui furent oubliés."*

What did it indicate?

Of only one thing was I certain; and that was that I was going to find out, for it had occurred to me that this was not the grave a beloved mistress had made for a dog. There was one dog's grave and that was in the moat. Someone who had lived in the year 1790—that most fateful and eventful year for the French people—was trying to send a message over the years.

It was a challenge and one I must accept.

I rose to my feet and left the graveyard, making my way through the small copse to the gardens. I remembered passing a shed in which I knew gardening tools were kept, and there I found a spade and went back to the graveyard.

As I made my way through the copse I had a sudden uneasy feeling that I was being watched. I stood still. There was silence except for the sudden flutter of a bird in the leaves above me.

"Is anyone there?" I called.

But there was no answer. You're being foolish, I told myself. You're nervous. You're reaching out for the past and it's making you uneasy. You've changed since you came to the *château*. You used to be a sensible young woman. Now you do all manner of foolish things . . .

What would anyone think if they found me with a spade intent on digging in the graveyard?

Then I would explain. But I didn't want to explain. I wanted to take my discovery complete and exciting to the Comte. Reaching the cross, I looked over my shoulder. I could see no one, but it would not be difficult for someone to have followed me through the copse, to be hiding now behind one of those houselike tombs which the French erect to their dead.

I began to dig.

The small box was very near the surface, and I saw at once that it was not big enough to contain the remains of a dog. I picked it up and brushed off the dirt. It was made of metal, and there were words scratched on this, similar to those on the cross: "1790. *N'oubliez pas ceux qui furent oubliés.*"

It was difficult to open the box, for it had become wedged with rust. But eventually I managed it; and I think I must have been expecting what was inside.

I knew as soon as I picked it up that when I had uncovered the wall-painting I had uncovered a message which had been intentionally left. For there in the box was the key which was lying beside the dog in the picture. I knew it because at one end was the *fleur-de-lis*.

Now I had to find the lock which fitted the key, and then I should know what the one who had drawn that message had wanted to say. It was a link with the past. It was the most thrilling discovery I or my father had ever made. I wanted to tell someone . . . not anyone . . . the Comte, of course.

I looked down at the key in my hand. Somewhere in the *château* there would be the lock to fit it.

I must find it.

I put the key carefully into the pocket of my dress. I closed the box and put it back in the earth. Then I covered it. In a few days no one would know that the ground had been disturbed.

I went to the toolshed and carefully replaced the spade. Then I went into the *château* and up to my room. But it was not until I was there and the door was shut that I could rid myself of the notion that someone had been watching me.

Those were days of burning heat. The Comte stayed in Paris, and I had now exposed the whole of the wall-painting and was cleaning it, a process which would not take me very long. When I had done that and the few pictures in the gallery, I should really have no excuse for staying. If I were wise I should tell Claude that I wanted to take up her suggestion.

The harvest was almost upon us. Very soon now the call would come to the workers to rise early and gather the grapes.

I had a feeling that we were moving towards a climax and when the harvest was over this episode in my life would be over too.

Wherever I went I carried the key with me in the pocket of one of my petticoats. It was a very secure pocket in which I carried anything I was afraid of losing, for it buttoned tightly and there was no way in which articles hidden there could be lost.

I had thought a great deal about the key, and I had come to the conclusion that if I could find the lock to it I should discover the emeralds. Everything pointed to this. The coffin had been painted over the dog in the picture in the year 1790—that very year when the revolutionaries had marched on the *château*. I was certain the emeralds had been taken from the strong room and hidden somewhere in the *château* and this was the key to open the receptacle in which they lay. This key was the property of the Comte, and I had no right to keep it; but I should give it to no one else, and together he and I should seek to find the lock which fitted it.

I had a great desire to find that lock myself. To await him on his return and say to him: "Here are your emeralds."

They could not be in a casket. That would have been discovered long ago. It must be a cupboard, a safe, somewhere which had gone undetected for a hundred years.

I began by examining every inch of my own room, tapping the paneling where I thought there might possibly be a cavity.

And as I did this I stopped short suddenly, remembering the tapping Geneviève and I had heard in the night. Someone else was searching as I was. Who? The Comte? That was understandable, but why should he, who owned the *château* and had every right to look for hidden treasure which belonged to him, seek to find it by stealth?

I thought of the treasure hunt when I had found the clues, and I knew that the words scratched on the box were a clue of a similar sort.

Could those who had been forgotten be those prisoners of the past who had been chained to their cages or dropped into the *oubliette?* The servants believed those dungeons to be haunted and refused to go there. That might have applied to the revolutionaries storming the *château*. Somewhere down there was the lock which would fit the key I carried in my petticoat pocket.

It must be in the *oubliette* of course. The word "forgotten" was the clue to that.

I remembered the trap door, the rope ladder and the occasion when Geneviève had shut me there. I longed to explore the *oubliette*, and yet, remembering how I had once been shut down there, I was reluctant to go alone.

Should I tell Geneviève of my discovery? I decided against it. No, I must go alone but I must make sure that it was known I was there so that if by some chance that trap door should be shut down I should be rescued.

I went along to Nounou.

"Nounou," I said, "I am going to explore the *oubliette* this afternoon. I think there may be something interesting under the lime-wash."

"Like that picture you've been finding?"

"Something like that. There's only the rope ladder for getting in and out, so if I should not be back in my room by four o'clock you would know where to find me."

Nounou nodded. "Though she wouldn't do it again," she said. "You need have no fear of that, Miss."

"No; but that's where I shall be."

"I'll remember."

I also took the precaution of mentioning where I should be to the maid who brought my lunch.

"Oh, will you, Miss?" she said. "Rather you than me."

"You don't like the place?"

"Well, Miss, when you think of what's gone on there. They say it's haunted. You know that, don't you?"

"That's often said about such places."

"Well, all those people . . . shut down there to pine away . . . ugh, rather you than me."

I touched the key beneath my skirts and thought of the pleasure I should have when I took the Comte to his *oubliette* and said to him: "I have found your treasure."

I was not going to let the fear of ghosts scare me.

As I stood in that room with its trap door which was the only entry to the *oubliette,* watching the play of sunlight on the weapons decorating the walls, it occurred to me that the lock which would fit the key might be in this room, for those who were about to be forgotten had first passed this way.

Guns of various shapes and kinds! Were they ever used now? I knew it was the duty of one of the servants to come to this room periodically and make sure everything was well kept. I had heard it said that the servants came in twos.

If there was anything here surely it would have been discovered long ago.

As I stood there my eye caught something gleaming on the floor and I went swiftly to it.

It was a pair of scissors—the kind which I had seen used for snipping off grapes that were not up to the required standard. There had been occasions when, as I had stood talking to him, I had seen Jean Pierre take such a pair of scissors from his pockets and use them on the vines.

I stooped and picked up the scissors. They were of an unusual shape. Could there be two pairs so much alike? And if not, how had Jean Pierre's scissors come to be here?

I slipped them into my pocket thoughtfully. Then, deciding that what I sought was more likely to be in the *oubliette,* I took out the rope ladder, opened the trap door, and descended to that place of doom where the forgotten had perished. I shivered as I relived those dreadful moments when Geneviève had pulled up the ladder and shut the trap door, leaving me to experience a little of what hundreds must have felt before within these walls.

It was an eerie place, close, confined, dark, except for the light which came through the trap door.

But I had not come to let my fancies rule my common sense. Here was where the forgotten had ended their days, and this was where the clue had led me. I believed that somewhere in this enclosed space was the lock which the key would open.

I examined the walls. Here was the familiar lime-wash which must have been done about eighty years ago. I tapped the wall gently to test it for cavities, but I could find nothing of interest. I looked about me, at the ceiling, at the flagged stone floors. I went into that aperture which Geneviève had told me was a maze. Could it be in there somewhere? The light was too poor for me to examine it well, but as I put out my hand to touch the stone pillar I could not imagine how anything could be secreted there.

I decided to make a thorough examination of the walls, and while I was doing this what little light there was disappeared.

I gave a little cry of horror and turned to the trap door.

Claude was looking down at me.

"Making discoveries?" she asked.

I stood looking up at her and moved towards the rope ladder. She pulled it a few inches from the ground rather playfully.

"I'm wondering whether there are any to make," I answered.

"You know so much about ancient castles. I saw you come here and guessed what you were up to."

I thought: She is watching me, all the time, hoping that I will make the decision to go.

I reached out to touch the ladder, but laughingly she jerked it upwards.

"Don't you feel a little alarmed down there, Mademoiselle Lawson?"

"Why should I?"

"Think of all the ghosts of dead men who have died horrible deaths cursing those who left them there to die."

"They would have no grudge against me."

I kept my eyes on the rope ladder, which she held just out of my reach.

"You might slip and fall down there. Anything could happen. You might be a prisoner there . . . like those others."

"Not for long," I answered. "They would come to look for me. I have told Nounou and others that I'd be here, so I shouldn't be left long."

"You're very practical as well as clever. Do you think you are going to find wall-paintings down there?"

"In castles like this, one never knows what one will find. That's where the excitement comes in."

"I should like to join you." She let the ladder fall, and I felt a relief as I was able to touch it. "But I don't think I will," she went on. "If you discover something you will let us know fast enough, I'm sure."

"I shall let it be known. I'm coming up now, in any case."

"And you'll be investigating again?"

"Very probably, although the examination I have made today makes me think I shan't find anything down here."

Firmly I grasped the ladder and climbed up to the room.

Claude had made me forget my discovery in the gun room, but no sooner had I returned to my own room than I remembered the scissors in my pocket.

It was early, so I decided I would take a walk to the Maison Bastide to ask if they belonged to Jean Pierre.

I found Madame Bastide alone. I showed her the scissors and asked if they were her grandson's.

"Why, yes," she said, "he's been looking for those."

"You're sure they are his?"

"Undoubtedly."

I laid them on the table.

"Where did you find them?"

"In the *château*."

I saw the fear leap into her eyes, and in that moment the incident seemed to take on a greater significance.

"Yes, in the gun room. I thought it was an odd place to find them."

There was a silence and I was deeply aware of the clock on the mantelpiece ticking away the seconds.

"He lost them some weeks ago—when he went to see Monsieur le Comte," said Madame Bastide, but I felt she was trying to excuse Jean Pierre's being in the *château* and to suggest that he had lost the scissors before the Comte's departure.

We avoided looking at each other. I knew Madame Bastide was alarmed.

I couldn't sleep very well that night. It had been a disturbing day. I wondered what Claude's motives had been when she had followed me to the *oubliette*. What would have happened if I had not taken the precaution of telling Nounou and the maid that I should be there? I shivered. Did Claude want me out of the way, and was she growing impatient because I was still hesitating to take the solution she had offered me?

And then finding Jean Pierre's scissors in the gun room had been disturbing—particularly in view of Madame Bastide's reaction when I returned them.

It was small wonder that I felt restless.

I was half dozing when the door of my room opened and I awoke with a start, my heart beating so fast that I felt it would burst. I sensed that there was something evil in my room.

Starting up in bed, I saw a figure swathed in blue at the foot of my bed. I was half dreaming I suppose, because for a few seconds I thought I really was face to face with one of the *château* ghosts. Then I saw it was Claude.

"I'm afraid I frightened you. I didn't think you would be asleep yet. I knocked at your door but you didn't answer."

"I was dozing," I said.

"I wanted to talk to you."

I looked surprised, and she went on: "You're thinking I've had better opportunities . . . but it's not easy to tell you. I had to wait until I could . . . and I kept putting it off."

"What have you to tell me?"

"I'm going to have a child," she said.

"Congratulations!" But why, I thought, wake me to tell me that?

"I want you to understand what this means."

"That you are going to have a child? I think this is good news and I suppose not wholly unexpected."

"You are a woman of the world."

I was a little surprised to hear myself referred to as such, and I did not protest, although I felt she was attempting to flatter me, which was strange.

"If he is a boy he will be the future Comte."

"You are presuming that the Comte will have no sons of his own."

"But surely you know enough of the family history to understand that Philippe is here because the Comte has no wish to marry. If he does not, then my son will inherit."

"That may be so," I said. "But what is it you are trying to tell me?"

"I'm telling you that you should accept the proposition I have put to you before it is too late. The offer won't remain open indefinitely. I was going to talk to you this afternoon, but I found it too difficult."

"What do you want to say to me?"

"I want to be quite frank. Whose child do you think I am going to have?"

"Your husband's, of course."

"My husband has no interest in women. In any case he is impotent. You see how this simplifies the plan. The Comte does not want to marry but he would like his son to inherit. Do you understand?"

"It is no concern of mine."

"No, that's true. But I'm trying to help you. I know you think that strange, but it's true. I haven't always been very pleasant to you, I know. So you wonder why I should bother to help you. I don't know why . . . except that people like you can get hurt even worse than most. The Comte is a man who will have his own way. His family have always been like that. They care for nothing but getting their own way. You should leave here. You should let me help you. I can do it now, but unless you make up your mind, you will lose this chance. You admit it's an excellent chance?"

I did not answer. I could only think of her implication that the child she carried was the Comte's. I didn't want to believe it, but it fitted in with what I knew. This would ensure his child's inheriting the title and estates. And Philippe, the complaisant, would pose as the child's father to the outside world. It was the price he must pay to be called Comte, should the real Comte die before him; it was the price he must pay to call the *château* his home.

She is right, I thought, I must get away.

She was watching me intently and she said gently, almost tenderly: "I know how you feel. He has been . . . attentive, hasn't he? He has never met anyone quite like you before. You are different from the rest of us, and he always was attracted by novelty. That is why nothing can last with him. You should go to prevent yourself being hurt . . . badly."

She was like a ghost at the foot of my bed, warning me to avert the tragedy which loomed over me.

She went on: "Shall I arrange for you to go on that tour?"

I answered quietly: "I will think about it."

She shrugged and turning, glided to the door. There she paused to look back at me.

"Good night," she said softly, and she was gone.

I lay awake for a long time.

I should be deeply hurt if I stayed. I had not realized until now how deeply, how bitterly.

❧ 11 ❧

When the Comte returned to the château a few days later, he seemed preoccupied and did not seek me out. As for myself I was so horrified by what Claude had told me that I was anxious to avoid him. I told myself that had I truly loved him I should not have believed Claude, but the fact was that I felt there was a possibility of her story's being true; and oddly enough it made no difference to my feelings for the Comte. I did not love him for his virtues. I had seen him for the man he was—in fact I had believed ill of him which had proved to be wrong as in the case of Gabrielle and Mademoiselle Dubois—and knowing all this, I had blindly allowed myself to be fascinated.

The fact was I could not understand my feelings. All I knew was that he dominated my life, that without him life would be flat, dull, meaningless. I could not even ask him now if Claude's story was true. There was too big a barrier between us. The man was an enigma to me —and yet it seemed to me that my whole world would be devoid of hope for happiness if he went out of it.

It was not sensible; it was not what I should have expected of myself; and yet I had done it.

I could only call that being recklessly and hopelessly involved. Involved! How typical of me to try to find another word for being in love because, I admonished myself scornfully, I was afraid to face up to the fact that I loved a man irrevocably.

There was a rising tension during those days. There was only one thing I was certain of. This situation could not remain static. It was explosive; we were working towards some crisis and when it came, my future would be decided.

There was always, I imagined, this atmosphere of excitement as the harvest approached. But this was my personal crisis. I was coming to the end of the work; I could not stay on indefinitely at the *château*. I should have to talk of my future, and I experienced complete desolation when I considered that I might tell the Comte that I was going and he would let me go.

I had strayed into this feudal life and I, with my strict English upbringing, had tried to become a part of it. How wrong I might have been! I clung to that word "might." It was the only hope I had.

Into this strange period of waiting there came suddenly the sense of danger . . . danger of a different sort from that into which a foolish woman allows herself to dream of an impossible romance. Imminent danger. It was because of an uneasy feeling that I was being watched. Little sounds—unmistakable yet unidentifiable—as I walked through the corridors to my room. The extra sense that comes unexpectedly and which sets one turning sharply to look over one's shoulder. This had suddenly crept upon me, and it persisted.

I was very conscious of the key which I carried about with me in my petticoat pocket. I had promised myself that I would show it to the Comte and that together we should search for the lock which it would fit. But since Claude had talked to me I felt unable to face him.

I had promised myself a few more days of exploration; secretly I pictured myself going to him and telling him I had discovered his emeralds, for I was growing more and more certain that that was what I should find. Perhaps, I thought in my heart, he would be so overwhelmed, so delighted that even if he had not thought seriously of me before, he would do so then.

What stupid ideas women in love will get! I reminded myself. They live in a world of romance which has little connection with reality. They make charming pictures and then convince themselves that they are true.

Surely I was beyond that sort of behavior.

He had not been to see how the wall-painting was progressing, which surprised me. At times I wondered whether Claude talked of me to him and they smiled together at my innocence. If it were true that she was to have his child, then they would be very intimate. I couldn't believe it —but that was the romantic woman in me. Looking at the situation from a practical point of view it seemed logical enough—and weren't the French noted for their logic? What to my English reasoning would seem an immoral situation, to their French logic would seem satisfactory. The Comte, having no desire for marriage, yet wishing to see his son inherit the name, fortune, estates, and everything that was important to him; Philippe as his reward would inherit before the boy if the Comte should die, and the *château* was his home; Claude could enjoy her relationship with her lover without suffering any loss of dignity. Of course it was reasonable; of course it was logical.

But to me it was horrible, and I hated it, and I did not try to see him for I feared I should betray my feelings. In the meantime I was watchful.

One afternoon I walked over to see Gabrielle who was now very obviously pregnant and contented. I enjoyed my visit, for we talked of the Comte, and Gabrielle was one of the people who had a high regard for him.

When I left her I took the short cut through the woods and it was while I was there that the feeling of being followed came upon me more strongly than before. On this occasion I was truly alarmed. Here was I alone in the woods—those very woods in which the Comte had received his injury. The fear had come suddenly upon me, with the crackle of undergrowth, the snapping of a twig.

I stopped and listened. All was silent; and yet I was conscious of danger.

An impulse came to me to run and I did so. Such panic possessed me that I almost screamed aloud when my skirt was caught by a bramble. I snatched it away leaving a little of the stuff behind, but I did not stop.

I was certain I heard the sound of hurrying steps behind me, and when the trees thinned out I looked behind me, but there was no one.

I came out of the copse. There was no sign of anyone emerging from the woods, but I did not pause long. I started the long walk back to the *château*.

Near the vineyards I met Philippe on horseback.

He rode up to me and as soon as he saw me exclaimed: "Why, Mademoiselle Lawson, is anything wrong?"

I guessed I still looked a little distraught, so there was no point in hiding it.

"I had rather an unpleasant experience in the woods. I thought I was being followed."

"You shouldn't go into the woods alone, you know."

"No, I suppose not. But I didn't think of it."

"Fancy, I daresay, but I can understand it. Perhaps you were remembering how you found my cousin there when he was shot, and that made you imagine someone was following you. It might have been someone after a hare."

"Probably."

He dismounted and stood still to look at the vineyards. "We're going to have a record harvest," he said. "Have you ever seen the gathering of the grapes?"

"No."

"You'll enjoy it. It won't be long now. They're almost ready. Would you care to take a look into the sheds? You'll see them preparing the baskets. The excitement is growing."

"Should we disturb them?"

"Indeed not. They like to think that everyone is as excited as they are."

He led me along a path towards the sheds and talked to me about the grapes. He admitted that he had not attended a harvest for years. I felt embarrassed in his company. I saw him now as the weak third party in a distasteful compact. But I could not gracefully make my escape.

"In the past," he was saying, "I used to stay at the *château* for long periods in the summer, and I always remembered the grape harvest. It seemed to go on far into the night, and I would get out of bed and listen to them singing as they trod the grapes. It was a most fascinating sight."

"It must have been."

"Oh yes, Mademoiselle Lawson. I never forgot the sight of men and women stepping into the trough and dancing on the grapes. And there were musicians who played the songs they knew and they danced and sang. I remember watching them sink lower and lower into the purple juice."

"So you are looking forward to this harvest."

"Yes, but perhaps everything seems more colorful when we are young. But I think it was the grape harvest which decided me that I'd rather live at Château Gaillard than anywhere else on earth."

"Well, now you have that wish."

He was silent and I noticed the grim lines about his mouth. I wondered what he felt about the relationship between the Comte and his wife. There was an air of effeminacy about him which made more plausible Claude's account, and the fact that his features did in some way resemble those of his cousin made this complete difference in their characters the more apparent. I could believe that he wanted more than anything to live at the *château,* to own the *château,* to be known as the Comte de la Talle, and for all this he had bartered his honor, had married the Comte's mistress and would accept the Comte's illegitimate son as his . . . all for the sake of one day, if the Comte should die, being King of the Castle, for I was sure that if he had refused to accept the terms laid down by the Comte, he would not have been allowed to inherit.

We talked of the grapes and the harvests he remembered from his childhood, and when we came to the sheds I was shown the baskets which were being prepared and I listened while Philippe talked to the workers.

He walked his horse back to the *château* and I thought him friendly, reserved, a little deprecating, and found myself making excuses for him.

I went up to my room and as soon as I entered it I was aware that someone had been there during my absence.

I looked about me; then I saw what it was. The book I had left on my bedside table was on the dressing table. I knew I had not left it there.

I hurried to it and picked it up. I opened the drawer. Everything appeared to be in order. I opened another and another. Everything was tidy.

But I was sure that the book had been moved.

Perhaps, I thought, one of the servants had been in. Why? No one usually came in during that time of day.

And then on the air I caught the faint smell of scent. A musk-rose scent which I had smelt before. It was feminine and pleasant. I had smelt it when Claude was near.

I was certain then that while I had been out Claude had been in my room. Why? Could it be that she knew I had the key and had she come to see if I had hidden it somewhere in my room?

I stood still, and my hands touched the pocket of my petticoat through my skirt. There was the key safe on my person. The scent had gone. Then again there it was—faint, elusive, but significant.

It was the next day when the maid brought a letter to my room from Jean Pierre, who said he must see me without delay. He wanted to speak to me alone, so would I come to the vineyards as soon as possible, where we could talk without being interrupted. He begged me to come.

I went out into the hot sunshine, across the drawbridge and towards the vineyards. The whole countryside seemed to be sleeping in the hot afternoon; and as I walked along the path through the vines now laden with their rich ripe fruit, Jean Pierre came to meet me.

"It's difficult to talk here," he said. "Let's go inside." He took me into the building and to the first of the cellars.

It was cool there and seemed dark after the glare of the sun; here the light came through small apertures and I remembered hearing how it was necessary to regulate the temperature by the shutters.

And there among the casks Jean Pierre said: "I am to go away."

"Go away," I repeated stupidly. And then: "But when?"

"Immediately after the harvest."

He took me by the shoulders. "You know why, Dallas?"

I shook my head.

"Because Monsieur le Comte wants me out of the way."

"Why?"

He laughed bitterly. "He does not give his reasons. He merely gives his orders. It no longer pleases him that I should be here—so, although I have been here all my life, I am now to move on."

"But surely if you explain . . ."

"Explain what? That this is my home . . . as the *château* is his? We, my dear Dallas, are not supposed to have such absurd sentiments. We are the serfs . . . born to obey. Did you not know that?"

"This is absurd, Jean Pierre."

"But no. I have my orders."

"Go to him . . . tell him . . . I am sure he will listen."

He smiled at me.

"Do you know why he wants me to go away? Can you guess? It is because he knows of my friendship with you. He does not like that."

"What should it mean to him?" I hoped Jean Pierre did not notice the excited note in my voice.

"It means that he is interested in you . . . in his way."

"But this is ridiculous."

"You know it is not. There have always been women . . . and you are

266

different from any he has ever known. He wants your undivided attention . . . for a time."

"How can you know?"

"How can I know? Because I know *him*. I have lived here all my life, and although he is frequently away, this is his home too. Here he lives as he can't live in Paris. Here he is lord of us all. Here we have stood still in time and he wants to keep it like that."

"You hate him, Jean Pierre."

"Once the people of France rose against such as he is."

"You've forgotten how he helped Gabrielle and Jacques."

He laughed bitterly. "Gabrielle like all women has a fondness for him."

"What are you suggesting?"

"That I don't believe in this goodness of his. There's always a motive behind it. To him we are not people with lives of our own. We are his slaves, I tell you. If he wants a woman, then anyone who stands in his way is removed, and when she is no longer required, well . . . you know what happened to the Comtesse."

"Don't dare say such things."

"Dallas! What's happened to you?"

"I want to know what you were doing in the gun room at the *château*."

"I?"

"Yes, I found your grape scissors there. Your mother said you had missed them and that they were yours."

He was taken aback a little. Then he said: "I had to go to the *château* to see the Comte on business . . . . that was just before he went away."

"And it took you to the gun room?"

"No."

"But that's where I found them."

"The Comte wasn't at home, so I thought I'd have a look round the *château*. You're surprised. It's a very interesting place. I couldn't resist looking round. That was the room, you know, where an ancestor of mine last saw the light of day."

"Jean Pierre," I said, "you shouldn't hate anyone so much."

"Why should it all be his? Do you know that he and I are blood relations? A great-great-grandfather of mine was half brother to a Comte—the only difference was that his mother was not a Comtesse."

"Please don't talk like this." A terrible thought struck me, and I said: "I believe you would kill him."

Jean Pierre did not answer, and I went on: "That day in the woods . . ."

"I didn't fire that shot. Do you imagine I'm the only one who hates him?"

"You have no reason to hate him. He has never harmed you. You hate him because he is what he is and you want what he has."

"It's a good reason for hating." He laughed suddenly. "It's just that I'm furious with him now because he wants to send me away. Wouldn't you hate anyone who wanted to send you away from your home and the one you loved? I did not come here to talk of hating the Comte but of loving you. I shall go to Mermoz when the harvest is over, and I want you to come with me, Dallas. You belong here among us. After all, we are your mother's people. Let us be married, and we will laugh at him then. He has no power over you."

No power over me! I thought: But you are wrong, Jean Pierre. No one has ever before had this power to regulate my happiness, to excite and depress me.

Jean Pierre had seized my hands; he drew me towards him, his eyes shining.

"Dallas, marry me. Think how happy that will make us all—you, me, my family. You are fond of us, aren't you?"

"Yes," I said, "I am fond of you all."

"And do you want to go away . . . back to England? What will you do there, Dallas, my darling? Have you friends there? Then why have you been content to leave them so long? You want to be here, don't you? You feel that you belong here?"

I was silent. I thought of it. The life Jean Pierre was offering me. I imagined myself being caught up in the excitement of the vineyards, taking my easel out and developing that little talent I had for painting. Visiting the family at the Maison Bastide . . . but no, then I should see the *château,* I should never be able to look at it without a pain in my heart; and there would be times when I should see the Comte perhaps. He would look at me and bow courteously. And perhaps he would say to himself: Who is that woman? I have seen her somewhere. Oh, she is that Mademoiselle Lawson who came to do the pictures and married Jean Pierre Bastide over at Mermoz.

Better to go right away than that—better to take the opportunity which Claude had offered and which was still open—although it would probably not remain so much longer.

"You hesitate," said Jean Pierre.

"No. It can't be."

"You do not love me?"

"I don't really know you, Jean Pierre." The words had escaped me, and I had not meant to say them.

"But we are old friends, I thought."

"There is so much that we don't know about each other."

"All I have to know of you is that I love you."

Love? I thought. Yet you do not speak of it as vehemently as you do of hate.

His hatred of the Comte was stronger than his love for me; and it occurred to me then that one had grown out of the other. Was Jean Pierre eager to marry me because he thought that the Comte was attracted by me? As that thought came to me I was conscious of a great revulsion against him and he no longer seemed like the old friend in whose home I had spent so many hours. He was a sinister stranger.

"Come, Dallas," he said, "say we'll be married. And I'll go to the Comte and tell him that I shall be taking a bride with me to Mermoz."

There it was! He would go to the Comte in triumph.

"I'm sorry, Jean Pierre," I said, "but this is not the way."

"You mean you will not marry me?"

"No, Jean Pierre, I can't marry you."

He dropped my hands and a look of baffled rage crossed his features. Then he lifted his shoulders.

"But," he said, "I shall continue to hope."

I had a great desire to escape from the cellar. Such hatred of one man towards another was terrifying; and I, who had felt so self-sufficient in the past, so able to take care of myself, had now begun to learn the meaning of fear.

I was glad to come out into the hot light of day.

I went straight to my room and thought about Jean Pierre's proposal. He had not the manner of a man in love. He had shown me how deeply he could feel when he talked of the Comte. To spite the Comte he would marry me. This horrifying thought brought with it its elation.

He had noticed, then, the Comte's interest in me. Yet since his return from Paris he had scarcely seemed aware of me.

The next morning I was working on the wall-painting to which I was putting the finishing touches when Nounou came to me in great distress.

"It's Geneviève," she said. "She's come in and gone straight to her room. She's half crying, half laughing and I can't get out of her what's wrong. I wish you'd come and help me."

I went with her to Geneviève's room. The girl was certainly in a wild mood. She had thrown her riding hat and crop into a corner of the room and when I entered was sitting on her bed glowering into space.

"What's wrong, Geneviève?" I asked. "I might be able to help."

"Help! How can you help? Unless you go and ask my father . . ." She looked at me speculatively.

I said coldly: "Ask what?"

She didn't answer; she clenched her fists and beat them on the bed. "I'm not a baby!" she cried. "I'm grown up. I won't stay here if I don't want to. I'll run away."

Nounou caught her breath in fear but asked: "Where to?"

"Anywhere I like, and you won't find me."

"I don't think I should be eager to if you remain in your present mood."

She burst out laughing but was sober almost at once. "I tell you, Miss, I won't be treated like a child."

"What has happened to upset you? How have you been treated like a child?"

She stared at the tips of her riding boots. "If I want friends, I shall have them."

"Who said you shouldn't?"

"I don't think people should be sent away just because . . ." She stopped and glared at me. "It's no business of yours. Nor yours, Nounou. Go away. Don't stand staring at me as though I'm a baby."

Nounou looked ready to burst into tears, and I thought I could handle this better if she were not there continually to remind Geneviève that she was her nurse. So I signed to her to leave us. She went readily.

I sat on the bed and waited. Geneviève said sullenly, "My father is sending Jean Pierre away because he's my friend."

"Who said so?"

"No one has to say so. I know."

"But why should he be sent away for that reason?"

"Because I'm Papa's daughter and Jean Pierre is one of the wine-growers."

"I don't see the point."

"Because I'm growing up, that's why. Because . . ." She looked at me and her lips quivered. Then she threw herself onto the bed and burst into loud sobs which shook her body.

I leaned over her. "Geneviève," I said gently, "do you mean that they're afraid you'll fall in love with him?"

"Now you laugh!" she cried, turning a hot face to glare at me. "I tell you I'm old enough. I'm not a child."

"I didn't say you were. Geneviève, are you in love with Jean Pierre?"

She didn't answer, so I went on: "And Jean Pierre?"

She nodded. "He told me that was why Papa is sending him away."

"I see," I said slowly.

She laughed bitterly. "It's only to Mermoz. I shall run away with him. I shan't stay here if he goes."

"Did Jean Pierre suggest this?"

"Don't keep questioning me. You're not on my side."

"I am, Geneviève. I am on your side."

She raised herself and looked at me. "Are you?"

I nodded.

"I thought you weren't because . . . because I thought you liked him too. I was jealous of you," she admitted naïvely.

"There's no need to be jealous of me, Geneviève. But you have to be reasonable, you know. When I was young I fell in love."

The thought made her smile. "Oh no, Miss, *you!*"

"Yes," I said tartly, "even I."

"That must have been funny."

"It seemed tragic rather."

"Why? Did your father send him away?"

"He couldn't do that. But he made me see how impossible it would have been."

"And would it have been?"

"It usually is when one is very young."

"Now you're trying to influence me. I tell you I won't listen. I'll tell you this though, that when Jean Pierre goes to Mermoz *I* am going with him."

"He'll go after the harvest."

"And so shall I," she said with determination.

I could see that it was no use talking to her when she was in this mood.

I was worried, asking myself what this meant. Had she imagined that Jean Pierre was in love with her, or had he told her so? Could he have done this at the same time that he was asking me to marry him?

I thought of Jean Pierre in the cellar, his eyes brilliant with hatred.

It seemed to me that the ruling passion of his life was hatred of the Comte, and because he thought that the Comte was interested in me he had asked me to marry him. Because Geneviève was the Comte's daughter . . . could it be that he was attempting to seduce her?

The following day had been fixed for the gathering of the grapes. All day long the sky overhead had been a cloudless blue; the sun was hot and the abundant grapes were ripe for picking.

I was not thinking of the next day. I was thinking of Jean Pierre and his desire for revenge on the Comte. I was watching Geneviève for, in her present mood, I could not guess what she would do next. Nor could I rid myself of that sinister feeling that I myself was being watched.

I longed for a *tête-à-tête* with the Comte but he seemed to ignore me, and I thought perhaps it was as well since my own feelings were in such a turmoil. Claude made several significant references to my work's growing near its termination. How she wanted to be rid of me! On the few occasions when I encountered him Philippe was as remote yet friendly as he had ever been.

After Geneviève's outburst I had been wondering how to act and I suddenly thought that the one person who might help me was Jean Pierre's grandmother.

The afternoon was almost turning into evening when I went to see her. I guessed she would be alone in the house, for there was a great deal of activity in the vineyards, preparing for the next day, and even Yves and Margot were not near the house.

She welcomed me as always, and without preamble I told her how worried I was.

"Jean Pierre has asked me to marry him," I said.

"And you do not love him."

I shook my head.

"He does not love me either," I went on. "But he hates the Comte."

I saw how the veins in her hands stood out as she clenched them together.

"There is Geneviève," I went on. "He has led her to believe . . ."

"Oh no!"

"She is excitable and vulnerable and I'm afraid for her. She's in a state of hysteria because he is being sent away. We must do something . . . I'm not sure what. But I'm afraid something dreadful will happen. This hatred of his . . . it's unnatural."

"It's born in him. Try to understand it. Every day he looks at the *château* there and he thinks: Why should it be the Comte's . . . that and the power that goes with it! Why not . . . ?"

"But this is absurd. Why should he feel this? Everyone in the neighborhood sees the *château* but they don't think it should be theirs."

"It's different. We Bastides have *château* blood in us. Bastide! Here in the south a *bastide* is a country house . . . but might it not once have been *Bâtard?* That is how names come about."

"There must be plenty of people hereabouts who, as they say, have *château* blood."

"That's so, but with the Bastides it was different. We were closer to the *château.* We belonged to it, and it is not so many years that we can forget. My husband's father was the son of a Comte de la Talle. Jean Pierre knows this; and when he looks at the *château,* when he sees the Comte, he thinks: So might I have ridden about the land. These vineyards might have been mine . . . and the *château* too."

"It's . . . unhealthy to think so."

"He has always been proud. He has always listened to the stories of the *château* which were handed down in our family. He knows how the Comtesse sheltered here in this house . . . how her son was born here, how he lived here until he went back to join his grandmother in the *château.* You see, the Madame Bastide who sheltered him had a son of her own; he was a year older than the little Comte—but they had the same father."

"It makes a strong link, I see, but it doesn't explain this envy and hatred going on over years."

Madame Bastide shook her head, and I burst out: "You must make him see reason. There'll be a tragedy if he goes on in this way. I sense it. In the woods when the Comte was shot . . ."

"That was not Jean Pierre."

"But if he hates him so much . . ."

"He is not a murderer."

"Then who . . . ?"

"A man such as the Comte has his enemies."

"None could hate him more than your grandson. I don't like it. It must be stopped."

"You must always restore people to what you think they should be, Dallas. Human beings are not pictures, you know. Nor . . ."

"Nor am I so perfect that I should seek to reform others. I know. But I find this alarming."

"If you could know the secret thoughts which go on in our minds there might often be cause for alarm. But, Dallas, what of yourself? You are in love with the Comte, are you not?"

I drew away from her in dismay.

"It is as clear to me as Jean Pierre's hatred is to you. You are alarmed not because Jean Pierre hates, but because he hates the Comte. You fear he will do him some harm. This hatred has been going on for years. It is necessary to Jean Pierre. It soothes his pride. You are in greater danger through your love, Dallas, than he is through his hate."

I was silent.

"My dear, you should go home. I, an old woman, who sees far more than you think, tell you that. Could you be happy here? Would the Comte marry you? Would you live here as his mistress? I don't think so. That would suit neither him nor you. Go home while there is still time. In your own country you will learn to forget, for you are still young and will meet someone whom you will learn to love. You will have children and they will teach you to forget."

"Madame Bastide," I said. "You are worried."

She was silent.

"You are afraid of what Jean Pierre will do."

"He has been different lately."

"He has asked me to marry him; he has convinced Geneviève that she is in love with him . . . what else?"

She hesitated. "Perhaps I should not tell you. It has been on my mind since I knew. When the Comtesse fled from the revolutionaries and took refuge here she was grateful to the Bastides and she left with them a small gold casket. Inside this casket was a key."

"A key!" I echoed.

"Yes, a small key. I have never before seen one like it. At one end was a *fleur-de-lis.*"

"Yes?" I prompted impatiently.

"The casket was for us. It is worth a great deal. It is kept locked away in case we should ever be in great need. The key was to be kept until it was asked for. It was not to be given up until then."

"And was it never asked for?"

"No, it never was. According to the story which had been handed down we were to tell no one we had it for fear the wrong people should ask. So we never mentioned the key . . . nor the casket. It was said that the Comtesse had talked of two keys . . . the one in our casket and the one hidden in the *château.*"

"Where is the key? May I see it?"

"It disappeared . . . a short time ago. I believe someone has taken it."

"Jean Pierre!" I whispered. "He is trying to find the lock in the *château* which fits the key."

"That could be so."

"And when he does?"

She gripped my hand. "If he finds what he seeks that will be the end of his hatred."

"You mean . . . the emeralds."

"If he had the emeralds he would think he had his share. I am afraid that that is what is in his mind. I am afraid that this . . . obsession is like a canker in his mind. Dallas, I am afraid of where it will lead him."

"Could you talk to him?"

She shook her head.

"It's no use. I have tried in the past. I'm fond of you. You must not be hurt too. Everything here seems peaceful on the surface . . . but nothing is what it seems. We none of us show our true face to the world. You should go away. You should not be involved in this years-old strife. Go home and start again. In time this will seem like a dream to you and we will all be like puppets in a shadow show."

"It could never be so."

"Yes, my dear, it could be . . . for that is life."

I left her and went back to the *château.*

I knew I could stand aside no longer. I had to act. How—I was not sure.

Half-past six in the morning—and this was the call of *vendange*. From all over the neighborhood, men, women, and children were making their ways to the vineyards where Jean Pierre and his father would give them instructions. At least, I told myself, for today there could be no concern for anything but the gathering of the grape.

In the *château* kitchens, according to ancient custom, food was being prepared to provide meals for all the workers, and as soon as the dew was off the grapes the gathering began.

The harvesters were working in pairs, one carefully cutting the grapes, making sure that those which were not perfect were discarded, while the other held the *osier* to receive them, keeping it steady so as not to bruise the grapes.

From the vineyards came the sound of singing as the workers joined together in the songs of the district. This again was an old custom Madame Bastide had once told me and there was a saying that *"Bouche qui mord à la chanson ne mord pas à la grappe."*

I did not work on that morning. I went to the vineyards to watch. I did not see Jean Pierre. He would have been too busy to pay much attention to me, too busy to pay attention to Geneviève, too busy to hate.

I felt that I was not part of all that. I had no job to do. I didn't belong, and that was symbolic.

I went to the gallery and looked at my work which in so very short a time would be finished.

Madame Bastide, who was my good friend, had advised me to leave. I wondered whether by avoiding me the Comte was telling me the same. He had some regard for me, I was sure, and that thought would sustain me a little when I went away. However sad I was, I should remind myself: But he had some regard for me. Love? Perhaps I was not one to inspire a *grande passion*. The thought almost made me laugh. If I could see this clearly I should see how absurd the whole thing was. Here was this man: worldly, experienced, fastidious . . . and there was I: the unattractive woman intense about one thing only, her work, all that he was not!—priding herself on her common sense, in which she had shown by her behavior she was sadly lacking. But I should remind myself: He had some regard for me.

His aloofness was the measure of that regard and he, like Madame Bastide, was saying to me: Go away. It is better so.

I took the key from my pocket. I must give it to the Comte and tell him how I had found it. Then I would say to him: "The work is almost finished. I shall be leaving shortly."

I looked at the key. Jean Pierre had one exactly like it. And he was searching for that lock even as I had.

I thought of those occasions when I had felt myself observed. Could it have been Jean Pierre? Had he seen me that day in the graveyard? Was he afraid that I should find what he was so desperately seeking?

He must not steal the emeralds, for whatever he told himself, it would be stealing and if he were caught . . .

It would be unbearable. I thought of the misery that would come to those people of whom I had grown so fond.

It would be no use remonstrating with him. There was only one thing to do: find the emeralds before he did. If they were here at all they must be in the dungeons because they were certainly not in the *oubliette*.

Here was an opportunity, for there was scarcely anyone in the *château* today. I remembered seeing a lantern near the door of the dungeon, and I promised myself that this time I would light it, so that I could explore properly. I made my way to the center of the *château* and descended the stone staircase. I reached the dungeons and as I opened the iron-studded door it creaked dismally.

I felt the chill of the place but I was determined to go on, so I lighted the lantern and held it up. It showed me the damp walls, the fungoid growth on them, the caves cut out of the wall, and here and there rings to which the chains were attached.

A gloomy place, dark, uninviting, still after all these years haunted by the sufferings of the forgotten men and women of a cruel age.

Where could there possibly be a lock here to fit the key?

I advanced into the gloom, and as I did so was aware of that sense of creeping horror. I knew exactly how men and women had felt in the past when they had been brought to this place. I sensed the terror, the hopelessness.

It seemed to me then that every nerve in my body was warning me: Get away. There's danger here. And I seemed to develop an extra sense of awareness as perhaps one does in moments of acute danger. I knew I was not alone, that I was being watched.

I remember thinking: Then if someone is waiting in lurk for me why doesn't that someone attack me now . . .

But I knew that whoever was there was waiting . . . waiting for me to do something and when I did, the danger would be upon me. Oh, Jean Pierre, I thought, you wouldn't hurt me—even for the Gaillard emeralds.

My fingers were trembling. I despised myself. I was no better than the servants who would not come here. I was afraid, even as they were, of the ghosts of the past.

"Who's there?" I cried, in a voice which sounded bold.

It echoed in a ghostly eerie way.

I knew that I must get out at once. It was that instinct warning me. Now! And don't come back here alone.

"Is anyone there?" I said. Then again speaking aloud: "There's nothing here . . ."

I didn't know why I had spoken aloud. It was some answer to the fear which possessed me. It was not a ghost who was lurking there in the shadows. But I had more to fear from the living than the dead.

I backed—trying to do so slowly and deliberately—to the door. I blew out the lantern and put it down. I was through that iron-studded door; I mounted the stone staircase and once at the top of it hurriedly went to my room.

I must never go there alone again, I told myself. I pictured that door shutting on me. I pictured the peril overtaking me. I was not sure in what form but I believed that I might then have had my wish to remain at the *château* forevermore.

I had come to a decision. I was going to talk to the Comte without delay.

It was characteristic that at Gaillard the grapes were trodden in the traditional way. In other parts of the country there might be presses but at Gaillard the old methods were retained.

"There are no ways like the old ways," Armand Bastide had said once. "No wine tastes quite like ours."

The warm air was filled with the sounds of revelry. The grapes were gathered and were three feet deep in the great trough.

The treaders, ready for the treading, had scrubbed their legs and feet until they shone; the musicians were tuning up. The excitement was high.

The scene touched by moonlight was fantastic to me, who had never seen anything like it before. I watched with the rest while the treaders, naked to the thighs, wearing short white breeches, stepped into the trough and began to dance.

I recognized the old song which Jean Pierre had first sung to me, and it had a special significance now:

> *"Qui sont-ils les gens qui sont riches?*
> *Sont-ils plus que moi qui n'ai rien . . ."*

I watched the dancers sink deeper and deeper into the purple morass; their faces gleaming, their voices raised in song. The music seemed to grow wilder; and the musicians closed in on the trough. Armand Bastide led the players with his violin; there was an accordion, a triangle and a drum, and some of the treaders used castinets as they went methodically round and round the trough.

Brandy was passed round to the dancers and they roared their appreciation as the singing grew louder, the dance more fervent.

I caught a glimpse of Yves and Margot; they with other children were wild with excitement, dancing together, shrieking with laughter as they pretended they were treading grapes.

Geneviève was there, her hair high on her head. She looked excited and secretive and I knew that her restless glances meant that she was looking for Jean Pierre.

And suddenly the Comte was beside me. He was smiling as though he was pleased, and I felt absurdly happy because I believed that he had been looking for me.

"Dallas," he said, and the use of my Christian name on his lips filled me with pleasure. Then: "Well, what do you think of it?"

"I have never seen anything like it."

"I'm glad we have been able to show you something you haven't seen before."

He had taken my elbow in the palm of his hand.

"I must speak to you," I said.

"And I to you. But not here. There is too much noise."

He drew me away from the crowd. Outside the air was fresh; I looked at the moon, gibbous, almost drunken-looking, the markings on its surface clear, so that it really did look like a face up there, laughing at us.

"It seems a long time since we have talked together," he said. "I could not make up my mind what to say to you. I wanted to think . . . about us. I did not want you to think me rash . . . impetuous. I did not think you would care for that."

"No," I replied.

We had started to walk towards the *château*.

"Tell me first what you wished to say," he said.

"In a few weeks I shall have finished my work. The time will have come for me to go."

"You must not go."

"But there will be no reason for me to stay."

"We must find a reason . . . Dallas."

I turned to him. It was no time for banter. I must know the truth. Even if I betrayed my feelings I must know it.

"What reason could there be?"

"That I asked you to stay because I should be unhappy if you left."

"I think you should tell me exactly what you mean."

"I mean that I could not let you go away. That I want you to stay here always . . . to make this place your home. I'm telling you that I love you."

"Are you asking me to marry you?"

"Not yet. There are things we must talk over first."

"But you have decided not to marry again."

"There was one woman in the world who could make me change my mind. I didn't even know she existed, and how was I to guess that chance should send her to me?"

"You are certain?" I asked and I heard the joy in my voice.

He stood still and took my hands in his; he looked solemnly into my face. "Never more certain in my life."

"And yet you do not ask me to marry you?"

"My dearest," he said, "I would not have you waste your life."

"Should I waste it . . . if I loved you?"

"Do not say if. Say you do. Let us be completely truthful with each other. Do you love me, Dallas?"

280

"I know so little of love. I know that if I left here, if I never saw you again I should be more unhappy than I have ever been in my life."

He leaned towards me and kissed me gently on the cheek. "That will do for a start. But how can you feel so . . . for me?"

"I don't know."

"You know me for what I am . . . I want you to. I could not let you marry me unless you really knew me. Have you thought of that, Dallas?"

"I have tried not to think of what seemed to me quite impossible, but secretly I have thought of it."

"And you thought it impossible?"

"I did not see myself in the role of *femme fatale*."

"God forbid."

"I saw myself as a woman—scarcely young, without any personal charm, but able to take care of herself, one who had put all foolish romantic notions behind her."

"And you did not know yourself."

"If I had never come here I should have become that person."

"If you had never met me . . . and if I had never met you . . . ? But we met and what did we do? We began to wipe off the bloom . . . the mildew . . . you know the terms. And now here we are. Dallas, I'll never let you leave me . . . but you must be sure . . ."

"I am sure."

"Remember you have become a little foolish . . . a little romantic. Why do you love me?"

"I don't know."

"You don't admire my character. You have heard rumors. What if I tell you that a great many of those rumors are true?"

"I did not expect you to be a saint."

"I have been ruthless . . . often cruel . . . I have been unfaithful . . . promiscuous . . . selfish . . . arrogant. What if I should be so again?"

"That I am prepared for. I am, as you know, self-opinionated . . . governessy, as Geneviève will tell you . . ."

"Geneviève . . ." he murmured and then with a laugh: "I am also prepared."

His hands were on my shoulders; I felt a rising passion in him and I was responding with all my being. But he was seeking for control; it was as though he was holding off that moment when he would take me in his arms and we should forget all else but the joy of being together at last in reality.

"Dallas," he said, "you must be *sure*."

"I am . . . I am . . . never more sure . . ."

"You would take me then?"

"Most willingly."

"Knowing . . . what you know."

"We will start again," I said. "The past is done with. What you were or what I was before we met is of no importance. It is what we shall be together."

"I am not a good man."

"Who shall say what is goodness?"

"But I have improved since you came."

"Then I must stay to see that you go on improving."

"My love," he said softly, and held me against him, but I did not see his face.

He released me and turned me towards the *château*.

It rose before us like a fairy castle in the moonlight, the towers seeming to pierce that midnight blue backcloth of the sky.

I felt like the Princess in a fairy story. I told him so.

"Who lived happy ever after," I said.

"Do you believe in happy endings?" he asked.

"Not perpetual ecstasy. But I believe it is for us to make our own happiness, and I am determined that we shall do that."

"You will make sure of it for both of us. I'm content. You will always achieve what you set out to do. I think you determined to marry me months ago. Dallas, when our plans are known there will be gossip. Are you prepared for that?"

"I shall not care for gossip."

"But I do not want you to have illusions."

"I believe I know the worst. You brought Philippe here because you had decided not to marry. How will he feel?"

"He will go back to his estates in Burgundy and forget he was once going to inherit when I died. After all, he might have had a long time to wait, and who knows when it came to him he might have been too old to care."

"But his son would have inherited. He might have cared for him."

"Philippe will never have a son."

282

"And his wife? What of her? I have heard that she was your mistress. It's true, isn't it?"

"At one time."

"And you married her to Philippe who you did not think would have a son so that she could bear yours?"

"I am capable of such a plan. I told you that I am a scoundrel, didn't I? But I need you to help me overcome my vices. You must never leave me, Dallas."

"And the child?" I asked.

"What child?"

"Her child . . . Claude's child."

"There is no child."

"But she has told me that she is to have a child . . . your child."

"It is not possible," he said.

"But if she is your mistress?"

"Was, I said, not is. You began to use your influence on me as soon as we met. Since she married Philippe there has been nothing between us. You look dubious. Does that mean you don't believe me?"

"I believe you," I said. "And . . . I'm glad. I can see that she wanted me to go. But it doesn't matter. Nothing matters now."

"You will probably hear of other misdeeds now and then."

"They will all be in the past. It will be the present and future which will be my affair."

"How I long for the time when my affairs are entirely yours."

"Could we say that they are from now on . . . ?"

"You delight me; you enchant me. Who would have believed I could hear such sweetness from your lips?"

"I should not have believed it myself. You have put a spell on me."

"My darling! But we must settle this. Please . . . please ask me more questions. You must know the worst now. What else have you heard of me?"

"I thought you were the father of Gabrielle's child."

"That was Jacques."

"I know now. I know too that you were kind to Mademoiselle Dubois. I know that you are good at heart . . ."

He put an arm round me and as we walked across the drawbridge, he said: "There is one thing you have not mentioned. You do not ask about my marriage."

"What do you expect me to ask?"

"You must have heard rumors."

"Yes, I have heard them."

"Little else was talked of in these parts at the time. I believe half the countryside believed I murdered her. They will think you are a brave woman to marry a man who, so many believed, murdered his wife."

"Tell me how she died."

He was silent.

"Please . . ." I said, "please tell me."

"I can't tell you."

"You mean . . ."

"This is what you must understand, Dallas."

"You know how she died?"

"It was an overdose of laudanum."

"How, tell me how?"

"You must never ask me."

"But I thought we were to be truthful with each other . . . always."

"That is why I can't tell you."

"Is the answer so bad then?"

"The answer is bad," he said.

"I don't believe you killed her. I won't believe it."

"Thank you . . . thank you, my dear. We must not talk of it again. Promise me not to."

"But I must know."

"It is what I feared. Now you look at me differently. You are uncertain. That is why I did not ask you to marry me. I could not until you had asked that question . . . and until you had heard my reply."

"But you have not replied."

"You have heard all I have to say. Will you marry me?"

"Yes . . . it is no use anyone's trying to tell me you're a murderer. I don't believe it. I'll never believe it."

He picked me up in his arms then.

"You've given your promise. May you never regret it."

"You are afraid to tell me . . ."

He put his lips to mine and the passion burst forth. I was limp clinging to him, bewildered, ecstatic, in my romantic dream.

When he released me he looked somber.

"There will be the gossip to face. There will be those who whisper behind our backs. They will warn you . . ."

"Let them."

"It will not be an easy life."

"It is the life I want."

"You will have a stepdaughter."

"Of whom I am already fond."

"A difficult girl who may become more so."

"I shall try to be a mother to her."

"You have done much for her already but . . ."

"You seem determined to tell me why I should not marry you. Do you want me to say no?"

"I should never allow you to say no."

"And what if I did?"

"I should carry you to one of the dungeons and keep you there."

Then I remembered the key and I told him how I had discovered it.

"I was hoping to present you with your long-lost emeralds," I said.

"If this is the key to them I'll present them to you," he told me.

"Do you think this key really does open wherever they are?"

"We can find out."

"When?"

"Now. The two of us. Yes, we'll go exploring together."

"Where do you think?"

"I think in the dungeons. There are *fleurs-de-lis* in one of the caves exactly like this. It may well be that one of them will give us the clue. You would like to go now?"

I was suddenly aware of others besides ourselves. Jean Pierre searching in the *château* for the emeralds. . . . We must find them before he did, for if he found them, he would steal them and bring disgrace on his family.

"Yes, please," I said. "Now."

He led the way to the stables, where he found a lantern; he lighted it and we made our way to the dungeons.

"I think I know where we will find the lock," he told me. "It's coming back now. I remember years ago when I was a boy there was an examination of the dungeons and this cave with the *fleur-de-lis* decorations was discovered. It was noticed because it was so unusual. A dado of *fleurs-de-lis* round the cave. It seemed such a strange idea to decorate such a place. Evidently there was a purpose."

"Didn't they look to see if there was a locked hiding place?"

"Evidently there was no sign of that. The theory was that some poor prisoner had somehow managed to make them—no one knew how—and fit them on the wall of his cage. How he worked in the gloom was a mystery."

We reached the dungeons and he swung open the iron-studded door. How different it was entering that dark and gloomy place with him; all fear was gone. I felt in a way it was symbolic. Whatever happens, if we're together, I can face it, I thought.

With one hand he held the lantern high; with the other he took my hand.

"The cave is somewhere here," he said.

The smell of decay and dampness was in the close atmosphere; my foot touched one of those iron rings to which a rusting chain was attached.

Horrible! And yet I was not afraid.

He gave a sudden exclamation.

"Come and look here."

I was beside him and there I saw the *fleurs-de-lis*. There were twelve of them placed at intervals round the cave about six inches from the ground.

He gave me the lantern and crouched down. He tried to push aside the first of the flowers but it would not move because it was so firmly attached to the wall. I watched him touch them in turn. At the sixth he paused.

"Just a minute," he said. "This one seems loose."

He gave an exclamation; I lifted the lantern higher and saw him push the flower aside. Beneath it was the lock.

The key fitted, and actually turned in the lock. "Can you see a door here?" he asked.

"There must be something," I answered. "The lock is there." I tapped the wall.

"There is a cavity behind this wall," I cried.

He threw his weight against the side of the cave and to our excitement there was a groaning sound and slowly a part of the wall appeared to move.

"It is a door," I said.

He tried again. A small door swung back suddenly and I heard him exclaim in triumph.

I went to stand beside him, the lantern bobbing in my hand.

I saw what was like a cupboard—a small space about two feet by two and inside it a casket that might have been silver.

He lifted it out and looked at me.

"It looks," he said, "as though we've found the emeralds."

"Open it," I cried.

Like the door it offered some resistance; but there they were—the rings, bracelets, girdle, necklaces, and tiara which I had restored to color on the portrait.

And as we stood there looking at each other over that casket I realized that he was looking at me, not at the stones. "So you have restored the treasure to the *château*," he said.

And I knew he wasn't thinking of the emeralds.

That was the happiest moment I was to know for a long time. It was like reaching the top of a mountain and, having done so, suddenly being flung down into despair.

Was it a creak of that iron-studded door? Was it a movement in the gloom?

The thought of danger came to us both simultaneously. We knew that we were not alone.

The Comte drew me quickly to his side and put an arm about me.

"Who is there?" he shouted.

A figure loomed out of the darkness.

"So you found them?" said Philippe.

I looked into his face and was terrified, for the dim light of the lantern, which I still held, showed me a man I had never seen before. Philippe's features, yes, but gone was the lassitude, the air of delicate effeminacy. Here was a desperate man, a man with one grim purpose.

"You were looking for them too?" asked the Comte.

"You got there before me. So it was you, Mademoiselle Lawson . . . I was afraid you would."

The Comte pressed my shoulder. "Go now," he began.

But Philippe interrupted. "Stay where you are, Mademoiselle Lawson."

"Have you gone mad?" demanded the Comte.

"By no means. Neither of you will leave here."

The Comte, still gripping me, took a step forward but stopped short when Philippe raised his hand. He was holding a gun.

"Don't be a fool, Philippe," said the Comte.

"You won't escape this time, Cousin, though you did in the woods."

"Give me the gun."

"I need it to kill you."

With a swift movement the Comte thrust me behind him. Philippe's short grim laugh echoed oddly in that place.

"You won't save her. I'm going to kill you both."

"Listen to me, Philippe."

"I've had to listen to you too often. Now it's your turn to listen to me."

"You propose to kill me because you want what is mine, is that it?"

"You're right. If you'd wanted to live you shouldn't have planned to marry Mademoiselle Lawson; you shouldn't have found those emeralds. You should have left something for me. Thank you, Mademoiselle Lawson, for leading me to them, but they're mine now. Everything is mine."

"And you think you're going to get away with . . . murder?"

"Yes, I've thought it out. I meant to catch you together . . . like this. I didn't know Mademoiselle Lawson would be so obliging as to find the emeralds for me first. So it couldn't be better. Murder and suicide. Oh, not mine, Cousin. I want to live . . . live in my own right . . . not under your shadow for once. Mademoiselle Lawson will have taken a gun from the gun room, killed you and then herself. You played into my hands so beautifully—your reputation being what it is."

"Philippe, you *fool*."

"I've done with talking. Now's the time for action. You first, Cousin . . . we must have it in the right order . . ."

I saw the gun raised. I tried to move to protect the Comte, but he held me firmly behind him. Involuntarily I shut my eyes. I heard the earsplitting sound. Then, after the explosion . . . silence. Faint with terror, I opened my eyes.

Two men were struggling on the floor—Philippe and Jean Pierre.

I was past surprise. I was scarcely aware of them. I just knew that I was not going to lose my life in the dungeons, but I was losing everything that would make that life worth living, for on the floor, bleeding from his wounds, lay the man I loved.

❧ 12 ❧

Outside the sounds of revelry went on. They did not know, those who celebrated the grape harvest, that the Comte lay on his bed near to death; that Philippe lay in his under the influence of the sleeping draught the doctor had given him; that Jean Pierre and I sat in the library waiting.

Two doctors were with the Comte. They had sent us down here to wait and the waiting seemed endless.

It was not yet eleven o'clock and I seemed to have lived through a lifetime since I had stood in the dungeons with the Comte and suddenly come face to face with death.

And so strangely, there sat Jean Pierre, his face pale, his eyes bewildered, as though he too did not understand what he was doing there.

"How long they are," I said.

"Don't fret. He won't die."

I shook my head.

"No," said Jean Pierre, almost bitterly. "He won't die until he wants to. Doesn't he always . . ." A smile twisted his lips. "Sit down," he said. "You can do no good by walking up and down. A second earlier and I'd have saved him. I left it that second too long."

He had taken on a new authority. Sitting there he might have been the Comte. For the first time I noticed the *château* features—an irrelevant detail with which to concern myself at such a time!

It was Jean Pierre who had dominated that grisly scene. He it was who had sent me to call the doctors, who had planned what we should do.

"We should as yet say little of what has happened in the dungeons," he cautioned, "for you can be sure that the Comte will want the story told his way. I expect the gun will have gone off accidentally. He wouldn't want Monsieur Philippe to be accused of attempted murder. We'd better be discreet until we know what he wants."

I clung to that. Until we know. Then we should know. He would open his eyes and live again.

"If he lives . . ." I began.

"He'll live," said Jean Pierre.

"If only I could be sure . . ."

"He wants to live." He paused for a moment, then went on: "I saw you leave. How could I help it? Monsieur Philippe saw you . . . why, everyone must have seen, and guessed how things were. I watched you. I followed you to the dungeons . . . as Philippe did. But the Comte will want to live . . . and if he wants to, he will."

"Then, Jean Pierre, *you* will have saved his life."

He wrinkled his brow. "I don't know why I did it," he said, "I could have let Philippe shoot him. He's a first-class shot. The bullet would have gone through his heart. That's what he was aiming for. I knew it . . . and I said to myself: 'This is the end of you, Monsieur le Comte.' And then . . . I did it . . . I sprang on Philippe; I caught his arm . . . just that second too late. Half a second, shall we say . . . if I'd been that half a second earlier the bullet would have hit the ceiling . . . half a second later and it would have pierced his heart. I couldn't have got there earlier though. I wasn't near enough. I don't know why I did it. I just didn't think."

"Jean Pierre," I repeated, "if he lives you will have saved his life."

"It's queer," he admitted.

And there was silence.

I had to talk of something else. I could not bear to think of him lying there unconscious . . . while his life slowly ebbed away, taking with it all my hopes of happiness.

"You were looking for the emeralds," I said.

"Yes. I meant to find them and go away. It would not have been stealing. I had a right to something . . . now, of course, I shall have nothing. I shall go to Mermoz and be his slave all my life . . . if he lives, and he will live because of what I did."

"We shall never forget it, Jean Pierre."

"You will marry him?"

"Yes."

"So I lose you too."

"You never wanted *me,* Jean Pierre. You wanted only what you thought he did."

"It's strange . . . how he's always been there . . . all my life. I hate him, you know. There have been times when I could have taken a gun to him . . . and to think . . . if he lives it will be because I saved his life. I wouldn't have believed it of myself."

"None of us knows how we'll act in certain circumstances . . . not until we come right face to face with them. It was a wonderful thing you did tonight, Jean Pierre."

"It was a crazy thing. I wouldn't have believed it. I hated him, I tell you. All my life I've hated him. He has all that I want. He *is* all that I want to be."

"All that Philippe wanted too. He hated him as you did. It was envy. That's one of the seven deadly sins, Jean Pierre, and I believe, the deadliest. But you triumphed over it. I'm so glad, Jean Pierre, so glad."

"But I tell you it wasn't meant. Or perhaps it was. Perhaps I never meant it when I thought I'd like to kill him. But I would have stolen the emeralds if I'd had a chance."

"But you would never have taken his life. You know that now. You would have even married me perhaps. You might have tried to marry Geneviève . . ."

His face softened momentarily: "I might yet," he said. "That would upset the noble Comte."

"And Geneviève? You would use her for your revenge?"

"She's a charming girl. Young . . . and wild . . . like myself perhaps, unaccountable. And she's the Comte's daughter. Don't think I'm a reformed character because I've done this crazy thing tonight. I won't make promises about Geneviève."

"She's a young and impressionable girl."

"She's fond of me."

"She must not be hurt. Life has not been easy for her."

"Do you think I'd hurt her?"

"No, Jean Pierre. I don't think you're half as wicked as you like to think you are."

"You don't know much about me, Dallas."

"I think I know a great deal."

"You'd be surprised if you did. I had my plans . . . I was going to see that my son was master of the *château* if I could never be."

"But how?"

"He had plans, you know, before he was going to marry you. He wasn't marrying again, so he decided he'd bring his mistress here and marry her to Philippe. His son and hers would inherit the *château*. Well, it wasn't going to be his son but mine."

"You . . . and Claude!"

He nodded triumphantly. "Why not? She was angry because he didn't notice her. Philippe's no man, and so . . . well, what do you think?"

I was listening for the approach of the doctors. I was only thinking of what was going on in that room above.

The doctors came into the room. There were two of them from the town, and they would know a great deal about us all. It was one of these who had attended the Comte when Philippe had shot him in the woods.

I had stood up and both doctors looked straight at me.

"He's . . ." I began.

"He's sleeping now."

I looked at them, mutely imploring them to give me some hope.

"It was a near thing," said one of them almost tenderly. "A few inches more and . . . he was fortunate."

"He'll recover?" My voice sounded loud and vibrant with emotion.

"He's by no means out of danger. If he gets through the night . . ."

I sank back into my chair.

"I propose to stay here until morning," said one of the doctors.

"Yes, please do."

"How did it happen?" asked the elder of the two.

"The gun Monsieur Philippe was carrying went off," said Jean Pierre. "Monsieur le Comte will be able to give an account of what happened . . . when he recovers."

The doctors nodded. And I wondered if they had both been here on the day Françoise died; and if then they waited for the Comte's account of that tragedy.

I didn't care what had happened then. All I asked was that he would recover.

"You're Mademoiselle Lawson, aren't you?" asked the younger doctor. I said I was.

"Is your name Dallas—or something like that?"

"Yes."

"I thought he was trying to say it: Perhaps you would care to sit by his bed. He won't speak to you, and just in case he's aware he might like to have you there."

I went to his bedroom and sat there through the night, watching him, praying that he would live. In the early morning he opened his eyes and looked at me and I was sure he was content to find me there.

I said: "You must live . . . you cannot die and leave me now."

He said later that he heard me, and for that reason he refused to die.

In a week we knew it was only a matter of time before he recovered. He had a miraculous constitution, said the doctors, and had had a miraculous escape; now it was for him to make a miraculous recovery.

He gave his account of what had happened. It was as we had thought. He had no wish for it to be known that his cousin had attempted to murder him. Philippe and Claude left for Burgundy, and in an interview between the two cousins Philippe was told that he should never come back to the *château*.

I was glad not to have to see Claude again now that I knew that she had hoped to find the emeralds, that she had become interested in the wall-painting when the words had been disclosed and she probably guessed that I had stumbled on some clue. She and Philippe would have worked together, watching me; she had searched my room while he detained me in the vineyards. It must have been Philippe who had followed me in the copse that day. Had he intended to shoot me as he had attempted to shoot the Comte? They had wanted to be rid of me and had tried their hardest to make me leave by offering me work elsewhere; that was when they had believed the Comte was becoming too interested in me, for if he married, their schemes would have been ruined.

Claude was a strangely complex woman. I was sure she had been sorry for me at one time and had, partly for my own good, wanted to save me from the Comte. She could not believe that a woman such as I could possibly arouse any lasting affection in such a man—for even an attractive woman like herself had been unable to. I pictured her working with her husband and with Jean Pierre—ready to go away with Jean Pierre if he found the emeralds, ready to stay with Philippe if he did.

I was glad, too, that Jean Pierre was free of her, for I would always have a fondness for him.

The Comte had said that the Mermoz vineyards should be his. "It is a small reward," he said, "for saving my life."

I did not tell him then what I knew; in fact I think he may have known already, for he did not ask what Jean Pierre had been doing in the dungeons.

Those were days of hopes and fears. It was with me that the doctors discussed his progress and I found I had an aptitude for nursing. But perhaps my special interest in the patient brought out this quality.

We would sit in the garden and talk of our future. We talked of Philippe and Jean Pierre. Philippe, I guessed, had first wanted me to stay at the *château* because he thought I should never attract the Comte, and when he found he was wrong sought to get rid of me. He must have planned with Claude that I should be offered the task of restoring her father's pictures so that I could be removed from Gaillard. And she had tried to lure me with a very tempting offer. Then of course he had planned my removal in a more sinister fashion.

We came to the conclusion that the secret cupboard had been constructed in that spot where a wretched prisoner had long ago tunneled his way from the *oubliette* to the dungeons. The Comte thought he remembered his grandfather's mentioning that this had happened.

The emeralds had been put away in the strong room. Perhaps one day I should wear them. The thought still seemed incongruous to me.

I wished that there could have been a neat ending to everything. I had a passion for neatness which I longed to satisfy. Sometimes I sat in the sunny garden and looked up at the machicolated towers of the *château* and felt that I was living in a fairy tale. I was a princess in disguise who had rescued a prince on whom a spell had been laid. I had lifted the spell, and he would be happy again, happy ever after. That was what I wanted to be sure of now . . . in the Indian summer of the pond garden, with the man I was soon to marry beside me, growing stronger every day.

But life is not a fairy tale.

Jean Pierre had left for Mermoz; Geneviève was sullen because he had left. Her head was full of wild plans; and one noble action had not changed Jean Pierre's character overnight.

And across my happiness there hung a dark shadow. I wondered if I should ever forget the first Comtesse.

They knew I was to marry the Comte. I had seen their glances . . . Madame Latière, Madame Bastide . . . all the servants.

It was a fairy tale. The humble young woman who came to the castle and married the Comte.

Geneviève, who was smarting under the loss of Jean Pierre, did not mince her words.

"You're brave, aren't you?"

"Brave? What do you mean?"

"If he murdered one wife why not another?"

No, there could be no neat happy ending.

I began to be haunted by Françoise. How strange it was. I had said I did not believe in the rumors I had heard; nor did I; but they haunted me.

He didn't kill her, I would say to myself a dozen times a day.

Yet why did he refuse to tell me the truth?

"There must be no lies between us," he had said.

And for this reason he could not tell me.

There came the opportunity and I found myself unable to resist it.

It happened like this. It was afternoon, and the *château* was quiet. I was anxious about Geneviève and went along to Nounou's room. I wanted to talk to her about the girl. I wanted to try to understand how deep this feeling for Jean Pierre had gone.

I knocked at the door of Nounou's sitting room. There was no answer so I went in. Nounou was lying on a couch; there was a dark handkerchief over her eyes and I guessed she was suffering from one of her headaches.

"Nounou," I said gently, but there was no answer.

My eyes went from the sleeping woman to the cupboard in which those little notebooks were kept, and I saw that Nounou's key was in the cupboard door. It was usually kept on the chain she wore about her waist, and it was unusual for her not to return it there immediately after using it.

I bent over her. She was breathing deeply; she was fast asleep. I looked again at the cupboard, and the temptation was irresistible. I had to know. I reasoned with myself: She showed you the others so why should you not see that one? After all, Françoise is dead; and if the books could be read by Nounou, why not by you?

It's important, I assured myself. It's of the utmost importance. I *must* know what is in that last book.

I went quietly to the cupboard; I looked over my shoulder at the sleeping woman and opened the cupboard door. I saw the bottle, the small glass. I lifted it up and smelt it. It had contained laudanum which she kept for her headaches, the same opiate which had killed Françoise.

Nounou had taken a dose because her headache was unbearable. I had to know. It was no use considering my scruples.

I picked the notebook at the end of the row; I knew that they would be in absolute order. I glanced inside. Yes. This was the one I wanted.

I went to the door.

Nounou had still not stirred. I sped to my own room and with wildly beating heart began to read.

"So I am going to have a child. This time it may be a boy. That will please him. I shall tell no one yet. Lothair must be the first to know. I shall say to him: 'Lothair, we are going to have a child. Are you pleased?' Of course I am frightened. I am frightened of so much. But when it is over it will be worth while. What will Papa say? He will be hurt . . . disgusted. How much happier he would be if I went to him and told him I was going into a convent. Away from the wickedness of the world, away from lust, away from vanity. That is what he would like. And I shall go to him and say, 'Papa, I am going to have a child.' But not yet. I shall choose the right time. That is why I must say nothing yet. In case Papa should get to know.

"They say a woman changes when she is going to have a child. I have changed. I could have been so happy. I almost am. I dream of the child. He will be a boy, for that is what we want. It is right that the Comtes de la Talle should have sons. That is why they marry. If it were not necessary they could be content with their mistresses. They are the ones they really care for. But now it will be different. He will look at me in a different light. I shall not be only the one he was obliged to marry for the sake of the family; I shall be the mother of his son."

"It is wonderful. I should have known this before. I should not have listened to Papa. Yesterday when I went to Carrefour I did not tell him. I could not bring myself to do so. And the reason that I am so happy is because it is so, and he will besmirch it. He will look at me with those stern cold eyes of his and he will be seeing it all . . . everything that led up to my having the child . . . not as it was . . . but as he believed it to be . . . horrible . . . sinful . . . I wanted to cry to him: 'No, Papa, it is not like that. You are wrong. I should never have listened to you.' Oh, that room where we knelt together and you prayed that I should be protected from the lusts of the flesh! It was because of that that I shrank from him. I keep thinking now of the night before my marriage. Why did he agree? He regretted it almost immediately afterwards. I remember after the night of the contrat de mariage *dinner* how we prayed together and he said: 'My child, I wish this need never take place.' And I said: 'Why, Papa, everyone is congratulating me!' And he answered: 'That's because a match with the de la Talles is considered a good one, but I would be happy if I thought you would be living a life of purity.' I did not understand then. I said I would try to be a pure woman; and he kept murmuring about the lusts of the flesh. And then the night before the church wedding we prayed together and I was ignorant and knew nothing of what was expected of me, except that it was shameful and that my father regretted he could not spare me such shame. And thus it was I came to my husband . . .

"But it is different now. I have come to understand that Papa is wrong. He should never have married. He wanted to be a monk. He was on the point of becoming one, and then he found that he wanted to marry and he changed his mind and married my mother. But he hated himself for his weakness, and his monk's robe was his greatest treasure. He is mistaken. I know that now. I might have been happy. I might have learned how to make Lothair love me if Papa had not frightened me, if he had not taught me that the marriage bed was shameful. I try not to blame him. All these years when my husband has turned from me, when he has spent his nights with other women —perhaps they need not have been. I begin to see that I have turned him from me with my shivering shrinking sense of sin. I shall go to Carrefour tomorrow and I shall tell Papa that I am going to have a child. I shall say: 'Papa, I feel no shame . . . only pride. Everything is going to be different from now on.'"

"I did not go to Carrefour as I promised myself. My wisdom tooth started to ache again. Nounou said to me: 'Sometimes when a woman has a baby she loses a tooth. You're not so, are you?' I flushed, and she knew. How could I keep a secret from Nounou? I said: 'Don't tell anyone yet, Nounou. I haven't told him. He should know first, shouldn't he? And I want to tell Papa too.' Nounou understood. She knows me so well. She knows how Papa makes me pray when I go there. She knows that Papa would like to see me in a convent. She knows what he thinks of marriage. She rubbed a clove on my gum and said that should make it better; and I sat on the footstool, leaning against her as I used to when I was little. And I talked to Nounou. I told her how I felt. I said: 'Papa was wrong, Nounou. He made me feel that marriage was shameful. It was because of this . . . because I made my marriage intolerable that my husband turned to others.' 'You're not to blame,' she said. 'You have broken none of the commandments.' 'Papa made me feel unclean,' I said. 'From the beginning it was so. So my husband turned from me. I could never explain to him. He thought me cold and you know, Nounou, he is not a cold man. He needed a warm affectionate clever woman. He has not been treated fairly.' Nounou wouldn't have it. She said I had done no wrong. I accused her of agreeing with Papa. I said: 'I believe you, too, would rather have seen me in a convent than married . . .' And she did not deny it. I said: 'You, too, think marriage is shameful, Nounou.' And she did not deny that either. My tooth was no better, so she gave me a few drops of laudanum in water and made me lie on the couch in her room. Then she locked the bottle in her cupboard and sat down beside me. 'That'll make you drowsy,' she said. 'That'll send you into a nice sleep.' And it did."

"This is too terrible. I do not believe I shall ever forget it as long as I live. It keeps coming in and out of my mind. Perhaps if I write it down I can stop going over and over it. Papa is very ill. It began like this: I went to see him today. I had made up my mind I would tell him about the child. He was in his room when I arrived, and I went straight to him. He was sitting at the table reading the Bible when I went in. He looked up and then laid the red silk bookmarker in the place and closed the book. 'Well, my child,' he said. I went to him and kissed him. He seemed to notice the change in me at once, for he looked startled and a little alarmed. He asked me about Geneviève, and if I had brought her. I told him I had not. Poor child, it is too much to expect her to pray for so long. She grows restive and that agitates him more than ever. I assured him that she was a good child. He said that he thought that she had a tendency to waywardness. It must be watched. Perhaps it was because I am about to become a mother again that I felt rebellious. I did not want Geneviève to go to her husband —when her time came—as I had gone to mine. I said rather sharply that I thought she was normal, as a child should be. One did not expect children to behave as the holy saints. He stood up and he looked terrible. 'Normal,' he said. 'Why do you say that?' And I answered: 'Because it is natural for a child to be a little wayward, as you call it, now and then. Geneviève is. I shall not punish her for it.' 'To spare the rod is to spoil the child,' he replied. 'If she is wicked she should be beaten.' I was horrified. 'You are wrong, Papa,' I said. 'I do not agree with you. Geneviève shall not be beaten. Nor shall any of my children.' He looked at me in astonishment and I blurted out: 'Yes, Papa, I am going to have a child. This time a boy, I hope. I shall pray for a boy . . . and you must pray too.' His mouth twitched. He said: 'You are to have a child . . .' I answered joyfully: 'Yes, Papa. And I'm happy . . . happy . . . happy . . .' 'You are hysterical,' he said. 'I feel hysterical. I feel I want to dance with joy.' Then he gripped the table and seemed to slide down to the floor. I caught at him and broke his fall. I could not understand what had happened to him. I knew that he was very ill. I called the Labisses and Maurice. They came and got him to his bed. I was faint myself. They sent for my husband and then I learned that my father was very ill. I believed he was dying."

"That was two days ago. He was asking for me. All day he asks for me. He likes me to sit with him. The doctor thinks it is good for him that I should. I am still at Carrefour. My husband is here too. I have told him. I said to him: 'It was when I told Papa that I was going to have a child that he became so ill. It was the shock, I believe.' And my husband comforted me. He said: 'He had been ill for a long time. This was a stroke and it could have happened at any time.' 'But,' I said, 'he did not want me to have children. He thinks it is sinful.' And my husband said I must not worry. It would be bad for the child. And he is pleased. I know he is pleased for I believe above all things he wants a son."

"I sat with Papa today. We were alone. He opened his eyes and saw me there. He said: 'Honorine . . . is that you Honorine?' And I said 'No. It is Françoise.' But he kept saying 'Honorine' so I knew that he was mistaking me for my mother. I sat there by the bed, thinking of the old days when she had been alive. I did not see her every day. Sometimes she was dressed in an afternoon gown with ribbons and laces and Madame Labisse brought her down to the drawing room. She would sit in her chair and say little, and I always thought what a strange mother she was. But she was very beautiful. Even as a child I knew that. She looked like a doll I once had; her face was smooth and pink and there were no wrinkles on it. She had a tiny waist, yet she was plump and curved like pictures I had seen of beautiful women. I sat by his bed, thinking of her and how one day I had come in and found her laughing, and laughing in such an odd way as though she couldn't stop and Madame Labisse's taking her off to her room where she seemed to stay for a long time. I knew her room because I had been there once. I had climbed the stairs to be with her. And I found her there sitting on her chair with her feet in little velvet slippers on her footstool. It was warm in the room, and it was snowing outside, I remember. There was a lamp very high on the wall and a guard round the fire such as I had in my nursery. And I noticed too the window, for there was only a small one and there were no curtains at it, but bars across. I went to her and sat at her feet and she said nothing to me but she liked having me there for she fondled my hair and ruffled it and pulled it, and made it very untidy and suddenly she started to laugh in that odd way I had heard. Madame Labisse came in and found me there and told me to go away at once. And she told Nounou, for I was scolded and told I was never to go up those stairs again. So I only saw Maman when she came to the drawing room. But when he kept talking of Honorine, I sat there remembering. He said suddenly: 'I must go, Honorine. I must go. No, I cannot stay.' Then he was praying: 'Oh God, I am a weak and sinful man. This woman tempted me and for her I became the sinner I am. And my punishment has come. You are testing me, O Lord, and Thy miserable servant has betrayed Thee—seventy times seven he has betrayed Thee.' I said: 'Papa, it is all right, this is not Honorine. It is I, Françoise, your daughter. And you are not sinful. You have been a good man.' And he answered: 'Eh? What's that?' And I went on talking to him, trying to soothe him."

"That night I understood a great deal about my father. As I lay in bed the picture became clear to me. He had yearned for sanctity; he had wanted to be a monk, but there was a sensual streak in him which fought with his piety. Being the man he was he would have suffered torture—knowing of this streak, seeking to suppress it. Then he met my mother and he desired her; he turned from the thought of a monastery and married instead. But even though married he had sought to suppress his desire and when he failed he despised himself. My mother was beautiful; as a child I had realized that; and to him she was irresistible. I pictured him, pacing up and down, steeling himself to stay away from her. He thought physical love sinful, but he had been unable to resist it. I could imagine those days and nights when he shut himself in his austere room, when he lay on his pallet, when he scourged himself. He would be awaiting vengeance, for he was a man who believed in vengeance. Every small fault of mine or the servants had to be punished. At morning prayers that was the theme of his daily sermon. 'Vengeance is mine, said the Lord.' Poor Papa! How unhappy he must have been! Poor Maman! What sort of marriage had she had? Then I saw what he had done to me and mine and I wept for the tragedy of it. Then I said to myself: 'But there is time yet. I am going to bear a child. So perhaps it is not too late.' And I wondered how I could help Papa. But I could see no way.

"This morning Nounou came in to draw the blinds and she looked at me anxiously. She said I looked drawn. I had had a sleepless night. It was true. I had lain awake for hours thinking of Papa and what he had done to my life. Was it the tooth? she asked. She thinks of me still as a child and does not seem to believe that I could be concerned with important problems. I let her think it was the tooth, for I knew it would be impossible to talk to her—nor did I want to. 'You must have some laudanum tonight, my child,' she said. I answered: 'Thank you, Nounou.'"

"When I went over to Carrefour, Maurice told me that Papa had been waiting for me. He kept watching the door and every time anyone went in he would say my name. They were all relieved that I had come. So I went in and sat by his bedside, although when I went in his eyes were closed and even when he opened them, after a while, he did not take much notice of me. Then I noticed that he was mumbling to himself. He kept saying: 'The Vengeance of the Lord . . .' over and over again. He was very anxious, I could see that. I bent over him and whispered: 'Papa, you have nothing to fear. You have done what you thought right. What more can anyone do?' 'I am a sinner,' he said. 'I was tempted into sin. 'Twas not her fault. She was beautiful . . . she loved the pleasures of the flesh and she lured me to follow her. Even after I knew I could not resist her. That is the sin, child. That was the greatest sin of all.' I said: 'Papa, you are distressing yourself. Lie still.' 'Is that Françoise?' he asked. 'Is that my daughter?' I answered that it was. He said: 'And is there a child?' 'Yes, Papa. Your little granddaughter, Geneviève.' His face puckered and I was frightened. He began to whisper: 'I have seen the signs. The sins of the fathers . . . Oh my God, the sins of the fathers . . .' I felt I had to comfort him. I said: 'Papa, I think I understand. You loved your wife. That was no sin. It is natural to love, natural for men and women to have children. That is the way the world goes on.' He kept murmuring to himself and I wondered whether to call Maurice. Occasionally a co-herent sentence emerged. 'I knew it. There was the hysteria . . . There was the time when we found her playing with the fire. There was the time when we found her building a fire in the bedroom, laying the sticks across each other . . . We were always finding sticks laid as though for a fire . . . in cupboards . . . under beds . . . She would run out to gather sticks . . . Then the doctors came.' 'Papa,' I said, 'do you mean that my mother was mad?' He did not answer, but went on as though I had not spoken: 'I could have sent her away. I should have sent her away . . . but I could not do without her . . . and I still went to her . . . even though I knew. And in time there was fruit of her madness. That is my sin and there will be vengeance . . . I watch for it . . . wait for it.' I was frightened, I forgot he was a sick man. I knew that what he was telling me was the truth as he saw it. I knew now why my mother had been kept in the room with the barred win-dows; I knew the reason for our strange household. My mother had been mad. It was for this reason that my father had not wanted me to marry. 'Françoise,' he mumbled. 'Françoise . . . my daughter.' 'I am

302

here, Papa.' 'I watched over Françoise,' he said. 'She was a good child
. . . quiet, shy, retiring . . . not like her mother. Not brazen, bold
. . . in love with the sins of the flesh. No, my daughter has escaped
. . . But it is written "unto the third and fourth generation . . ."
She was sought in marriage by the de la Talles . . . and I gave my
consent. That was my sin of pride. I could not say to the Comte when
he asked for my daughter for his son: "Her mother is mad." So I said
my daughter should marry and then I scourged myself for my pride
and my lust for I was guilty of two of the deadliest sins. But I did not
stop the marriage and so my daughter went to the château.' I tried
to soothe him. 'All is well, Papa. There is nothing to fear. The past is
done with. All is well now.' '"Unto the third and fourth generations . . ."' he whispered. '"The sins of the fathers . . ." I have seen
it in the child. She is wild and she has the look of her grandmother. I
know the signs. She will be like her grandmother . . . unable to resist
the pleasures of the flesh . . . and the evil seed will pass on and on
through the generations to come.' 'You can't mean Geneviève . . .
my little girl.' He whispered: 'The seed is there in Geneviève . . . I
have seen it. It will grow and grow until it destroys her. I should have
warned my daughter. She has escaped, but her children will not!' I
was frightened. I began to see so much more than I ever had before.
I knew now why he had been overcome with horror when I had told
him I was to have another child. I sat by my bed numb with horror.

"There is no one I can talk to. When I returned from Carrefour I
went into one of the flower gardens and sat alone for a long time
thinking of it. Geneviève! My daughter! Incidents from the past rose
in my mind. It was like watching a play in a series of scenes, all significant leading to a climax. I remembered violent rages; her way of
laughing immoderately; and I heard her laughter mingling with echoes
from the past. My mother . . . my daughter. They even looked alike
. . . The more I tried to recall my mother's face the more she looked
like Geneviève. I knew now that I should watch my daughter as my
father had watched me. Every little misdemeanor of her childhood
which I had once thought of as a prank took on a new significance.
The evil seed had passed on through me to the coming generation.
My father, who had wanted to be a monk, had been unable to suppress
his passion for his wife even though he knew her to be mad, and as a

result I had been born—and I in my turn had borne a child. Then the horror of my situation made me tremble with fear for not only was there my poor Geneviève. There was the unborn child."

"I did not go to Carrefour yesterday. I could not. I made the excuse that my tooth was bad. Nounou fussed over me. She gave me a few drops of her laudanum and that sent me to sleep. I felt refreshed when I awoke, but my anxieties were soon nagging at my mind. The child I longed for . . . what would it be like? What of my poor Geneviève? She came in this morning, as she always does first thing. I heard her with Nounou outside the door. Nounou said: 'Your mother is not well. She has a toothache and wants to rest.' 'But I always go in,' replied my daughter. 'Not today, my dear. Let your Maman rest.' But Geneviève flew into a rage. She stamped her feet and when Nounou tried to hold her off she bit poor Nounou's hand. I lay there shivering. He is right. These sudden passions are more than childish temper. Nounou can't control them . . . nor can I. I called that she was to come in, and she came, her eyes bright with angry tears, her lips sullen. She threw herself at me; she hugged me far too wildly, far too passionately. 'Nounou is trying to keep us apart. I won't let her. I'll kill her.' That was how she talked, wildly, extravagantly. She doesn't mean it, I always said. It is just her way. Just her way! Honorine's way. My father had noticed the seed in her. I believed it was there . . . and I was seized with terror."

"Papa was asking for me. So I went over to Carrefour. 'He waits for you to come all the time,' they told me. 'He watches the door. He asks for your mother,' they say. 'He thinks you are your mother perhaps.' So I sat by his bed and he looked at me with those wild glazed eyes and he said my name and sometimes that of my mother. He murmured of sin and vengeance, but he was not as coherent as he had been. I thought he was dying. I could see that he was working himself up to an excitement and I bent over him to hear what he was saying. 'A child?' he said. 'There is going to be a child?' I thought he was thinking of what I had told him until I realized he was farther back in time. 'A child . . . Honorine is going to have a child. How could this have happened? Oh, but it is God's vengeance. I knew . . . and in spite of my knowledge . . . I went to her and this is the vengeance of the Lord . . . *unto the third and fourth generation . . . and the seed . . . the evil seed . . . will live forever.' 'Papa,' I said, 'it is all long ago. Honorine is dead and I am well. There is nothing wrong with me.' His wild uncomprehending eyes were on me. He murmured: 'They told me she was with child. I remember the day well. "You are to be a father," they said. And they smiled at me . . . not knowing the horror that was in my heart. It had come. Vengeance had come. My sin would not die with me. It would live to the third and fourth generation. I went to her room that night . . . I stood over her. She was sleeping. I held the pillow in my hands. I could press it over her face . . . that would be the end . . . the end of her and the child. But she was beautiful . . . her black hair . . . the round childishness of her face . . . and I was a coward, so I fell upon her, embracing her, and I knew I could never kill her.' 'You distress yourself, Papa,' I said. 'It is over. Nothing can change what is done. I am here now . . . and I am well, I assure you.' He was not listening to me and I was thinking of Geneviève and the child who was not yet born."*

"I couldn't sleep last night. I kept thinking of Papa's grief. And I could not forget Geneviève. I thought of the wildness in her, which frightened Nounou. I knew why. Nounou had known my mother. Nounou's fears were a reflection of my father's. I had seen Nounou watching my daughter. I dozed and suffered a nightmare. There was someone in a room with a barred window. I had to kill her; I stood there with a pillow in my hand. It was my mother . . . but she had Geneviève's face and in her arms she carried a child . . . a child who was not yet born. I made her lie down and I stood over her with the pillow. I woke up crying: 'No! No!' I was shivering. I couldn't rest after that. I was afraid to sleep for fear of more nightmares so I took some of Nounou's laudanum and then I fell into a long dreamless sleep.

"When I awoke this morning my mind was very clear. If my child is a boy, I thought, he will carry on the line of the de la Talles. And I thought of that evil seed of madness entering the château like a ghost that would haunt it for the centuries to come. I should have brought that to them. Geneviève? She has Nounou to care for her. And Nounou knows. Nounou will watch over her. She will see that she never marries. Perhaps Nounou will persuade her to go into a convent as

Papa wanted to persuade me. But the child . . . if it is a boy . . . Papa lacked the courage. It needs courage. Had Papa killed my mother I should never have been born. I should have known no pain . . . nothing. And that is how it would be with the child."

"Last night a strange thing happened. I awoke from a nightmare, and I remembered the peaceful sleep which comes from the little green bottle with the crinkly sides. Crinkly, Nounou told me, because if you should pick it up in the dark you would know it for a poison bottle. Poison! But it gives such sweet sleep, such relief! I thought how easy it would be to take twice . . . three times . . . the dose Nounou gave me for my toothache . . . and then no more fears . . . no more worries. The child would know nothing. The child would be saved from coming into the world, to be continually watched for the first sign of the evil seed. I reached for the bottle and thought: 'I will not be a coward as Papa was.' I thought of myself old as he is now . . . lying on my deathbed, reproaching myself for all the unhappiness I had brought to my children. I looked at the bottle, and I was afraid. I took a few drops and slept and in the morning I told myself: 'That is not the way.' "

"It is night and the fears are with me again. I can't sleep. I keep thinking of Papa and my mother in the room with the bars, and I am very conscious of the child I am carrying. Nounou, please take care of Geneviève. I leave her to your care. I am wondering now whether I have the courage which Papa lacked. I believe that had he succeeded it would have been better for so many of us. My little Geneviève would never have been born . . . Nounou would have been saved her fears . . . I should never have been born. I believe my father was right. I can see the bottle. Green with the crinkly side. I will put my notebook with the others in the cupboard and Nounou will find them. She loved reading about the days when I was little and says my books bring them back. She will explain to them why . . . I wonder if I can. I wonder if it is right . . . Now I shall try to sleep . . . but if I can't . . . In the morning I shall write that this is how one feels at night . . . By daylight it seems different. But Papa lacked the courage . . . I wonder if I shall have enough. I wonder . . ."

The writing stopped there. But I knew what had happened. She had found what she would call the courage and because of it she and her unborn child had died that night.

The pictures conjured up by Françoise's writing filled my mind. I saw it all so clearly; the house with the grim secret; the room with the barred window, the guarded fire; the lamp high in the wall; the wild and passionate woman; the austere husband who yet found her irresistible; his battle with his senses; his abandonment to passion and the result which to his fanatical mind seemed like a vengeance. The birth of Françoise, the watchful eyes, the secluded upbringing . . . and then marriage to the Comte. I saw why that marriage had been a failure from the beginning. The girl, innocent and ignorant, had been taught to regard marriage with horror; the disillusion of them both; she in finding a virile young husband, he a frigid wife.

And everyone in the *château* had been aware of the unsatisfactory nature of the marriage, and when Françoise died through an overdose of laudanum they would have asked themselves: Did her husband have a hand in it?

It was so cruelly unfair, and Nounou was to blame. She had read what I had read; she knew what I had just discovered, and yet she had allowed the Comte to be suspected of murdering his wife. Why had she not produced this book which explained so clearly?

Well, the truth should be known now.

I looked at the watch pinned to my blouse. The Comte would be in the garden. He would be wondering why I had not joined him as I always did when he was there. We would sit looking at the pond, making plans for our marriage, which would take place as soon as he was sufficiently recovered.

I went down to join him and found him alone, impatiently awaiting me. He saw immediately that something had happened.

"Dallas!" He said my name with that note of tenderness which never failed to move me; now it filled me with anger that he, an innocent man, should have been so unjustly accused.

"I know the truth about Françoise's death," I blurted out. "Everyone shall know now. It is all here . . . she wrote it herself. It is a clear explanation. She killed herself."

I saw the effect those words had on him and I went on triumphantly. "She kept notebooks . . . little diaries. Nounou has had them all this time. Nounou *knew* . . . and she said nothing. She allowed you to be blamed. It's monstrous. But now everyone shall know."

"Dallas, my dear, you are excited."

"Excited! I have discovered this secret. I can now show this . . . admission . . . to the world. No one else will dare say that you killed Françoise."

He laid his hand over mine. "Tell me what you have discovered," he said.

"I was determined to find out. I knew of the notebooks. Nounou had shown me some. So I went to her room. She was asleep, her cupboard was open . . . so I took the last one. I had guessed that there might be some clue there but I had not thought I should find the answer so clear . . . so indisputable."

"What did you find?"

"She killed herself because of the fear of madness. Her mother was mad and her father told her this when he was rambling after his stroke. He told her how he tried to kill her mother . . . how he had failed . . . how much better it would have been if he had. Don't you see? She was so . . . unworldly. That comes through in her diaries. She would accept . . . fatalistically what was put into her mind. . . . But it's here . . . as clear as we could wish. Never again will anyone accuse you of murder."

"I am glad you found this. Now there need be no secrets between us. Perhaps I should have told you. I think I should have done in time. But I was afraid that even you might have betrayed by some look . . . by some gesture . . ."

I looked at him searchingly. "Of course I knew that you had not killed her. You don't think for a moment I believed that absurd gossip . . ."

He took my face in his hands and kissed me. "I like to think," he said, "that you doubted me and loved me just the same."

"Perhaps it's true," I admitted. "I can't understand Nounou. How could she have known and kept quiet?"

"For the same reason that I did."

"As . . . you did?"

"I knew what happened. She left a note for me, explaining."

"You knew she took her own life and why and yet let them . . ."

"Yes, I knew and I let them."

"But why . . . why? It's so unfair . . . so cruel . . ."

"I was used to being gossiped about . . . slandered. I deserved most of it. You know I warned you you would not marry a saint."

"But . . . murder."

"It's your secret now, Dallas."

"Mine. But I'm going to make this known . . ."

"No. There's something you've forgotten."

"What?"

"Geneviève."

I stared at him in understanding.

"Yes, Geneviève," he went on. "You know her nature. It is wild, excitable. How easy it would be to send her the way her grandmother went. Since you have been here she has changed a little. Oh, not a great deal. We can't expect it . . . but I think that one of the easiest ways to send a highly strung person toppling into madness would be the continual watching, the suggestion that there is some seed in her which could develop. I don't want her watched in that way. I want her to have every chance to grow up normally. Françoise took her life for the sake of the child she was to have; I at least can face a little gossip for the sake of our daughter. You understand now, Dallas?"

"Yes, I understand."

"I'm glad for now there are no secrets between us."

I looked across the grass to the pond. It was hot now, but the afternoon was already late and the evening was drawing in. It was only a year ago that I had come here. So much, I thought, to happen in one short year.

"You are silent," he said. "Tell me what you are thinking."

"I was thinking of all that has happened since I first came here. Nothing is as it seemed when I came to the *château* . . . when I saw you all for the first time. I saw you so differently from what you are . . . and now I find you capable of this . . . great sacrifice."

"My darling, you are too dramatic. This . . . sacrifice has cost me little. What do I care for what is said of me? You know I am arrogant enough to snap my fingers at the world and say: Think what you will. But although I snap my fingers at the world there is one whose good opinion is of the greatest importance to me. . . . That is why I sit here basking in her approval, allowing her to set the halo on my head. I know of course that she will soon discover it was an illusion . . . but it's pleasant to wear it for a while."

"Why do you always want to denigrate yourself?"

"Because I'm afraid beneath my arrogance."

"Afraid. You. Of what?"

"That you will stop loving me."

"And what of me? Don't you think I have a similar fear?"

"It is comforting to know you can be capable of folly now and then."

"I think," I said, "that this is the happiest moment of my life."

He put an arm about me and we sat close together for some minutes looking over the peaceful garden.

"Let's make it last," he said.

He took the notebook from me and tore off the cover. Then he struck a match and applied it to the leaves.

I watched the blue and yellow flame creep over the childish handwriting.

Soon there was nothing left of Françoise's confession.

He said: "It was unwise to keep it. Will you explain to Nounou?"

I nodded. I picked up the cover of the notebook and slipped it into my pocket.

Together we watched a piece of blackened paper tossed across the lawn. I thought of the future—of whispers that would now and then reach me, of the wildness of Geneviève, of the complex nature of the man I had inexplicably chosen to love. The future was a challenge. But then I had always been one to accept a challenge.